DEATH IS NOW MY NEIGHBOUR and THE SECRET OF ANNEXE 3

THE INSPECTOR MORSE NOVELS

Last Bus to Woodstock
Last Seen Wearing
The Silent World of Nicholas Quinn
Service of All the Dead
The Dead of Jericho
The Riddle of the Third Mile
The Secret of Annexe 3
The Wench is Dead
The Jewel That Was Ours
The Way Through the Woods
The Daughters of Cain
Death is Now My Neighbour
The Remorseful Day

Also available in Pan Books

Morse's Greatest Mystery and other stories
The First Inspector Morse Omnibus
The Second Inspector Morse Omnibus
The Third Inspector Morse Omnibus
The Fourth Inspector Morse Omnibus

Colin Dexter graduated from Cambridge University in 1953 and has lived in Oxford since 1966. His first novel, *Last Bus to Woodstock*, was published in 1975. There are now thirteen novels in the series, of which *The Remorseful Day* is, sadly, the last.

Colin Dexter has won many awards for his novels, including the CWA Silver Dagger twice, and the CWA Gold Dagger for *The Wench is Dead* and *The Way Through the Woods*. In 1997 he was presented with the CWA Diamond Dagger for outstanding services to crime literature, and in 2000 was awarded the OBE in the Queen's Birthday Honours List.

The Inspector Morse novels have, of course, been adapted for the small screen with huge success by Carlton/Central Television, starring John Thaw and Kevin Whately.

COLIN DEXTER

DEATH
IS NOW MY
NEIGHBOUR
and
THE SECRET
OF ANNEXE 3

PAN BOOKS

Death is Now my Neighbour first published 1996 by Macmillan
First published in paperback 1997 by Pan Books
The Secret of Annexe 3 first published 1986 by Macmillan
First published in paperback 1987 by Pan Books

This omnibus edition published 2004 by Pan Books
an imprint of Pan Macmillan Ltd
Pan Macmillan, 20 New Wharf Road, London N1 9RR
Basingstoke and Oxford
Associated companies throughout the world
www.panmacmillan.com

ISBN 0330 43263 X

1 3 5 7 9 8 6 4 2

A CIP catalogue record for this book is available from
the British Library.

Typeset by CentraCet limited, Cambridge
Printed and bound in Great Britain by
Mackays of Chatham plc, Chatham, Kent

DEATH IS NOW MY NEIGHBOUR

For
Joan Templeton
with gratitude

Acknowledgements

The author and publishers wish to thank the following who have kindly given permission for use of copyright materials:
Extract from *The Dance* by Philip Larkin reproduced by permission of Faber & Faber Ltd;
Extract from the *News of the World* reproduced by permission of the *News of the World*;
Extract from Fowler's *Modern English Usage* reproduced by permission of Oxford University Press;
Ace Reporter by Helen Peacocke reproduced by kind permission of the author;
Extract from *Major Barbara* by Bernard Shaw reproduced by permission of The Society of Authors on behalf of the Bernard Shaw Estate;
Extract from *The Brontës* by Juliet Barker reproduced by permission of Weidenfeld and Nicolson;
Extract from *The Dry Salvages* by T. S. Eliot reproduced by permission of Faber & Faber Ltd;
Extract from *Summoned by Bells* by John Betjeman reproduced by permission of John Murray (Publishers) Ltd;
Extract from *Aubade* by Philip Larkin reproduced by permission of Faber & Faber Ltd;
Extract from *May-Day Song for North Oxford* by John

Betjeman, from *Collected Poems of John Betjeman*, reproduced by permission of John Murray (Publishers) Ltd;
Extract from *This Be the Verse* by Philip Larkin reproduced by permission of Faber & Faber Ltd;
Extract by Philip Larkin on p. 345 reproduced by permission of Faber & Faber Ltd.

Quickly, bring me a beaker of wine,
so that I may wet my mind and say
something clever

(ARISTOPHANES)

Prolegomenon

January, 1996

A decided boon, therefore, are any multiple-choice items for those pupils in our classrooms who are either inured to idleness, or guilty of wilful ignorance. Such pupils, if simply and appropriately instructed, have only to plump for the same answer on each occasion – let us say, choice (a) from choices (a) (b) (c) (d) – in order to achieve a reasonably regular score of some 25% of the total marks available. This is a wholly satisfactory return for academic incompetence

(*Crosscurrents in Assessment Criteria: Theory and Practice*, HMSO, 1983)

'WHAT TIME DO you call this, Lewis?'

'The missus's fault. Not like her to be late with the breakfast.'

Morse made no answer as he stared down at the one remaining unsolved clue:

'Stand for soldiers? (5–4)'

Lewis took the chair opposite his chief and sat waiting for some considerable while, leafing through a magazine.

'Stuck, sir?' he asked finally.

'If I was – if I *were* – I doubt I'd get much help from you.'

'You never know,' suggested Lewis good-naturedly. 'Perhaps—'

'Ah!' burst out Morse triumphantly – as he wrote in TOASTRACK. He folded *The Times* away and beamed across at his sergeant.

'You – are – a – genius, Lewis.'

'So you've often told me, sir.'

'*And* I bet you had a boiled egg for breakfast – with *soldiers*. Am I right?'

'What's that got—?'

'What are you reading there?'

Lewis held up the title page of his magazine.

'Lew-is! There are more important things in life than the *Thames Valley Police Gazette*.'

'Just thought you might be interested in one of the articles here . . .'

Morse rose to the bait. 'Such as?'

'There's a sort of test – you know, see how many points you can score: ARE YOU REALLY WISE AND CULTURED?'

'Very doubtful in your case, I should think.'

'You reckon you could do better than I did?'

'Quite certain of it.'

Lewis grinned. '*Quite* certain, sir?'

'Absolutely.'

'Want to have a go, then?' Lewis's mouth betrayed gentle amusement as Morse shrugged his indifference.

'Multiple-choice questions – you know all about—?'

'Get *on* with it!'

'All you've got to do is imagine the world's going to end in exactly one week's time, OK? Then you've got to answer five questions, as honestly as you can.'

'And you've already answered these questions yourself?'

Lewis nodded.

'Well, if *you* can answer them . . . Fire away!'

Lewis read aloud from the article:

Question One

Given the choice of only four CDs or cassettes, which one of the following would you be likely to play at least once?

(a) A Beatles album
(b) Fauré's *Requiem*
(c) *An Evening with Victor Borge*
(d) The complete overtures to Wagner's operas

With a swift flourish, Morse wrote down a letter.

Question Two

Which of these videos would you want to watch?

(a) *Casablanca* (the film)
(b) England's World Cup victory (1966)
(c) *Copenhagen Red-Hot Sex* (2 hours)
(d) *The Habitat of the Kingfisher* (RSPB)

A second swift flourish from Morse.

Question Three

With which of the following women would you wish to spend some, if not all, of your surviving hours?

(a) Lady Thatcher
(b) Kim Basinger
(c) Mother Teresa
(d) Princess Diana

A third swift flourish.

Question Four
If you could gladden your final days with one of the following, which would it be?

(a) Two dozen bottles of vintage champagne
(b) Five hundred cigarettes
(c) A large bottle of tranquillizers
(d) A barrel of real ale

Flourish number four, and the candidate (confident of imminent success, it appeared) sat back in the black-leather armchair.

Question Five
Which of the following would you read during this period?

(a) Cervantes' *Don Quixote*
(b) Dante's *The Divine Comedy*
(c) A bound volume of *Private Eye* (1995)
(d) Homer's *Iliad*

This time Morse hesitated some while before writing on the pad in front of him. 'You did the test yourself, you say?'

Lewis nodded. 'Victor Borge; the football; Princess

Diana; the champagne; and *Private Eye.* Just hope Princess Di likes Champers, that's all.'

'There must be worse ways of spending your last week on earth,' admitted Morse.

'I didn't do so well, though – not on the marking. I'm not up there among the cultured and the wise, I'm afraid.'

'Did you expect to be?'

'Wouldn't you?'

'Of course.'

'Let's hear what you picked, then.'

'My preferences, Lewis' (Morse articulated his words with precision) 'were as follows: (b); (c); (b); (c); none of them.'

Turning to the back page, Lewis reminded himself of the answers putatively adjudged to be correct.

'I don't believe it,' he whispered to himself. Then, to Morse: 'You scored the maximum!'

'Are you surprised?'

Lewis shook his head in mild bewilderment.

'You chose, what, the *Requiem*?'

'Well?'

'But you've never believed in all that religious stuff.'

'It's important if it's *true*, though, isn't it? Let's just say it's a bit like an insurance policy. A beautiful work, anyway.'

'Says here: "Score four marks for (b). Sufficient recommendation that it was chosen by three of the last four Popes for their funerals."'

Morse lifted his eyebrows. 'You didn't know that?'

Lewis ignored the question and continued:

'Then you chose the sex video!'

'Well, it was either that or the kingfisher. I've already seen *Casablanca* a couple of times – and no one's ever going to make me watch a football match again.'

'But I mean, a sex video . . .'

Morse, however, was clearly unimpressed by such obvious disapprobation. 'It'd be the choice of those three Popes as well, like as not.'

'But it all gets – well, it gets so plain *boring* after a while.'

'So you keep telling me, Lewis. And all I'm asking is the chance to get as bored as everybody else. I've only got a *week*, remember.'

'I like your next choice, though. Beautiful girl, Kim Basinger. *Beautiful*.'

'Something of a toss-up, that – between her and Mother Teresa. But I'd already played the God-card.'

'Then' (Lewis considered the next answer) 'Arrghh, come off it, sir! You didn't even go for the beer! You're supposed to answer these questions *honestly*.'

'I've already got plenty of booze in,' said Morse. 'Certainly enough to see me through to Judgment Day. And I don't fancy facing the Great Beyond with a blinding hangover. It'll be a new experience for me – tranquillizers . . .'

Lewis looked down again, and proceeded to read out the reasons for Morse's greatest triumph. 'It says here, on Question Five, "Those choosing any of the suggested titles are clearly unfit for high honours. If any choice whatsoever is made, four marks will therefore be deducted from the final score. If the answer is a timid dash – or similar – no marks will be awarded, but no marks will be deducted. A more positively negative answer – e.g. 'Come off it!' – will be rewarded with a bonus of four marks."' Again Lewis shook his head. 'Nonsense, isn't it? "Positively negative", I mean.'

'Rather nicely put, I'd've thought,' said Morse.

'Anyway,' conceded Lewis, 'you score twenty out of twenty according to this fellow who seems to have all the answers.' Lewis looked again at the name printed below the article. '"Rhadamanthus" – whoever he is.'

'Lord Chief Justice of Appeal in the Underworld.'

Lewis frowned, then grinned. 'You've been cheating! You've got a copy—'

'No!' Morse's blue eyes gazed fiercely across at his sergeant. 'The first I saw of that *Gazette* was when you brought it in just now.'

'If you say so.' But Lewis sounded less than convinced.

'Not surprised, are you, to find me perched up there on the topmost twig amongst the intelligentsia?'

'"The wise and the cultured", actually.'

'And that's another thing. I think I shall go crackers if I hear three things in my life much more: "Hark the Herald Angels Sing"; *Eine Kleine Nachtmusik*; and that wretched bloody word "actually".'

'Sorry, sir.'

Suddenly Morse grinned. 'No need to be, old friend. And at least you're right about one thing. I did cheat – in a way.'

'You don't mean *you* . . . ?'

Morse nodded.

It had been a playful, pleasant interlude. Yet it would have warranted no inclusion in this chronicle had it not been that one or two of the details recorded herein were to linger significantly in the memory of Chief Inspector E. Morse, of the Thames Valley Police HQ.

PART ONE

Chapter One

> In hypothetical sentences introduced by 'if' and referring to past time, where conditions are deemed to be 'unfulfilled', the verb will regularly be found in the pluperfect subjunctive, in both protasis and apodosis
>
> (Donet, *Principles of Elementary Latin Syntax*)

It is perhaps unusual to begin a tale of murder with a reminder to the reader of the rules governing conditional sentences in a language that is incontrovertibly dead. In the present case, however, such a course appears not wholly inappropriate.

If (*if*) Chief Inspector Morse had been on hand to observe the receptionist's dress – an irregularly triangled affair in blues, greys, and reds – he might have been reminded of the uniform issued to a British Airways stewardess. More probably, though, he might not, since he had never flown on British Airways. His only flight during the previous decade had occasioned so many fears concerning his personal survival that he had determined to restrict all future travel to those (statistically) far more precarious means of conveyance – the car, the coach, the train, and the steamer.

Yet almost certainly the Chief Inspector would have noted, with approval, the receptionist herself, for in Yorkshire she would have been reckoned a bonny lass: a vivacious, dark-eyed woman, long-legged and well figured; a woman – judging from her ringless, well-manicured fingers – not overtly advertising any marital commitment, and not averse, perhaps, to the occasional overture from the occasional man.

Pinned at the top-left of her colourful dress was a name-tag: 'Dawn Charles'.

Unlike several of her friends (certainly unlike Morse) she was quite content with her Christian name. Sometimes she'd felt *slightly* dubious about it; but no longer. Out with some friends in the Bird and Baby the previous month, she'd been introduced to a rather dashing, rather dishy undergraduate from Pembroke College. And when, a little later, she'd found herself doodling inconsequentially on a Burton beer-mat, the young man, on observing her sinistrality, had initiated a wholly memorable conversation.

'Dawn? That *is* your name?'

She'd nodded.

'Left-handed?'

She'd nodded.

'Do you know that line from Omar Khayyam? "Dreaming when Dawn's left hand was in the sky ..." Lovely, isn't it?'

Yes, it was. Lovely.

She'd peeled the top off the beer-mat and made him write it down for her.

Then, very quietly, he'd asked her if he could see her again. At the start of the new term, perhaps?

She'd known it was silly, for there must have been at least twenty years difference in their ages. If only . . . if only he'd been ten, a dozen years older . . .

But people *did* do silly things, and hoped their silly hopes. And that very day, 15 January, was the first full day of the new Hilary Term in the University of Oxford.

Her Monday–Friday job, 6–10 p.m., at the clinic on the Banbury Road (just north of St Giles') was really quite enjoyable. Over three years of it now, and she was becoming a fixture there. Most of the consultants greeted her with a genuine smile; several of them, these days, with her Christian name.

Nice.

She'd once stayed at a four-star hotel which offered a glass of sherry to incoming guests; and although the private Harvey Clinic was unwilling (perhaps on medical grounds?) to provide such laudable hospitality, Dawn ever kept two jugs of genuine coffee piping hot for her clients, most of them soberly suited and well-heeled gentlemen. A number of whom, as she well knew, were most seriously ill.

Yes, there had been several occasions when she had heard a few brief passages of conversation between consultant and client which she *shouldn't* have heard; or which, having heard, she should have forgotten; and which she should never have been willing to report to anyone.

Not even to the police.

Quite certainly not to the Press . . .

As it happened, 15 January was to prove a day unusually easy for her to recall, since it marked the twenty-fifth anniversary of the clinic's opening in 1971. By prior negotiation and arrangement, the clinic was visited that evening, between 7 p.m. and 8.30 p.m., by Radio Oxford, by the local press, and by Mr Wesley Smith and his crew from the Central TV studios out at Abingdon. And particularly memorable for Dawn had been those precious moments when the camera had focused upon her: first, when (as instructed) she had poured a cup of genuine coffee for a wholly bogus 'client'; second, when the cameraman had moved behind her left shoulder as she ran a felt-tipped pen through a name on the appointments list in front of her – but only, of course, after a full assurance that no viewer would be able to read the name itself when the feature was shown the following evening.

Yet Dawn Charles was always to remember the name:

Mr J. C. Storrs.

It had been a fairly new name to her – another of those patients, as Dawn suspected (correctly), whose influence and affluence afforded the necessary leverage and £ s d to jump the queues awaiting their calls to the hospitals up in Headington.

There was something else she would always remember, too . . .

By one of those minor coincidences (so commonplace in Morse's life) it had been just as most of the personnel from the media were preparing to leave, at almost exactly 8.30 p.m., that Mr Robert Turnbull, the Senior Cancer

Consultant, had passed her desk, nodded a greeting, and walked slowly to the exit, his right hand resting on the shoulder of Mr J. C. Storrs. The two men were talking quietly together for some while – Dawn was certain of that. But certain of little else. The look on the consultant's face, as far as she could recall, had been neither that of a judge who has just condemned a man to death, nor that of one just granting a prisoner his freedom.

No obvious grimness.

No obvious joy.

And indeed there was adequate cause for such uncertainty on Dawn's part, since the scene had been partially masked from her by the continued presence of several persons: a pony-tailed reporter scribbling a furious shorthand as he interviewed a nurse; the TV crew packing away its camera and tripods; the Lord Mayor speaking some congratulatory words into a Radio Oxford microphone – all of them standing between her and the top of the three blue-carpeted stairs which led down to the double-doored exit, outside which were affixed the vertical banks of well-polished brass plates, ten on each side, the fourth from the top on the left reading:

ROBERT H. TURNBULL

If only Dawn Charles could have recalled a little more.

'If' – that little conjunction introducing those unfulfilled conditions in past time which, as Donet reminds us, demand the pluperfect subjunctive in both clauses – a syntactical rule which Morse himself had mastered early on in an education which had been far more fortunate than that enjoyed by the receptionist at the Harvey Clinic.

Indeed, over the next two weeks, most people in Oxford were destined to be considerably more fortunate than Dawn Charles: she received no communication from the poetry-lover of Pembroke; her mother was admitted to a psychiatric ward out at Littlemore; she was (twice) reminded by her bank manager of the increasing problems arising from the large margin of negative equity on her small flat; and finally, on Monday morning, 29 January, she was to hear on Fox FM Radio that her favourite consultant, Mr Robert H. Turnbull, MB, ChB, FRCS, had been fatally injured in a car accident on Cumnor Hill.

Chapter Two

The Master shall not continue in his post beyond the age of sixty-seven. As a simple rule, therefore, the incumbent Master will be requested to give notice of impending retirement during the University term immediately prior to that birthday. Where, however, such an accommodation does not present itself, the Master is required to propose a particular date not later than the end of the first week of the second full term after the statutory termination (*vide supra*)

(Paragraph 2 (a), translated from the Latin, from the Founders' Statutes of Lonsdale College, Oxford)

SIR CLIXBY BREAM would be almost sixty-nine years old when he retired as Master of Lonsdale. A committee of Senior Fellows, including two eminent Latin scholars, had found itself unable to interpret the gobbledegook of the Founders' Statutes (*vide supra*); and since no 'accommodation' (whatever that was) had presented itself, Sir Clixby had first been persuaded to stay on for a short while – then for a longer while.

Yet this involved no hardship.

He was subject to none of the normal pressures about

moving to somewhere nearer the children or the grand-children, since his marriage to Lady Muriel had been *sine prole.* Moreover, he was blessedly free from the usual uxorial bleatings about a nice little thatched cottage in Dorset or Devon, since Lady Muriel had been in her grave these past three years.

The position of Head of House at any of the Oxbridge Colleges was just about the acme of academic ambition; and since three of the last four Masters had been knighted within eighteen months of their appointments, it had been natural for him to be attracted by the opportunity of such pleasing preferment. And he *had* been so attracted; as, even more strongly, had the late Lady Muriel.

Indeed, the incumbent Master, a distinguished mathematician in his earlier days, had never enjoyed living anywhere as much as in Oxford – ten years of it now. He'd learned to love the old city more and more the longer he was there: it was as simple as that. Of course he was somewhat saddened by the thought of his imminent retirement: he would miss the College – miss the challenges of running the place – and he knew that the sight of the furniture van outside the wisteria-clad front of the Master's Lodge would occasion some aching regret. But there were a few unexpected consolations, perhaps. In particular, he would be able (he supposed) to sit back and survey with a degree of detachment and sardonic amusement the in-fighting that would doubtless arise among his potential successors.

It was the duty of the Fellows' Appointments Committee (its legality long established by one of the more readily comprehensible of the College Statutes) to stipulate three conditions for those seeking election as Master: first, that any candidate should be 'of sound mind and in good health'; second, that the candidate should 'not have taken Holy Orders'; third, that the candidate should have no criminal record within 'the territories administered under the governance of His (or Her) Most Glorious Majesty'.

Such stipulations had often amused the present Master. If one judged by the longevity of almost all the Masters appointed during the twentieth century, physical well-being had seldom posed much of a problem; yet mental stability had never been a particularly prominent feature of his immediate predecessor, nor (by all accounts) of his predecessor's predecessor. And occasionally Sir Clixby wondered what the College would say of himself once he was gone ... With regard to the exclusion of the clergy, he assumed that the Founders (like Edward Gibbon three centuries later) had managed to trace the source of all human wickedness back to the Popes and the Prelates, and had rallied to the cause of anticlericalism ... But it was the possibility of the candidate's criminality which was the most amusing. Presumably any convictions for murder, rape, sodomy, treason, or similar misdemeanours, were to be discounted if shown to have taken place *outside* the jurisdiction of His (or Her) Most Glorious Majesty. Very strange.

Strangest of all, however, was the absence of any mention in the original Statute of academic pedigree;

and, at least theoretically, there could be no bar to a candidate presenting himself with only a Grade E in GCSE Media Studies. Nor was there any stipulation that the successful candidate should be a senior (or, for that matter, a junior) member of the College, and on several occasions 'outsiders' had been appointed. Indeed, he himself, Sir Clixby, had been imported into Oxford from 'the other place', and then (chiefly) in recognition of his reputation as a resourceful fund-raiser.

On this occasion, however, outsiders seemed out of favour. The College itself could offer at least two candidates, each of whom would be an admirable choice; or so it was thought. In the Senior Common Room the consensus was most decidedly in favour of such 'internal' preferment, and the betting had hardened accordingly.

By some curious omission no entry had hitherto been granted to either of these ante-post favourites in the pages of *Who's Who*. From which one may be forgiven for concluding that the aforesaid work is rather more concerned with the third cousins of secondary aristocrats than with eminent academics. Happily, however, both of these personages had been considered worthy of mention in Debrett's *People of Today 1995*:

> STORRS, Julian Charles; *b* 9 July 1935; *Educ* Christ's Hosp, Services S Dartmouth, Emmanuel Coll Cambridge (BA, MA); *m* Angela Miriam Martin 31 March 1974; *Career* Capt RA (Indian Army Secondment); Pitt Rivers Reader in Social Anthropology and Senior Fellow Lonsdale Coll Oxford; *Recreations* taking taxis, playing bridge.

CORNFORD, Denis Jack; *b* 23 April 1942; *Educ* Wyggeston GS Leicester, Magdalen Coll Oxford (MA, DPhil); *m* Shelly Ann Benson 28 May 1994; *Career* University Reader in Mediaeval History and Fellow Lonsdale Coll Oxford; *Recreations* kite-flying, cultivation of orchids.

Each of these entries may appear comparatively uninformative. Yet perhaps in the more perceptive reader they may provoke one or two interesting considerations.

Was, for example, the Senior Fellow of Lonsdale so affluent that he could afford to take a taxi everywhere? Did he never travel by car, coach, or train? Well, quite certainly on special occasions he would travel by train.

Oh, yes.

As we shall see.

And why was Dr Cornford, soon to be fifty-four years old, so recently converted to the advantages of latter-day matrimony? Had he met some worthy woman of comparable age?

Oh, no.

As we shall see.

Chapter Three

How right
I should have been to keep away, and let
You have your innocent–guilty–innocent night
Of switching partners in your own sad set:
How useless to invite
The sickening breathlessness of being young
Into my life again

(Philip Larkin, *The Dance*)

DENIS CORNFORD, *omnium consensu*, was a fine historian. Allied with a mind both sharp and rigorously honest was a capacity for the assemblage and interpretation of evidence that was the envy of the History Faculty at Oxford. Yet in spite of such qualities, he was best known for a brief monograph on the Battle of Hastings, in which he maintained that the momentous conflict between Harold of England and William of Normandy had taken place one year earlier than universally acknowledged. In 1065.

In the Trinity Term of 1994, Cornford – a slimly-built, smallish, pleasantly featured man – had taken sabbatical leave at Harvard; and there – somehow and somewhere, in Cambridge, Massachusetts – something quite extraordinary had occurred. For six months later, to the amazement and amusement of his colleagues, the confirmed bachelor of Lonsdale had returned to Oxford with a woman who had agreed to change her name from Shelly Benson to Shelly Cornford: a student from Harvard who had just gained her Master's degree in American History, twenty-six years old – exactly half the age of her new husband (for this was her second marriage).

It is perhaps not likely that Shelly would have reached the semi-final heats of any Miss Massachusetts beauty competition: her jawline was slightly too square, her shoulders rather too strong, her legs perhaps a little on the sturdy side. Yet there were a good many in Lonsdale College – both dons and undergraduates – who were to experience a curious attraction to the woman now putting in fairly regular appearances in Chapel, at Guest Nights, and at College functions during the Michaelmas Term of 1994. Her wavy, shoulder-length brown hair framed a face in which the widely set dark brown eyes seemed sometimes to convey the half-promise of a potential intimacy, whilst her quietly voiced New England accent could occasionally sound as sweetly sensual as some enchantress's.

Many were the comments made about the former Shelly Benson during those first few terms. But no one could ever doubt what Denis Cornford had seen in her, for it was simply what others could now so clearly see for themselves. So from the start Shelly Cornford was regularly lusted after; her husband secretly envied. But the couple themselves appeared perfectly happy: no hint of infidelity on her part; no cause for jealousy on his.

Not yet.

Frequently during those days they were to be seen walking hand-in-hand the short distances from their rooms in Holywell Street to the King's Arms, or the Turf Tavern ('Find Us If You Can!'), where in bars blessedly free from juke-box and fruit-machine Shelly had quickly acquired a taste for real ale and a love for the ambience of the English public house.

Occasionally the two of them ventured further afield in and around Oxford; and one evening, just before Christmas 1994, they had taken the No. 2 bus from Cornmarket up to another King's Arms, the one in the Banbury road, where amid many unashamedly festive young revellers Cornford watched as his (equally young) wife, with eyes half-closed, had rocked her shoulders sensuously to the thudding rhythm of some pop music, her black-stockinged thighs alternately lifted and lowered as though she were mentally disco-dancing. And at that point he was conscious of being the oldest person in the bar, by about twenty years; inhabiting alien territory there; wholly excluded from the magic circle of the night; and suddenly sadly aware that he could never even begin to share the girlish animality of the woman he had married.

Cornford had said nothing that evening.

Nor had he said anything when, three months later, at the end-of-term Gaudy, he had noticed, beneath the table, the left hand of Julian Storrs pressed briefly against Shelly's right thigh as she sat drinking rather a lot of

Madeira, after drinking rather a lot of red wine at dinner, after drinking rather a lot of gin at the earlier reception . . . her chair perhaps unnecessarily close to the Senior Fellow seated on her right, the laughing pair leaning together in some whispered, mutual, mouth-to-ear exchange. Perhaps it was all perfectly harmless; and Cornford sought to make little of it. Yet he ought (he knew it!) to have said a few words on that occasion – lightly, with a heavy heart.

It was only late in the Michaelmas Term 1995 that Cornford finally did say something to his wife . . .

They had been seated one Tuesday lunchtime in the Turf Tavern, he immediately opposite his wife as she sat in one of the wooden wall-seats in the main bar, each of them enjoying a pint of London Pride. He was eagerly expounding to her his growing conviction that the statistical evidence concerning the number of deaths resultant from the Black Death in 1348 had been wildly misinterpreted, and that the supposed demographic effects consequent upon that plague were – most decidedly! – extremely suspect. It should all have been of some interest, surely? And yet Cornford was conscious of a semi-preoccupied gaze in Shelly's eyes as she stared over his left shoulder into some more fascinating area.

All right. She *ought* to have been interested – but she wasn't. Not everyone, not even a trained historian like his wife, was going to be automatically enthralled by any re-evaluation of some abstruse mediaeval evidence.

He'd thought little of it.

And had drunk his ale.

They were about to leave when a man, in his early thirties or so, walked over to them – a tall, dark, slimly built Arab with a bushy moustache. Looking directly into Shelly's eyes, he spoke softly to her:

'Madame! You are the most beautiful lady I see!'

Then, turning to Cornford: 'Please excuse, sir!' With which, picking up Shelly's right hand, he imprinted his full-lipped mouth most earnestly upon the back of her wrist.

After the pair of them had emerged into the cobbled lane that led up again into Holywell Street, Cornford stopped and so roughly pushed his wife's shoulder that she had no choice but to stand there facing him.

'You – are – a – bloody – flirt! Did you know that? All the time we were in there – all the time I was telling you—'

But he got no further.

The tall figure of Sir Clixby Bream was striding down towards them.

'Hell-*o*! You're both just off, I can see that. But what about another little snifter? Just to please me?'

'Not for me, Master.' Cornford trusted that he'd masked the bitterness of his earlier tone. 'But if . . . ?' He turned to his wife.

'No. Not now. Another time. Thank you, Master.'

With Shelly still beside him, Cornford walked rather blindly on, suspecting (how otherwise?) that the Master had witnessed the awkward, angry scene. And then, a few steps later – almost miraculously – he felt his wife's arm link with his own; heard the wonderful words spoken in her quiet voice: 'Denis, I'm so very sorry. Do please forgive me, my darling.'

As the Master stooped slightly to pass beneath the entrance of the Turf Tavern, an observer skilled in the art of labiomancy would have read the two words on his smoothly smiling mouth:

'Well! Well!'

Chapter Four

Wednesday, 7 February

DISCIPLE (weeping):	O Master, I disturb thy meditations.
MASTER:	Thy tears are plural; the Divine Will is one.
DISCIPLE:	I seek wisdom and truth, yet my thoughts are ever of lust and the necessary pleasures of a woman.
MASTER:	Seek not wisdom and truth, my son; seek rather forgiveness. Now go in peace, for verily hast thou disturbed my meditations – of lust and of the necessary pleasures of a woman

(K'ung-Fu-Tsu, from *Analects XXIII*)

'WELL, AT LEAST it's *left* on time.'

'Not surprising, is it? The bloody thing *starts* from Oxford. Give it a chance, though. We'll probably run into signalling failure somewhere along the line.'

She smiled, attractively. 'Funny, really. They've been

signalling on the railways for – what? – a hundred and fifty years, and with all these computers and things . . .'

'Over one hundred and seventy years, if we want to be accurate – and why shouldn't we? Eighteen twenty-five when the Stockton to Darlington line was opened.'

'Yeah. We learned about that in school. You know, Stephenson's *Rocket* and all that.'

'No, my dear girl. A few years later, that was. Stephenson's first locomotive was called *The Locomotion* – not very difficult to remember, is it?'

'No.'

The monosyllable was quietly spoken, and he knew that he'd made her feel inadequate again.

She turned away from him to look through the carriage window, spotting the great sandstone house in Nuneham Park, up towards the skyline on the left. More than once he'd told her something of its history, and about Capability Brown and Somebody Adams; but she was never able to remember things as accurately as he seemed to expect. He'd told her on their last train journey, for example, about the nationalization of the railways after World War II: 1947 (or was it 1948?).

So what?

Yet there was one year she would *never* forget: the year the network changed its name to 'British Rail'. Her father had told her about that; told her she'd been born on that very same day. In that very same year, too.

In 1965.

'Drinks? Refreshments?'

An overloaded trolley was squeezing a squeaky passage

along the aisle; and the man looked at his wristwatch (10.40 a.m.) as it came alongside, before turning to the elegantly suited woman seated next to him:

'Fancy anything? Coffee? Bit too early for anything stronger, perhaps?'

'Gin and tonic for me. And a packet of plain crisps.'

Sod him! He'd been pretty insufferable so far.

A few minutes later, after pouring half his can of McEwan's Export Ale into a plastic container, he turned towards her again; and she felt his dry, slightly cracked lips pressed upon her right cheek. Then she heard him say the wonderful word that someone else had heard a month or two before; heard him say 'Sorry'.

She opened her white-leather handbag and took out a tube of lip-salve. As she passed it to him, she felt his firm, slim fingers move against the back of her wrist; then move along her lower arm, beneath the sleeve of her light-mauve Jaeger jacket: the fingers of a pianist. And she knew that very soon – the Turbo Express had just left Reading – the pianist would have been granted the licence to play with her body once more, as though he were rejoicing in a gentle Schubert melody.

She had never known a man so much in control of himself.

Or of her.

The train stopped just before Slough.

When, ten minutes later, it slowly began to move forward again, the Senior Conductor decided to introduce himself over the intercom.

'Ladies and Gentlemen. Due to a signalling failure at Slough, this train will now arrive at Paddington approximately fifteen minutes late. We apologize to customers for this delay.'

The man and the woman, seated now more closely together, turned to each other – and smiled.

'What are you thinking?' she asked.

'You often ask me that, you know. Sometimes I'm not thinking of anything.'

'Well?'

'I was only thinking that our Senior Conductor doesn't seem to know the difference between "due to" and "owing to".'

'Not sure *I* do. Does it matter?'

'Of course it matters.'

'But you won't let it come between us?'

'I won't let anything come between us,' he whispered into her ear.

For a few seconds they looked lovingly at each other. Then he lowered his eyes, removed a splayed left hand from her stockinged thigh, and drank his last mouthful of beer.

'Just before we get into Paddington, Rachel, there's something important I ought to tell you.'

She turned to him – her eyes suddenly alarmed.

He wanted to put a stop to the affair?

He wanted to get rid of her?

He'd found another woman? (Apart from his wife, of course.)

'Tickets, please!'

He looked as if he might be making his maiden

voyage, the young ticket-collector, for he was scrutinizing each ticket proffered to him with preternatural concentration.

The man took both his own and the young woman's ticket from his wallet: cheap-day returns.

'This yours, sir?'

'Yes.'

'You an OAP?'

'As a matter of fact I am not, no.' (The tone of his voice was quietly arrogant.) 'To draw a senior-citizen pension in the United Kingdom a man has to be sixty-five years of age. But a Senior Railcard is available to a man who has passed his sixtieth birthday – as doubtless you know.'

'Could I see your Railcard, sir?'

With a sigh of resignation, the man produced his card. And the slightly flustered, spotty-faced youth duly studied the details.

Valid: until 07 MAY 96,
Issued to: Mr J C Storrs

'How the hell does he think I got my ticket at Oxford without showing *that*?' asked the Senior Fellow of Lonsdale.

'He's only doing his duty, poor lad. And he's got awful acne.'

'You're right, yes.'

She took his hand in hers, moving more closely again. And within a few minutes the PADDINGTON sign passed by as the train drew slowly into the long platform. In a rather sad voice, the Senior Conductor now made his second announcement: 'All change, please! All change! This train has now terminated.'

They waited until their fellow-passengers had alighted; and happily, just as at Oxford, there seemed to be no one on the train whom either of them knew.

In the Brunel Bar of the Station Hotel, Storrs ordered a large brandy (two pieces of ice) for his young companion, and half a pint of Smith's bitter for himself. Then, leaving his own drink temporarily untouched, he walked out into Praed Street, thence making his way down to the cluster of small hotels in and around Sussex Gardens, several of them displaying VACANCIES signs. He had 'used' (was that the word?) two of them previously, but this time he decided to explore new territory.

'Double room?'

'One left, yeah. Just the one night, is it?'

'How much?'

'Seventy-five pounds for the two – with breakfast.'

'How much without breakfast?'

Storrs sensed that the middle-aged peroxide blonde was attuned to his intentions, for her eyes hardened knowingly behind the cigarette-stained reception counter.

'Seventy-five pounds.'

One experienced campaigner nodded to another experienced campaigner. 'Well, thank you, madam. I promise I'll call back and take the room – after I've had a look at it – if I can't find anything a little less expensive.'

He turned to go.

'Just a minute! . . . No breakfast, you say?'

'No. We're catching the sleeper to Inverness, and we just want a room for the day – you know? – a sort of habitation and a place.'

She squinted up at him through her cigarette smoke.

'Sixty-five?'

'Sixty.'

'OK.'

He counted out six ten-pound notes as, pushing the register forward, she reached behind her for Key Number 10.

It was, one may say, a satisfactory transaction.

Her glass was empty, and without seating himself he drained his own beer at a draught.

'Same again?'

'Please!' She pushed over the globed glass in which the semi-melted ice-cubes still remained.

Feeling most pleasantly relaxed, she looked around the thinly populated bar, and noticed (again!) the eyes of the middle-aged man seated across the room. But she gave no sign that she was aware of his interest, switching her glance instead to the balding, grey-white head of the man leaning nonchalantly at the bar as he ordered their drinks.

Beside her once more, he clinked their glasses, feeling (just as she did) most pleasantly relaxed.

'Quite a while since we sat here,' he volunteered.

'Couple o' months?'

'Ten weeks, if we wish to be exact.'

'Which, of course, we do, sir.'

Smiling, she sipped her second large brandy. Feeling good; feeling increasingly good.

'Hungry?' he asked.

'What for?'

He grinned. 'An hour in bed, perhaps – before we have a bite to eat?'

'Wine thrown in?'

'I'm trying to bribe you.'

'Well . . . if you *want* to go to bed for a little while first . . .'

'I *think* I'd quite enjoy that.'

'One condition, though.'

'What?'

'You tell me what you were going to tell me – on the train.'

He nodded seriously. 'I'll tell you over the wine.'

It was, one may say, a satisfactory arrangement.

As they got up to leave, Storrs moved ahead of her to push open one of the swing-doors; and Rachel James (for such was she), a freelance physiotherapist practising up in North Oxford, was conscious of the same man's eyes upon her. Almost involuntarily she leaned her body backward, thrusting her breasts against the smooth white silk of her blouse as she lifted both her hands behind her head to tighten the ring which held her light brown hair in its pony-tail.

A pony-tail ten inches long.

Chapter Five

Then the smiling hookers turned their attention to our shocked reporters.

'Don't be shy! You paid for a good time, and that's what we want to give you.'

Our men feigned jet-lag, and declined

(Extract from the *News of the World*, 5 February, 1995)

GEOFFREY OWENS had a better knowledge of Soho than most people.

He'd been only nineteen when first he'd gone to London as a junior reporter, when he'd rented a room just off Soho Square, and when during his first few months he'd regularly walked around the area there, experiencing the curiously compulsive attraction of names like Brewer Street, Greek Street, Old Compton Street, Wardour Street . . . a sort of litany of seediness and sleaze.

In those days, the mid-seventies, the striptease parlours, the porno cinemas, the topless bars – all somehow had been more wholesomely sinful, in the best sense of that word (or was it the worst?). Now, Soho had quite definitely changed for the better (or was it the worse?): more furtive and tawdry, more dishonest in its exploitation of the lonely, unloved men who would ever pace the pavements there and occasionally stop like rabbits in the headlights.

Yet Owens appeared far from mesmerized when in the early evening of 7 February he stopped outside Le Club Sexy. The first part of this establishment's name was intended (it must be assumed) to convey that *je-ne-sais-quoi* quality of Gallic eroticism; yet the other two parts perhaps suggested that the range of the proprietor's French was somewhat limited.

'Lookin' for a bit o' fun, love?'

The heavily mascara'd brunette appeared to be in her early twenties – quite a tall girl in her red high-heels, wearing black stockings, a minimal black skirt, and a low-cut, heavily sequined blouse stretched tightly over a large bosom – largely exposed – beneath the winking light-bulbs.

Déjà vu.

And, ever the voyeur, Owens was momentarily aware of all the old weaknesses.

'Come in! Come down and join the fun!'

She took a step towards him and he felt the long, blood-red fingernails curling pleasingly in his palm.

It was a good routine, and one that worked with many and many a man.

One that seemed to be working with Owens.

'How much?'

'Only three-pound membership, that's all. It's a private club, see – know wha' I mean?' For a few seconds she raised the eyes beneath the empurpled lids towards Elysium.

'Is Gloria still here?'

The earthbound eyes were suddenly suspicious – yet curious, too.

'Who?'

'If Gloria's still here, she'll let me in for nothing.'

'Lots o' names 'ere, mistah: real names – stage names . . .'

'So what's your name, beautiful?'

'Look, you wanna come in? Three pound – OK?'

'You're not being much help, you know.'

'Why don't you just fuck off?'

'You don't know Gloria?'

'What the 'ell do you *want*, mate?' she asked fiercely.

His voice was very quiet as he replied. 'I used to live fairly close by. And she used to work here, then – Gloria did. She was a stripper – one of the best in the business, so everybody said.'

For the second time the eyes in their lurid sockets seemed to betray some interest.

'When was that?'

'Twenty-odd years ago.'

'Christ! She must be a bloody granny by now!'

'Dunno. She had a child, though, I know that – a daughter . . .'

A surprisingly tall, smartly suited Japanese man had been drawn into the magnetic field of Le Club Sexy.

'Come in! Come down and—'

'How much is charge?'

'Only three pound. It's a private club, see – and you gotta be a member.'

With a strangely trusting, wonderfully polite smile, the

man took a crisp ten-pound note from his large wallet and handed it to the hostess, bowing graciously as she reached a hand behind her and parted the multicoloured vertical strips which masked from public view the threadbare carpeting on the narrow stairs leading down to the secret delights.

'You give me change, please? I give you ten pound.'

'Just tell 'em downstairs, OK?'

'Why you not give me seven pound?'

'It'll be OK – OK?'

'OK.'

Halfway down the stairs, the newly initiated member made a little note in a little black book, smiling (we may say) scrutably. He was a member of a Home Office Committee licensing all 'entertainment premises' in the district of Soho.

His expenses were generous: needed to be.

Sometimes he enjoyed his job.

'Don't you ever feel bad about that sort of thing?'

'What d'you mean?'

'He'll never get his change, will he?'

'Like I said, why don't you just fuck off!'

'Gloria used to feel bad sometimes – quite a civilized streak in that woman somewhere. You'd have liked her ... Anyway, if you do come across her, just say you met me, Geoff Owens, will you? She'll remember me – certain to. Just tell her I've got a little proposition for her. She may be a bit down on her luck. You never know these days, and I wouldn't want to think she was on her uppers ... or her daughter was, for that matter.'

'What's her daughter got to do with it?' The voice was sharp.

Owens smiled, confidently now, lightly rubbing the back of his right wrist lightly across her blouse.

'Quite a lot, perhaps. You may have quite a lot to do with it, sweetheart!'

She made no attempt to contradict him. 'In the pub' (she pointed across the street) 'half an hour, OK?'

She watched him go, the man with a five o'clock shadow who said his name was Owens. She'd never seen him before; but she'd recognize him again immediately, the dark hair drawn back above his ears, and tied in a pony-tail about eight or nine inches long.

Apart from the midnight 'milk-float', which gave passengers the impression that it called at almost every hamlet along the line the 11.20 p.m. was the last train from Paddington. And a panting Owens jumped into its rear coach as the Turbo Express suddenly juddered and began to move forward. The train was only half-full, and he found a seat immediately.

He felt pleased with himself. The assignation in the pub had proved to be even more interesting than he'd dared to expect; and he leaned back and closed his eyes contentedly as he pondered the possible implications of what he had just learned . . .

He jolted awake at Didcot, wondering where he was – realizing that he had missed the Reading stop completely. Determined to stay awake for the last twelve minutes of the journey, he picked up an *Evening Standard* someone had left on the seat opposite, and was reading the sports page when over the top of the newspaper he saw a man walking back down the carriage – *almost* to where he himself was sitting – before taking his place next to a woman. And Owens recognized him.

Recognized Mr Julian Storrs of Lonsdale.

Well! Well! Well!

At Oxford, his head still stuck behind the *Evening Standard*, Owens waited until everyone else had left the rear carriage. Then, himself alighting, he observed Storrs arm-in-arm with his companion as they climbed the steps of the footbridge which led over the tracks to Platform One. And suddenly, for the second time that evening, Owens felt a shiver of excitement – for he immediately recognized the woman, too.

How could he fail to recognize her?

She was his next-door neighbour.

Chapter Six

Monday, 19 February

Many is the gracious form that is covered with a veil; but on withdrawing this thou discoverest a grandmother

(Musharrif-Uddin, *Gulistan*)

PAINSTAKINGLY, in block capitals, the Chief Inspector wrote his name, E. MORSE; and was beginning to write his address when Lewis came into the office at 8.35 a.m. on Monday, 19 February.

'What's that, sir?'

Morse looked down at a full page torn from one of the previous day's colour supplements.

'Special offer: two free CDs when you apply to join the Music Club Library.'

Lewis looked dubious. 'Don't forget you have to buy a book every month with that sort of thing. Life's not all freebies, you know.'

'Well, it is in this case. You've just got to have a look at the first thing they send you, that's all – then send it back if you don't like it. I think they even refund the postage.'

Lewis watched as Morse completed and snipped out the application form.

'Wouldn't it be fairer if you agreed to have *some* of the books?'

'You think so?'

'At least *one* of them.'

Intense blue eyes, slightly pained, looked innocently across the desk at Sergeant Lewis.

'But I've already got this month's book – I bought it for myself for Christmas.'

He inserted the form into an envelope, on which he now wrote the Club's address. Then he took from his wallet a sheaf of plastic cards: Bodleian Library ticket; Lloyds payment card; RAC Breakdown Service; blood donor card; Blackwell's Bookshops; Oxford City Library ticket; phonecard . . . but there appeared to be no booklet of first-class stamps there. Or of second-class.

'You don't, by any chance, happen to have a stamp on you, Lewis?'

'What CDs are you going for?'

'I've ordered Janáček, the *Glagolitic Mass* – you may not know it. Splendid work – beautifully recorded by Simon Rattle. And Richard Strauss, *Four Last Songs* – Jessye Norman. I've got several recordings by other sopranos, of course.'

Of course . . .

Lewis nodded, and looked for a stamp.

It was not infrequent for Lewis to be reminded of what he had lost in life; or rather, what he'd never had in the first place. The one Strauss he knew was the 'Blue Danube' man. And he'd only recently learned there were two of *those*, as well – Senior and Junior; and which was which he'd no idea.

'Perhaps you'll be in for a bit of a let-down, sir. Some of these offers – they're not exactly up to what they promise.'

'You're an expert on these things?'

'No . . . but . . . take Sergeant—' Lewis stopped himself in time. Just as well to leave a colleague's weakness cloaked in anonymity. 'Take this chap I know. He read this advert in one of the tabloids about a free video – sex video – sent in a brown envelope with no address to say where it had come from. You know, in case the wife . . .'

'No, I don't know, Lewis. But please continue.'

'Well, he sent for one of the choices—'

'*Copenhagen Red-Hot Sex*?'

'No. *Housewives on the Job* – that was the title; and he expected, you know . . .'

Morse nodded. 'Housewives "on the job" with the milkman, the postman, the itinerant button-salesmen . . .'

Lewis grinned. 'But it wasn't, no. It just showed all these fully dressed Swedish housewives washing up the plates and peeling the potatoes.'

'Serves Sergeant Dixon right.'

'You won't mention it, sir!'

'Of course I won't. And you're probably right. You never really get something for nothing in this life. I never seem to, anyway.'

'Really, sir?'

Morse licked the flap of the white envelope. Then licked the back of the first-class stamp that Lewis had just given him.

The phone had been ringing for several seconds, and

Lewis now took the call, listening briefly but carefully, before putting his hand over the mouthpiece:

'There's been a murder, sir. On the doorstep, really – up in Bloxham Drive.'

PART TWO

Chapter Seven

> In addition to your loyal support on the ballot paper, we shall be grateful if you can agree to display the enclosed sticker in one of your windows
>
> (Extract from a 1994 local election leaflet distributed by the East Oxford Labour Party)

IT REMINDED Morse of something – that rear window of Number 17.

As a young lad he'd been fascinated by a photograph in one of his junior school text-books of the apparatus frequently fixed round the necks of slaves in the southern states of America: an iron ring from whose circumference, at regular intervals, there emanated lengthy, fearsome spikes, also of iron. The caption, as Morse recalled, had maintained that such a device readily prevented any absconding cotton-picker from passing himself off as an enfranchised citizen.

Morse had never really understood the caption.

Nor indeed, for some considerable while, was he fully to understand the meaning of the neat bullet-hole in the centre of the shattered glass, and the cracks that radiated from it regularly, like a young child's crayoning the rays of the sun.

Looking around him, Morse surveyed the area from the wobbly paving-slabs which formed a pathway at the rear of the row of terraced houses stretching along the northern side of Bloxham Drive, Kidlington, Oxfordshire. About half of the thirty-odd young trees originally planted in a staggered design beside and behind this path had been vandalized to varying degrees: some of them wholly extirpated; some cruelly snapped in the middle of their gradually firming stems; others, with many of their burgeoning branches torn off, standing wounded and forlorn amid the unkempt litter-strewn area, once planned by some Environmental Officer as a small addendum to England's green and pleasant land.

Morse felt saddened.

As did Sergeant Lewis, standing beside him.

Yet it is appropriate here to enter one important qualification. Bloxham Drive, in the view of most of its residents, was showing some few signs of unmistakable improvement. The installation of sleeping-policemen had virtually eliminated the possibilities of joy-riding; many denizens were now lying more peacefully in their beds after the eviction of one notoriously anti-social household; and over the previous two or three years the properties had fallen in price to such an extent as to form an attractive proposition to those few of the professional classes who were prepared to give the street the benefit of the doubt. To be more specific, three such persons had taken out mortgages on properties there: the properties standing at Number 1, Number 15, and Number 17.

But – yes, agreed! – Bloxham Drive and the surrounding streets was still an area a league and a league from the peaceful, leafy lanes of Gerrards Cross; and still the scene of some considerable crime.

Crime which now included murder . . .

The call had come through to Lewis at 8.40 a.m.

Just over one hour previously, whilst the sky was still unusually dark, Mrs Queenie Norris, from Number 11, had (as was her wont) taken out her eight-year-old Cavalier King Charles along the rear of the terrace, ignoring (as was her wont) the notices forbidding the fouling of pavements and verges. That was when she'd noticed it: noticed the cracked back window at Number 17 – yet failed to register too much surprise, since (as we have seen) vandalism there had become commonplace, and any missile, be it bottle or brick, would have left some similar traces of damage.

Back from her walk, Mrs Norris, as she was later to explain to the police, had felt increasingly uneasy. And just before the weather forecast on Radio 4, she had stepped out once again, now minus the duly defecated Samson, and seen that the light in the kitchen of Number 17 was still on, the blind still drawn down to the bottom of the casement.

This time she had knocked quietly, then loudly, against the back door.

But there had been no reply to her reiterated raps; and only then had she noticed that behind the hole in the kitchen window – *immediately* behind it – was a corresponding hole in the thin beige-brown material of the blind. It was at that point that she'd felt the horrid crawl of fear across her skin. Her near-neighbour worked in North Oxford, almost invariably leaving home at about a quarter to eight. And now it was coming up to the hour. Had reached the hour.

Something was wrong.

Something, Mrs Norris suspected, was seriously wrong; and she'd rung 999 immediately.

It had been ten minutes later when PCs Graham and Swift had finally forced an entry through the front door of the property to discover the grim truth awaiting them in the back kitchen: the body of a young woman lying dead upon her side, the right cheek resting on the cold red tiles, the light brown hair of her pony-tail soaked and stiffened in a pool of blood. Indeed it was not only the dreams of the two comparatively inexperienced constables, but also those of the hardened Scenes-of-Crime Officers, that would be haunted by the sight of so much blood; such a copious outpouring of blood.

And now it was Morse's turn.

'Oh dear,' said Lewis very quietly.

Morse said nothing, holding back (as ever) from any close inspection of a corpse, noting only the bullet wound, somewhere at the bottom of the neck, which clearly had been the cause of death, the cause of all the blood. Yet (as ever, too) Morse, who had never owned a camera in his life, had already taken several mental flashes of his own.

It seemed logical to assume that the murder had occurred towards the end of a fairly conventional breakfast. On the side of a wooden kitchen table – the side nearest the window – a brown plastic-topped stool had been moved slightly askew. On the table itself was a plate, a small heap of salt sprinkled with pepper at its edge, on which lay a brown egg-shell beside a wooden egg-cup; and alongside, on a second plate, half a round of toasted brown bread, buttered, and amply spread from a jar of Frank Cooper's Oxford Marmalade. And one other item: a white mug bearing the legend GREETINGS FROM GUERNSEY; bearing, too, the remains of some breakfast coffee, long since cold and muddily brown.

That was what Morse saw. And for the present that was enough; he wished to be away from the dreadful scene.

Yet before he left, he forced himself to look once more at the woman who lay there. She was wearing a white nightdress, with a faded-pink floral motif, over which was a light blue dressing-gown, reaching about halfway down the shapely, slim, unstockinged legs. It was difficult to be sure about things, of course; but Morse suspected that the twisted features of the face had been – until so very recently – just as comely as the rest of her. And for a few seconds his own face twisted, too, as if in sympathy with the murdered woman lying at his feet.

The SOCOs had now arrived; and after brief, perfunctory greetings, Morse was glad to escape and leave them to it. Bidding Lewis to initiate some immediate house-to-house enquiries, on both sides of the street, he himself stepped out of the front door into Bloxham Drive, now the scene of considerable police activity, with checkered-capped officers, the flashing blue lights of their cars, and a cordon of blue-and-white tape being thrown round the murder-house. A knot of local inhabitants, too, stood whispering there, shivering occasionally in the early morning cold, yet determined to witness the course of events unfolding.

And the media.

Recognizing the Chief Inspector, two press-men (how so early there?) pleaded for just the briefest interview – a sentence even; a TV crew from Abingdon had already covered Morse's exit from the house; and a Radio Oxford reporter waved a bulbous microphone in front of his face.

But Morse ignored them all with a look of vacuous incomprehension worthy of some deaf-mute, and proceeded to walk slowly to the end of the street (observing, all the time *observing*), where he turned left down one side of the terraced row, then left again, retracing his earlier steps along the uneven paving slabs behind the houses, stopping briefly where he and Lewis had stopped before; then completing the circuit and again curtly dismissing the converging reporters with a wave of his right hand as he walked back along the front of the terrace.

It would be untrue to say that Morse's mind had been

particularly acute on this peripatetic reconnaissance. Indeed, only one single feature of the neighbourhood had made much of an impression upon him.

A political impression.

Very soon (the evidence was all around him) there was to be an election for one of the local council seats – death of an incumbent, perhaps? – and clearly, if unusually, there appeared to be considerable interest in the matter. Stickers were to be observed in all but two of the front windows of the north-side terrace: green stickers with the red lettering of the Labour candidate's name; white stickers with the royal blue lettering of the Conservative's. With little as yet upon which his mind could fix itself, Morse had taken a straw-poll of the support shown, from Number 1 to Number 21. And hardly surprisingly, perhaps, in this marginally depressed and predominantly working-class district, the advantage was significantly with the Labour man, with six stickers to the Tory's two.

One of the stickers favouring the latter cause was displayed in the ground-floor window of Number 15. And for some reason Morse had found himself standing and wondering for a while outside the only other window in the Drive parading its confidence in the Conservative Party – and in a candidate with the splendidly patriotic name of Jonathan Bull; standing and wondering outside Number 1, at the main entrance to Bloxham Drive.

Chapter Eight

Oft have we seen him at the peep of dawn
Brushing with hasty steps the dews away
(Thomas Gray, *Elegy Written in a Country Churchyard*)

In his earlier years Geoffrey Owens had been an owl, preferring to pursue whatever tasks lay before him into the late hours of the night, often through into the still, small hours. But now, in his mid-forties, he had metamorphosed into a lark, his brain seeming perceptibly clearer and fresher in the morning. It had been no hardship, therefore, when he was invited, under the new flexi-time philosophy of his employers, to start work early and finish work early – thereby receiving a small bonus into the bargain. And, since the previous September, Owens had made it his regular practice to leave his home in Bloxham Drive just before 7 a.m., incidentally thus avoiding the traffic jams which began to build up in the upper reaches of the Banbury Road an hour or so later; and, on his return journey, missing the corresponding jams the other way, as thousands of motorists left the busy heart of Oxford for the comparative peace of the northern outskirts, and the neighbouring villages – such as Kidlington.

It was, all in all, a happy enough arrangement. And one which had applied on Monday, 19 February.

Owens had left his house at about ten minutes to seven that morning, when he had, of course, passed the house on the corner, Number 1, where a woman had watched him go. But if he in turn had spotted her, this was in no way apparent, for he had passed without a wave of recognition, and driven up to the junction, where he had turned right, on his way down into Oxford. But if he had not seen her, quite definitely she had seen him.

Traffic had been unusually light for a Monday (more often than not the busiest morning of the week) even at such a comparatively early hour; and without any appreciable hold-up Owens soon reached the entrance barrier of the large car park which serves the Oxfordshire Newspapers complex down in Osney Mead, just past the railway station along the Botley Road.

Owens had come to Oxford three years previously with an impressive-looking CV, in which the applicant asserted his 'all-round experience in the fields of reporting, copy-editing, advertising, and personnel management'. And he had been the unanimous choice of the four members of the interviewing panel. Nor had there been the slightest reason since for them to rue their decision. In fact, Owens had proved a profitable investment. With his knowledge of English grammar way above average, his job description had quickly been modified, with an appropriate increase in salary, to include responsibility for recasting the frequently ill-constructed paragraphs of his junior colleagues, and for correcting the heinous errors in orthography which blighted not a few of their offerings; and, in addition to these new tasks, to stand in as required when the Personnel Manager was called away on conferences.

As a result of these changes, Owens himself, nominally the group's senior reporter, had become more and more desk-bound, venturing out only for the big stories. Like now. For as he stood in Bloxham Drive that morning, he was never in doubt that this would be one of those 'big stories' – not just for himself but also for the steadily increasing number of media colleagues who were already joining him.

All of them waiting . . .

Waiting, in fact, until 11.30 a.m. – well before which time, as if by some sort of collective instinct, each was aware that something grotesque and gruesome had occurred in the house there numbered 17.

Chapter Nine

Instead of being arrested, as we stated, for kicking his wife down a flight of stairs and hurling a lighted kerosene lamp after her, the Revd James P. Wellman died unmarried four years ago

(Correction in a US journal, quoted by Burne-Jones in a letter to Lady Horner)

AT 11.15 A.M. LEWIS suggested that someone perhaps ought to say something.

For the past hour and a half a group of police officers had been knocking on neighbourhood doors, speaking to residents, taking brief preliminary statements. But as yet nothing official had been released to the representatives of the media assembled in a street now increasingly crowded with curious onlookers.

'Go ahead!' said Morse.

'Shall I tell them all we know?'

'That won't take you long, will it?'

'No need to keep anything back?'

'For Chrissake, Lewis! You sound as if we've *got* something to hide. If we have, why don't you tell *me*?'

'Just wondered.'

Morse's tone softened. 'It won't matter much what you tell 'em, will it?'

'All right.'

'Just one thing, though. You can remind 'em that we'd all welcome a bit of accuracy for a change. Tell 'em to stick an "h" in the middle of Bloxham Close – that sort of thing.'

'Bloxham *Drive*, sir.'

'Thank you, Lewis.'

With which, a morose-looking Morse eased himself back in the armchair in the front sitting-room, and continued his cursory examination of the papers, letters, documents, photographs, taken from the drawers of a Queen-Anne-style escritoire – a rather tasteful piece, thought Morse. Family heirloom, perhaps.

Family . . .

Oh dear!

That was always one of the worst aspects of suicides and murders: the family. This time with Mum and Dad and younger sister already on their way up from Torquay. Still, Lewis was wonderfully good at that sort of thing. Come to think of it, Lewis was quite good at several things, really – including dealing with the Press. And as Morse flicked his way somewhat fecklessly through a few more papers, he firmly resolved (although in fact he forgot) to tell his faithful sergeant exactly that before the day was through.

Immediately on confronting his interlocutors, Lewis was invited by the TV crew to go some way along the street so that he could be filmed walking before appearing in front of the camera talking. Normal TV routine, it was explained: always see a man striding along somewhere before seeing his face on the screen. So, would Sergeant Lewis please oblige with a short perambulation?

No, Sergeant Lewis wouldn't.

What he would do, though, was try to tell them what they wanted to know. Which, for the next few minutes, he did.

A murder had occurred in the kitchen of Number 17 Bloxham Drive: B-L-O-X-H-A-M –

One of the neighbours (unspecified) had earlier alerted the police to suspicious circumstances at that address –

A patrol car had been on the scene promptly; forced open the front door; discovered the body of a young woman –

The woman had been shot dead through the rear kitchen window –

The body had not as yet been officially identified –

The property appeared to show no sign – no *other* sign – of any break-in –

That was about it, really.

Amid the subsequent chorus of questions, Lewis picked out the raucous notes of the formidable female reporter from the *Oxford Star*:

'What time was all this, Sergeant?'

As it happened, Lewis knew the answer to that question very well. But he decided to be economical with the details of the surprisingly firm evidence already gleaned . . .

*

The Jacobs family lived immediately opposite Number 17, where the lady of the house, in dressing-gown and curlers, had opened her front door a few minutes after 7 a.m. in order to pick up her two pints of Co-op milk from the doorstep. Contemporaneously, exactly so, her actions had been mirrored across the street where another woman, also in a dressing-gown (though without curlers), had been picking up her own single pint. Each had looked across at the other; each had nodded a matutinal greeting.

'You're quite *sure*?' Lewis had insisted. 'It was still a bit dark, you know.'

'We've got some streetlamps, haven't we, Sergeant?'

'You *are* sure, then.'

'Unless she's got – unless she had a twin sister.'

'Sure about the *time*, too? That's very important.'

She nodded. 'I'd just watched the news headlines on BBC1 – I like to do that. Then I turned the telly off. I might have filled the kettle again . . . but, like I say, it was only a few minutes past seven. Five past, at the outside.'

It therefore seemed virtually certain that there was a time-span of no more than half an hour during which the murder had occurred: between 7.05 a.m., when Mrs Jacobs had seen her neighbour opposite, and 7.35 a.m. or so, when Mrs Norris had first noticed the hole in the window. It was unusual – *very* unusual – for such exactitude to be established at so early a stage in a murder enquiry; and there would be little need in this case for the police to be dependent upon (what Morse always called) those prevaricating pathologists . . .

*

'About quarter past seven,' answered the prevaricating Lewis.

'You're quite *sure*?' It was exactly the same question Lewis himself had asked.

'No, not sure at all. Next question?'

'Why didn't everybody hear the shot?' (The same young, ginger-headed reporter.)

'Silencer, perhaps?'

'There'd be the sound of breaking glass surely?' (A logically minded man from the *Oxford Star*.)

A series of hand gestures and silent lip-movements from the TV crew urged Lewis not to look directly into the camera.

Lewis nodded. 'Yes. In fact several of the neighbours think they heard something – two of them certainly did. But it could have been lots of things, couldn't it?'

'Such as?' (The importunate ginger-knob again.)

Lewis shrugged. 'Could have been the milkman dropping a bottle—?'

'No broken glass here, though, Sergeant.'

'Car backfiring? We don't know.'

'Does what the neighbours heard fit in with the time all right?' (The TV interviewer with his fluffy cylindrical microphone.)

'Pretty well, yes.'

The senior reporter from the *Oxford Mail* had hitherto held his peace. But now he asked a curious question, if it was a question:

'Not the two *immediate* neighbours, were they?'

Lewis looked at the man with some interest.

'Why do you say that?'

'Well, the woman who lives there' (a finger pointed to Number 19) 'she was probably still asleep at the time, and she's stone-deaf without her hearing-aid.'

'Really?'

'And the man who lives there' (a finger pointed to Number 15) 'he'd already left for work.'

Lewis frowned. 'Can you tell me how you happen to know all this, sir?'

'No problem,' replied Geoffrey Owens. 'You see, Sergeant, *I* live at Number 15.'

Chapter Ten

Where lovers lie with ardent glow,
Where fondly each forever hears
The creaking of the bed below –
Above, the music of the spheres
(Viscount Mumbles, 1797–1821)

WHEN LEWIS RETURNED from his encounter with the media, Morse was almost ready to leave the murder-house. The morning had moved towards noon, and he knew that he might be thinking a little more clearly if he were drinking a little – or at least be starting to think when he started to drink.

'Is there a real-ale pub somewhere near?'

Lewis, pleasantly gratified with his handling of the Press and TV, was emboldened to sound a note of caution.

'Doesn't do your liver much good – all this drinking.'

Surprisingly Morse appeared to accept the reminder with modest grace.

'I'm sure you're right; but my medical advisers have warned me it may well be unwise to give up alcohol at my age.'

Lewis was not impressed, for he had heard the same words – exactly the same words – on several previous occasions.

'You've had a good look around, sir?'

'Not really. I know I always find the important things. But I want *you* to have a look around. You usually manage to find the *un*important things – and often they're the things that really matter in the end.'

Lewis made little attempt to disguise his pleasure, and straightway relented.

'We could go up to the Boat at Thrupp?'

'Excellent.'

'You don't want to stay here any longer?'

'No. The SOCOs'll be another couple of hours yet.'

'You don't want to see . . . *her* again?'

Morse shook his head. 'I know what she looks like – *looked* like.' He picked up two coloured photographs and one postcard, and made towards the front door, handing over the keys of the maroon Jaguar to Lewis. 'You'd better drive – if you promise to stick to the orange juice.'

Once on their way, Lewis reported the extraordinarily strange coincidence of the press-man, Owens, living next-door to the murdered woman. But Morse, who always looked upon any coincidence in life as the norm rather than the exception, was more anxious to set forth the firm details he had himself now gleaned about Ms Rachel James, for there could now be no real doubt of her identity.

'Twenty-nine. Single. No offspring. Worked as a freelance physiotherapist at a place in the Banbury Road. CV says she went to school at Torquay Comprehensive; left there in 1984 with a clutch of competent O-levels, three A-levels – two Bs, in Biology and Geography, and an E in Media Studies.'

'Must have been fairly bright.'

'What do you mean? You need to be a moron to get an E in Media Studies,' asserted Morse, who had never seen so much as a page of any Media Studies syllabus, let alone a question paper.

He continued:

'Parents, as you know, still alive, on their way here—'

'You'll want me to see them?'

'Well, you *are* good at that sort of thing, aren't you? And if the mother's like most women she'll probably smell the beer as soon as I open the door.'

'Good reason for you to join me on the orange juice.'

Morse ignored the suggestion. 'She bought the property there just over four years ago for £65,000 and the value's been falling ever since by the look of things, so the poor lass is one of those figuring in the negative equity statistics; took out a mortgage of £55,000 – probably Mum and Dad gave her the other £10,000; and the saleable value of Number 17 is now £40,000, at the most.'

'Bought at the wrong time, sir. But some people *were* a bit irresponsible, don't you think?'

'I'm not an economist, as you know, Lewis. But I'll tell you what would have helped her. Helped so many in her boots.'

'A win on the National Lottery?'

'Wouldn't help *many*, that, would it? No. What she

could have done with is a healthy dose of inflation. It's a good thing – inflation – you know. Especially for people who've got nothing to start with. One of the best things that happened to some of us. One year I remember I had three jumps in salary.'

'Not many would agree with you on that, though, would they? Conservative and Labour both agree about inflation.'

'Ah! Messrs Bull and Thomas, you mean?'

'You noticed the stickers?'

'I notice most things. It's just that some of them don't register – not immediately.'

'What'll you have, sir?'

'Lew-is! We've known each other long enough, surely.'

As Morse tasted the hostelry's Best Bitter, he passed over a photograph of Rachel James.

'Best one of her I could find.'

Lewis looked down at the young woman.

'Real good-looker,' he said softly.

Morse nodded. 'I bet she'd have set a few hearts all a-flutter.'

'Including yours, sir?'

Morse drank deeply on his beer before replying. 'She'd probably have a good few boyfriends, that's all I'm suggesting. As for my own potential susceptibility, that's beside the point.'

'Of course.' Lewis smiled good-naturedly. 'What else have we got?'

'What do you make of this? One of the few interesting things there, as far as I could see.'

Lewis now considered the postcard handed to him. First, the picture on the front: a photograph of a woodland ride, with a sunlit path on the left, and a pool of azured bluebells to the right. Then turning over the card, he read the cramped lines amateurishly typed on the left-hand side:

Ten Times I beg, dear Heart, let's Wed!
(Thereafter long may Cupid reigne)
Let's tread the Aisle, where thou hast led
The fifteen Bridesmaides in thy Traine.
Then spend our honeyed Moon a-bed,
With Springs that creake againe – againe!
(John Wilmot, 1672)

That was all.

No salutation.

No valediction.

And on the right-hand side of the postcard – nothing: no address, with the four dotted, parallel lines devoid of any writing, the top right-hand rectangle devoid of any stamp.

Lewis, a man not familiar with seventeenth-century love-lyrics, read the lines, then read them again, with only semi-comprehension.

'Pity she didn't get round to filling in the address, sir. Looks as if she might be proposing to somebody.'

'Aren't you making an assumption?'

'Pardon?'

'Did you see a typewriter in the house?'

'She could have typed it at work.'

'Yes. You must get along there soon.'

'You're the boss.'

'Nice drop o' beer, this. In good nick.' Morse drained the glass and set it down in the middle of the slightly rickety table, whilst Lewis took a gentle sip of his orange juice; and continued to sit firmly fixed to his seat.

Morse continued:

'No! You're making a false assumption – I *think* you are. You're assuming she'd just written this to somebody and then forgotten the fellow's address, right? Pretty unlikely, isn't it? If she was proposing to him.'

'Perhaps she couldn't find a stamp.'

'Perhaps . . .'

Reluctantly Morse got to his feet and pushed his glass across the bar. 'You don't want anything more yourself, do you, Lewis?'

'No thanks.'

'You've nothing less?' asked the landlady, as Morse tendered a twenty-pound note. 'You're the first ones in today and I'm a bit short of change.'

Morse turned round. 'Any change on you, by any chance, Lewis?'

'You see,' continued Morse, 'you're still assuming she wrote it, aren't you?'

'And she didn't?'

'I think someone wrote the card to *her*, put it in an

envelope, and then addressed the envelope – not the card.'

'Why not just address the card?'

'Because whoever wrote it didn't want anyone else to read it.'

'Why not just phone her up?'

'Difficult – if he was married and his wife was always around.'

'He could ring her from a phone-box.'

'Risky – if anyone saw him.'

Lewis nodded without any conviction: 'And it's only a bit of poetry.'

'Is it?' asked Morse quietly.

Lewis picked up the card again. 'Perhaps it's this chap called "Wilmot", sir – the date's just there to mislead us.'

'Mislead *you*, perhaps. John Wilmot, Earl of Rochester, was a court poet to Charles II. He wrote some delightfully pornographic lyrics.'

'So it's – it's all genuine?'

'I didn't say that, did I? The name's genuine, but not the poem. Any English scholar would know that's not seventeenth-century verse.'

'I'm sure you're right, sir.'

'And if I'm right about the card coming in an envelope – fairly recently – we might be able to find the envelope, agreed? Find a postmark, perhaps? Even a bit of handwriting?'

Lewis looked dubious. 'I'd better get something organized, then.'

'All taken care of! I've got a couple of the DCs looking through the wastepaper baskets and the dustbin.'

'You reckon this is important, then?'

'Top priority! You can see that. She's been meeting some man – meeting him secretly. Which means he's probably married, probably fairly well known, probably got a prominent job, probably a local man—'

'Probably lives in Peterborough,' mumbled Lewis.

'That's exactly why the postmark's so vital!' countered an unamused Morse. 'But if he's an Oxford man . . .'

'Do you know what the population of Oxford *is*?'

'I know it to the nearest *thousand*!' snapped Morse.

Then, of a sudden, the Chief Inspector's mood completely changed. He tapped the postcard.

'Don't be despondent, Lewis. You see, we know just a little about this fellow already, don't we?'

He smiled benignly after draining his second pint; and since no other customers had as yet entered the lounge, Lewis resignedly got to his feet and stepped over to the bar once more.

Lewis picked up the postcard again.

'Give me a clue, sir.'

'You know the difference between nouns and verbs, of course?'

'How could I forget something like that?'

'Well, at certain periods in English literature, all the nouns were spelt with capital letters. Now, as you can see, there are *eight* nouns in those six lines – each of them spelt with a capital letter. But there are *nine* capitals

– forgetting the first word of each line. Now which is the odd one out?'

Lewis pretended to study the lines once more. He'd played this game before, and he trusted he could get away with it again, as his eyes suddenly lit up a little.

'Ah . . . I think – I *think* I see what you mean.'

'Hits you in the eye, doesn't it, that "Wed" in the first line? And that's what it was *intended* to do.'

'Obviously.'

'What's it mean?'

'What, "Wed"? Well, it means "marry" – you know, get hitched, get spliced, tie the knot—'

'What else?'

'Isn't that enough?'

'What *else*?'

'I suppose you're going to tell me it's Anglo-Saxon or something.'

'Not exactly. Not far off, though. Old English, in fact. And what's it short for?'

'"Wednesday"?' suggested Lewis tentatively.

Morse beamed at his sergeant. 'Woden's day – the fourth day of the week. So we've got a *day*, Lewis. And what else do you need, if you're going to arrange a date with a woman?'

Lewis studied the lines yet again. 'Time? Time, yes! I see what you mean, sir. "Ten Times" . . . "fifteen Bridesmaides" . . . Well, well, well! Ten-fifteen!'

Morse nodded. 'With a.m. likelier than p.m. Doesn't say where though, does it?'

Lewis studied the lines for the fifth time.

'"Traine", perhaps?'

'Well done! "Meet me at the station to catch the ten-fifteen a.m. train" – that's what it says. And we know where that train goes, don't we?'

'Paddington.'

'Exactly.'

'If only we knew who he was . . .'

Morse now produced his second photograph – a small passport-sized photograph of two people: the woman, Rachel James (no doubt of that), turning partially round and slightly upward in order to kiss the cheek of a considerably older man with a pair of smiling eyes beneath a distinguished head of greying hair.

'Who's he, sir?'

'Dunno. We could find out pretty quickly, though, if we put his photo in the local papers.'

'*If* he's local.'

'Even if he's not local, I should think.'

'Bit dodgy, sir.'

'Too dodgy at this stage, I agree. But we can try another angle, can't we? Tomorrow's Tuesday, and the day after that's Wednesday – Woden's day . . .'

'You mean he may turn up at the station?'

'If the card's fairly recent, yes.'

'Unless he's heard she's been murdered.'

'Or unless he murdered her himself.'

'Worth a try, sir. And if he *does* turn up, it'll probably mean he didn't murder her . . .'

Morse made no comment.

'Or, come to think of it, it might be a fairly clever thing to do if he *did* murder her.'

Morse drained his glass and stood up.

'You know something? I reckon orange juice occasionally germinates your brain cells.'

As he drove his chief down to Kidlington, Lewis returned the conversation to where it had begun.

'You haven't told me what you think about this fellow Owens – the dead woman's next-door neighbour.'

'Death is always the next-door neighbour,' said Morse sombrely. 'But don't let it affect your driving, Lewis!'

Chapter Eleven

Wednesday, 21 February

Orandum est ut sit mens sana in corpore sano
(Our aim? Just a brain that's not addled with pox,
And a guaranteed clean bill-of-health from the docs)
(Juvenal, *Satires X*)

THE NEXT MEETING of the Lonsdale Fellows had been convened for 10 a.m.

In the Stamper Room.

William Leslie Stamper, b. 1880, had graduated from Oxford University in 1903 with the highest marks (it is said) ever recorded in Classical Moderations. The bracketed caveat in the previous sentence would be unnecessary were it not that the claim for such distinction was perpetuated, in later years, by one person only – by W. L. Stamper himself. And it is pointless to dwell upon the matter since no independent verification is available: the relevant records had been removed from Oxford to a safe place, thereafter never to be seen again, during the First World War – a war in which Stamper had not been an active participant, owing to an illness which was unlikely to prolong his eminently promising career as a don for more than a couple of years or so. Such nonparticipation in the great events of 1914–18 was a major sadness (it is said) to Stamper himself, who was frequently heard to lament his own failure to figure among the casualty lists from the fields of Flanders or Passchendaele.

Now, the reader may readily be forgiven for assuming from the preceding paragraph that Stamper had been a time-server; a dissembling self-seeker. Yet such an assumption is highly questionable, though not necessarily untrue. When, for example, in 1925, the Mastership of Lonsdale fell vacant, and nominations were sought amid the groves of Academe, Stamper had refused to let his name go forward, on the grounds that if ten years earlier he had been declared unfit to fight in defence of his country he could hardly be considered fit to undertake the governance of the College; specifically so, since the Statutes stipulated a candidate whose body was no less healthy than his brain.

Thereafter, in his gentle, scholarly, pedantic manner, Stamper had passed his years teaching the esoteric skills of Greek Prose and Verse Composition – until retiring at the age of sixty-five, two years before the statutory limit, on the grounds of ill-health. No one, certainly not Stamper himself (it is said), anticipated any significant continuation of his life, and the College Fellows unanimously backed a proposal that the dear old boy should have the privilege, during the few remaining years of his life, of living in the finest set of rooms that the College had to offer.

Thus it was that the legendary Stamper had stayed on in Lonsdale as an honorary Emeritus Fellow, with full dining rights, from the year of his retirement, 1945, to 1955; and then to 1965 . . . and 1975; and almost indeed until 1985, when he had finally died at the age of 104 – and then not through any dysfunction of the bodily organs, but from a fall beside his rooms in the front quad after a heavy bout of drinking at a Gaudy, his last words (it is said) being a whispered request for the Madeira to be passed round once again.

The agenda which lay before Sir Clixby Bream and his colleagues that morning was short and fairly straightforward:

(i) To receive apologies for absence
(ii) To approve the minutes of the previous meeting (already circulated)
(iii) To consider the Auditors' statement on College expenditure, Michaelmas 1995
(iv) To recommend appropriate procedures for the election of a new Master
(v) AOB

Items (i)–(iii) took only three minutes, and would have taken only one, had not the Tutor for Admissions sought an explanation of why the 'Stationery etc' bill for the College Office had risen by four times the current rate of inflation. For which increase the Domestic Bursar admitted full responsibility, since instead of ordering 250 Biros he had inadvertently ordered 250 *boxes* of Biros.

This confession put the meeting into good humour, as it passed on to item (iv).

The Master briefly restated the criteria to be met by potential applicants: first, that he be not in Holy Orders; second, that he be mentally competent, and particularly so in the 'Skills of the Arithmetick' (as the original Statute had it); third, that he be free from serious bodily infirmity. On the second criterion, the Master suggested that since it was now virtually impossible (a gentle glance here at the innumerate Professor of Arabic) to fail GCSE Mathematics, there could be little problem for anyone. As far as the third criterion was concerned however (the Master grew more solemn now) there was a sad announcement he had to make. One name previously put forward had been withdrawn – that of Dr Ridgeway, the brilliant micro-biologist from Balliol, who had developed serious heart trouble at the comparatively youthful age of forty-three.

Amid murmurs of commiseration round the table, the Master continued:

'Therefore, gentlemen, we are left with two nominations only . . . unless we . . . unless anyone . . . ? No?'

No.

Well, that was pleasing, the Master declared: he had always wished his successor to be appointed from within the College. And so it would be. Voting would take place in the time-honoured way: a single sheet of paper bearing the handwritten name of the preferred candidate, with the signature of the Voting Fellow beneath it, must be delivered to the Master's Lodge before noon on the nineteenth of March, one month away.

The Master proceeded to wish the two candidates well; and Julian Storrs and Denis Cornford, by chance seated next to each other, shook hands smilingly, like a couple of boxers before the weigh-in for a bruising fight.

That was not quite all.

Under AOB, the Tutor for Admissions was moved to make his second contribution of the morning.

'Perhaps it may be possible, Master, in view of the current plethora of pens in the College Office, for the Domestic Bursar to send us each a free Biro with which we can write down our considered choices for Master?'

It was a nice touch, typical of an Oxford SCR; and when at 10.20 a.m. they left the Stamper Room and moved outside into the front quad, most of the Fellows were grinning happily.

But not the Domestic Bursar.

Nor Julian Storrs.

Nor Denis Cornford.

Chapter Twelve

The virtue of the camera is not the power it has to transform the photographer into an artist, but the impulse it gives him to keep on looking – and looking

(Brooks Atkinson, *Once Around the Sun*)

EARLIER THAT SAME morning Morse and Lewis had been sitting together drinking coffee in the canteen at Kidlington Police HQ.

'Well, that's them!' said an unwontedly ungrammatical Morse as he pointed to the photograph which some darkroom boy had managed to enlarge and enhance. 'Our one big clue, that; one *small* clue, anyway.'

As Lewis saw things, the enlargement appeared to have been reasonably effective as far as the clothing was concerned; yet, to be truthful, the promised 'enhancement' of the two faces, those of the murdered woman and of the man so close beside her, seemed to have blurred rather than focused any physiognomical detail.

'Well?' asked Morse.

'Worse than the original.'

'Nonsense! Look at that.' Morse pointed to the tight

triangular knot of the man's tie, which appeared – just – above a high-necked grey sweater.

Yes. Lewis acknowledged that the colour and pattern of the tie were perhaps a little clearer.

'I think I almost recognize that tie,' continued Morse slowly. 'That deepish maroon colour. And that' (he pointed again) 'that narrow white stripe . . .'

'We never had ties at school,' ventured Lewis.

But Morse was too deeply engrossed to bother about his sergeant's former school uniform, or lack of it, as with a magnifying glass he sought further to enhance(?) the texture of the small relevant area of the photograph.

'Bit o' taste there, Lewis. Little bit o' class. I wouldn't be surprised if it's the tie of the Old Wykehamists' Classical Association.'

Lewis said nothing.

And Morse looked at him almost accusingly. 'You don't seem very interested in what I'm telling you.'

'Not too much, perhaps.'

'All right! Perhaps it's not a public-school tie. So what tie do *you* think it is?'

Again Lewis said nothing.

After a while, a semi-mollified Morse picked up the photograph, returned it to its buff-coloured Do-Not-Bend envelope, and sat back in his seat.

He looked tired.

And, as Lewis knew, he was frustrated too, since necessarily the whole of the previous day had been spent on precisely those aspects of detective work that Morse disliked the most: admin, organization, procedures –

with as yet little opportunity for him to indulge in the things he told himself he did the best: hypotheses, imaginings, the occasional leap into the semi-darkness.

It was now 9 a.m.

'You'd better get off to the station, Lewis. And good luck!'

'What are *you* planning to do?'

'Going down into Oxford for a haircut.'

'We've got a couple of new barbers' shops opened here. No need to—'

'I – am – going – down – into – Oxford, all right? A bit later, I'm going to meet a fellow who's an expert on ties, all right?'

'I'll give you a lift, if you like.'

'No. It only takes one of those shapely lasses in Shepherd and Woodward's about ten minutes to trim my locks – and I'm not meeting this fellow till eleven.'

'King's Arms, is it?'

'Ah! You're prepared to guess about *that*.'

'Pardon?'

'So why not have a guess about the tie? Come on!'

'I dunno.'

'Nor do *I* bloody know. That's exactly why we've got to guess, man.'

Lewis stood by the door now. It was high time he went.

'I haven't got a clue about all those posh ties you see in the posh shops in the High. For all I know he probably got it off the tie-rack in Marks and Spencer's.'

'No. I don't think so.'

'Couldn't we just cut a few corners? Perhaps we ought to put the photo in the *Oxford Mail*. We'd soon find out who he was then.'

Morse considered the possibility anew.

'Ye-es ... and if we find he's got nothing to do with the murder ...'

'We can eliminate him from enquiries.'

'Ye-es. Eliminate his marriage, too – '

' – if he's married – '

' – and ruin his children – '

' – if he's got any.'

'You just get off to the railway station, Lewis.'

Morse had had enough.

Chapter Thirteen

> It is the very temple of discomfort
> (John Ruskin, *The Seven Lamps of Architecture* –
> referring to the building of a railway station)

At 9.45 a.m. Lewis was seated strategically at one of the small round tables in the refreshment area adjacent to Platform One. Intermittently an echoing loudspeaker announced arrivals or apologies for delays; and, at 9.58, recited a splendid litany of all the stops on the slow train to Reading: Radley, Culham, Appleford, Didcot Parkway, Cholsey, Goring and Streatley . . .

Cholsey, yes.

Mrs Lewis was a big fan of Agatha Christie, and he'd often promised to take her to Cholsey churchyard where the great crime novelist was buried. But one way or another he'd never got round to it.

The complex was busy, with passengers constantly leaving the station through the two automatic doors to Lewis's right, to walk down the steps outside to the taxi-rank and buses for the city centre; passengers constantly entering through those same doors, making for the ticket-windows, the telephones, the Rail Information office; passengers turning left, past Lewis, in order to buy newspapers, sweets, paperbacks, from the Menzies shop – or sandwiches, cakes, coffee, from the Quick Snack counter alongside.

From where he sat, Lewis could just read one of the display screens: the 10.15 train to Paddington, it appeared, would be leaving on time – no minutes late. But he had seen no one remotely resembling the man whose photograph he'd tucked inside his copy of the *Daily Mirror*.

At 10.10 a.m. the train drew in to Platform One, and passengers were now getting on. But still there was no one to engage Lewis's attention; no one standing around impatiently as if waiting for a partner; no one sitting anxiously consulting a wristwatch every few seconds, or walking back and forth to the exit doors and scanning the occupants of incoming taxis.

No one.

Lewis got to his feet and went out on to the platform, walking quickly along the four coaches which comprised the Turbo Express for Paddington, memorizing as best he could the face he'd so earnestly been studying that morning. But, again, he could find no one resembling the man who had once sat beside the murdered woman in a photographic booth.

No one.

It was then, at the last minute (quite literally so), that the idea occurred to him.

A young-looking ticket-collector was leaning out of one of the rear windows whilst a clinking refreshment-trolley was being lifted awkwardly aboard. Lewis showed him his ID; showed him the photograph.

'Have you ever seen either of these two on the Paddington train? Or any other train?'

The acne-faced youth examined the ID card as if suspecting, perchance, that it might be a faulty ticket; then, equally carefully, looked down at the photograph before looking up at Lewis.

Someone blew a whistle.

'Yes, I have. Seen *him*, anyway. Do you want to know his name, Sergeant? I remember it from his Railcard.'

Chapter Fourteen

A well-tied tie is the first serious step in life
(Oscar Wilde)

Morse caught a No. 2A bus into the centre of Oxford, alighting at Carfax, thence walking down the High and entering Shepherd and Woodward's, where he descended the stairs to Gerrard's hairdressing saloon.

'The usual, sir?'

Morse was glad that he was being attended to by Gerrard himself. It was not that the proprietor was gifted with trichological skills significantly superior to those of his attractive female assistants; it was just that Gerrard had always been an ardent admirer of Thomas Hardy, and during his life had acquired an encyclopaedic knowledge of the great man's works.

'Yes, please,' answered Morse, looking morosely into the mirror at hair that had thinly drifted these last few years from ironish-grey to purish-white.

As Morse stood up to wipe the snippets of hair from his face with a hand-towel, he took out the photograph and showed it to Gerrard.

'Has he ever been in here?'

'Don't think so. Shall I ask the girls?'

Morse considered. 'No. Leave it for the present.'

'Remember the Hardy poem, Mr Morse? "The Photograph"?'

Morse did. Yet only vaguely.

'Remind me.'

'I used to have it by heart but . . .'

'We all get older,' admitted Morse.

Gerrard now scanned the pages of his extraordinary memory.

'You remember Hardy'd just burnt a photo of one of his old flames – he didn't know if she was alive or not – she was someone from the back of beyond of his life – but he felt awfully moved – as if he was putting her to death somehow – when he burned the photo . . . Just a minute . . . just a minute, I think I've got it:

Well – she knew nothing thereof did she survive,
And suffered nothing if numbered among the dead;
    Yet – yet – if on earth alive
Did she feel a smart, and with vague strange anguish strive?
If in heaven, did she smile at me sadly and shake her head?'

Morse felt saddened as he walked out into the High. Hardy always managed to make him feel sad. And particularly so now, since only a few days earlier he'd consigned a precious photograph to the flames: a photograph hitherto pressed between pages 88–89 of his *Collected Poems of A. E. Housman* – the photograph of a dark-haired young woman seated on a broken classical column somewhere in Crete. A woman named Ellie Smith; a woman whom he'd loved – and lost.

Morse pondered the probabilities. Had other photographs been burned or torn to little pieces since the murder of Rachel James – photographs hitherto kept in books or secret drawers?

Perhaps Lewis was right. Why not publish the photo in the *Oxford Mail*? Assuredly, there'd be hundreds of incoming calls: so many of them wrong, of course – but some few of them probably right . . .

Morse turned left into Alfred Street, and walked down the narrow cobbled lane to the junction with Blue Boar Street, where he tried the saloon-bar door of the Bear Inn.

Locked – with the opening hour displayed disappointingly as midday. It was now 11.20 a.m., and Morse felt thirsty. Perhaps he was always thirsty. That morning, though, he felt preternaturally thirsty. In fact he would gladly have swallowed a pint or two of ice-cold lager – a drink which at almost any other time would have been considered a betrayal by a real-ale addict like Morse.

He tapped lightly on the glass of the door. Tapped again. The door was opened.

A few minutes later, after offering identification, after a brief explanation of his purpose, Morse was seated with the landlord, Steven Lowbridge, at a table in the front bar.

'Would you like a coffee or something?' asked Sonya, his wife.

Morse turned round and looked towards the bar,

where a row of beers paraded their pedigrees on the hand-pumps.

'Is the Burton in good nick?'

The landlord (Morse learned) had been at the Bear Inn for five years, greatly enjoying his time there. A drinking-house had been on the site since 1242, and undergraduates and undergraduettes were still coming in to crowd the comparatively small pub: from Oriel and Christ Church mostly; from Lincoln and Univ, too.

And the ties?

The Bear Inn was nationally – internationally – renowned for its ties: about five thousand of them at the last count. Showcases of ties covered the walls, covered the ceilings, in each of the bars: ties from Army regiments, sports clubs, schools and OB associations; ties from anywhere and everywhere. The collection started (Morse learned) in 1954, when the incumbent landlord had invited any customer with an interesting-looking tie to have the last three or four inches of its back-end cut off – in exchange for a couple of pints of beer. Thereafter, the snipped-off portions were put on display in cabinets, with a small square of white card affixed to each giving provenance and description.

Morse nodded encouragingly as the landlord told his well-rehearsed tale, occasionally casting a glance at the cabinet on the wall immediately opposite: Yale University Fencing Club; Kenya Police; Welsh Schoolboys' Hockey Association; Women's Land Army . . .

Ye gods!

What a multitude of ties!

Morse's glass was empty; and the landlady tentatively suggested that the Chief Inspector would perhaps enjoy a further pint?

Morse had no objection; and made his way to the Gents where, as he washed his hands, he wondered whither all the washbasin plugs in the world could have disappeared – plugs from every pub, from every hotel, from every public convenience in the land. Somewhere (Morse mused) there must surely be a prodigious pile of basin-plugs, as high as some Egyptian pyramid.

Back in the bar, Morse produced his photograph and pointed to the little patch of tie.

'Do you think there's anything like that here?'

Lowbridge looked down at the slimly striped maroon tie, shaking his head dubiously.

'Don't *think* so . . . But make yourself at home – please have a look round – for as long as you like.'

Morse experienced disappointment.

If only Lewis were there! Lewis – so wonderfully competent with this sort of thing: checking, checking, checking, the contents of the cabinets.

Help, Lewis!

But Lewis was elsewhere. And for twenty-five minutes or so, Morse moved round the two bars, with increasing fecklessness and irritation.

Nothing was matching . . .

Nothing.

'Find what you're after?' It was the darkly attractive Sonya, just returned from a shopping expedition to the Westgate Centre.

'No, sadly no,' admitted Morse. 'It's a bit like a farmer looking for a lost contact lens in a ploughed field.'

'That what you're looking for?'

Sonya Lowbridge pointed to the tie in the photograph that still lay on the table there.

Morse nodded. 'That's it.'

'But I can tell you where you can find that.'

'You can?' Morse's eyes were suddenly wide, his mouth suddenly dry.

'Yep! I was looking for a tie for Steve's birthday. And you'll find one just like that on the tie-rack in Marks and Spencer's.'

CHAPTER FIFTEEN

A Slave has but one Master; yet ambitious folk have as many masters as there are people who may be useful in bettering their position

(La Bruyère, *Characters*)

'WELL?'

Julian Storrs closed the front door behind him, hung up his dripping plastic mac, and took his wife into his arms.

'No external candidates – just the two of us.'

'That's wonderful news!' Angela Storrs moved away from her husband's brief, perfunctory embrace, and led the way into the lounge of the splendidly furnished property in Polstead Road, a thoroughfare linking the Woodstock Road with Aristotle Lane (the latter, incidentally, Morse's favourite Oxford street-name).

'Certainly not bad news, is it? If the gods just smile on us a little . . .'

'Drink?'

'I think I may have earned a small brandy.'

She poured his drink; poured herself a large Dry Martini; lit a cigarette; and sat beside him on the brown-leather settee. She clinked her glass with his, and momentarily her eyes gleamed with potential triumph.

'To *you*, Sir Julian!'

'Just a minute! We've got to win the bloody thing first. No pushover, old Denis, you know: good College man – fine scholar – first-class brain—'

'Married to a second-class tart!'

Storrs shook his head with an uneasy smile.

'You're being a bit cruel, love.'

'Don't call me "love" – as if you come from Rotherham, or somewhere.'

'What's wrong with Rotherham?' He put his left arm around her shoulders, and forced an affectionate smile to his lips as he contemplated the woman he'd married just over twenty years previously – then pencil-slim, fresh-faced, and wrinkle-free.

Truth to tell, she was aging rather more quickly than most women of her years. Networks of varicose veins marred the long, still-shapely legs; and her stomach was a little distended around the waistband of the elegant trouser-suits which recently she almost invariably wore. The neck had grown rather gaunt, and there were lines and creases round her eyes. Yet the face itself was firmly featured still; and to many a man she remained an attractive woman – as she had appeared to Julian Storrs when first he had encountered her . . . in those extraordinary circumstances. And few there were who even now could easily resist the invitation of those almond eyes when after some dinner party or drinks reception she removed the dark glasses she had begun to wear so regularly.

Having swiftly swallowed her Martini, Angela Storrs got to her feet and poured herself another – her husband making no demur. In fact, he was quite happy when she decided to indulge her more than occasional craving for alcohol, since then she would usually go to bed, go to sleep, and reawaken in a far more pleasant frame of mind.

'What are your chances – honestly?'

'Hope is a Christian virtue, you know that.'

'Christ! Can't you think of anything better to say than that?'

He was silent awhile. 'It means a lot to you, Angela, doesn't it?'

'It means a lot to you, too,' she replied, allowing her slow words to take their full effect. 'It *does*, doesn't it?'

'Yes,' he replied softly, 'it means almost everything to me.'

Angela got up and poured herself another Martini.

'I'm glad you said that. You know why? Because it doesn't just mean *almost* everything to me – it means *literally* everything. I want to be the Master's Wife, Julian. I want to be Lady Storrs! Do you understand how much I want that?'

'Yes . . . yes, I think I do.'

'So . . . so if we have to engage in any "dirty-tricks" business . . .'

'What d'you mean?'

'Nothing specific.'

'What d'you mean?' he repeated.

'As I say . . .'

'Come on! Tell me!'

'Well, let's say if it became known in the College that Shelly Cornford was an insatiable nymphomaniac . . . ?'

'That just isn't *fair*!'

Angela Storrs got to her feet and drained the last drop of her third drink:

'Who said it *was*?'

'Where are you going?'

'Upstairs, for a lie-down, if you don't object. I'd had a few before you got back – hadn't you noticed? But I don't suppose so, no. You haven't really noticed me much at all recently, have you?'

'What's that supposed to mean?'

But she was already leaving the room, and seemed not to hear.

Storrs took another small sip of his brandy, and pulled the copy of the previous evening's *Oxford Mail* from the lower shelf of the coffee-table, its front-page headline staring at him again:

MURDER AT KIDLINGTON
Woman Shot Through Kitchen Window

*

'What did you tell Denis?'

'He's got a tutorial, anyway. I just said I'd be out shopping.'

'He told you about the College Meeting?'

She nodded.

'You pleased?'

'Uh, uh!'

'It'll be a bit of a nerve-racking time for you.'

'You should know!'

'Only a month of it, though.'

'What d'you think his chances are?'

'Difficult to say.'

'Will *you* vote for him?'

'I don't have a vote.'

'Unless it's a tie.'

'Agreed. But that's unlikely, they tell me. Arithmetically quite impossible – if all twenty-three Fellows decide to vote.'

'So you won't really have much say in things at all.'

'Oh, I wouldn't say that. I'll be a bit surprised if one or two of the Fellows don't ask me for a little advice about, er, about their choice.'

'And?'

'And I shall try to be helpful.'

'To Denis, you mean?'

'Now I didn't *say* that, did I?'

The great cooling-towers of Didcot power-station loomed into view on the left, and for a while little more was said as the two of them continued the drive south along the A34, before turning off, just before the Ridgeway, towards the charming little village of West Ilsley.

'I feel I'm letting poor old Denis down a bit,' he said, as the dark blue Daimler pulled up in front of the village pub.

'Don't you think *I* do?' she snapped. 'But I don't keep on about it.'

At the bar, he ordered a dry white wine for Shelly Cornford and a pint of Old Speckled Hen for himself;

and the pair of them studied the Egon Ronay menu chalked up on a blackboard before making their choices, and sitting down at a window-table overlooking the sodden village green.

'Do you think we should stop meeting?' He asked it quietly.

She appeared to consider the question more as an exercise in logical evaluation than as any emotional dilemma.

'I don't want that to happen.'

She brushed the back of her right wrist down the front of his dark grey suit.

'Pity we've ordered lunch,' he said quietly.

'We can always give it a miss.'

'Where shall we go?'

'Before we go anywhere, I shall want *you* to do something for *me*.'

'You mean something for Denis?'

She nodded decisively.

'I can't really promise you too much, you know that.'

She looked swiftly around the tables there, before moving her lips to his ear. '*I* can, though. I can promise you everything, Clixby,' she whispered.

From his room in College, Denis Cornford had rung Shelly briefly just before 11 a.m. She'd be out later, as she'd mentioned, but he wanted to tell her about the College Meeting as soon as possible.

He told her.

He was pleased – she could sense that.

She was pleased – he could sense that.

Cornford had half an hour to spare before his next tutorial with a very bright first-year undergraduette from Nottingham who possessed one of the most astonishingly retentive memories he had ever encountered, and a pair of the loveliest legs that had ever folded themselves opposite him. Yet he experienced not even the mildest of erotic day-dreams as now, briefly, he thought about her.

He walked over to the White Horse, the narrow pub between the two Blackwell's shops just opposite the Sheldonian; and soon he was sipping a large Glenmorangie, and slowly coming to terms with the prospect that in a month's time he might well be the Master of Lonsdale College. By nature a diffident man, he was for some curious reason beginning to feel a little more confident about his chances. Life was a funny business – and the favourite often failed to win the Derby, did it not?

Yes, odd things were likely to happen in life.

Against all the odds, as it were.

His black-stockinged student was sitting cross-legged on the wooden steps outside his room, getting to her feet as soon as she saw him. Being with Cornford, talking with him for an hour every week – that had become the highlight of her time at Oxford. But History was the great fascination in his life – not her.

She knew that.

Chapter Sixteen

Prosōpagnoia (n.): the failure of any person to recognize the face of any other person, howsoever recently the aforementioned persons may have mingled in each other's company

(*Small's Enlarged English Dictionary*,
13th Edition, 1806)

FROM OXFORD RAILWAY station, at 10.20 a.m., Lewis had tried to ring Morse at HQ. But to no avail. The dramatic news would have to wait awhile, and at least Lewis now had ample time to execute his second order of the day.

There had been just the two of them at the Oxford Physiotherapy Centre – although 'Centre' seemed a rather grandiloquent description of the ground-floor premises of the large, detached red-brick house halfway down the Woodstock Road ('1901' showing on the black drainpipe): the small office, off the spacious foyer; the single treatment room, to the right, its two beds separated by mobile wooden screens; and an inappropriately luxurious loo, to the left.

Rachel James's distressed partner, a plain-featured,

muscular divorcée in her mid-forties, could apparently throw little or no light on the recent tragedy. Each of them a fully qualified physiotherapist, they had gone freelance after a difference of opinion with the Hospital Trust, and two years earlier had decided to join forces and form their own private practice: women for the most part, troubled with ankles and knees and elbows and shoulders. The venture had been fairly successful, although they would have welcomed a few more clients – especially Rachel, perhaps, who (as Lewis learned for a second time) had been wading deeper and deeper into negative equity.

Boyfriends? – Lewis had ventured.

Well, she was attractive – face, figure – and doubtless there had been a good many admirers. But no specific beau; no one that Rachel spoke of as anyone special; no incoming calls on the office phone, for example.

'That hers?' Lewis had asked.

'Yes.'

Lewis took down a white coat from its hook behind the door and looked at the oval badge: CHARTERED SOCIETY OF PHYSIOTHERAPY printed round a yellow crest. He felt inside the stiffly starched pockets.

Nothing.

Not even Morse (Lewis allowed the thought) could have made much of *that*.

Each of the two women had a personal drawer in the office desk, and Lewis looked carefully through the items which Rachel had kept at hand during her own working hours: lip-stick; lip-salve; powder-compact; deodorant stick; a small packet of tissues; two Biros, blue and red; a yellow pencil; a pocket English dictionary (OUP); and a library book. Nothing else. No personal diary; no letters.

Again Lewis felt (though wrongly this time) that Morse would have shared his disappointment.

As for Morse, he had called in at his bachelor flat in North Oxford before returning to Police HQ. Always, after a haircut, he went through the ritual of washing his hair – and changing his shirt, upon which even a few stray hairs left clinging seemed able to effect an intense irritation on what, as he told himself (and others), was a particularly sensitive skin.

When he finally returned to HQ he found Lewis already back from his missions.

'You're looking younger, sir.'

'No, you're wrong. I reckon this case has put years on me already.'

'I meant the haircut.'

'Ah, yes. Rather nicely done, isn't it?'

'You had a good morning, sir – apart from the haircut?'

'Well, you know – er – satisfactory. What about you?'

Lewis smiled happily.

'Do you want the good news first or the bad news?'

'The bad news.'

'Well, not "bad" – just not "news" at all, really. I don't think we're going to get many leads from her work-place. In fact I don't think we're going to get any.' And Lewis proceeded to give an account of his visit to the Oxford Physiotherapy Centre.

'What time did she get there every morning?'

Lewis consulted his notes. 'Five past, ten past eight – about then. Bit early. But if she left it much later she'd hit the heavy Kidlington traffic down into Oxford, wouldn't she?'

'Mm ... The first treatments don't begin till quarter to nine, you say.'

'Or nine o'clock.'

'What did she do before the place opened?'

'Dunno.'

'*Read*, Lewis!'

'Well, like I said, there was a library book in her drawer.'

'What was it?'

'I didn't make a note.'

'Can't you remember?'

Ye-es, Lewis thought he could. Yes!

'Book called *The Masters*, sir – by P. C. Snow.'

Morse laughed and shook his head.

'He wasn't a bloody police constable, Lewis! You mean *C. P.* Snow.'

'Sorry, sir.'

'Interesting, though.'

'In what way?'

But Morse ignored the question.

'*When* did she get it from the library?'

'How do I know?'

'You just,' said Morse slowly, sarcastically, 'take fourteen days from the date printed for the book's return, which you could have found, if you'd looked, by gently opening the front cover.'

'Perhaps they let you have three weeks – at the library she borrowed it from.'

'And which library was that?'

Somehow Lewis managed to maintain his good humour.

'Well, at least I can give you a very straight answer to that: I haven't the faintest idea.'

'And what's the good news?'

This time, it was Lewis's turn to make a slow, impressive pronouncement:

'I know who the fellow is – the fellow in the photo.'

'You do?' Morse looked surprised. 'You mean he turned up at the station?'

'In a way, I suppose he did, yes. There was no one like him standing around waiting for his girlfriend. But I had a word with this ticket-collector – young chap who's only been on the job for a few weeks. And he recognized him straightaway. He'd asked to look at his rail pass and he remembered him because he got a bit shirty with him – and probably because of that he remembered his name as well.'

'A veritable plethora of pronouns, Lewis! Do you know how many *he*'s and *him*'s and *his*'s you've just used?'

'No. But I know *one* thing – he told me his name!' replied Lewis, happily adding a further couple of potentially confusing pronouns to his earlier tally. 'His name's *Julian Storrs.*'

For many seconds Morse sat completely motionless, feeling the familiar tingling across his shoulders. He picked up his silver Parker pen and wrote some letters on the blotting pad in front of him. Then, in a whispered voice, he spoke:

'*I know him, Lewis.*'

'You didn't recognize him, though—?'

'Most people,' interrupted Morse, 'as they get older, can't remember names. For them "A name is troublesome" – anagram – seven letters – what's that?'

'"Amnesia"?'

'Well done! I'm all right on names, usually. But as I get older it's *faces* I can't recall. And there's a splendid word for this business of not being able to recognize familiar faces—'

'"Pro-sop-a-something", isn't it?'

Morse appeared almost shell-shocked as he looked across at his sergeant. 'How in heaven's name . . . ?'

'Well, as you know, sir, I didn't do all that marvellously at school – as I told you, we didn't even have a school tie – but I was ever so good at one thing' (a glance at the blotting pad) 'I was best in the class at reading things upside-down.'

Chapter Seventeen

Facing the media is more difficult than bathing a leper
(Mother Teresa of Calcutta)

There had been little difficulty in finding out information on Julian Charles Storrs – a man to whom Morse (as he now remembered) had been introduced only a few months previously at an exhibition of Thesiger's desert photography in the Pitt Rivers Museum. But Morse said nothing of this to Lewis as the pair of them sat together that same evening in Kidlington HQ; said nothing either of his discovery that the tie whose provenance he had so earnestly sought was readily available from any Marks & Spencer's store, priced £6.99.

'We shall have to see this fellow Storrs soon, sir.'

'I'm sure we shall, yes. But we've got nothing against him, have we? It's not a criminal offence to get photographed with some attractive woman ... Interesting, though, that she was reading *The Masters.*'

'I've never read it, sir.'

'It's about the internal shenanigans in a Cambridge College when the Master dies. And recently I read in the

University Gazette that the present Master of Lonsdale is about to hang up his mortar-board – see what I mean?'

'I think I do,' lied Lewis.

'Storrs is a Fellow at Lonsdale – the Senior Fellow, I think. So if he suggested she might be interested in reading that book . . .'

'Doesn't add up to much, though, does it? It's *motive* we've got to look for. Bottom of everything – motive is.'

Morse nodded. 'But perhaps it does add up a bit,' he added quietly. 'If he wants the top job badly enough – and if she reminded him she could go and queer his pitch . . .'

'Kiss-and-tell sort of thing?'

'Kiss-and-*not*-tell, if the price was right.'

'Blackmail?' suggested Lewis.

'She'd have letters.'

'The postcard.'

'Photographs.'

'*One* photograph.'

'Hotel records. Somebody would use a credit card, and it wouldn't be *her*.'

'He'd probably pay by cash.'

'You're not trying to *help* me by any chance, are you, Lewis?'

'All I'm trying to do is be honest about what we've got – which isn't much. I agree with you, though: it wouldn't have been *her* money. Not exactly rolling in it, that's for sure. Must have been a biggish lay-out – setting up the practice, equipment, rent, and everything. And she'd got a mortgage on her own place, and a car to run.'

Yes, a car. Morse, who never took the slightest interest

in any car except his own, visualized again the white Mini which had been parked outside Number 17.

'Perhaps you ought to look a bit more carefully at that car, Lewis.'

'Already have. Log-book in the glove-compartment, road atlas under the passenger seat, fire-extinguisher under the back seat—'

'No drugs or pornography in the boot?'

'No. Just a wheel-brace and a Labour Party poster.'

Lewis looked at his watch: 8.35 p.m. It had been a long day, and he felt very tired. And so, by the look of him, did his chief. He got to his feet.

'Oh, and two cassettes: Ella Fitzgerald and a Mozart thing.'

'*Thing?*'

'Clarinet thing, yes.'

'Concerto or Quintet, was it?'

Blessedly, before Lewis could answer (for he had no answer), the phone rang.

Chief Superintendent Strange.

'Morse? In your office? I almost rang the Red Lion.'

'How can I help, sir?' asked Morse wearily.

'TV – that's how you can help. BBC want you for the *Nine O'clock News* and ITV for *News at Ten.* One of the crews is here now.'

'I've already told 'em all we know.'

'Well, you'd better think of something else, hadn't you? This isn't just a murder, Morse. This is a *PR exercise.*'

Chapter Eighteen

Thursday, 22 February

For example, in such enumerations as 'French, German, Italian and Spanish', the two commas take the place of 'ands'; there is no comma after 'Italian', because, with 'and', it would be otiose. There are, however, some who favour putting one there, arguing that, since it may sometimes be needed to avoid any ambiguity, it may as well be used always for the sake of uniformity

(Fowler, *Modern English Usage*)

JUST AFTER LUNCHTIME on Thursday, Morse found himself once again wandering aimlessly around Number 17 Bloxham Drive, a vague, niggling instinct suggesting to him that earlier he'd missed something of importance there.

But he was beginning to doubt it.

In the (now-cleared) kitchen, he switched on the wireless, finding it attuned to Radio 4. Had it been *on* when the police had first arrived? Had she been listening to the *Today* programme when just for a second, perhaps, she'd looked down at the gush of blood that had spurted over the front of her night-clothes?

So what if she had been? – Morse asked himself, conscious that he was getting nowhere.

In the front living-room, he looked again along the single shelf of paperbacks. Women novelists, mostly: Jackie Collins, Jilly Cooper, Danielle Steel, Sue Townsend . . . He read four or five of the authors' opening sentences, without once being instantly hooked, and was about to leave when he noticed Craig Raine's *A Choice of Kipling's Prose* – its white spine completely uncreased, as if it had been a very recent purchase. Or a gift? Morse withdrew the book and flicked through some of the short stories that once had meant – still meant – so very much to him. 'They' was there, although Morse confessed to himself that he had never really understood its meaning. But genius? Christ, ah! And 'On Greenhow Hill'; and 'Love-o'-Women' – the latter (Morse was adamant about it) the greatest short story in the English language. He looked at the title page: no words *to* anyone; *from* anyone. Then, remembering a book he'd once received from a lovely, lost girl, he turned to the inside of the back cover: and there, in the bottom right-hand corner, he saw the pencilled capitals: FOR R FROM J – RML.

'Remember My Love.'

It could have been anyone though – so many names beginning with 'J': Jack, James, Jason, Jasper, Jeremy, John, Joseph, Julian . . .

So what?

Anyway, these days, Morse, it could have been a woman, could it not?

*

Upstairs, in the front bedroom, he looked down at the double-bed that almost monopolized the room, and noted again the two indented pillows, one atop the other, in their Oxford blue pillowcases, whereon for the very last time Rachel James had laid her pretty head. The winter duvet, in matching blue, was still turned back as she had left it, the under-sheet only lightly creased. Nor was it a bed (of this Morse felt certain) wherein the murdered woman had spent the last night of her life in passionate lovemaking. Better, perhaps, if she had . . .

Standing on the bedside table was a glass of stale-looking water, beside which lay a pair of bluish earrings whose stones (Morse suspected) had never been fashioned from earth's more precious store.

But the Chief Inspector was forming something of a picture, so he thought.

Picture . . . Pictures . . .

Two framed pictures only on the bedroom walls: the statutory Monet; and one of Gustav Klimt's gold-patterned compositions. Plenty of posters and stickers, though: anti deer-hunting; anti export of live animals; anti French nuclear tests; pro the NHS; pro the whales; pro legalized abortion. About par for the course at her age, thought Morse. Or at *his* age, come to think of it.

He pulled the side of the curtains slightly away from the wall, and briefly surveyed the scene below. An almost reverent hush now seemed to have settled upon Rachel's side of the street. One uniformed policeman stood at the front gate – but only the one – talking to a representative of the Press – but only the one: the one who had lived next-door to the murdered woman, at Number 15; the one with the pony-tail; the one whom Morse would have to interview so very soon; the one he ought already to have interviewed.

Then, from the window, he saw his colleague, Sergeant Lewis, getting out of a marked police car; and thoughtfully he walked down the stairs. Odd – very odd, really – that with all those stickers around the bedroom, the one for the party the more likely (surely?) to further those advertised causes had been left in the boot of her car, where earlier Lewis had found it. Why hadn't she put it up, as so many other householders in the terrace had done, in one of her upper or lower windows?

Aware that whatever had been worrying him had still not been identified, Morse turned the Yale lock to admit Lewis, the latter carrying the lunchtime edition of the *Oxford Mail*.

'I reckon it's about time we interviewed *him*,' began Lewis, pointing through the closed door.

'All in good time,' agreed Morse, taking the newspaper where, as on the previous two days, the murder still figured on page one, although no longer as the lead story.

POLICE PUZZLED BY KIDLINGTON KILLING

THE BRUTAL murder of the physiotherapist Rachel James, which has caused such a stir in the local community, has left the police baffled, according to Inspector Morse of the Thames Valley CID.

The murdered woman was seen as a quietly unobtrusive member of the community with no obvious enemies, and as yet the police have been unable to find any plausible motive for her murder.

Neighbours have been swift to pay their tributes. Mrs Emily Jacobs, who waved a greeting just before Rachel was murdered, said she was a friendly, pleasant resident who would be sadly missed.

Similar tributes were paid by other local inhabitants who are finding it difficult to come to terms with their neighbourhood being the scene of such a terrible murder and a centre of interest for the national media.

For the present, however, Bloxham Drive has been sealed off to everyone except local residents, official reporters and a team of police officers carefully searching the environs of No. 17.

But it seems inevitable that the street will soon be a magnet for sightseers, drawn by a ghoulish if natural curiosity, once police activity is scaled down and restrictions are lifted.

A grim-faced Sergeant Lewis, after once again examining the white Mini still parked outside the property, would make no comment other than confirming that various leads were being followed.

Rachel's parents, who live in Devon, have identified the body as that of their daughter, and a bouquet of white lilies bearing the simple inscription 'To our darling daughter' lies in cellophaned wrapping beside the front gate of No. 17.

The tragedy has cast a dark cloud over the voting taking place today for the election of a councillor to replace Terry Burgess who died late last year following a heart attack.

'Nicely written,' conceded Morse. 'Bit pretentious, perhaps . . . and I do wish they'd all stop *demoting* me!'

'No mistakes?'

Morse eyed his sergeant sharply. 'Have I missed something?'

Lewis said nothing, smiling inexplicably, as Morse read through the article again.

'Well, I'd've put a comma after "reporters" myself. Incidentally, do you know what such a comma's called?'

'Remind me.'

'The "Oxford Comma".'

'Of course.'

'Why are you grinning?'

'That's just it, sir. It's that "grim-faced". Should be "grin-faced", shouldn't it? You see, the missus rang me up half an hour ago: she's won fifty pounds on the Premium Bonds. Bond, really. She's only got one of 'em.'

'Congratulations!'

'Thank you, sir.'

For a final time Morse looked through the article, wondering whether the seventeenth word from the beginning and the seventeenth word from the end had anything to do with the number of the house in which Rachel James had been murdered. Probably not. (Morse's life was bestrewn with coincidences.)

'Is that pony-tailed ponce still out there?' he asked suddenly.

Lewis looked out of the front window.

'No, sir. He's gone.'

'Let's hope he's gone to one of those new barbers' shops you were telling me about?' (Morse's views were beset with prejudices.)

Chapter Nineteen

She is disturbed
When the phone rings at 5 a.m.
And with such urgency
Aware that one of these calls
Will summon her to witness another death
Commanding more words than she
The outside observer can provide – and yet
Note-pad poised and ready
She picks up the receiver
(Helen Peacocke, *Ace Reporter*)

AT 2.25 P.M. THAT same day, Morse got into the maroon Jaguar and after looking at his wristwatch drove off. First, down to the Cutteslowe Roundabout, thence straight over and along the Banbury Road to the Martyrs' Memorial, where he turned right into Beaumont Street, along Park End Street, and out under the railway bridge into Botley Road, where just beyond the river bridge he turned left into the Osney Industrial Estate.

There was, in fact, one vacant space in the limited parking-lots beside the main reception area to Oxford City and County Newspapers; but Morse pretended not to notice it. Instead he asked the girl at the reception desk for the open-sesame to the large staff car-park, and was soon watching the black-and-white barrier lift as he inserted a white plastic card into some electronic contraption there. Back in reception, the same young girl retrieved the precious ticket before giving Morse a VISITOR badge, and directing him down a corridor alongside, on his left, a vast open-plan complex, where hundreds of newspaper personnel appeared too preoccupied to notice the 'Visitor'.

Owens (as Morse discovered) was one of the few employees granted some independent square-footage there, his small office hived off by wood-and-glass partitions.

'You live, er, she lived next-door, I'm told,' began Morse awkwardly.

Owens nodded.

'Bit of luck, I suppose, in a way – for a reporter, I mean?'

'For me, yes. Not much luck for her, though, was it?'

'How did you first hear about it? You seem to have been on the scene pretty quickly, sir.'

'Della rang me. She lives in the Drive – Number 1. She'd seen me leave for work.'

'What time was that?'

'Must have been . . . ten to seven, five to seven?'

'You usually leave about then?'

'I do now, yes. For the past year or so we've been working a fair amount of flexi-time and, well, the earlier I leave home the quicker I'm here. Especially in term-time when—' Owens looked shrewdly across his desk at

Morse. 'But you know as much as I do about the morning traffic from Kidlington to Oxford.'

'Not really. I'm normally going the other way – North Oxford to Kidlington.'

'Much more sensible.'

'Yes . . .'

Clearly Owens was going to be more of a heavyweight than he'd expected, and Morse paused awhile to take his bearings. He'd made a note only a few minutes since of exactly how long the same distance had taken him, from Bloxham Drive to Osney Mead. And even with quite a lot of early afternoon traffic about – even with a couple of lights against him – he'd done the journey in fourteen and a half minutes.

'So you'd get here at about . . . about *when*, Mr Owens?'

The reporter shrugged his shoulders. 'Quarter past? Twenty past? Usually about then.'

A nucleus of suspicion was beginning to form in Morse's brain as he sensed that Owens was perhaps exaggerating the length of time it had taken him to reach work that Monday morning. If he *had* left at, say, ten minutes to seven, he could well have been in the car park at – what? – seven o'clock? With a bit of luck? So why . . . why had Owens suggested quarter past – even twenty past?

'You can't be more precise?'

Again Morse felt the man's shrewd eyes upon him.

'You mean the later I got here the less likely I am to be a suspect?'

'You realize how important times are, Mr Owens – a sequence of times – in any murder enquiry like this?'

'Oh yes, I know it as well as you do, Inspector. I've covered quite a few murders in my time ... So ... so why don't you ask Della what time she saw me leave? Della Cecil, that is, at Number 1. She'll probably remember better than me. And as for getting here ... well, that'll be fairly easy to check. Did you know that?'

Owens took a small white rectangular card from his wallet, with a number printed across the top – 008 14922 – and continued: 'I push that in the thing there and the whatsit goes up and something somewhere records the time I get into the car park.'

Clearly the broad-faced, heavy-jowled reporter had about as much specialist knowledge of voodoo-technology as Morse, and the latter switched the thrust of his questions.

'This woman who saw you leave, I shall have to see her – you realize that?'

'You wouldn't be doing your job if you didn't. Cigarette, Inspector?'

'Er, no, no thanks. Well, er, perhaps I will, yes. Thank you. This woman, as I say, do you know her well?'

'Only twenty houses in the Drive, Inspector. You get to know most people, after a while.'

'You never became, you know, more friendly? Took her out? Drink? Meal?'

'Why do you ask that?'

'I've just got to find out as much as I can about

everybody there, that's all. Otherwise, as you say, I wouldn't be doing my job, would I, Mr Owens?'

'We've had a few dates, yes – usually at the local.'

'Which is?'

'The Bull and Swan.'

'Ah, "Brakspear", "Bass", "Bishop's Finger" . . .'

'I wouldn't know. I'm a lager man myself.'

'I see,' said a sour-faced Morse. Then, after a pause, 'What about Rachel James? Did you know her well?'

'She lived next-*door*, dammit! Course I knew her fairly well.'

'Did you ever go inside her house?'

Owens appeared to consider the question carefully. 'Just the twice, if I've got it right. Once when I had a few people in for a meal and I couldn't find a corkscrew and I knocked on her back door and she asked me in, because it was pissing the proverbials, while she looked around for hers. The other time was one hot day last summer when I was mowing the grass at the back and she was hanging out her smalls and I asked her if she wanted me to do her patch and she said she'd be grateful, and when I'd done it she asked me if I'd like a glass of something and we had a drink together in the kitchen there.'

'Lager, I suppose.'

'Orangeade.'

Orangeade, like water, had never played any significant rôle in Morse's dietary, but he suddenly realized that at that moment he would have willingly drunk a pint of anything, so long as it was ice-cold.

Even lager.

'It was a hot day, you say?'

'Boiling.'

'What was she wearing?'

'Not much.'

'She was an attractive girl, wasn't she?'

'To me? I'm always going to be attracted to a woman with not much on. And, as I remember, most of what she'd got on that day was mostly off, if you follow me.'

'So she'd have a lot of boyfriends?'

'She was the sort of woman men would lust after, yes.'

'Did you?'

'Let's put it this way, Inspector. If she'd invited me to bed that afternoon, I'd've sprinted up the stairs.'

'But she didn't invite you?'

'No.'

'Did she invite other men?'

'I doubt it. Not in Bloxham Drive, anyway. We don't just have Neighbourhood Watch here; we've got a continuous Nosey-Parker Surveillance Scheme.'

'Even in the early morning?'

'As I told you, somebody saw me go to work on Monday morning.'

'You think others may have done?'

'Bloody sure they did!'

Morse switched tack again. 'You wouldn't remember – recognize – any of her occasional boyfriends?'

'No.'

'Have you heard of a man called Julian Storrs?'

'Yes.'

'You know him?'

'Not really, no. But he's from Lonsdale, and I interviewed him for the *Oxford Mail* last year – December, I think it was – when he gave the annual Pitt Rivers Lecture. On Captain Cook, as I recall. I'd never realized how much the natives hated that fellow's guts – you know, in the Sandwich Islands or somewhere.'

'I forget,' said Morse, as if at some point in his life he *had* known . . .

At his local grammar school, the young Morse had been presented with a choice of the 3 Gs: Greek, Geography, or German. And since Morse had joined the Greek option, his knowledge of geography had ever been fatally flawed. Indeed, it was only in his late twenties that he had discovered that the Balkan States and the Baltic States were not synonymous. Yet about Captain Cook's voyages Morse should (as we shall see) have known at least a little – *did* know a little – since his father had adopted that renowned British navigator, explorer, and cartographer as his greatest hero in life – unlike (it seemed) the natives of those 'Sandwich Islands or somewhere'. . .

'You never saw Mr Storrs in Bloxham Drive?'

In their sockets, Owens' eyes shot from bottom left to top right, like those of a deer that has suddenly sniffed a predator.

'Never. Why?'

'Because' (Morse leaned forward a few inches as he summoned up all his powers of creative ingenuity) 'because someone in the Drive – this is absolutely confidential, sir! – says that he was seen, fairly recently, going into, er, another house there.'

'*Which* house?' Owens' voice was suddenly sharp.

Morse held up his right hand and got to his feet. 'Just a piece of gossip, like as not. But we've got to check out every lead, you know that.'

Owens remained silent.

'You've always been a journalist?'

'Yes.'

'Which papers . . . ?'

'I started in London.'

'Whereabouts?'

'Soho – around there.'

'When was that?'

'Mid-seventies.'

'Wasn't that when Soho was full of sex clubs and striptease joints?'

'*And* more. Gets a bit boring, all that stuff though, after a time.'

'Yes. So they tell me.'

'I read your piece today in the *Oxford Mail*,' said Morse as the two men walked towards reception. 'You write well.'

'Thank you.'

'I can't help remembering you said "comparatively" crime-free area.'

'That was in yesterday's.'

'Oh.'

'Well . . . we've only had one burglary this last year, and we've had no joy-riders around since the council put the sleeping-policemen in. We still get a bit of mindless vandalism, of course – you'll have seen the young trees we tried to plant round the back. And litter – litter's always a problem – and graffiti . . . And someone recently unscrewed most of the latches on the back gates – you know, the things that click as the gates shut.'

'I didn't know there was a market for those,' muttered Morse.

'And you're wasting your time if you put up a name for your house, or something like that. I put a little notice on my front gate. Lasted exactly eight days. Know what it was?'

Morse glanced back at the corporate work-force seated in front of VDU screens at desks cluttered with in-trays, out-trays, file-cases, handbooks, and copy being corrected and cosseted before inclusion in forthcoming editions of Oxford's own *Times, Mail, Journal, Star* . . .

'"No Free Newspapers"?' he suggested *sotto voce.*

Morse handed in his Visitor badge at reception.

'You'll need to give me another thing to get out with.'

'No. The barrier lifts automatically when you leave.'

'So once you're in . . .'

She smiled. 'You're in! It's just that we used to get quite a few cars from the Industrial Estate trying it on.'

Morse turned left into the Botley Road and drove along to the Ring-Road junction where he took the north-bound A34, coming off at the Pear Tree Roundabout, and thence driving rather too quickly up the last stretch to Kidlington HQ – where he looked at his wristwatch again.

Nine and a half minutes.

Only nine and a half minutes.

Chapter Twenty

It is a capital mistake to theorize before one has data

(Conan Doyle, *Scandal in Bohemia*)

As Morse climbed the stairs to Lewis's office he was experiencing a deep ache in each of his calves.

'Hardest work I've done today, that!' he admitted as, panting slightly, he flopped into a chair.

'Interview go OK, sir?'

'Owens? I wouldn't trust that fellow as far as I could kick him.'

'Which wouldn't be too far, in your present state of health.'

'Genuine journalist he may be – but he's a phoney witness, take it from me!'

'Before you go on, sir, we've got the preliminary post-mortem report here.'

'You've read it through?'

'Tried to. Bullet-entry in the left sub-mandibular—'

'Lew-is! Spare me the details! She was shot through the window, through the blind, in the morning twilight. You mustn't expect much accuracy about the thing! You've been watching too many old cowboy films where they mow down the baddies at hundreds of yards.'

'Distance of about eighteen inches to two feet, that's what it says, judging from—'

'What's it say about the *time*?'

'She's not quite so specific there.'

'Why the hell not? We told her *exactly* when the woman was shot!'

'Dr Hobson says the temperature in the kitchen that morning wasn't much above zero.'

'Economizing everywhere, our Rachel,' said Morse rather sadly.

'And it seems you get this sort of "refrigeration factor"—'

'In which we are not particularly interested, Lewis, because we *know*—' Morse suddenly stopped. 'Unless . . . unless our distinguished pathologist is suggesting that Rachel may have been murdered just a *little* earlier than we've been assuming.'

'I don't think she's trying to suggest anything, sir. Just giving us the facts as far as she sees them.'

'I suppose so.'

'Do you want to read the report?'

'I shall have to, shan't I, if *you* can't understand it?'

'I didn't say that—'

But again Morse interrupted him, almost eagerly now recounting his interview with Owens . . .

'. . . So don't you see, Lewis? *He* could have done it. Quarter of an hour it took me, to the newspaper offices via Banbury Road; ten minutes back via the Ring Road. So if he left home about ten to seven – clocked into the car park at seven, say – hardly anything on the roads – then drove straight *out* of the car park – there's no clocking out there – that's the system they have – drove hell for leather back to Bloxham Close – '

'*Drive*, sir.'

' – parks his car up on the road behind the houses' (Morse switched now to the vivid present tense) ' – goes through the vandalized fence there – down the grass slope – taps on her window – the thin blinds still drawn' (Morse's eyes seemed almost mesmerized) ' – sees her profile more clearly as she gets nearer – for a second or two scrutinizes the dark outline at the gas-lit window – '

'It's electric there.'

' – then he fires through the window into her face – and hits her just below the jaw.'

Lewis nodded this time. 'The sub-mandibular bit, you're right about that.'

'Then he goes up the bank again – gets in his car – back to Osney Mead. But he daren't go into the car park again – of course not! So he leaves his car somewhere near, and goes into the office from the rear of the car park. Nobody much there to observe his comings and goings – most of the people get in there about eightish, so I learn. *Quod erat demonstrandum!* I know you're going to ask me what his motive was, and I don't know. But this time we've found the murderer before we've found the motive. Not grumbling too much about that, are you?'

'Yes! It just won't hold water.'

'And why's that?'

'There's this woman from Number 1, for a start. Miss Cecil—'

'Della – Owens called her Della.'

'She saw him leave, didn't she? About seven o'clock? That's why she knew he'd be at his desk when she rang him as soon as she saw the police arrive – just after eight.'

'One hour – one whole hour! You can do a lot in an hour.'

'You still can't put a quart into a pint pot.'

'We've now gone metric, by the way, Lewis. Look, what if they're in it *together* – have you thought of that? Owens is carrying a torch for that Miss Cecil, believe me! When I happened to mention Julian Storrs – '

'You didn't do that, surely?'

' – and when I said he'd been seen knocking at one of the other doors there – '

'But nobody—'

' – he was jealous, Lewis! And there are only two houses in the Close' (Lewis gave up the struggle) 'occupied by nubile young women: Number 17 and Number 1, Miss James and Miss Cecil, agreed?'

'I thought you just said they were in it *together*.'

'I said they might be, that's all. I'm just thinking aloud, for Christ's sake! One of us has got to think. And I'm a bit weary and I'm much underbeered. So give me a chance!'

Lewis waited a few seconds. Then:

'Is it my turn to speak, sir?'

Morse nodded weakly, contemplating the threadbare state of Lewis's carpet.

'I don't know whether you've been down the Botley

Road in the morning recently – even in the fairly early morning – but it's one of the worst bottlenecks in Oxford. You drove there and back in mid-afternoon, didn't you? But you want Owens to do three journeys between Kidlington and Osney Mead. First he drives to work – perhaps fairly quickly, agreed. Twenty minutes, say? He drives back – a bit quicker? Quarter of an hour, say. He parks his car somewhere – it's not going to be in Bloxham Drive, though. He murders his next-door neighbour. Drives back into Oxford after that – another twenty, twenty-five minutes *at least* now. Finds a parking space – and this time it's not going to be in the car park, as you say. Walks or runs to his office, not going in the front door, either – for obvious reasons. Gets into his office and is sitting there at his desk when his girlfriend – if you're right about that – rings him up and tells him he'll be in for a bit of a scoop if he gets out again to Bloxham Drive. It's just about possible, sir, if *all* the lights are with him *every* time, if almost everybody's decided to walk to work that morning. But it's very improbable even then. And remember it's *Monday* morning – the busiest morning of the week in Oxford.'

Morse looked hurt.

'You still think it's just *about* possible?'

Lewis considered the question again.

'No, sir. I know you always like to think that most murders are committed by next-door neighbours or husbands or wives—'

'But what if this woman at Number 1 isn't telling us the truth?' queried Morse. 'What if she never made that phone-call at all? What if she's in it with him? What if she's more than willing to provide him with a nice little alibi? You see, you're probably right about the time-scale of things. He probably *wouldn't* have had time to get back here to Kidlington, commit the murder, and then return to the office and be sitting quietly at his desk when she rang him.'

'So?'

'So she's lying. Just like *he* is! He got back here – easy! – murdered Rachel James – and *stayed* here, duly putting in an appearance as the very first reporter on the scene!'

'I'm sorry, sir, but she *isn't* lying, not about this. I don't know what you think the rest of us have been doing since Monday morning but we've done quite a bit of checking up already. And she's *not* lying about the phone-call to Owens' office. One of the lads went along to BT and confirmed it. The call was monitored and it'll be listed on the itemized telephone bill of the subscriber – Number 1 Bloxham Drive!'

'Does it give the *time*?'

Lewis appeared slightly uneasy. 'I'm not quite sure about that.'

'And if our ace-reporter Owens is privileged enough to have an answerphone in his office – which he *is* . . .'

Ye-es. Perhaps Morse was on to something after all. Because if the two of them *had*, for some reason, been working together . . . Lewis put his thoughts into words:

'You mean he needn't have gone in to work at all . . . Ye-es. You say that electronic gadget records the number on your card, and the time – but it doesn't record the car itself, right?'

Morse nodded encouragement. And Lewis, duly encouraged, continued:

'So if somebody *else* had taken his card – and if *he* stayed in the Drive all the time . . .'

Morse finished it off for him: 'He's got a key to Number 1 – he's in there when she drives off – he walks along the back of the terrace – shoots Rachel James – goes back to Number 1 – rings up his own office number – waits for the answerphone pips – probably doesn't say anything – just keeps the line open for a minute or two – and Bob's your father's brother.'

Lewis sighed. 'I'd better get on with a bit of fourth-grade clerical checking, sir – this parking business, the phone-call, any of his colleagues who might have seen him—'

'Or her.'

'It's worth checking, I can see that.'

'Tomorrow, Lewis. We're doing nothing more today.'

'And this woman at Number 1?'

'Is she a nice-looking lass?'

'Very much so.'

'You leave that side of things to me, then.'

Morse got to his feet and went to the door. But then returned, and sat down again.

'That "refrigeration factor" you mentioned, Lewis – time of death and all that. Interesting, isn't it? So far, we've been assuming that the bullet went through the window and ended up in the corpse, haven't we? But if – just *if* – Rachel James had been murdered a bit *earlier*, inside Number 17, and then someone had fired through the window *at some later stage* . . . You see what I mean? Everybody's alibi is up the pole, isn't it?'

'There'd be another bullet, though, wouldn't there?

We've got the one from Rachel's neck; but there'd be another one somewhere in the kitchen if someone fired—'

'Not necessarily the murderer, remember!'

'But if *someone* fired just through the window, without aiming at anything . . .'

'Did the SOCOs have a good look at the ceiling, the walls – the floorboards?'

'They did, yes.'

'Somebody might have picked it up and pocketed it.'

'Who on earth—'

'I've not the faintest idea.'

'Talking of bullets, sir, we've got another little report – from ballistics. Do you want to read it?'

'Not tonight.'

'Very short, sir.'

He handed Morse the single, neatly typed paragraph:

Ballistics Report: Prelim.
17 Bloxham Dnve, Kıdlıngton, Oxon

.577 heavy-calibre revolver. One of the Howdah pıstols probably – perhaps the Lancaster Patent four-barrel An old firing-piece but if reasonably well cared for could be ın good working nick like as not ın 1996

Acc. to recent catalogues readily avaılable ın USA· $370 to $700 Tests progressing

ASH
22.ii.96

Morse handed the report back. 'I'm not at all sure I know what "calibre" means. Is it the diameter of the bullet or the diameter of the barrel?'

'Wouldn't they be the same, sir?'

Morse got up and walked wearily to the door once more.

'Perhaps so, Lewis. Perhaps so.'

Chapter Twenty-One

A Conservative is one who is enamored of existing evils, as distinguished from the Liberal, who wishes to replace them with others

(Ambrose Bierce, *The Devil's Dictionary*)

MORSE DID NOT go straight home to his North Oxford flat that evening; nor, *mirabile dictu*, did he make for the nearest hostelry – at least not immediately. Instead, he drove to Bloxham Drive, pulling in behind the single police car parked outside Number 17, in which a uniformed officer sat reading the *Oxford Mail*.

'Constable Brogan, sir,' was the reply in answer to Morse's question.

'Happen to know if Number 1's at home?'

'The one with the N-reg Rover, you mean?'

Morse nodded.

'No. But she keeps coming backwards and forwards all the time. She seems a very busy woman, that one.'

'Anything to report?'

'Not really, sir. We keep getting a few gawpers, but I just ask them to move along.'

'Gently, I trust.'

'Very gently, sir.'

'How long are you on duty for?'

'Finish at midnight.'

Morse pointed to the front window. 'Why don't you nip in and watch the telly?'

'Bit cold in there.'

'You can put the gas-fire on.'

'It's electric, sir.'

'Please yourself!'

'Would that be official, sir?'

'*Anything* I say's official, lad.'

'My lucky night, then.'

Mine, too, thought Morse as he looked over his shoulder to see an ash-blonde alighting from her car outside Number 1.

He hastened along the pavement in what could be described as an arrested jog, or perhaps more accurately as an animated walk.

'Good *evening*.'

She turned towards him as she inserted her latchkey.

'Yes?'

'A brief word – if it's possible . . . er . . .'

Morse fumbled for his ID card. But she forestalled the need.

'Another police sergeant, are you?'

'Police, yes.'

'I can't spare much time – not tonight. I've got a busy few hours ahead.'

'I shan't keep you long.'

She led the way through into a tastefully furbished and furnished front room, taking off her ankle-length white mackintosh, placing it over the back of the red-leather settee, and bidding Morse sit opposite her as she smoothed the pale blue dress over her hips and crossed her elegant, nylon-clad legs.

'Do you mind?' she asked, lifting a cigarette in the air.

'No, no,' muttered Morse, wishing only that she'd offered one to him.

'What can I do for you?' She had a slightly husky, upper-class voice, and Morse guessed she'd probably attended one of the nation's more prestigious public schools.

'Just one or two questions.'

She smiled attractively: 'Go ahead.'

'I understand that my colleague, Sergeant Lewis, has spoken to you already.'

'Nice man – in a gentle, shy sort of way.'

'Really? I'd never quite thought of him . . .'

'Well, you're a bit older, aren't you?'

'What job do you do?'

She opened her handbag and gave Morse her card.

'I'm the local agent for the Conservative Party.'

'Oh dear! I *am* sorry,' said Morse, looking down at the small oblong card:

Adèle Beatrice Cecil
Conservative Party Agent
1 Bloxham Drive
Kidlington, Oxon, OX5 2NY
For information please ring
01865 794768

'Was that supposed to be a sick joke?' There was an edge to her voice now.

'Not really. It's just that I've never had a friend who's a Tory, that's all.'

'You mean you didn't vote for us today?'

'I don't live in this ward.'

'If you give me your address, I'll make sure you get some literature, Sergeant.'

'Chief Inspector, actually,' corrected Morse, oblivious of the redundant adverb.

She tugged her dress a centimetre down her thighs. 'How can I help?'

'Do you know Mr Owens well?'

'Well enough.'

'Well enough to hand him a newspaper scoop?'

'Yes.'

'Have you ever slept with him?'

'Not much finesse about you, is there?'

'Just a minute,' said Morse softly. 'I've got a terrible job to do – just up the street here. And part of it's to ask some awkward questions about what's going on in the Close—'

'*Drive.*'

'To find out who knows who – *whom*, if you prefer it.'

'They did teach us English grammar at Roedean, yes.'

'You haven't answered my question.'

Adèle breathed deeply, and her grey eyes stared across almost fiercely.

'Once, yes.'

'But you didn't repeat the experience?'

'I said "once" – didn't you hear me?'

'You still see him?'

'Occasionally. He's all right: intelligent, pretty well read, quite good fun, sometimes – and he promised he'd vote Conservative today.'

'He sounds quite compatible.'

'Are you married, Inspector?'

'*Chief* Inspector.'

'Are you?'

'No.'

'Do you wish you were?'

Perhaps Morse didn't hear the question.

'Did you know Rachel James fairly well?'

'We had a heart-to-heart once in a while.'

'You weren't aware of any one particular boyfriend?'

She shook her head.

'Would you say she was attractive to men?'

'Wouldn't you?'

'I only saw her the once.'

'I'm sorry.' She said it quietly. 'Please, forgive me.'

'Do you know a man called Storrs? Julian Storrs?'

'Good gracious, yes! Julian? He's one of our Vice-Presidents. We often meet at do's. In fact, I'm seeing him next week at a fund-raising dinner at The Randolph. Would you like a complimentary ticket?'

'No, perhaps not.'

'Shouldn't have asked, should I? Anyway,' she got to her feet, 'I'll have to be off. They'll be starting the count fairly soon.'

They walked to the front door.

'Er ... when you rang Mr Owens on Monday morning, just after eight o'clock you say, you did *speak* to him, didn't you?'

'Of course.'

Morse nodded. 'And one final thing, please. My sergeant found some French letters—'

'French letters? How old *are* you, Chief Inspector? Condoms, for heaven's sake.'

'As I say, we found two packets of, er, condoms in one of her bedroom drawers.'

'Big deal!'

'You don't know if she ever invited anyone home to sleep with her?'

'No, I don't.'

'I thought,' said Morse hesitantly, 'most women were on the pill these days?'

'A lot of them *off* it, too – after that thrombosis scare.'

'I suppose so, yes. I'm ... I'm not really an expert in that sort of thing.'

'And don't forget safe sex.'

'No. I'll ... I'll try not to.'

'Did she keep them under her nighties?'

Morse nodded sadly, and bade goodnight to Adèle Beatrice Cecil.

ABC.

As he walked slowly along to the Jaguar, he felt a slight tingling behind the eyes at the thought of Rachel James, and the nightdress she'd been wearing when she was murdered; and the condoms so carefully concealed in her lingerie drawer – along with the hopes and fears she'd had, like everyone. And he thought of Auden's immortal line on A. E. Housman:

Kept tears like dirty postcards in a drawer.

As he started the Jaguar, Morse noticed the semi-stroboscopic light inside the lounge; and trusted that PC Brogan had managed to activate the heating system in Number 17 Bloxham Drive.

Chapter Twenty-Two

O Beer! O Hodgson, Guinness, Allsopp, Bass!
Names that should be on every infant's tongue!
(Charles Stuart Calverly)

Morse headed south along the Banbury Road, turning left just after the Cutteslowe Roundabout, and through the adjoining Carlton and Wolsey Roads (why hadn't the former been christened 'Cardinal'?); then, at the bottom of the Cutteslowe Estate, down the steeply sloping entry to the Cherwell, a quietly civilized public house where the quietly civilized landlord kept an ever-watchful eye on the Brakspear and the Bass. The car-phone rang as he unfastened his safety belt.

Lewis.

Speaking from HQ.

'I thought I'd told you to go home! The eggs and chips are getting cold.'

Lewis, as Morse earlier, showed himself perfectly competent at ignoring a question.

'I've had a session on the phone with Ox and Cow Newspapers, sir – still at work there, quite a few of them. Owens' car-park card is number 14922 and it was registered by the barrier contraption there at 7.04 on Monday morning. Seems he's been in fairly early these last couple of months. Last week, for example, Monday to Friday, 7.37, 7.06, 7.11, 7.00, 7.18.'

'So what? Shows he can't get up that early on Monday mornings.'

'That's not all, though.'

'It *is*, Lewis! It's still the *card* you're on about – not the *car*! Can't you see that?'

'Please listen to me for a change, sir. The personnel fellow who looked out the car-park things for me, he just happened to be in earlyish last Monday morning himself: 7.22. There weren't many others around then, but one of the ones who was . . . Guess who, sir?'

'Oh dear!' said Morse for the second time that evening.

'Yep. Owens! Pony-tail 'n' all.'

'Oh.'

In that quiet monosyllable Lewis caught the depth of Morse's disappointment. Yet he felt far from dismayed himself, knowing full well as he did, after so many murder investigations with the pair of them in harness, that Morse's mind was almost invariably at its imaginative peak when one of his ill-considered, top-of-the-head hypotheses had been razed to the ground – in this case by some lumbering bulldozer like himself. And so he understood the silence at the other end of the line: a long silence, like that at the Cenotaph in commemoration of the fallen.

Lewis seldom expected (seldom received) any thanks. And in truth such lack of recognition concerned him little, since only rarely did Morse show the slightest sign of graciousness or gratitude to anyone.

Yet he did so now.

'Thank you, my old friend.'

At the bar Morse ordered a pint of Bass and proceeded to drink it speedily.

At the bar Morse ordered a second pint of Bass and proceeded to drink it even more speedily – before leaving and driving out once more to Bloxham Drive, where no one was abroad and where the evening's TV programmes appeared to be absorbing the majority of the households.

Including Number 17.

The Jaguar door closed behind him with its accustomed aristocratic click, and he walked slowly through the drizzle along the street. Still the same count: six for Labour; two for the Tories; and two apparently unprepared to parade their political allegiances.

Yes! YES!

Almost everything (he saw it now so clearly) had been pushing his mind towards that crucial clue – towards the breakthrough in the case.

It had not been Owens who had murdered Rachel James – almost certainly he *couldn't* have done it, anyway.

And that late evening, as if matching his slow-paced walk, a slow and almost beatific smile had settled round the mouth of Chief Inspector Morse.

Chapter Twenty-Three

Friday, 23 February

Thirteen Unlucky: The Turks so dislike the number that the word is almost expunged from their vocabulary. The Italians never use it in making up the numbers of their lotteries. In Paris, no house bears that number

(*Brewer's Dictionary of Phrase and Fable*)

As Lewis pulled into Bloxham Drive, he was faced with an unfamiliar sight: a smiling, expansive-looking Morse was leaning against the front gate of Number 17, engaged in a relaxed, impromptu press conference with one camera crew (ITV), four reporters (two from national, two from local newspapers – but no Owens), and three photographers. Compared with previous mornings, the turn-out was disappointing.

It was 9.05 a.m.

Lewis just caught the tail-end of things. 'So it'll be a waste of time – staying on here much longer. You won't expect me to go into details, of course, but I can tell you that we've finished our investigations in this house.'

If the 'this' were spoken with a hint of some audial semi-italicization, it was of no moment, for no one appeared to notice it.

'Any leads? Any new leads?'

'To the murder of Rachel James, you mean?'

'Who else?'

'No. No new leads at all, really . . . Well, perhaps one.'

On which cryptic note, Morse raised his right hand to forestall the universal pleas for clarification, and with a genial – perhaps genuine? – smile, he turned away.

'Drive me round the block a couple of times, Lewis. I'd rather all these people buggered off, and I don't think they're going to stay much longer if they see us go.'

Nor did they.

Ten minutes later the detectives returned to find the Drive virtually deserted.

'How many houses are there here, Lewis?'

'Not sure.' From Number 17 Lewis looked along to the end of the row. Two other houses – presumably Numbers 19 and 21, although the figures from the front gate of the latter had been removed. Then he looked across to the other side of the street where the last even-numbered house was 20. The answer, therefore, appeared to be reasonably obvious.

'Twenty-one.'

'That's an *odd* number, isn't it?'

Lewis frowned. 'Did you think I thought it was an *even* number?'

Morse smiled. 'I didn't mean "odd" as opposed to "even"; I meant "odd" as opposed to "normal".'

'Oh!'

'Lew-is! You don't build a street of terraced houses with one side having ten and the other side having eleven, now do you? You get a bit of symmetry into things; a bit of regularity.'

'If you say so.'

'And I *do* say so!' snapped Morse, with the conviction of a fundamentalist preacher asserting the divine authority of Holy Writ.

'No need to be so sharp, sir.'

'I should have spotted it from day one! From those political stickers, Lewis! Let's count, OK?'

The two men walked along the odd-numbered side of Bloxham Drive. And Lewis nodded: six Labour; two Tory; two don't-knows.

Ten.

'You see, Lewis, we've perhaps been a little misled by these minor acts of vandalism here. We've got several houses minus the numbers originally screwed into their front gates – *and their back gates.* So we were understandably confused.'

Lewis agreed. 'I still am, sir.'

'How many odd numbers are there between one and twenty-one – inclusive?'

'I reckon it's ten, sir. So I suppose there must be eleven.'

Morse grinned. 'Write 'em down!'

So Lewis did, in his notebook: 1, 3, 5, 7, 9, 11, 13, 15, 17, 19, 21. Then counted them.

'I was right, sir. Eleven.'

'But only ten houses, Lewis.'

'I don't quite follow.'

'Of course you do. It happens quite often in hotel floors and hotel room numbers . . . and street numbers. They miss one of them out.'

Enlightenment dawned on Lewis's honest features.

'Number thirteen!'

'Exactly! Do you know there used to be people in France called "fourteeners" who made a living by going along to dinner parties where the number of guests was thirteen?'

'Where do you find all these bits and pieces?'

'Do you know, I think I saw that on the back of a matchbox in a pub in Grimsby. I've learned quite a lot in life from the back of matchboxes.'

'What's it all got to do with the case, though?'

Morse reached for Lewis's notebook, and put brackets round the seventh number. Then, underneath the first few numbers, he wrote in an arrow, →, pointing from left to right.

'Lewis! If you were walking along the back of the houses, starting from Number 1 – she must be feeling a bit sore about the election, by the way . . . Well, let's just go along there.'

The two men walked to the rear of the terrace, where (as we have seen) several of the back gates had been sadly, if not too seriously, vandalized.

'Get your list, Lewis, and as we go along, just put a ring round those gates where we *haven't* got a number, all right?'

At the end of the row, Lewis's original list, with its successive emendations, appeared as follows:

1, 3, 5, ⑦ 9, 11, (13), ⑮⑰ 19, ㉑

⟶

'You see,' said Morse, 'the vandalism gets worse the further you get into the Close, doesn't it? As it gets further from the main road.'

'Yes.'

'So just picture things. You've got a revolver and you walk along the back here in the half-light. *You know the number you want.* You know the morning routine, too: breakfast at about seven. All you've got to do is knock on the kitchen window, wait till you see the silhouette behind the thin blind, the silhouette of a face with one distinctive feature – a pony-tail. You walk along the back; you see Number 11; you move along to the next house – Number 13 – *you think*! And so the house after that *must* be Number 15. And to confirm things, there's the pony-tailed silhouette. You press the trigger – and there you have it, Lewis! The Horseman passes by. But you've got it wrong, haven't you? Your intended victim is living at Number 15, not Number 17!'

'So,' said Lewis slowly, 'whoever stood at the kitchen window thought he – or she – was firing . . .'

Morse nodded sombrely. 'Yes. Not at Rachel James, but *Geoffrey Owens*.'

Chapter Twenty-Four

Men entitled to bleat BA after their names
(D. S. MacColl)

THE SENIOR COMMON Room at Lonsdale is comparatively small, and for this reason has a rather more intimate air about it than some of the spacious SCRs in the larger Oxford Colleges. Light-coloured, beautifully grained oak-panelling encloses the room on all sides, its colouring complemented by the light-brown leather sofas and armchairs there. Copies of almost all the national dailies, including the *Sun* and the *Mirror*, are to be found on the glass-topped coffee-tables; and indeed it is usually these tabloids which are flipped through first – sometimes intently studied – by the majority of the dons.

Forgathered here on the evening of Friday, 23 February (7.00 for 7.30) was a rather overcrowded throng of dons, accompanied by wives, partners, friends, to enjoy a Guest Night – an occasion celebrated by the College four times per term. A white-coated scout stood by the door with a silver tray holding thinly fluted glasses of sherry: either the pale-amber 'dry' variety or the darker brown 'medium', for it was a basic assumption in such a setting that no one could ever wish for the deeply umbered 'sweet'.

A begowned Jasper Bradley took a glass of dry, drained it at a swallow, put the glass back on to the tray, and took another. He was particularly pleased with himself that day; *and* with the *Classical Quarterly*, whose review of *Greek Moods and Tenses* (J. J. Bradley, 204 pp, £45.50, Classical Press) contained the wonderful lines which Bradley had now by heart:

> A small volume, but one which plumbs the unfathomed mysteries of the aorist subjunctive with imaginative insights into the very origins of language.

Yes. He felt decidedly chuffed.

'How's tricks?' he asked, looking up at Donald Franks, a very tall astrophysicist, recently head-hunted from Cambridge, whose dark, lugubrious features suggested that for his part he'd managed few imaginative insights that week into the origins of the universe.

'So-so.'

'Who d'you fancy then?'

'What – of the women here?'

'For the Master's job.'

'Dunno.'

'Who'll you vote for?'

'Secret ballot, innit?'

Mr and Mrs Denis Cornford now came in, each taking a glass of the medium sherry. Shelly looked extremely attractive and perhaps a little skimpily dressed for such a chilly evening. She wore a lightweight white two-piece suit; and as she bent down to pick up a cheese-nibble her low-cut, bottle-green blouse gaped open to reveal a splendid glimpse of her beautiful breasts.

'Je-sus!' muttered Bradley.

'She certainly flouts her tits a bit,' mumbled the melancholy Franks.

'You mean "flaunts" 'em, I think.'

'If you say so,' said Franks, slightly wounded.

Bradley moved to the far end of the room where Angela Storrs stood talking to a small priest, clothed all in black, with buckled shoes and leggings.

'Ah, Jasper! Come and meet Father Dooley from Sligo.'

Clearly Angela Storrs had decided she had now done her duty; for soon she drifted away – tall, long-legged, wearing a dark-grey trouser-suit with a white high-necked jumper. There was about her an almost patrician mien, her face high-cheekboned and pale, with the hair swept back above her ears and fastened in a bun behind. It was obvious to all that she had been a very attractive woman. But she was aging a little too quickly perhaps; and the fact that over the last two or three years she had almost invariably worn trousers did little to discourage the belief that her legs had succumbed to an unsightly cordage of varicose veins. If she were on sale in an Arab wife-market (in the cruel words of one of the younger dons) she would have passed her best-before date several years earlier.

'I knew the Master many years ago – and his poor wife. Yes . . . that was long ago,' mused the little priest.

Bradley was ready with the appropriate response of scholarly compassion.

'Times change, yes. *Tempora mutantur: et nos mutamur in illis.*'

'I think,' said the priest, 'that the line should read: *Tempora mutantur:* nos et *mutamur in illis.* Otherwise the hexameter won't scan, will it?'

'Of course it won't, sorry.'

The scout now politely requested dons – wives – partners – guests – to proceed to the Hall. And Jasper Bradley, eminent authority on the aorist subjunctive in Classical Greek, walked out of the SCR more than slightly wounded.

Sir Clixby Bream brought up the rear as the room emptied, and lightly touched the bottom of Angela Storrs standing just in front of him.

Sotto voce he lied into her ear: 'You're looking ravishing tonight. And I'll tell you something else – I'd far rather be in bed with you now than face another bloody Guest Night.'

'So would I!' she lied, in a whisper. 'And I've got a big favour to ask of *you*, too.'

'We'll have a word about it after the port.'

'*Before* the port, Clixby! You're usually blotto after it.'

Sir Clixby banged his gavel, mumbled *Benedictus benedicat*, and the assembled company seated themselves, the table-plan having positioned Julian Storrs and Denis Cornford at diagonally opposite ends of the thick oak table, with their wives virtually opposite each other in the middle.

'I love your suit!' lied Shelly Cornford, in a not unpleasing Yankee twang.

'You look very nice, too,' lied Angela Storrs, smiling widely and showing such white and well-aligned teeth that no one could be in much doubt that her upper plate had been disproportionately expensive.

After which preliminary skirmish, each side observed a dignified truce, with neither a further word nor a further glance between them during the rest of the dinner.

At the head of the table, the little priest sat on the Master's right.

'Just the two candidates, I hear?' he said quietly.

'Just the two: Julian Storrs and Denis Cornford.'

'The usual shenanigans, I assume? The usual horse-trading? Clandestine cabals?'

'Oh no, nothing like that. We're all very civilized here.'

'How do you know that?'

'Well, you've only got to hear what people say – the way they say it.'

The little priest pushed away his half-eaten guinea-fowl.

'You know, Clixby, I once read that speech often gets in the way of genuine communication.'

Chapter Twenty-Five

Saturday, 24 February

There never was a scandalous tale without some foundation
(Richard Brinsley Sheridan, *The School for Scandal*)

WHILST THE GUEST NIGHT was still in progress, whilst still the port and Madeira were circulating in their time-honoured directions, an over-wearied Morse had decided to retire comparatively early to bed, where almost unprecedentedly he enjoyed a deep, unbroken slumber until 7.15 the following morning, when gladly would he have turned over and gone back to sleep. But he had much to do that day. He drank two cups of instant coffee (which he preferred to the genuine article); then another cup, this time with one slice of brown toast heavily spread with butter and Frank Cooper's Oxford Marmalade.

By 8.45 he was in his office at Kidlington HQ, where he found a note on his desk:

Please see Chief Sup. Strange a s a p

The meeting, almost until the end, was an amiable enough affair, and Morse received a virtually uninterrupted hearing as he explained his latest thinking on the murder of Rachel James.

'Mm!' grunted Strange, resting his great jowls on his palms when Morse had finished. 'So it *could* be a contract-killing that went cockeyed, you think? The victim gets pinpointed a bit too vaguely, and the killer shoots at the wrong pig-tail—'

'Pony-tail, sir.'

'Yes – through the wrong window. Right?'

'Yes.'

'What about the motive? The key to this sort of mess is almost always the *motive*, you know that.'

'You sound just like Sergeant Lewis, sir.'

Strange looked dubiously across the desk, as if a little uncertain as to whether he *wanted* to sound just like Sergeant Lewis.

'Well?'

'I agree with you. That's one of the reasons it could have been a case of misidentity. We couldn't really find any satisfactory motive for Rachel's murder anywhere. But if somebody wanted *Owens* out of the way – well, I can think of a dozen possible motives.'

'Because he's a news-hound, you mean?'

Morse nodded. 'Plenty of people in highish places who've got some sort of skeleton in the sideboard—'

'Cupboard.'

'Who'd go quite a long way to keep the, er, cupboard firmly locked.'

'Observed openly masturbating on the M40, you mean? Weekend away with the PA? By the way, *you've* got a pretty little lass for a secretary, I see. Don't you ever lust after her?'

'I seem to have lost most of my lust recently, sir.'

'We all do. It's called getting old.'

Strange lifted his large head, and eyed Morse over his half-lenses.

'Now about the case. It won't be easy, will it? You've no reason to think he's got a lot of stuff stashed under his mattress?'

'No . . . no, I haven't.'

'You'd no real reason for thinking he'd killed Rachel?'

'No . . . no, I hadn't.'

'So he's definitely out of the frame?'

Morse considered the question awhile. ''Fraid so, yes. I wish he weren't.'

'So?'

'So I'll – *we'll* think of some way of approaching things.'

'Nothing irregular! You promise me that! We're just about getting over one or two unsavoury incidents in the Force, aren't we? And we're not going to start anything here. Is that clear, Morse?'

'To be fair, sir, I usually do go by the book.'

Strange pointed a thick finger.

'Well, *usually*'s not bloody good enough for me! You – go – by – the book, matey! Understood?'

Morse walked heavily back to his office, where a refreshed-looking Lewis awaited him.

'Everything all right with the Super?'

'Oh, yes. I just told him about our latest thinking—'

'*Your* latest thinking.'

'He understands the difficulties. He just doesn't want us to bend the rules of engagement too far, that's all.'

'So what's the plan?'

'Just nip and get me a drink first, will you?'

'Coffee?'

Morse pondered. 'I think I'll have a pint of natural, lead-free orange juice. Iced.'

'So what's the plan?' repeated Lewis, five minutes later.

'Not quite sure, really. But if I'm right, if it *was* something like a contract-killing, it must have been arranged because Owens was threatening to expose somebody. And if he was—'

'Lot of "if's", sir.'

'*If* he was, Lewis, he must have some evidence tucked away somewhere: vital evidence, damning evidence. It could be in the form of newspaper-cuttings or letters or photographs – anything. *And* he must have been pretty sure about his facts if he's been trying to extort some money or some favours or whatever from any disclosures. Now, as I see it, he must have come across most of his evidence in the course of his career as a journalist. Wouldn't you think so? Sex scandals, that sort of thing.'

'Like as not, I suppose.'

'So the plan's this. I want you, once you get the chance, to go and see the big white chief at the newspaper offices and get a look at all the confidential stuff on Owens. They're sure to have it in his appointment-file or somewhere: previous jobs, references, testimonials, CV, internal appraisals, comments—'

'Gossip?'

'Anything!'

'Is that what you mean by not bending the rules too much?'

'We're *not* bending the rules – not too much. We're on a *murder* case, Lewis, remember that! Every member of the public's got a duty to help us in our enquiries.'

'I just hope the editor agrees with you, that's all.'

'He does,' said Morse, a little shamefacedly. 'I rang him while you went to the canteen. He just wants us to do it privately, that's all, and confidentially. Owens only works alternate Saturdays, and this is one of his days off.'

'You don't want to do it yourself?'

'It's not that I don't *want* to. But you're so much better at that sort of thing than I am.'

A semi-mollified Lewis elaborated: 'Then, if anything sticks out as important . . . just follow it up . . . and let you know?'

'Except for one thing, Lewis. Owens told me he worked for quite a while in Soho when he started. And if there's anything suspicious or interesting about that period of his life . . .'

'You'd like to do that bit of research yourself.'

'Exactly. I'm better at that sort of thing than you are.'

'What's your programme for today, then?'

'Quite a few things, really.'

'Such as?' Lewis looked up quizzically.

'Well, there's one helluva lot of paperwork, for a start.

And filing. So you'd better stay and give me a hand for a while – after you've fetched me another orange juice. And please tell the girl not to dilute it quite so much this time. And just a cube or two more ice perhaps.'

'And then?' persisted Lewis.

'And then I'm repairing to the local in Cutteslowe, where I shall be trying to thread a few further thoughts together over a pint, perhaps. And where I've arranged to meet an old friend of mine who may possibly be able to help us a little.'

'Who's that, sir?'

'It doesn't matter.'

'Not—?'

'Where's my orange juice, Lewis?'

Chapter Twenty-Six

Maria: No, I've just got the two O-levels – and the tortoise, of course. But I'm fairly well known for some other accomplishments.

Judge: Known to whom, may I ask?

Maria: Well, to the police for a start.

(Diana Doherty, *The Re-trial of Maria Macmillan*)

At ten minutes to noon Morse was enjoying his pint of Brakspear's bitter. The Chief Inspector had many faults, but unpunctuality had never been one of them. He was ten minutes early.

JJ, a sparely built, nondescript-looking man in his mid-forties, walked into the Cherwell five minutes later.

When Morse had rung at 8.30 a.m., Malcolm 'JJ' Johnson had been seated on the floor, on a black cushion, only two feet away from the television screen, watching a hard-core porn video and drinking his regular breakfast of two cans of Beamish stout – just after the lady of the household had left for her job (mornings only) in one of the fruiterers' shops in Summertown.

Accepted wisdom has it that in such enlightened times as these most self-respecting burglars pursue their trade by day; but JJ had always been a night-man, relying firmly on local knowledge and reconnaissance. And often in the daylight hours, as now, he wondered why he didn't spend his leisure time in some more purposeful pursuits. But in truth he just couldn't think of any. At the same time, he did realize, yes, that sometimes he was getting a bit bored. Over the past two years or so, the snooker table had lost its former magnetism; infidelities and fornication were posing too many practical problems, as he grew older; and even darts and dominoes were beginning to pall. Only gambling, usually in Ladbrokes' premises in Summertown, had managed to retain his undivided attention over the years: for the one thing that never bored him was acquiring money.

Yet JJ had never been a miser. It was just that the acquisition of money was a necessary prerequisite to the *spending* of money; and the spending of money had always been, and still was, the greatest purpose of his life.

Educated (if that be the word) in a run-down comprehensive school, he had avoided the three Bs peculiar to many public-school establishments: beating, bullying, and buggery. Instead, he had left school at the age of sixteen with a delight in a different triad: betting, boozing, and bonking – strictly in that order. And to fund such expensive hobbies he had come to rely on one source of income, one line of business only: burglary.

He now lived with his long-suffering, faithful, strangely influential, common-law wife in a council house on the Cutteslowe Estate that was crowded with crates of lager and vodka and gin, with all the latest computer games, and with row upon row of tasteless seaside souvenirs. And home, after two years in jail, was where he wanted to stay.

No! JJ didn't want to go back inside. And that's why Morse's call had worried him so. So much, indeed, that he had turned the video to 'Pause' even as the eager young stud was slipping between the sheets.

What did Morse want?

'Hello, Malcolm!'

Johnson had been 'Malcolm' until the age of ten, when the wayward, ill-disciplined young lad had drunk from a bottle of Jeyes Fluid under the misapprehension that the lavatory cleaner was lemonade. Two stomach-pumpings and a week in hospital later, he had emerged to face the world once more; but now with the sobriquet 'Jeyes' – an embarrassment which he sought to deflect, five years on, by the rather subtle expedient of having the legend 'JJ – all the Js' tattooed longitudinally on each of his lower arms.

Morse drained his glass and pushed it over the table.

'Coke, is it, Mr Morse?'

'Bit early for the hard stuff, Malcolm.'

'Half a pint, was it?'

'Just tell the landlord "same again".'

A Brakspear it was – and a still mineral water for JJ.

'One or two of those gormless idiots you call your pals seem anxious to upset the police,' began Morse.

'Look. I didn't 'ave nothin' to do with that – 'onest!

You know me.' Looking deeply unhappy, JJ dragged deeply on a king-sized cigarette.

'I'm not really interested in that. I'm interested in your doing me a favour.'

JJ visibly relaxed, becoming almost his regular, perky self once more. He leaned over the table, and spoke quietly:

'I'll tell you what. I got a red-'ot video on up at the country mansion, if you, er . . .'

'Not this morning,' said Morse reluctantly, conscious of a considerable sacrifice. And it was now *his* turn to lean over the table and speak the quiet words:

'I want you to break into a property for me.'

'Ah!'

The balance of power had shifted, and JJ grinned broadly to reveal two rows of irregular and blackened teeth. He pushed his empty glass across the table.

'Double vodka and lime for me, Mr Morse. I suddenly feel a bit thirsty, like.'

For the next few minutes Morse explained the mission; and JJ listened carefully, nodding occasionally, and once making a pencilled note of an address on the back of a pink betting-slip.

'OK,' he said finally, 'so long as you promise, you know, to see me OK if . . .'

'I can't promise anything.'

'But you will?'

'Yes.'

'OK, then. Gimme a chance to do a bit o' recce, OK?

Then gimme another buzz on the ol' blower, like, OK? When had you got in mind?'

'I'm not quite sure.'

'OK – that's it then.'

Morse drained his glass and stood up, wondering whether communication in the English language could ever again cope without the word 'OK'.

'Before you go . . .' JJ looked down at his empty glass.

'Mineral water, was it?' asked Morse.

'Just tell the landlord "same again".'

Almost contented with life once more, JJ sat back and relaxed after Morse had gone. Huh! Just the one bleedin' door, by the sound of it. Easy. Piece o' cake!

Morse, too, was pleased with the way the morning had gone. Johnson, as the police were well aware, was one of the finest locksmen in the Midlands. As a teenager he'd held the reputation of being the quickest car-thief in the county. But his incredible skills had only really begun to burgeon in the eighties, when all manner of house-locks, burglar-alarms, and safety-devices had surrendered meekly to his unparalleled knowledge of locks and keys and electrical circuits.

In fact 'JJ' Johnson knew almost as much about burglary as J. J. Bradley knew about the aorist subjunctive.

Perhaps more.

Chapter Twenty-Seven

The faults of the burglar are the qualities of the financier
(Bernard Shaw, *Major Barbara*)

In fact, Morse's campaign was destined to be launched that very day.

Lewis had called back at HQ at 2 p.m. with a slim folder of photocopied documents – in which Morse seemed little interested; and with the news that Geoffrey Owens had left his home the previous evening to attend a weekend conference on Personnel Management, in Bournemouth, not in all likelihood to be back until late p.m. the following day, Sunday. In this latter news Morse seemed more interested.

'Well done, Lewis! But you've done quite enough for one day. You look weary and I want you to go home. Nobody can keep up the hours you've been setting yourself.'

As it happened, Lewis was feeling wonderfully fresh; but he *had* promised that weekend to accompany his wife (if he could) on her quest for the right sort of dish-washer. They could well afford the luxury now, and Lewis himself would welcome some alleviation of his domestic duties at the sink.

'I'll accept your offer – on one condition, sir. You go off home, too.'

'Agreed. I was just going anyway. I'll take the folder with me. Anything interesting?'

'A few little things, I suppose. For instance—'

'Not now!'

'Aren't you going to tell me how *your* meeting went?'

'*Not now!* Let's call it a day.'

As the two detectives walked out of the HQ block, Morse asked his question casually:

'By the way, did you discover which swish hotel they're at in Bournemouth?'

Back in his flat, Morse made two phone-calls: the first to Bournemouth; the second to the Cutteslowe Estate. Yes, a Mr Geoffrey Owens was present at the conference there. No, Mr Malcolm Johnson had not yet had a chance to make his recce – of course he hadn't! But, yes, he would repair the omission forthwith in view of the providential opportunity now afforded (although Johnson's own words were considerably less pretentious).

'And no more booze today, Malcolm!'

'What me – drink? On business? Never! And you better not drink, neither.'

'Two sober men – that's what the job needs,' agreed Morse.

'What time you pickin' me up then?'

'No. You're picking *me* up. Half past seven at my place.'

'OK. And just remember you got more to lose than I 'ave, Mr Morse.'

Yes, far more to lose, Morse knew that; and he felt a shudder of apprehension about the risky escapade he was undertaking. His nerves needed some steadying.

He poured himself a goodly measure of Glenfiddich; and shortly thereafter fell deeply asleep in the chair for more than two hours.

Bliss.

Johnson parked his filthy F-reg Vauxhall in a fairly convenient lay-by on the Deddington Road, the main thoroughfare which runs at the rear of the odd-numbered houses in Bloxham Drive. As instructed, Morse stayed behind, in the murky shadow of the embankment, as Johnson eased himself through a gap in the perimeter fence, where vandals had smashed and wrenched away several of the vertical slats, and then, with surprising agility, descended the steep stretch of slippery grass that led down to the rear of the terrace.

The coast seemed clear.

Morse looked on nervously as the locksman stood in his trainers at the back of Number 15, patiently and methodically doing what he did so well. Once, he snapped to taut attention hard beside the wall as a light was switched on in one of the nearby houses, throwing a yellow rectangle over the glistening grass – and then switched off.

Six minutes.

By Morse's watch, six minutes before Johnson turned the knob, carefully eased the door open, and disappeared within – before reappearing and beckoning a tense and jumpy Morse to join him.

'Do you want the lights on?' asked Johnson as he played the thin beam of his large torch around the kitchen.

'What do *you* think?'

'Yes. Let's 'ave 'em on. Lemme just go and pull the curtains through 'ere.' He moved into the front living-room, where Morse heard a twin swish, before the room burst suddenly into light.

An ordinary, somewhat spartan room: settee; two rather tatty armchairs; dining-table and chairs; TV set; electric fire installed in the old fireplace; and above the fireplace, on a mantelshelf patinated deep with dust, the only object perhaps which any self-respecting burglar would have wished to take – a small, beautifully fashioned ormolu clock.

Upstairs, the double-bed in the front room was unmade, an orange bath-towel thrown carelessly across the duvet; no sign of pyjamas. On the bedside table two items only: Wilbur Smith's *The Seventh Scroll* in paperback, and a packet of BiSoDoL Extra indigestion tablets. An old-fashioned mahogany wardrobe monopolized much of the remaining space, with coats/suits/trousers on their hangers, and six pairs of shoes neatly laid in parallels at the bottom; and on the shelves, to the left, piles of jumpers, shirts, pants, socks, and handkerchiefs.

The second bedroom was locked.

'Malcolm!' whispered Morse down the stairwell.

Two and a half minutes later, Morse was taking stock of a smaller but clearly more promising room: a large book-case containing a bestseller selection from over the years; one armchair; one office chair; the latter set beneath a veneered desk with an imitation leather top, four drawers on either side, and between them a longer drawer with two handles – locked.

'Malcolm!' whispered Morse down the stairwell.

Ninety seconds only this time, and clearly the locksman was running into form.

The eight side-drawers contained few items of interest: stationery, insurance documents, car documents, bank statements, pens and pencils – but in the bottom left-hand drawer a couple of pornographic paperbacks. Morse opened *Topless in Torremolinos* at random and read a short paragraph.

In its openly titillating way, it seemed to him surprisingly well written. And there was that one striking simile where the heroine's bosom was compared to a pair of fairy-cakes – although Morse wasn't at all sure what a fairy-cake looked like. He made a mental note of the author, Ann Berkeley Cox, and read the brief dedication on the title page, 'For Geoff From ABC', before slipping the book into the pocket of his mackintosh.

Johnson was seated in an armchair, in the living-room, in the dark, when Morse came down the stairs holding a manila file.

'Got what you wanted, Mr Morse?'

'Perhaps so. Ready?'

With the house now in total darkness, the two men felt their way to the kitchen, when Morse stopped suddenly.

'The torch! Give me the torch.'

Retracing his steps to the living-room, he shone the beam along an empty mantelpiece.

'Put it back!' he said.

Johnson took the ormolu clock from his overcoat-pocket and replaced it carefully on its little dust-free rectangle.

'I'm glad you made me do that,' confided Johnson quietly. 'I shouldn't 'a done it in the first place. Anyway, me conscience'll be clear now.'

There was a streak of calculating cruelty in the man, Morse knew that. But in several respects he was a lovable rogue; even sometimes, as now perhaps, a reasonably honest one. And oddly it was Morse who was beginning to worry – about his own conscience.

He went quickly up to the second bedroom once more and slipped the book back in its drawer.

At last, as quietly as it had opened, the back door closed behind them and the pair now made their way up the grassy gradient to the gap in the slatted perimeter fence.

'You've not lost your old skills,' volunteered Morse.

'Nah! Know what they say, Mr Morse? Old burglars never die – they simply steal away.'

*

In the darkened house behind them, on the mantelshelf in the front living-room, a little dust-free rectangle still betrayed the spot where the beautifully fashioned ormolu clock had so recently stood.

Chapter Twenty-Eight

When you have assembled what you call your 'facts' in logical order, it is like an oil-lamp you have fashioned, filled, and trimmed; but which will shed no illumination unless first you light it

(Saint-Exupéry, *The Wisdom of the Sands*)

BACK IN HIS flat, Morse closed the door and shot the bolts, both top and bottom. It was an oddly needless precaution, yet an explicable one, perhaps. As a twelve-year-old boy, he remembered so vividly returning from school with a magazine, and locking all the doors in spite of his certain knowledge that no other member of the family would be home for several hours. And then, even then, he had waited awhile, relishing the anticipatory thrill before daring to open the pages.

It was just that sensation he felt now as he switched on the electric fire, poured a glass of Glenfiddich, lit a cigarette, and settled back in his favourite armchair – not this time, however, with the *Naturist Journal* which (all those years ago now) had been doing the rounds in Lower IVA, but with the manila file just burgled from the house in Bloxham Drive.

The cover was well worn, with tears and creases along its edges; and maroon rings where once a wine glass had rested, amid many doodles of quite intricate design. Inside the file was a sheaf of papers and cuttings, several of them clipped or stapled together, though not arranged in any chronological or purposeful sequence.

Nine separate items.

– Two newspaper cuttings, snipped from one of the less inhibited of the Sunday tabloids, concerning a Lord Hardiman, together with a photograph of the aforesaid peer fishing in his wallet (presumably for Deutschmarks) outside a readily identifiable sex establishment in Hamburg's Reeperbahn. Clipped to this material was a further photograph of Lord Hardiman arm-in-arm with Lady Hardiman at a polo match in Great Windsor Park (September 1984).

– A letter (August 1979) addressed to Owens from a firm of solicitors in Cheltenham informing the addressee that it was in possession of letters sent by him (Owens) to one of their clients (unspecified); and that some arrangement beneficial to each of the parties might possibly be considered.

– A glossy, highly defined photograph showing a paunchy elderly man fondling a frightened-looking prepubescent girl, both of them naked. Pencilled on the back was an address in St Albans.

– A stapled sheaf of papers showing the expenses of a director in a Surrey company manufacturing surgical appliances, with double exclamation-marks against several of the mammoth amounts claimed for foreign business trips.

– A brief, no-nonsense letter (from a woman, perhaps?) in large, curly handwriting, leaning italic-fashion to the right: 'If you contact me again I shall take your letters to the police – I've kept them all. You'll get no more money from me. You're a despicable human being. I've got nothing more to lose, not even my money.' No signature but (again) a pencilled address, this time in the margin, in Wimbledon.

– Four sets of initials written on a small page probably torn from the back of a diary:

AM✓ DC✓ JS✓ CB

Nothing more – except a small tick in red Biro against the first three.

– Two further newspaper cuttings, paper-clipped together. The first (*The Times* Diary, 2.2.96) reporting as follows:

After a nine-year tenure Sir Clixby Bream is retiring as Master of Lonsdale College, Oxford. Sir Clixby would, indeed should, have retired earlier. It is only the inability of anyone in the College(including the classicists) to understand the Latin of the original Statutes that has prolonged Sir Clixby's term. The present Master has refused to speculate whether such an extension has been the result of some obscurity in the language of the Statutes themselves; or the incompetence of his classical colleagues, none of whom appears to have been nominated as a possible successor.

The second, a cutting from the *Oxford Mail* (November 1995) of an article written by Geoffrey Owens; with a photograph alongside, the caption reading, 'Mr Julian Storrs and his wife Angela at the opening of the Polynesian Art Exhibition at the Pitt Rivers Museum.'

– A smudgy photocopy of a typed medical report, marked 'Strictly Private and Confidential', on the notepaper of a private health clinic in the Banbury Road:

Ref:	Mr J. C Storrs
Diagnosis:	Inoperable liver cancer confirmed For second opn see letter Dr O V Maxim (Churchill)
Prognosis:	Seven/eight months, or less Possibly(??) a year No longer
Patient Notes:	Honesty best in this case. Strong personality.
Next Appt:	See book, but a s a p
	RHT

Clipped to this was a cutting from the obituary columns of one of the national dailies – *The Independent*, by the look of it – announcing the death of the distinguished cancer specialist Robert H. Turnbull.

– Finally, three photographs, paper-clipped together:
(i) A newspaper photograph of a strip-club, showing in turn (though indistinguishably) individual photographs of the establishment's principal performers, posted on each side of the narrow entrance; showing also (with complete clarity) the inviting legend: SEXIEST RAUNCHIEST SHOW IN SOHO.
(ii) A full-length, black-and-white photograph of a tallish bottle-blonde in a dark figure-hugging gown, the thigh-slit on the left revealing a length of shapely leg. About the woman there seemed little that was less than genuinely attractive – except the smile perhaps.
(iii) A colour photograph of the same woman seated completely naked, apart from a pair of extraordinarily thin stiletto heels, on a bar-stool somewhere – her overfirm breasts suggesting that the smile in the former photograph was not the only thing about her that might be semi-artificial. The legs, now happily revealed in all their lengthy glory, were those of a young dancer – the legs of a Cyd Charisse or a Betty Grable, much better than those in the *Naturist Journal*...

Morse closed the file, and knew what he had read: an agenda for blackmail – and possibly for murder.

Chapter Twenty-Nine

Sunday, 25 February

He was advised by a friend, with whom he afterwards lost touch, to stay at the Wilberforce Temperance Hotel

(Geoffrey Madan, *Notebooks*)

I hate those who intemperately denounce beer – and call it Temperance

(G. K. Chesterton)

SOCRATES, ON HIS last day on earth, avowed that death, if it be but one long and dreamless sleep, was a blessing most devoutly to be wished. Morse, on the morning of Sunday, 25 February – without going quite so far as Socrates – could certainly look back on his own long and dreamless sleep with a rare gratitude, since the commonest features of his nights were regular visits to the loo, frequent draughts of water, occasional doses of Nurofen and Paracetamol, an intake of indigestion tablets, and finally (after rising once more from his crumpled bed-linen) a tumbler of Alka-Seltzer.

The Observer was already poking thickly through the

letter-box as he hurriedly prepared himself a subcontinental breakfast.

10.30 a.m.

It was 11.15 a.m. when he arrived at HQ, where Lewis had already been at work for three hours, and where he was soon regaling the chief about his visit to the newspaper offices.

A complete picture of Owens – built up from testimonials, references, records, impressions, gossip – showed a competent, hard-working, well-respected employee. That was the good news. And the bad? Well, it seemed the man was aloof, humourless, unsympathetic. In view of the latter shortcomings (Lewis had suggested) it was perhaps puzzling to understand why Owens had been sent off on a personnel management course. Yet (as the editor had suggested) some degree of aloofness, humourlessness, lack of sympathy, was perhaps precisely what was required in such a rôle.

Lewis pointed to the cellophane folder in which his carefully paginated photocopies were assembled.

'And one more thing. He's obviously a bit of a hit with some of the girls there – especially the younger ones.'

'In spite of his pony-tail?'

'Because of it, more likely.'

'You're not serious?'

'And you're never going to catch up with the twentieth century, are you?'

'One or two possible leads?'

'Could be.'

'Such as?'

'Well, for a start, the Personnel Manager who saw Owens on Monday. I'll get a statement from him as soon as he gets back from holiday – earlier, if you'd like.'

Morse looked dubious. 'Ye-es. But if somebody intended to murder Owens, not Rachel James . . . well, Owens' alibi is neither here nor there really, is it? You're right, though. Let's stick to official procedure. I've always been in favour of rules and regulations.'

As Lewis eyed his superior officer with scarce disguised incredulity, he accepted the manila file handed to him across the desk; and began to read.

Morse himself now opened the 'Life' section of *The Observer* and turned to the crossword set by Azed (for Morse, the Kasparov of cruciverbalists) and considered 1 across: 'Elephant-man has a mouth that's deformed (6)'. He immediately wrote in MAHOUT, but then put the crossword aside, trusting that the remaining clues might pose a more demanding challenge, and deciding to postpone his hebdomadal treat until later in the day. Otherwise, he might well have completed the puzzle before Lewis had finished with the file.

'How did you come by this?' asked Lewis finally.

'Yours not to reason how.'

'He's a blackmailer!'

Morse nodded. 'We've found no evidential motive for Rachel's murder, but . . .'

'. . . dozens of 'em for his.'

'About *nine*, Lewis – if we're going to be accurate.'

Morse opened the file, and considered the contents once more. Unlike that of the obscenely fat child-fondler, neither photograph of the leggy blonde stripper was genuinely pornographic – certainly not the wholly nude one, which seemed to Morse strangely unerotic; perhaps the one of her in the white dress, though ... 'Unbuttoning' had always appealed to Morse more than 'unbuttoned'; 'undressing' than 'undressed'; 'almost naked' to completely so. It was something to do with Plato's idea of process; and as a young classical scholar Morse had spent so many hours with that philosopher.

'Quite a bit of leg-work there, sir.'

'Yes. Lovely legs, aren't they?'

'No! I meant there's a lot of work to do there – research, going around.'

'You'll need a bit of help, yes.'

'Sergeant Dixon – couple of his lads, too – that'd help.'

'Is Dixon still eating the canteen out of jam doughnuts?'

Lewis nodded. '*And* he's still got his pet tortoise—'

'—always a step or two in front of him, I know.'

For half an hour the detectives discussed the file's explosive material. Until just after noon, in fact.

'Coffee, sir?'

'Not for me. Let's nip down to the King's Arms in Summertown.'

'Not for me,' echoed Lewis. 'I can't afford the time.'

'As you wish.' Morse got to his feet.

'Do you think you should be going out quite so much – on the booze, I mean, sir?' Lewis took a deep breath and prepared for an approaching gale, force ten. 'You're getting worse, not better.'

Morse sat down again.

'Let me just tell you something, Lewis. I care quite a bit about what you think of me as a boss, as a colleague, as a detective – as a *friend*, yes! But I don't give two bloody monkeys about what you think of me as a boozer, all right?'

'No, it's not all right,' said Lewis quietly. 'As a professional copper, as far as solving murders are concerned – '

'*Is* concerned!'

' – it doesn't matter. Doesn't matter to me at all.' (Lewis's voice grew sharper now.) 'You do your job – you spend all your time sorting things out – I'm not worried about that. And if the Chief Constable told me you *weren't* doing your job, I'd resign myself. But he *wouldn't* say that – never. What he'd say – what others would say – what others *are* saying – is that you're ruining yourself. Not the Force, not the department, not the murder enquiries – nothing! – *except yourself*.'

'Just hold on a second, will you?' Morse's eyes were blazing.

'No! No, I won't. You talked about me as a friend, didn't you, just now? Well, as a friend I'm telling you that you're buggering up your health, your retirement, your life – everything!'

'Listen!' hissed Morse. 'I've never myself tried to tell

any other man how to live his life. And I will *not* be told, at my age, how I'm supposed to live mine. Even by you.'

After a prolonged silence, Lewis spoke again.

'Can I say something else?'

Morse shrugged indifferently.

'Perhaps it doesn't matter much to most people whether you kill yourself or not. You've got no wife, no family, no relatives, except that aunt of yours in Alnwick—'

'She's dead, too.'

'So, what the hell? What's it matter? Who cares? Well, *I* care, sir. And the missus cares. And for all I know that girl Ellie Smith, *she* cares.'

Morse looked down at his desk. 'Not any longer, no.'

'And *you* ought to care – care for yourself – just a bit.'

For some considerable while Morse refrained from making any answer, for he was affected by his sergeant's words more deeply than he would ever be prepared to admit.

Then, finally:

'What about that coffee, Lewis?'

'And a sandwich?'

'And a sandwich.'

By early afternoon Morse had put most of his cards on the table, and he and Lewis had reached an agreed conclusion. No longer could either of them accept that Rachel James had been the intended victim: each of them now looked towards Geoffrey Owens as by far the likelier target. Pursuance of the abundant clues provided by the Owens file would necessarily involve a great deal of extra work; and fairly soon a strategy was devised, with Lewis and Dixon allocated virtually everything except the Soho slot.

'You know, I could probably fit that in fairly easily with the Wimbledon visit,' Lewis had volunteered.

But Morse was clearly unconvinced:

'The Soho angle's the most important of the lot.'

'Do you honestly believe that?'

'Certainly. That's why—'

The phone rang, answered by Morse.

Owens (he learned) had phoned HQ ten minutes earlier, just after 3 p.m., to report that his property had been burgled over the weekend, while he was away.

'And you're dealing with it? . . . Good . . . Just the one item you say, as far as he knows? . . . I see . . . Thank you.'

Morse put down the phone; and Lewis picked up the file, looking quizzically across the desk.

But Morse shook his head. 'Not the file, no.'

'What, then?'

'A valuable little ormolu clock from his living-room.'

'Probably a professional, sir – one who knows his clocks.'

'Don't ask me. I know nothing about clocks.'

Lewis grinned. 'We both know somebody who does though, don't we, sir?'

Chapter Thirty

This world and the next – and after that *all* our troubles will be over

(Attributed to General Gordon's aunt)

No knock. The door opened. Strange entered.

'Haven't they mentioned it yet, Morse? The pubs are open all day on Sundays now.'

As Strange carefully balanced his bulk on the chair opposite, Morse lauded his luck that Lewis had taken the Owens material down the corridor for photocopying.

'Just catching up on a bit of routine stuff, sir.'

'Really?'

'Why are *you* here?'

'It's the wife,' confided Strange. 'Sunday afternoons she always goes round the house dusting everything. Including me!'

Morse was smiling dutifully as Strange continued: 'Making progress?'

'Following up a few things, yes.'

'Mm . . . Is your brain as bright as it used to be?'

'I'm sure it's not.'

'Mm . . . You don't *look* quite so bright, either.'

'We're all getting older.'

'Worse luck!'

'Not really, surely? "No wise man ever wished to be younger."'

'Bloody nonsense!'

'Not my nonsense – Jonathan Swift's.'

Elbows on the desk, Strange rested his large head on his large hands.

'I'm probably finishing in September, I suppose you'd heard.'

Morse nodded. 'I'm glad they're letting you go.'

'What the 'ell's *that* supposed to mean?'

'Well, I should think Mrs Strange'll be pleased to have you around, won't she? Retirement, you know . . . Getting up late and watching all the other poor sods go off to work, especially on Monday mornings. That sort of thing. It's what we all work for, I suppose. What we all wait for.'

'You mean,' muttered Strange, '*that's* what I've been flogging me guts out all this time for – thirty-two years of it? I used to do your sort of job, you know. Caught nearly as many murderers as you in me day. It's just that I used to do it a bit different, that's all. Mostly used to wait till they came to *me*. No problem, often as not: jealousy, booze, sex, next-door neighbour between the sheets with the missus. *Motive* – that's what it's all about.'

'Not always quite so easy, though, is it?' ventured Morse, who had heard the sermon several times before.

'Certainly not when *you're* around, matey!'

'This case needs some very careful handling, sir. Lots of sensitive enquiries—'

'Such as?'

'About Owens, for a start.'

'You've got some new evidence?'

'One or two vague rumours, yes.'

'Mm ... I heard a vague rumour myself this afternoon. I heard Owens' place got burgled. I suppose you've heard that, too?' He peered at Morse over his half-lenses.

'Yes.'

'Only one thing pinched. Hm! A clock, Morse.'

'Yes.'

'We've only got one or two clock specialists on the patch, as far as I remember. Or is it just the one?'

'The one?'

'You've not seen him – since they let him out again?'

'Ah, Johnson! Yes. I shall have to call round to see him pretty soon, I suppose.'

'What about tomorrow? He's probably your man, isn't he?'

'I'm away tomorrow.'

'Oh?'

'London. Soho, as a matter of fact. Few things to check out.'

'I don't know why you don't let Sergeant Lewis do all that sort of tedious leg-work.'

Morse felt the Chief Superintendent's small, shrewd eyes upon him.

'Division of labour. Someone's got to do it.'

'You know,' said Strange, 'if I hadn't got a Supers' meeting in the morning, I'd join you. See the sights ... and everything.'

'I don't think Mrs Strange'd approve.'

'What makes you think I'd tell her?'

'She's – she's not been all that well, has she?'

Strange slowly shook his head, and looked down at the carpet.

'What about you, sir?'

'Me? I'm fine, apart from going deaf and going bald and haemorrhoids and blood pressure. Bit overweight, too, perhaps. What about you?'

'I'm fine.'

'How's the drinking going?'

'Going? It's going, er . . .'

'"Quickly"? Is that the word you're looking for?'

'That's the word.'

Strange appeared about to leave. And – blessedly! – Lewis (Morse realized) must have been aware of the situation, since he had put in no appearance.

But Strange was not quite finished: 'Do you ever worry how your liver's coping with all this booze?'

'We've all got to die of something, they say.'

'Do you ever think about that – about dying?'

'Occasionally.'

'Do you believe in life after death?'

Morse smiled. 'There was a sign once that Slough Borough Council put up near one of the churches there: NO ROAD BEYOND THE CEMETERY.'

'You don't think there is, then?'

'No,' answered Morse simply.

'Perhaps it's just as well if there isn't – you know, rewards and punishments and all that sort of thing.'

'I don't want much reward, anyway.'

'Depends on your ambition. You never had much o' that, did you?'

'Early on, I did.'

'You could've got to the top, you know that.'

'Not doing a job I enjoyed, I couldn't. I'm not a form-filler, am I? Or a committee-man. Or a clipboard-man.'

'Or a *procedure*-man,' added Strange slowly, as he struggled to his feet.

'Pardon?'

'Bloody piles!'

Morse persisted. 'What did you mean, sir?'

'Extraordinary, you know, the sort of high-tech stuff we've got in the Force these days. We've got a machine here that even copies colour photos. You know, like the one— Oh! Didn't I mention it, Morse? I had a very pleasant little chat with Sergeant Lewis in the photocopying room just before I came in here. By the look of things, you've got quite a few alternatives to go on there.'

'Quite a lot of "choices", sir. Strictly speaking, you only have "alternatives" if you've just got the two options.'

'Fuck off, Morse!'

That evening Morse was in bed by 9.45 p.m., slowly reading but a few more pages of Juliet Barker's *The Brontës*, before stopping at one sentence, and reading it again:

> Charlotte remarked, 'I am sorry you have changed your residence as I shall now again lose my way in going up and down stairs, and stand in great tribulation,

contemplating several doors, and not knowing which to open.'

It seemed as good a place to stop as any; and Morse was soon nodding off, in a semi-upright posture, the thick book dropping on to the duvet, the whisky on his bedside table (unprecedentedly) unfinished.

Chapter Thirty-One

A time
Older than the time of chronometers, older
Than time counted by anxious worried women
Lying awake, calculating the future,
Trying to unweave, unwind, unravel
And piece together the past and the future
(T. S. Eliot, *The Dry Salvages*)

The result of one election had already been declared, with Mr Ivan Thomas, the Labour candidate, former unsuccessful aspirant to municipal honours, now preparing to assume his duties as councillor for the Gosforth ward at Kidlington, near Oxford.

At Lonsdale College, five miles further south, in the golden heart of Oxford, the likely outcome of another election was still very much in the balance, with the wives of the two nominees very much – and not too discreetly, perhaps – to the fore in the continued canvassing. As it happened, each of them (like Morse) was in bed – or in *a* bed – comparatively early that Sunday evening.

*

Shelly Cornford was always a long time in the bathroom, manipulating her waxed flossing-ribbon in between and up and down her beautifully healthy teeth. When finally she came into the bedroom, her husband was sitting up against the pillows reading the *Sunday Times* Books Section. He watched her as she took off her purple Jaeger dress, and then unfastened her black bra, her breasts bursting free. So very nearly he said something at that point; but the back of his mouth was suddenly dry, and he decided not to. Anyway, it had been only a small incident, and his wife was probably completely unaware of how she could affect some other men – with a touch, a look, a movement of her body. But he'd never been a jealous man.

Not if he could help it.

She got into bed in her Oxford blue pyjamas and briefly turned towards him.

'Why wasn't Julian at dinner tonight?'

'Up in Durham – some conference he was speaking at. He's back tonight – Angela's picking him up from the station, so she said.'

'Oh.'

'Why do you ask?'

'No reason, darling. Night-night! Sweet dreams, my sweetie!'

She blew a kiss across the narrow space between their beds, turned her back towards him, and snuggled her head into the green pillows.

'Don't be too long with the light, please.'

A few minutes later she was lying still, breathing quite rhythmically, and he thought she was asleep.

As quietly as he could, he manoeuvred himself down beneath the bedclothes, and straightway turned off the light. And tried, tried far too hard, to go to sleep himself . . .

. . . After evensong earlier that same evening in the College Chapel, the Fellows and their guests had been invited (as was the custom) to the Master's Lodge, where they partook of a glass of sherry before dining at 7.30 p.m. at the top-table in the main hall, the students seated on the long rows of benches below them. It was just before leaving the Master's Lodge that Denis had looked round for his wife and found her by the fireplace speaking to David Mackenzie, one of the younger dons, a brilliant mathematician, of considerable corpulence, who hastily folded the letter he had been showing to Shelly and put it away.

Nothing in that, perhaps? Not in itself, no. But he, Denis Cornford, knew what was in the letter. And that, for the simplest of all reasons, since Mackenzie had shown him the same scented purple sheets in the SCR the previous week; and Cornford could recall pretty accurately, though naturally not verbatim, the passage he'd been invited to consider. Clearly the letter had been, thus far, the highlight of Mackenzie's term:

> Remember what you scribbled on my menu that night? Your handwriting was a bit wobbly(!) and I couldn't quite make out just that one word: 'I'd love to take you out and make a f— of you'. I *think* it was

'fuss' and it certainly begins with an 'f'. Could be naughty; could be perfectly innocent. *Please* enlighten me!

Surely it was ridiculous to worry about such a thing. But there was something else. The two of them had been giggling together like a pair of adolescents, and looking at each other, and she had put a hand on his arm. And it was almost as if they had established a curious kind of intimacy from which he, Denis Cornford, was temporarily excluded.

Could be naughty.

Could be perfectly innocent . . .

'Would you still love me if I'd got a spot on my nose?'

'Depends how big it was, my love.'

'But you still want my body, don't you,' she whispered, 'in spite of my varicose veins?'

Metaphorically, as he lay beside her, Sir Clixby sidestepped her full-frontal assault as she turned herself towards him.

'You're a very desirable woman, and what's more you know it!' He moved his hands down her naked shoulders and fondled the curves of her bosom.

'I *hope* I can still do something for you,' she whispered. 'After all, you've promised to do something for me, haven't you?'

Perhaps Sir Clixby should have been a diplomat:

'Do you know something? I thought the Bishop was never going to finish tonight, didn't you? I shall have to have a word with the Chaplain. God knows where he found *him*?'

She moved even closer to the Master. 'Come on! We haven't got all night. Julian's train gets in at ten past ten.'

Two of the College dons stood speaking together on the cobblestones outside Lonsdale as the clock on Saint Mary the Virgin struck ten o'clock; and a sole undergraduate passing through the main gate thought he heard a brief snatch of their conversation:

'Having a woman like *her* in the Lodge? The idea's unthinkable!'

But who the woman was, the passer-by was not to know.

Chapter Thirty-Two

Monday, 26 February

How shall I give thee up, O Ephraim? How shall I cast thee off, O Israel?

(*Hosea*, ch. 11, v. 8)

At 8.45 a.m. there were just the two of them, Morse and Lewis, exchanging somewhat random thoughts about the case, when the young blonde girl (whom Strange had already noticed) came in with the morning post. She was a very recent addition to the typing pool, strongly recommended by the prestigious Marlborough College in the High, her secretarial skills corroborated by considerable evidence, including a Pitman Shorthand Certificate for 120 wpm.

'Your mail, sir. I'm . . .' (she looked frightened) 'I'm terribly sorry about the one on top. I just didn't notice.'

But Morse had already taken the letter from its white envelope, the latter marked, in the top left-hand corner, 'Strictly Private and Personal'.

Hullo Morse

Tried you on the blower at Christmas but they said you were otherwise engaged probably in the boozer.

I'm getting spliced. No, don't worry! I'm not asking you for anything this time!! He's nice and he's got a decent job and he says he loves me and he's okay in bed so what the hell. I don't really love him and you bloody well know why that is, don't you, you miserable stupid sod. Because I fell in love with you and I'm just as stupid as you are. St Anthony told me to tell you something but I'm not going to. I want to put my arms round you and hug you tight. God help me! Why didn't you look for me a bit harder Morse?

Ellie

No address.

Of course, there was no address.

'Did you read this?' Morse spoke in level tones, looking up at his secretary with unblinking eyes.

'Only till . . . you know, I realized . . .'

'You shouldn't have opened it.'

'No, sir,' she whispered.

'You can type all right?'

She nodded.

'And you can take shorthand?'

She nodded, despairingly.

'But you can't read?'

'As I said, sir . . .' The tears were starting.

'I heard what *you* said. Now just you listen to what *I'm* saying. This sort of thing will never happen again!'

'I promise, sir, it'll—'

'Listen!' Morse's eyes suddenly widened with an almost manic gleam, his nostrils flaring with suppressed fury as he repeated in a slow, soft voice: 'It won't happen again – not if you want to work for me any longer. Is that clear? *Never.* Now get out,' he hissed, 'and leave me, before I get angry with you.'

After she had left, Lewis too felt almost afraid to speak.

'What was all that about?' he asked finally.

'Don't you start poking your bloody nose—' But the sentence went no further. Instead, Morse picked up the letter and passed it over, his saddened eyes focused on the wainscoting.

After reading the letter, Lewis said nothing.

'I don't have much luck with the ladies, do I?'

'She's still obviously wearing the pendant.'

'I hope so,' said Morse; who might have said rather more, but there was a knock on the door, and DC Learoyd was invited into the sanctum.

Morse handed over the newspaper cuttings concerning Lord Hardiman, together with the photograph, and explained Learoyd's assignment:

'Your job's to find out all you can. It doesn't look all that promising, I know. Hardly blackmail stuff these days, is it? But Owens thinks it is. And that's the point. We're not really interested in how many times he's been knocking on the doors of the knocking-shops. It's finding the nature of his connection with *Owens.*'

Learoyd nodded his understanding, albeit a little unhappily.

'Off you go, then.'

But Learoyd delayed. 'Whereabouts do you think would be a good place to start, sir?'

Morse's eyeballs turned ceilingward.

'What about looking up His Lordship in *Debrett's Peerage*, mm? It might just tell you where he lives, don't you think?'

'But where can I find a copy?'

'What about that big building in the centre of Oxford – in Bonn Square. You've heard of it? It's called the Central Library.'

Item 2 in the manila file, as Lewis had discovered earlier that morning, was OBE (Overtaken By Events, in Morse's shorthand). The Cheltenham firm of solicitors had been disbanded in 1992, its clientèle dispersed, to all intents and purposes now permanently incommunicado.

Item 3 was to be entrusted into the huge hands of DC Elton, who now made his entrance; and almost immediately his exit, since he passed no observations, and asked no questions, as he looked down at the paunchy paedophiliac from St Albans.

'Leave it to me, sir.'

'And while you're at it, see how the land lies *here*.' Morse handed over the documentation on Item 4 – the accounts-sheets from the surgical appliances company in Croydon.

'Good man, that,' commented Lewis, as the door closed behind the massive frame of DC Elton.

'Give me Learoyd every time!' confided Morse. 'At least he's got the intelligence to ask a few half-witted questions.'

'I don't quite follow you.'

'Wouldn't *you* need a bit of advice if you called in at some place selling surgical appliances? With Elton's great beer-gut they'll probably think he's called in for a temporary truss.'

Lewis didn't argue.

He knew better.

Also OBE, as Lewis had already discovered, was Item 5. The address Owens had written on the letter was – had been – that of a home for the mentally handicapped in Wimbledon. A Social Services inspection had uncovered gross and negligent malpractices; and the establishment had been closed down two years previously, its management and nursing staff redeployed or declared redundant. Yet no prosecutions had ensued.

'Forlorn hope,' Lewis had ventured.

And Morse had agreed. 'Did you know that "forlorn hope" has got nothing to do with "forlorn" or "hope"? It's all Dutch: "Verloren hoop" – "lost troop".'

'Very useful to know, sir.'

Seemingly oblivious to such sarcasm, Morse contemplated once more the four sets of initials that comprised Item 6:

AM✓ DC✓ JS✓ CB

with those small ticks in red Biro set against the first three of them.

'Any ideas?' asked Lewis.

'"Jonathan Swift", obviously, for "JS". I was only talking about him to the Super yesterday.'

'Julian Storrs?'

Morse grinned. 'Perhaps *all* of 'em are dons at Lonsdale.'

'I'll check.'

'So that leaves Items seven and eight – both of which I leave in your capable hands, Lewis. And lastly my own little assignment in Soho, Item nine.'

'Coffee, sir?'

'Glass of iced orange juice!'

After Lewis had gone, Morse re-read Ellie's letter, deeply hurt, and wondering whether people in the ancient past had found it quite so difficult to cope with disappointments deep as his. But at least things were over; and in the long run that might make things much easier. He tore the letter in two, in four, in eight, in sixteen, and then in thirty-two – would have torn it in sixty-four, had his fingers been strong enough – before dropping the little square pieces into his wastepaper basket.

'No ice in the canteen, sir. Machine's gone kaput.'

Morse shrugged indifferently and Lewis, sensing that the time might be opportune, decided to say something which had been on his mind:

'Just one thing I'd like to ask . . .'

Morse looked up sharply. 'You're not going to ask me where Lonsdale is, I hope!'

'No. I'd just like to ask you not to be too hard on that new secretary of yours, that's all.'

'And what the hell's that got to do with you?'

'Nothing really, sir.'

'I *agree*. And when I want your bloody advice on how to handle my secretarial staff, I'll come and ask for it. Clear?'

Morse's eyes were blazing anew. And Lewis, his own temperature now rising rapidly, left his superior's office without a further word.

Just before noon, Jane Edwards was finalizing an angry letter, spelling out her resignation, when she heard the message over the intercom: Morse wanted to see her in his office.

'Si' down!'

She sat down, noticing immediately that he seemed tired, the whites of his eyes lightly veined with blood.

'I'm sorry I got so cross, Jane. That's all I wanted to say.'

She remained where she was, almost mesmerized.

Very quietly he continued: 'You *will* try to forgive me – please?'

She nodded helplessly, for she had no choice.

And Morse smiled at her sadly, almost gratefully, as she left.

Back in the typing pool Ms Jane Edwards surreptitiously dabbed away the last of the slow-dropping tears, tore up her letter (so carefully composed) into sixty-four pieces; and suddenly felt, as if by some miracle of St Anthony, most inexplicably happy.

Chapter Thirty-Three

A recent survey has revealed that 80.5% of Oxford dons seek out the likely pornographic potential on the Internet before making use of that facility for purposes connected with their own disciplines or research. The figure for students, in the same university, is 2% lower

(Terence Benczik, *A Possible Future for Computer Technology*)

Until the age of twelve, Morse's reading had comprised little beyond a weekly diet of the *Dandy* comic, and a monthly diet of the *Meccano Magazine* – the legacy of the latter proving considerably the richer, in that Morse had retained a lifelong delight in model train-sets and in the railways themselves. Thus it was that as he stood on Platform One at Oxford Station, he was much looking forward to his journey. Usually, he promised himself a decent read of a decent book on a trip like this. But such potential pleasures seldom materialized; hadn't materialized that afternoon either, when the punctual 2.15 p.m. from Oxford arrived fifty-nine minutes later at Paddington, where Morse immediately took a taxi to New Scotland Yard.

Although matters there had been prearranged, it was

purely by chance that Morse happened to meet Paul Condon, the Metropolitan Commissioner, in the main entrance foyer.

'They're ready for you, Morse. Can't stay myself, I'm afraid. Press conference. It's not just the ethnic minorities I've upset this time – it's the ethnic majorities, too. All because I've published a few more official crime-statistics.'

Morse nodded. He wanted to say something to his old friend: something about never climbing in vain when you're going up the Mountain of Truth. But he only recalled the quotation after stepping out of the lift at the fourth floor, where Sergeant Rogers of the Porn Squad was awaiting him.

Once in Rogers' office, Morse produced the photograph of the strip-club. And immediately, with the speed of an experienced ornithologist recognizing a picture of a parrot, Rogers had identified the premises.

'Just off Brewer Street.' He unfolded a detailed map of Soho. 'Here – let me show you.'

The early evening was overcast, drizzly and dank, when like some latter-day Orpheus Morse emerged from the depths of Piccadilly Circus Underground; whence, after briefly consulting his A–Z, he proceeded by a reasonably direct route to a narrow, seedy-looking thoroughfare, where a succession of establishments promised XXXX videos and magazines (imported), sex shows (live), striptease (continuous) – and a selection of freshly made sandwiches (various).

And there it was! *Le Club Sexy.* Unmistakably so, but prosaically and repetitively now rechristened *Girls Girls Girls.* It made the former proprietors appear comparatively imaginative.

Something – some aspiration to the higher things in life, perhaps – prompted Morse to raise his eyes from the ground-floor level of the gaudily lurid fronts there to the architecture, some of it rather splendid, above.

Yet not for long.

'Come in out of the drizzle, sir! Lovely girls here.'

Morse showed his ID card, and moved into the shelter of the tiny entrance foyer.

'Do you know *her*?'

The young woman, black stockings and black mini-skirt meeting at the top of her thighs, barely glanced at the photograph thrust under her eyes.

'No.'

'Who runs this place? I want to see him.'

'*Her.* But she ain't 'ere now, is she? Why don't you call back later, handsome?'

A helmeted policeman was ambling along the opposite pavement, and Morse called him over.

'OK,' the girl said quickly. 'You bin 'ere before, right?'

'Er – one of my officers, yes.'

'Me mum used to know her, like I told the other fellah. Just a minute.'

She disappeared down the dingy stairs.

'How can I help you, sir?'

Morse showed his ID to the constable.

'Just keep your eyes on me for a few minutes.'

But there was no need.

Three minutes later, Morse had an address in Praed Street, no more than a hundred yards from Paddington Station where earlier, at the entrance to the Underground, he had admired the bronze statue of one of his heroes, Isambard Kingdom Brunel.

So Morse now took the Tube back. It had been a roundabout sort of journey.

She was in.

She asked him in.

And Morse, from a moth-eaten settee, agreed to sample a cup of Nescafé.

'Yeah, Angie Martin! Toffee-nosed little tart, if you know wo' I mean.'

'Tell me about her.'

'You're the *second* one, encha?'

'Er – one of my officers, yes.'

'Nah! He wasn't from the fuzz. Couldna bin! Giv me a couple o' twennies 'e did.'

'What did he want to know?'

'Same as you, like as not.'

'She was quite a girl, they say.'

'Lovely on 'er legs, she was, if you know wo' I mean. Most of 'em, these days, couldn't manage the bleedin' Barn Dance.'

'But *she* was good?'

'Yeah. The men used to love 'er. Stick fivers down 'er boobs and up 'er suspenders, if you know wo' I mean.'

'She packed 'em in?'

'Yeah.'

'And then?'

'Then there was this fellah, see, and he got to know 'er and see 'er after the shows, like, and 'e got starry-eyed, the silly sod. Took 'er away. Posh sort o' fellah, if you know wo' I mean. Dresses, money, 'otels – all that sort o' thing.'

'Would you remember *his* name?'

'Yeah. The other fellah – 'e showed me his photo, see?'

'His name?'

'Julius Caesar, I fink it was.'

Morse showed her the photograph of Mr and Mrs Julian Storrs.

'Yeah. That's 'im an' 'er. That's Angie.'

'Do you know why I'm asking about her?'

She looked at him shrewdly, an inch or so of grey roots merging into a yellow mop of wiry hair.

'Yeah, I got a good idea.'

'My, er, colleague told you?'

'Nah! Worked it out for meself, dint I? She was tryin' to forget wo' she was, see? She dint want to say she were a cheap tart who'd open 'er legs for a fiver, if you know wo' I mean. Bi' o' class, tho', Angie. Yeah. Real bi' o' class.'

'Will you be prepared to come up to Oxford – we'll pay your expenses, of course – to sign a statement?'

'Oxford? Yeah. Why not? Bi' o' class, Oxford, innit?'

'I suppose so, yes.'

'Wo' she done? Wo' sort of enquiry you workin' on?'

'Murder,' said Morse softly.

*

Mission accomplished Morse walked across Praed Street and into the complex of Paddington Station, where he stood under the high Departures Board and noted the time of the next train: Slough, Maidenhead, Reading, Didcot, Oxford.

Due to leave in forty minutes.

He retraced his steps to the top of the Underground entrance, crushed a cigarette-stub under his heel, and walked slowly down towards the ticket-office, debating the wisdom of purchasing a second Bakerloo line ticket to Piccadilly Circus – from which station he might take the opportunity of concentrating his attention on the ground-floor attractions of London's Soho.

Chapter Thirty-Four

The average, healthy, well-adjusted adult gets up at seven-thirty in the morning feeling just plain terrible

(Jean Kerr, *Where Did You Put the Aspirin?*)

WITH A LECTURE A.M. and a Faculty Meeting early p.m., Julian Storrs had not been able to give Lewis much time until late p.m.; but he was ready and waiting when, at 4 o'clock precisely, the front doorbell rang at his home, a large red-bricked property in Polstead Road, part of the Victorian suburb that stretches north from St Giles' to Summertown.

Lewis accepted the offer of real coffee, and the two of them were soon seated in armchairs opposite each other in the high-ceilinged living-room, its furniture exuding a polished mahogany elegance, where Lewis immediately explained the purpose of his call.

As a result of police investigations into the murder of Rachel James, Storrs' name had moved into the frame; well, at least his photograph had moved into the frame.

Storrs himself said nothing as he glanced down at the twin passport photograph that Lewis handed to him.

'That *is* you, sir? You and Ms James?'

Storrs took a deep breath, then exhaled. 'Yes.'

'You were having an affair with her?'

'We . . . yes, I suppose we were.'

'Did anybody know about it?'

'I'd hoped not.'

'Do you want to talk about it?'

Storrs talked. Though not for long . . .

He'd first met her just over a year earlier when he'd pulled a muscle in his right calf following an ill-judged decision to take up jogging. She was a physiotherapist, masseuse, manipulator – whatever they called such people now; and after the first two or three sessions they had met together *outside* the treatment room. He'd fallen in love with her a bit – a lot; must have done, when he considered the risks he'd taken. About once a month, six weeks, they'd managed to be together when he had some lecture to give or meeting to attend. Usually in London, where they'd book a double room, latish morning, in one of the hotels behind Paddington, drink a bottle or two of champagne, make love together most of the afternoon and – well, that was it.

'Expensive sort of day, sir? Rail-fares, hotel, champagne, something to eat . . .'

'Not really expensive, no. Off-peak day returns, one of the cheaper hotels, middle-range champagne, and we'd go to a pub for a sandwich at lunchtime. Hundred and twenty, hundred and thirty pounds – that would cover it.'

'You didn't give Ms James anything for her services?'

'It wasn't like that. I think – I hope – she enjoyed

being with me. But, yes, I did sometimes give her something. She was pretty short of money – you know, her mortgage, HP commitments, the rent on the clinic.'

'How much, sir?'

'A hundred pounds. Little bit more sometimes, perhaps.'

'Does Mrs Storrs know about this?'

'No – and she mustn't!' For the first time Lewis was aware of the sharp, authoritative tone in the Senior Fellow's voice.

'How did you explain spending so much?'

'We have separate accounts. I give my wife a private allowance each month.'

Lewis grinned diffidently. 'You could always have said they were donations to Oxfam.'

Storrs looked down rather sadly at the olive-green carpet. 'You're right. That's just the sort of depths I would have sunk to.'

'Why didn't you get in touch with us? We made several appeals for anybody who knew Rachel to come forward. We guaranteed every confidence.'

'You must understand, surely? I was desperately anxious not to get drawn into things in any way.'

'Nothing else?'

'What do you mean?'

'Was someone trying to blackmail you, sir, about your affair with her?'

'Good God, no! What on earth makes you think that?'

Lewis drank the rest of his never-hot now-cold real coffee, before continuing quietly:

'I don't believe you, sir.'

And slowly the truth, or some of it, was forthcoming.

Storrs had received a letter about a fortnight earlier from someone – no signature – someone giving a PO Box address; someone claiming to have 'evidence' about him which would be shouted from the rooftops unless a payment was duly made.

'Of?' asked Lewis.

'Five thousand pounds.'

'And you paid it?'

'No. But I was stupid enough to send a thousand, in fifty-pound notes.'

'And did you get this "evidence" back?'

Storrs again looked down at the carpet, and shook his head.

'You didn't act very sensibly, did you, sir?'

'In literary circles, Sergeant, that is what is called "litotes".'

'Did you keep the letter?'

'No,' lied Storrs.

'Did you keep a note of the PO Box number?'

'No,' lied Storrs.

'Was it care of one of the local newspapers?'

'Yes.'

'*Oxford Mail?*'

'*Oxford Times.*'

The living-room door opened, and there entered a darkly elegant woman, incongruously wearing a pair of sunglasses, and dressed in a black trouser-suit – 'Legs right up to the armpits', as Lewis was later to report.

Mrs Angela Storrs briefly introduced herself, and picked up the empty cups.

'Another coffee, Sergeant?'

Her voice was Home Counties, rather deep, rather pleasing.

'No thanks. That was lovely.'

Her eyes smiled behind the sunglasses – or Lewis thought they smiled. And as she closed the living-room door softly behind her, he wondered where she'd been throughout the interview. Outside the door, perhaps, listening? Had she heard what her husband had said? Or had she known it all along?

Then the door quietly opened again.

'You won't forget you're out this evening, darling? You haven't *all* that much time, you know.'

Lewis accepted the cue and hurried on his questioning apace:

'Do you mind telling me exactly what you were doing between seven a.m. and eight a.m. last Monday, sir?'

'Last Monday morning? Ah!' Lewis sensed that Julian Storrs had suddenly relaxed – as if the tricky part of the examination was now over – as if he could safely resume his wonted donnish idiom.

'How I wish every question my students asked were susceptible to such an unequivocal answer! You see, I was in bed with my wife and we were having sex together. And why do I recall this so readily, Sergeant? Because such an occurrence has not been quite so common these past few years; nor, if I'm honest with you, quite so enjoyable as once it was.'

'Between, er, between seven and eight?' Lewis's voice was hesitant.

'Sounds a long time, you mean? Huh! You're right. More like twenty past to twenty-five past seven. What I do remember is Angela – Mrs Storrs – wanting the news on at half past. She's a great *Today* fan, and she likes to know what's going on. We just caught the tail-end of the sports news – then the main headlines on the half-hour.'

'Oh!'

'Do you believe me?'

'Would Mrs Storrs remember . . . as clearly as you, sir?'

Storrs gave a slightly bitter-sounding laugh. 'Why don't you ask her? Shall I tell her to come through? I'll leave you alone.'

'Yes, I think that would be helpful.'

Storrs got to his feet and walked towards the door.

'Just one more question, sir.' Lewis too rose to his feet. 'Don't you think you were awfully naïve to send off that money? I think anyone could have told you you weren't going to get anything back – except another blackmail note.'

Storrs walked back into the room.

'Are you a married man, Sergeant?'

'Yes.'

'How would you explain – well, say a photograph like the one you showed me?'

Lewis took out the passport photo again.

'Not too difficult, surely? You're a well-known man, sir – quite a distinguished-looking man, perhaps? So let's just say one of your admiring undergraduettes sees you at a railway station and says she'd like to have a picture taken with you. You know, one of those "Four colour photos in approximately four minutes" places. Then she could carry the pair of you around with her, like some girls carry pictures of pop stars around.'

Storrs nodded. 'Clever idea! I wish *I'd* thought of it. Er . . . can I ask *you* a question?'

'Yes?'

'Why are you still only a sergeant?'

Lewis made no comment on the matter, but asked a final question:

'You're standing for the Mastership at Lonsdale, I understand, sir?'

'Ye-es. So you can see, can't you, why all this business, you know . . . ?'

'Of course.'

Storrs' face now suddenly cleared.

'There are just the two of us: Dr Cornford – Denis Cornford – and myself. And may the better man win!'

He said it lightly, as if the pair of them were destined to cross swords in a mighty game of Scrabble – and called through to Angela, his wife.

Chapter Thirty-Five

Keep your eyes wide open before marriage,
half shut afterwards

(Benjamin Franklin,
Poor Richard's Almanack)

In Oxford that same early evening the clouds were inkily black, the forecast set for heavy rain, with most of those walking along Broad Street or around Radcliffe Square wearing raincoats and carrying umbrellas. The majority of these people were students making their way to College Halls for their evening meals, much as their predecessors had done in earlier times, passing through the same streets, past the same familiar buildings and later returning to the same sort of accommodation, and in most cases doing some work for the morrow, when they would be listening to the same sort of lectures. Unless, perhaps, they were students of Physics or some similar discipline where breakthroughs ('Breaksthrough, if we are to be accurate, dear boy') were as regular as inaccuracies in the daily weather forecasts.

But that evening the forecast was surprisingly accurate; and at 6.45 p.m. the rains came.

Denis Cornford looked out through the window on to Holywell Street where the rain bounced off the surface of the road like arrowheads. St Peter's (Dinner, 7.00 for 7.30 p.m.) was only ten minutes' walk away but he was going to get soaked in such a downpour.

'What do you think, darling?'

'Give it five minutes. If it keeps on like this, I should get a cab. You've got plenty of time.'

'What'll you be doing?' he asked.

'Well, I don't think I'll be venturing out too far, do you?' She said it in a gentle way, and there seemed no sarcasm in her voice. She came up behind him and placed her hands on his shoulders as he stood indecisively staring out through the sheeted panes.

'Denis?'

'Mm?'

'Do you really want to be Master all *that* much?'

He turned towards her and looked directly into her dazzlingly attractive dark eyes, with that small circular white light in the centre of their irises – eyes which had always held men, and tempted them, and occasioned innumerable capitulations.

'Yes, Shelly. Yes, I do! Not quite so badly as Julian, perhaps. But badly enough.'

'What would you give – to be Master?'

'Most things, I suppose.'

'Give up your work?'

'A good deal of that would go anyway. It would be different work, that's all.'

'Would you give *me* up?'

He took her in his arms. 'Of course, I would!'

'You don't really mean—?'

He kissed her mouth with a strangely passionate tenderness.

A few minutes later they stood arm-in-arm at the window looking out at the ceaselessly teeming rain.

'I'll ring for a cab,' said Shelly Cornford.

On Mondays the dons' attendance at Lonsdale Dinner was usually fairly small, but Roy Porter would be there, Angela Storrs knew that: Roy Porter was almost always there. She rang him in his rooms at 6.55 p.m.

'Roy?'

'Angela! Good to hear your beautiful voice.'

'Flattery will get you exactly halfway between nowhere and everywhere.'

'I'll settle for that.'

'You're dining tonight?'

'Yep.'

'Would you like to come along afterwards and cheer up a lonely old lady.'

'Julian away?'

'Some Brains Trust at Reading University.'

'Shall I bring a bottle?'

'Plenty of bottles here.'

'Marvellous.'

'Nine-ish?'

'About then. Er . . . Angela? Is it something you want to talk about or is it just . . . ?'

'Why not both?'

'You want to know how things seem to be going with the election?'

'I'm making no secret of that.'

'You do realize I don't know anything definite at all?'

'I don't expect you to. But I'd like to talk. You can understand how I feel, can't you?'

'Of course.'

'And I've been speaking to Julian. There *are* one or two little preferments perhaps in the offing, if he's elected.'

'Really?'

'But like you, Roy, I don't know anything definite.'

'I understand. But it'll be good to be together again.'

'Oh, yes. Have a drink or two together.'

'Or three?'

'Or four?' suggested Angela Storrs, her voice growing huskier still.

The phone rang at 7.05 p.m.

'Shelly?'

'Yes.'

'You're on your own?'

'You know I am.'

'Denis gone?'

'Left fifteen minutes ago.'

'One or two things to tell you, if we could meet?'

'What sort of things?'

'Nothing definite. But there's talk about a potential benefaction from the States, and one of the trustees met

Denis – met *you*, I gather, too – and, well, I can tell you all about it when we meet.'

'*All* about it?'

'It's a biggish thing, and I think we may be slightly more likely to pull it off, perhaps, if Denis . . .'

'And you'll be doing your best?'

'I can't promise anything.'

'I know that.'

'So?'

'So?'

'So you're free and I'm free.'

'On a night like this? Far too dangerous. Me coming to the Master's Lodge? No chance.'

'I agree. But, you see, one of my old colleagues is off to Greece – he's left me his key – just up the Banbury Road – lovely comfy double-bed – crisp clean sheets – central heating – *en suite* facilities – mini bar. Tariff? No pounds, no shillings, no pence.'

'You remember pre-decimalization?'

'I'm not *too* old, though, am I? And I'd just love to be with you now, at this minute. More than anything in the world.'

'You ought to find a new variation on the theme, you know! It's getting a bit of a cliché.'

'Cleesháy', she'd said; but however she'd pronounced it, the barb had found its mark; and Sir Clixby's voice was softer, more serious as he answered her.

'I need you, Shelly. Please come out with me. I'll get a taxi round to you in ten minutes' time, if that's all right?'

There was silence on the other end of the line.

'Shelly?'

'Yes?'

'Will that be all right?'

'No,' she replied quietly. 'No it won't. I'm sorry.'

The line was dead.

Just before nine o'clock, Cornford rang home from St Peter's:

'Shelly? Denis. Look, darling, I've just noticed in my diary . . . You've not had a call tonight, have you?'

Shelly's heart registered a sudden, sharp stab of panic.

'No, why?'

'It's just that the New York publishers said they might be ringing. So, if they do, please make a note of the number and tell 'em I'll ring them back. All right?'

'Fine. Yes.'

'You having a nice evening?'

'Mm. It's lovely to sit and watch TV for a change. No engagements. No problems.'

'See you soon.'

'I hope so.'

Shelly put down the phone slowly. 'I've just noticed in my diary', he'd said. But he hadn't, she knew that. She'd looked in his diary earlier that day, to make sure of the time of the St Peter's do. That had been the only entry on the page for 26.2.96.

Or, as she would always think of it, 2/26/96.

Just before ten o'clock, Julian Storrs rang his wife from Reading; rang three times.

The number was engaged.

He rang five minutes later.

The number was still engaged.

He rang again, after a further five minutes.

She answered.

'Angie? I've been trying to get you these last twenty minutes.'

'I've only been talking to Mum, for Christ's sake!'

'It's just that I shan't be home till after midnight, that's all. So I'll get a taxi. Don't worry about meeting me.'

'OK.'

After she had hung up, Angela Storrs took a Thames Trains timetable from her handbag and saw that Julian could easily be catching an earlier train: the 22.40 from Reading, arriving Oxford 23.20. Not that it mattered. Perhaps he was having a few drinks with his hosts? Or perhaps – the chilling thought struck her – he was checking up on her?

Hurriedly she rang her mother in South Kensington. And kept on kept on kept on talking. The call would be duly registered on the itemized BT lists and suddenly she felt considerably easier in her mind.

Morse had caught the 23.48 from Paddington that night, and at 01.00 sat unhearing as the Senior Conductor made his lugubrious pronouncement: 'Oxford, Oxford. This train has now terminated. Please be sure to take all your personal possessions with you. Thank you.'

From a deeply delicious cataleptic state, Morse was

finally prodded into consciousness by no less a personage than the Senior Conductor himself.

'All right, sir?'

'Thank you, yes.'

But in truth things were not all right, since Morse had been deeply disappointed by his evening's sojourn in London. And as he walked down the station steps to the taxi-rank, he reminded himself of what he'd always known – that life was full of disappointments: of which the most immediate was that not a single taxi was in sight.

CHAPTER THIRTY-SIX

Tuesday, 27 February

Initium est dimidium facti
(Once you've started, you're halfway there)
(Latin proverb)

AN UNSHAVEN MORSE was still dressed in his mauve and Cambridge blue pyjamas when Lewis arrived at 10 o'clock the following morning. Over the phone half an hour earlier he had learned that Morse was feeling 'rough as a bear's arse' – whatever that was supposed to mean.

For some time the two detectives exchanged information about their previous day's activities; and fairly soon the obvious truth could be simply stated: Owens was a blackmailer. Specifically, as far as investigations had thus far progressed, with the Storrs' household being the principal victims: he, for his current infidelity; she, for her past as a shop-soiled Soho tart. One thing seemed certain: that *any* disclosure was likely to be damaging, probably fatally damaging, to Julian Storrs' chances of election to the Mastership of Lonsdale.

Morse considered for a while.

'It still gives us a wonderful motive for one of them

murdering Owens – not much of a one for murdering Rachel.'

'Unless Mrs Storrs was just plain jealous, sir?'

'Doubt it.'

'Or perhaps Rachel got to know something, and was doing a bit of blackmailing herself? She needed the money all right.'

'Yes.' Morse stroked his bristly jaw and sighed wearily. 'There's such a lot we've still got to check on, isn't there? Perhaps you ought to get round to Rachel's bank manager this morning.'

'Not this morning, sir – or this afternoon. I'm seeing his lordship, Sir Clixby Bream, at a quarter to twelve; then I'm going to find out who's got access to the photocopier and whatever at the Harvey Clinic.'

'Waste o' time,' mumbled Morse.

'I dunno, sir. I've got a feeling it may all tie in together somehow.'

'What with?'

'I'll know more after I've been to Lonsdale. You see, I've already learned one or two things about the situation there. The present Master's going to retire soon, as you know, and the new man's going to be taking up the reins at the start of the summer term – '

'*Trinity* term.'

' – and they've narrowed it down to two candidates: Julian Storrs and a fellow called Cornford, Denis Cornford – he's a Lonsdale man himself, too. And they say the odds are fairly even.'

'Who's this "they" you keep talking about?'

'One of the porters there. We used to play cricket together.'

'Ridiculous game!'

'What's *your* programme today, sir?'

But Morse appeared not to hear his sergeant's question.

'Cup o' tea, Lewis?'

'Wouldn't say no.'

Morse returned a couple of minutes later, with a cup of tea for Lewis and a pint glass of iced water for himself. He sat down and looked at his wristwatch: twenty-five past ten.

'What's your programme today?' repeated Lewis.

'I've got a meeting at eleven-thirty this morning. Nothing else much. Perhaps I'll do a bit of thinking – it's high time I caught up with you.'

As Lewis drank his tea, talking of this and that, he was aware that Morse seemed distanced – seemed almost in a world of his own. Was he listening at all?

'Am I boring you, sir?'

'What? No, no! Keep talking! That's always the secret, you know, if you want to start anything – start *thinking*, say. All you've got to do is listen to somebody talking a load of nonsense, and somehow, suddenly, something emerges.'

'I wasn't talking nonsense, sir. And if I was, *you* wouldn't have known. You weren't listening.'

Nor did it appear that Morse was listening even now – as he continued: 'I wonder what time the postman comes to Polstead Road. Storrs usually caught the ten-fifteen train from Oxford, you say ... So he'd leave the house about a quarter to ten – bit earlier, perhaps? He's got to get to the station, park his car, buy a ticket – buy *two* tickets ... So if the postman called about then ... perhaps Storrs met him as he left the house and took his letters with him, and read them as he waited for Rachel, then stuffed 'em in his jacket-pocket.'

'So?'

'So if ... What do most couples do after they've had sex together?'

'Depends, I suppose.' Lewis looked uneasily at his superior. 'Go to sleep?'

Morse smiled waywardly. 'It's as tiring as that, is it?'

'Well, if they did it more than once.'

'Then she – *she*, Lewis – stays awake and goes quietly through his pockets and finds the blackmail letter. By the way, did you ask him *when* he received it?'

'No, sir.'

'Well, find out! She sees the letter and she knows she can blackmail *him*. Not about the affair they're having, perhaps – they're both in that together – but about something else she discovered from the letter ... You know, I suspect that our Ms James was getting a bit of a handful for our Mr Storrs. What do *you* think?' (But Lewis was given no time at all to think.) 'What were the last couple of dates they went to London together?'

'That's something else I shall have to check, sir.'

'Well, check it! You see, we've been coming round to the idea that somebody was trying to murder Owens, haven't we? And murdered Rachel by mistake. But perhaps we're wrong, Lewis. Perhaps we're wrong.'

Morse looked flushed and excited as he drained his iced water and got to his feet.

'I'd better have a quick shave.'

'What else have you got on your programme—?'

'As I say, you see what happens when you start talking nonsense! You're indispensable, old friend. Absolutely *indispensable*!'

Lewis, who had begun to feel considerable irritation at Morse's earlier brusque demands, was now completely mollified.

'I'll be off then, sir.'

'No you won't! I shan't be more than a few minutes. You can run me down to Summertown.'

(*Almost* completely mollified.)

'You still haven't told me what—' began Lewis as he waited at the traffic-lights by South Parade.

But a clean-shaven Morse had suddenly stiffened in his safety-belt besidc him.

'What did you say the name of that other fellow was, Lewis? The chap who's standing against Storrs?'

'Cornford, Denis Cornford. Married to an American girl.'

'"DC", Lewis! Do you remember in the manila file? Those four sets of initials?'

Lewis nodded, for in his mind's eye he could see that piece of paper as clearly as Morse:

AM✓ DC✓ JS✓ CB

'There they are,' continued Morse, 'side-by-side in the middle – Denis Cornford and Julian Storrs, flanked on either side by Angela Martin – I've little doubt! – and – might it be? – Sir Clixby Bream.'

'So you think Owens might have got something on all—?'

'Slow down!' interrupted Morse. 'Just round the corner here.'

Lewis turned left at the traffic-lights into Marston Ferry Road and stopped immediately outside the Summertown Health Centre.

'Wish me well,' said Morse as he alighted.

PART THREE

Chapter Thirty-Seven

Tuesday, 27 February

> The land of Idd was a happy one. Well, almost. There was one teeny problem. The King had sleepless nights about it and the villagers were very scared. The problem was a dragon called Diabetes. He lived in a cave on top of a hill. Every day he would roar loudly. He never came down the hill but everyone was still very scared just in case he did
>
> (Victoria Lee, *The Dragon of Idd*)

FROM THE WAITING-ROOM on the first floor, Morse heard his name called.

'How can I help?' asked Dr Paul Roblin, a man Morse had sought so earnestly to avoid over the years, unless things were bordering on the desperate.

As they were now.

'I think I've got diabetes.'

'Why do you think that?'

'I've got a book. It mentions some of the symptoms.'

'Which are?'

'Loss of weight, tiredness, a longing for drink.'

'You've had the last one quite a while though, haven't you?'

Morse nodded wearily. 'I've lost weight; I could sleep all the time; and I drink a gallon of tap-water a day.'

'As *well* as the beer?'

Morse was silent, as Roblin jabbed a lancet into the little finger of his left hand, squeezed the skin until a domed globule appeared, then smeared the blood on to a test-strip. After thirty seconds, he looked down at the reading. And for a while sat motionless, saying nothing. 'How did you get here, Mr Morse?'

'Car.'

'Is your car here?'

'No, I had a lift. Why?'

'Well, I'm afraid I couldn't let you drive a car now.'

'Why's that?'

'It's serious. Your blood sugar level's completely off the end of the chart. We shall have to get you to the Radcliffe Infirmary as soon as we can.'

'What are you telling me?'

'You should have seen me way before this. Your pancreas has packed in completely. You'll probably be on three or four injections of insulin a day for the rest of your life. You may well have done God-knows-what damage to your eyes and your kidneys – we shall have to find out. The important thing is to get you in hospital immediately.'

He reached for the phone.

'I only live just up the road,' protested Morse.

Roblin put his hand over the mouthpiece. 'They'll have a spare pair of pyjamas and a toothbrush. Don't worry!'

'You don't realize—' began Morse.

'Hello? Hello! Can you get an ambulance here – Summertown Health Centre – straightaway, please ... The Radcliffe Infirmary ... Thank you.'

'You don't realize I'm in the middle of a murder enquiry.'

But Roblin had dialled a second number, and was already speaking to someone else.

'David? Ah, glad you're there! Have you got a bed available? ... Bit of an emergency, yes ... He'll need an insulin-drip, I should think. But you'll know ... Yes ... Er, Mr Morse – initial "E". He's a chief inspector in the Thames Valley CID.'

Half an hour later – weight (almost thirteen stone), blood pressure (alarmingly high), blood sugar level (still off the scale), details of maternal and paternal grandparents' deaths (ill-remembered), all of these duly recorded – Morse found himself lying supine, in a pair of red-striped pyjamas, in the Geoffrey Harris Ward in the Radcliffe Infirmary, just north of St Giles', at the bottom of the Woodstock Road. A tube from the insulin-drip suspended at the side of his bed was attached to his right arm by a Sellotaped needle stuck into him just above the inner wrist, allowing little, if any, lateral movement without the sharpest reminder of physical agony.

It was this tube that Morse was glumly considering when the Senior Consultant from the Diabetes Centre came round: Dr David Matthews, a tall, slim, Mephistophelian figure, with darkly ascetic, angular features.

'As I've told you all, I'm in the middle of a murder enquiry,' reiterated Morse, as Matthews sat on the side of the bed.

'And can I tell *you* something? You're going to forget all about that, unless you want to kill yourself. With a little bit of luck you may be all right, do you understand? So far you don't seem to have done yourself all that much harm. Enough, though! But you're going to have to forget everything about work – *everything* – if you're going to come through this business without too much damage. You do know what I mean, don't you?'

Morse didn't. But he nodded helplessly.

'Only here four or five days, if you do as we tell you.'

'But, as I say—'

'No "buts", I'm afraid. Then you might be home Saturday or Sunday.'

'But there's so much to do!' remonstrated Morse almost desperately.

'Weren't those the words of Cecil Rhodes?'

'Yes, I think they were.'

'The last words, if I recall aright.'

Morse was silent.

And the Senior Consultant continued: 'Look, there are three basic causes of diabetes – well, that's an oversimplification. But you're not a medical man.'

'Thank you,' said Morse.

'Hereditary factors, stress, excessive booze. You'd score five . . . six out of ten on the first. Your father had diabetes, I see.'

'Latish in life.'

'Well, you're not exactly a youngster yourself.'

'Perhaps not.'

'Stress? You're not too much of a worryguts?'

'Well, I worry about the future of the human race – does that count?'

'What about booze? You seem to drink quite a bit, I see?'

So Morse told him the truth; or, to be more accurate, told him between one-half and one-third of the truth.

Matthews got to his feet, peered at the insulin-drip, and marginally readjusted some control thereon.

'Six out of ten on the second; ten out of ten on the third, I'm afraid. And by the way, I'm not allowing you any visitors. None at all – not even close relatives. Just me and the nurses here.'

'I haven't got any close relatives,' said Morse.

Matthews now stood at the foot of his bed. 'You've already had *somebody* wanting to see you, though. Fellow called Lewis.'

After Matthews had gone, Morse lay back and thought of his colleague. And for several minutes he felt very low, unmanned as he was with a strangely poignant gratitude.

CHAPTER THIRTY-EIGHT

Thursday, 29 February

> The relations between us were peculiar. He was a man of habits, narrow and concentrated habits, and I had become one of them. But apart from this I had uses. I was a whetstone for his mind, I stimulated him. He liked to think aloud in my presence
>
> (Conan Doyle, *The Adventures of the Creeping Man*)

'AND 'OW IS 'E TODAY, then?' asked Mrs Lewis when her husband finally returned home on Thursday evening, and when soon the fat was set a-sizzling in the chip-pan, with the two eggs standing ready to be broken in the frying pan.

'On the mend.'

'They always say that.'

'No. He's genuinely on the mend.'

'Why can't 'e 'ave visitors then? Not contagious, is it, this diabetes?'

Lewis smiled at her. Brought up as she had been in the Rhondda Valley, the gentle Welsh lilt in her voice was an abiding delight with him – though not, to be quite truthful, with everyone.

'He'll probably be out this weekend.'

'And back to work?'

Lewis put his hands on his wife's shoulders as she stood watching the pale chips gradually turning brown.

'This weekend, I should think.'

'You've always enjoyed working with 'im, 'aven't you?'

'Well . . .'

'I've often wondered why. It's not as if 'e's ever treated you all that well, is it?'

'I'm the only one he's ever treated well,' said Lewis quietly.

She turned towards him, laterally shaking the chips with a practised right hand.

'And 'ow are *you* today, then? The case going OK?'

Lewis sat down at the red Formica-topped kitchen table and surveyed the old familiar scene: lacy white doily, knife and fork, bottle of tomato ketchup, bread and butter on one side, and a glass of milk on the other. He should have felt contented; and as he looked back over another long day, perhaps he did.

Temporarily, Chief Superintendent David Blair from the Oxford City Force had been given overall responsibility for the Rachel James murder enquiry, and he had spent an hour at Kidlington Police HQ earlier that afternoon, where Lewis had brought him up to date with the latest developments.

Not that they had amounted to much . . .

*

The reports from DCs Learoyd and Elton were not destined significantly to further the course of the investigation. Lord Hardiman, aged eighty-seven, a sad victim of Alzheimer's disease, and now confined to his baronial hall in Bedfordshire, was unlikely, it seemed, to squander any more of his considerable substance in riotous living along the Reeperbahn. Whilst the child-fondler, recognized immediately by his erstwhile neighbours, was likewise unlikely to disturb the peace for the immediate future, confined as he was at Her Majesty's Pleasure in Reading for the illegal publication and propagation of material deemed likely to deprave and corrupt.

More interestingly, Lewis had been able to report on his own enquiries, particularly on his second interview with Julian Storrs, who had been more willing now to divulge details of dates, times, and hotels for his last three visits to Paddington with Rachel James.

And after that, to report on his interview with Sir Clixby Bream, who had informed Lewis of the imminent election of a new Master, and who had given him a copy of the College Statutes (fortunately, rendered *Anglice*) with their emphasis upon the need for any candidate for the Mastership to be in good physical health (*in corpore sano*).

'Nobody can guarantee good health,' Blair had observed.

'No, but sometimes you can almost guarantee *bad* health, perhaps, sir?'

'We're still no nearer to finding how Owens got a copy of that letter?'

'No. I went round to the Harvey Clinic again yesterday. No luck, though. The doc who wrote the letter got himself killed, as you know, and all his records have been distributed around . . . reallocated, sort of thing.'

'They're all in a mess, you mean?'

Lewis nodded. 'Somehow Owens got to know that he hadn't got much time left, didn't he? So he's got three things on him: he knows a good deal about Angela Storrs' past; he knows he was having an affair with Rachel James; and he knows he's pretty certainly hiding his medical reports from his colleagues in College – from everybody, perhaps.'

Quite certainly Morse would have complained about the confusing profusion of third-person pronouns in the previous sentence. But Blair seemed to follow the account with no difficulty.

'From his wife, too?' he asked.

'I wouldn't be surprised.'

'You know, Morse once told me that any quack who tells you when you're going to die is a bloody fool.'

Lewis grinned. 'He's told me the same thing about a dozen times.'

'He's getting better, you say?'

'Out by the weekend, they think.'

'You hope so, don't you?'

Lewis nodded, and Blair continued quietly:

'You're peculiar companions, you know, you and Morse. Don't you think? He can be an ungrateful, ungracious sod at times.'

'Almost always, sir,' admitted Lewis, smiling to himself as if recalling mildly happy memories.

'He'll have to take things more easily now.'

'Would you care to tell him that?'

'No.'

'Just one thing more, sir – about Owens. I really think we ought to consider the possibility that he's in a bit of danger. There must be quite a few people who'd gladly see him join Rachel in the mortuary.'

'What do you suggest, Sergeant?'

'That's the trouble, isn't it? We can't just give him a bodyguard.'

'There's only one way of keeping an eye on him all the time.'

'Bring him in, you mean, sir? But we can't do that – not yet.'

'No. No good bringing him in and then having to let him go. We shall need something to charge him with. I don't suppose ...' Blair hesitated. 'I don't suppose there's any chance that *he* murdered Rachel James?'

'I don't think so, myself, no.'

'What's Morse think?'

'He *did* think so for a start, but ... Which reminds me, sir. I'd better make another trip to the newspaper offices tomorrow.'

'Don't go and do everything yourself, Sergeant.'

'Will you promise to tell the Chief Inspector that?'

'No,' replied Blair as he prepared to leave; but hesitantly so, since he was feeling rather worried himself now about what Lewis had said.

'What did Morse think about the possibility of Owens getting himself murdered?'

'Said he could look after himself; said he was a streetwise kid from the start; said he was a survivor.'

'Let's hope he's right.'

'Sometimes he is, sir,' said Lewis.

Chapter Thirty-Nine

> We forget ourselves and our destinies in health; and the chief use of temporary sickness is to remind us of these concerns
>
> (Ralph Waldo Emerson, *Journals*)

SISTER JANET MCQUEEN – an amply bosomed woman now in her early forties, single and darkly attractive to the vast majority of men – had been considerably concerned about her new patient: one E. Morse. Patently, in spite of his superficial patter, the man knew nothing whatsoever of medicine, and appeared unaware, and strangely unconcerned, about his physical well-being; ill-being, rather.

On several occasions during the following days she'd spent some time with him, apologizing for the two-hourly check on his blood sugar levels (even during the night); explaining the vital rôle of the pancreas in the metabolic processes; acquainting him with the range, colour, purpose, and possible efficacy, of the medication and equipment now prescribed – single-use insulin syringes, Human Ultratard, Human Actrapid, Unilet Lancets,

Exactech Reagent Strips, Enalapril Tablets, Frusemide Tablets, Nifedipine Capsules . . .

He'd seemed to understand most of it, she thought. And from their first meeting she'd realized that the prematurely white-haired man was most unusual.

'Glad about the pills,' he'd said.

'You are?'

'Different colours, aren't they? White, pink, brown-and-orange. Good, that is. Gives a man a bit of psychological confidence. In the past, I've always thought that confidence was a bit overrated. Not so sure now, though, Sister.'

She made no answer. But his words were to remain in her mind; and she knew that she would look forward to talking with this man again.

By Tuesday evening, Morse's blood sugar level had fallen dramatically. And at coffee-time on Wednesday morning, Sister McQueen came to his bedside, the fingers of her right hand almost automatically feeling his pulse as she flicked the watch from the starched white lapel of her uniform.

'Shall I survive till the weekend?'

'You hardly deserve to.'

'I'm OK now, you mean?'

She snorted in derision; but winsomely so.

'You know why we didn't want you to have any visitors?'

'You wanted me all to yourself?' suggested Morse.

She shook her head slowly, her sensitive, slim lips widening into a saddened smile.

'No. Dr Matthews thought you were probably far too

worried about life – about your work – about other things, perhaps. And he didn't want to take any chances. Visitors are always a bit of a stress.'

'He needn't have worried too much about that.'

'But you're wrong, aren't you?' She got to her feet. 'You've had four people on the phone every day, regular callers – regular as well-adjusted bowels.'

Morse looked up at her.

'Four?'

'Somebody called Lewis – somebody called Strange – somebody called Blair. All from the police, I think.'

'*Four*, you said?'

'Ah yes. Sorry. And somebody called Jane. She works for you, she said. Sounds awfully sweet.'

As he lay back after Sister had gone, and switched on the headphones to Classic FM, Morse was again aware of how low he had sunk, since almost everything – a kindly look, a kindly word, a kindly thought, even the *thought* of a kindly thought – seemed to push him ever nearer to the rim of tears. Forget it, Morse! Forget yourself and forget your health! For a while anyway. He picked up *The ABC Murders* which he'd found in the meagre ward-library. He'd always enjoyed Agatha Christie: a big fat puzzle ready for the reader from page one. Perhaps it might help a little with the big fat puzzle waiting for him in the world outside the Radcliffe Infirmary . . .

ABC.

Alexander Bonaparte Cust.

Adèle Beatrice Cecil.

Ann Berkeley Cox . . .

Within five minutes Morse was asleep.

On Thursday afternoon, a slim, rather prissy young dietitian came to sit beside Morse's bed and to talk quickly, rationally, and at inordinate length, about such things as calories and carrots and carbohydrates.

'And if you ever feel like a pint of beer once a week, well, you just go ahead and have one! It shouldn't do you much harm.'

Morse's spirit groaned within him.

The Senior Consultant himself came round again the following morning. The insulin-drip had long gone; blood-readings were gradually reverting to a manageable level; blood pressure was markedly down.

'You've been very lucky,' said Matthews.

'I don't deserve it,' admitted Morse.

'No. You don't.'

'When are you going to let me go?'

'Home? Tomorrow, perhaps. Work? Up to you. I'd take a fortnight off myself – but then I've got far more sense than you have.'

Well before lunchtime on Saturday, already dressed and now instructed to await an ambulance, Morse was seated in the entrance corridor of the Geoffrey Harris Ward when Sister McQueen came to sit beside him.

'I'm almost sorry to be going,' said Morse.

'You'll miss us?'

'I'll miss *you*.'

'Really?'

'Could I ring you – here?' asked Morse diffidently.

'In those immortal words: "Don't ring us – we'll ring you."'

'You mean you *will* ring me?'

She shook her head. 'Perhaps not. And it doesn't matter, does it? What matters is that you look after yourself. You're a nice man – a very nice man! – and I'm so glad we met.'

'If I did come to see you, would you look after me?'

'Bed and Breakfast, you mean?' She smiled. 'You'd always be welcome in the McQueen Arms.'

She stood up as an ambulance-man came through the flappy doors.

'Mr Morse?' he asked.

'I'd love to be in the McQueen arms,' Morse managed to say, very quietly.

As he was driven past the Neptune fountain in the forecourt of the Radcliffe Infirmary, he wondered if Sister had appreciated that shift in key, from the upper-case Arms to the lower-case arms.

He hoped she had.

Chapter Forty

Sunday, 3 March

Important if true
(Inscription A.W. Kinglake wished
to see on all churches)

Forgive us for loving familiar hymns and religious feelings more than Thee, O Lord
(From the United Presbyterian Church Litany)

'But I'd better not call before the *Archers*' omnibus?' Lewis had suggested the previous evening.

'Don't worry about that. I've kept up with events in Ambridge all week. And I don't want to hear 'em again. I just wonder when these scriptwriters will understand that beautiful babies are about as boring as happy marriages.'

'About ten then, sir?'

Morse, smartly dressed in clean white shirt and semi-well-pressed grey flannels, was listening to the last few minutes of the *Morning Service* on Radio 4 when Lewis was quickly admitted – and cautioned.

'Sh! My favourite hymn.'

In the silence that followed, the two men sat listening with Morse's bleating, uncertain baritone occasionally accompanying the singing.

'Didn't know you were still interested in that sort of thing,' volunteered Lewis after it had finished.

'I still love the old hymns – the more sentimental the better, for my taste. Wonderful words, didn't you think?' And softly, but with deep intensity, he recited a few lines he'd just sung:

'I trace the rainbow through the rain
And feel the promise is not vain
That Morn shall tearless be.'

But Lewis, who had noted the moisture in Morse's eyes, and who had sensed that the promise of the last line might soon be broken, immediately injected a more joyful note into the conversation.

'It's really good to have you back, sir.'

Apparently unaware that any reciprocal words of gratitude were called for, Morse asked about the case; and learned that the police were perhaps 'treading water' for the time being, and that Chief Superintendent Blair was nominally i/c pro tem.

'David Blair. Best copper in the county' (Lewis was about to nod a partial agreement) 'apart from me, of course.'

And suddenly Lewis felt very happy that he was back in harness with this arrogant, ungracious, vulnerable, lovable man with whom he had worked so closely for so many years; a man who looked somewhat slimmer, somewhat paler than when he had last seen him, but who sounded not a whit less brusque as he now asked whether Lewis had checked up on the time when Storrs had left home for his last visit with Rachel to Paddington, and the time when the postman had delivered the mail in Polstead Road that same morning.

And Lewis had.

9.45–9.50 a.m.

9.10–9.20 a.m.

Respectively.

'From which, Lewis, we may draw *what* conclusions?'

'Precious few, as far as I can see.'

'Absolutely! What other new facts have you got for me?'

So Lewis told him.

It was ten minutes short of noon when Morse dropped the mini-bombshell.

'The Cherwell, do you think, Lewis? The landlord there always keeps a decent pint.'

'But beer's full of sugar, isn't it? You can't—'

'Lewis! This diabetes business is all about *balance*, that's all. I've got to take all this insulin because I can't produce any insulin *myself* – to counteract any sugar intake. But if I didn't have any sugar intake to counteract, I'd be in one helluva mess. I'd become *hypoglycaemic*, and you know what that means.'

Not having the least idea, Lewis remained silent as Morse took out a black pen-like object from his pocket, screwed off one end, removed a white plastic cap from the needle there, twisted a calibrator at the other end, unbuttoned his shirt, and plunged the needle deep into his midriff.

Lewis winced involuntarily.

But Morse, looking up like some young child expecting praise after taking a very nasty-tasting medicine, seemed wholly pleased with himself.

'See? That'll take care of things. No problem.'

With great care, Lewis walked back from the bar with a pint of Bass and a glass of orange juice.

'I've been waiting a long time for this,' enthused Morse, burying his nose into the froth, taking a gloriously gratifying draught of real ale, and showing, as he relaxed back, a circle of blood on his white shirt just above the waist.

After a period of silence, during which Morse several times raised his glass against the window to admire the colour of the beer, Lewis asked the key question.

'What have they said about you starting work again?'

'What do you say about us seeing Storrs and Owens this afternoon?'

'You'll have a job with Storrs, sir. Him and his missus are in Bath for the weekend.'

'What about Owens?'

'Dunno. Perhaps he's away, too – on another of his personnel courses.'

'One easy way of finding out, Lewis. There's a telephone just outside the Gents.'

'Look, sir! For heaven's sake! You've been in hospital a week—'

'Five days, to be accurate, and only for observation. They'd never have let me out unless—'

But he got no further.

The double-doors of the Cherwell had burst open and there, framed in the doorway, jowls a-quiver, stood Chief Superintendent Strange – looking around, spying Morse, walking across, and sitting down.

'Like a beer, sir?' asked Lewis.

'Large single-malt Scotch – no ice, no water.'

'And it's the same again for me,' prompted Morse, pushing over his empty glass.

'I might have known it,' began Strange, after regaining his breath. 'Straight out of hospital and straight into the nearest boozer.'

'It's *not* the nearest.'

'Don't remind me! Dixon's already carted me round to the Friar Bacon – the King's Arms – the Dew Drop – and now here. And it's about time somebody reminded you that you're in the Force to reduce the crime-level, not the bloody beer-level.'

'We were talking about the case when you came in, sir.'

'*What* case?' snapped Strange.

'The murder case – Rachel James.'

'Ah yes! I remember the case well; I remember the address, too: Number 17 Bloxham Drive, wasn't it? Well, you'd better get off your arse, matey' (at a single swallow, he drained the Scotch which Lewis had just placed in front of him) 'because if you *are* back at work, you can just forget that beer and get over smartish to Bloxham Drive again. Number 15, this time. Another murder. Chap called Owens – Geoffrey Owens. I think you've heard of him?'

PART FOUR

Chapter Forty-One

For now we see through a glass darkly; but then face to face
(*I Corinthians*, ch. 13, v. 12)

Déjà vu.

The street, the police cars, the crowd of curious onlookers, the SOCOs – repetition almost everywhere, as if nothing was found only once in the world. Just that single significant shift: the shift from one terraced house to another immediately adjacent.

Morse himself had said virtually nothing since Strange had brought the news of Owens' murder; and said nothing now as he sat in the kitchen of Number 15, Bloxham Drive, elbows resting on the table there, head resting on his hands. For the moment his job was to bide his time, he knew that, during the interregnum between the activities of other professionals and his own assumption of authority: a necessary yet ever frustrating interlude, like that when an in-flight air-stewardess rehearses the safety drill before take-off.

By all rights he should have felt weary and defeated; but this was not the case. Physically, he felt considerably fitter than he had the week before; and mentally, he felt eager for that metaphorical take-off to begin. Some people took little or no mental exercise except that of jumping to conclusions; while Morse was a man who took excessive mental exercise and who *still* jumped to dubious conclusions, as indeed he was to do now. But as some of his close colleagues knew – and most especially as Sergeant Lewis knew – it was at times like this, with preconceptions proved false and hypotheses undone, that Morse's brain was wont to function with astonishing speed, if questionable lucidity.

As it did now.

Lewis walked through just before 2 p.m.

'Anything I can do for the minute, sir?'

'Just nip out and get me the *Independent on Sunday*, will you? And a packet of Dunhill.'

'Do you think—?' But Lewis stopped; and waited as Morse reluctantly took a five-pound note from his wallet.

For the next few minutes Morse was aware that his brain was still frustrated and unproductive. And there was something else, too. For some reason, and for a good while now, he had been conscious that he might well have missed a vital clue in the case (cases!) which so far he couldn't quite catch. It was a bit like going through a town on a high-speed train when the eyes had *almost* caught the name of the station as it flashed so tantalizingly across the carriage-window.

Lewis returned five minutes later with the cigarettes, which Morse put unopened into his jacket-pocket; and with the newspaper, which Morse opened at the Cryptic

Crossword ('Quixote'), glanced at 1 across: 'Some show dahlias in the Indian pavilion (6)' and immediately wrote in 'HOWDAH'.

'Excuse me, sir – but how do you get that?'

'Easiest of all the clue-types, that. The letters are all there, in their proper, consecutive order. It's called the "hidden" type.'

'Ah, yes!' Lewis looked and, for once, Lewis saw. 'Shall I leave you for two or three minutes to finish it off, sir?'

'No. It'll take me at least five. And it's time you sat down and gave me the latest news on things here.'

Owens' body Morse had already viewed, howsoever briefly, sitting back, as it had been, against the cushions of the living-room settee, the green covers permeated with many pints of blood. His face unshaven, his long hair loose down to the shoulders, his eyes open and staring, almost (it seemed) as if in permanent disbelief; and two bullet wounds showing raggedly in his chest. Dead four to six hours, that's what Dr Laura Hobson had already suggested – a margin narrower than Morse had expected, though wider than he'd hoped; death, she'd claimed, had fairly certainly been 'instant' (or 'instantaneous', as Morse would have preferred). There were no signs of any forcible entry to the house: the front door had been found still locked and bolted; the tongue of the Yale on the back door still engaged, though not clicked to the locked position from the inside. On the mantelpiece above the electric fire (not switched on) was a small oblong virtually free of the generally pervasive dust.

The body would most probably not have been discovered

that day had not John Benson, a garage mechanic from Hartwell's Motors, agreed to earn himself a little untaxed extra income by fixing a few faults on Owens' car. But Benson had been unable to get any answer when he called just after 11.15 a.m.; had finally peered through the open-curtained front window; had rapped repeatedly, and increasingly loudly, against the pane when he saw Owens lying asleep on the settee there.

But Owens was not asleep. So much had become gradually apparent to Benson, who had dialled 999 at about 11.30 a.m. from the BT phone-box at the entrance to the Drive.

Thus far no one, it appeared, had seen or heard anything untoward that morning between seven and eight o'clock, say. House-to-house enquiries would soon be under way, and might provide a clue or two. But concerning such a possibility Morse was predictably (though, as it happened, mistakenly) pessimistic. Early Sunday morning was not a time when many people were about, except for dog-owners and insomniacs: the former, judging from the warnings on the lamp-posts concerning the fouling of verges and footpaths, not positively encouraged to parade their pets along the street; the latter, if there were any, not as yet coming forward with any sightings of strangers or hearings of gunshots.

No. On the face of it, it had seemed a typical, sleepy Sunday morning, when the denizens of Bloxham Drive had their weekly lie-in, arose late, walked around their homes in dressing-gowns, sometimes boiled an egg, perhaps – and settled down to read in the scandal sheets about the extra-marital exploits of the great and the not-so-good.

But one person had been given no chance to read his Sunday newspaper, for the *News of the World* lay unopened on the mat inside the front door of Number 15; and few of the others in the Drive that morning were able to indulge their delight in adulterous liaisons, stunned as they were by disbelief and, as the shock itself lessened, by a growing sense of fear.

At 2.30 p.m. Morse was informed that few if any of the neighbours were likely to be helpful witnesses – except the old lady in Number 19. Morse should see her himself, perhaps?

'Want me to come along, sir?'

'No, Lewis. You get off and try to find out something about Storrs – *and* his missus. Bath, you say? He probably left details of where he'd be at the Porters' Lodge – that's the usual drill. And do it from HQ. Better keep the phone here free.'

Mrs Adams was a widow of some eighty summers, a small old lady who had now lost all her own teeth, much of her wispy white hair, and even more of her hearing. But her wits were sharp enough, Morse sensed that immediately; and her brief evidence was of considerable interest. She had slept poorly the previous night; got up early; made herself some tea and toast; listened to the news on the radio at seven o'clock; cleared away; and then gone out the back to empty her waste-bin. *That*'s when she'd seen him!

'Him?'

'Pardon?'

'You're sure it was a *man*?'

'Oh yes. About twenty – twenty-five past seven.'

The case was under way.

'You didn't hear any shots or bangs?'

'Pardon?'

Morse let it go.

But he managed to convey his thanks to her, and to explain that she would be asked to sign a short statement. As he prepared to leave, he gave her his card.

'I'll leave this with you, Mrs Adams. If you remember anything else, please get in touch with me.'

He thought she'd understood; and he left her there in her kitchen, holding his card about three or four inches from her pale, rheumy eyes, squinting obliquely at the wording.

She was not, as Morse had quickly realized, ever destined to be called before an identity parade; for although she might be able to spot that all of them were men, any physiognomical differentiation would surely be wholly beyond the capacity of those tired old eyes.

Poor Mrs Adams!

Sans teeth, sans hair, sans ears, sans eyes – and very soon, alas, sans everything.

Seldom, in any investigation, had Morse so badly mishandled a key witness as now he mishandled Mrs Arabella Adams.

Chapter Forty-Two

Alibi (*adv.*): in another place, elsewhere
(*Small's Latin-English Dictionary*)

Some persons in life eschew all sense of responsibility, and are never wholly at ease unless they are closely instructed as to what to do, and how and when to do it. Sergeant Lewis was not such a person, willing as he was always to shoulder his share of responsibility and, not infrequently, to face some apportionment of blame. Yet, to be truthful, he was ever most at ease when given some specific task, as he had been now; and he experienced a pleasing sense of purpose as he drove up to Police HQ that same afternoon.

One thing only disturbed him more than a little. For almost a week now Morse had forgone, been forced to forgo, both beer and cigarettes. And what foolishness it was to capitulate, as Morse *had* done, to both, within the space of only a couple of hours! But that's what life was all about – personal decisions; and Morse had clearly decided that the long-term disintegration of his liver and his lungs was a price well worth paying, even with diabetes, for the short-term pleasures of alcohol and nicotine.

Yet Morse was still on the ball. As he had guessed, Storrs had left details of his weekend whereabouts at the Porters' Lodge. And very soon Lewis was speaking to the Manager of Bath's Royal Crescent Hotel – an appropriately cautious man, but one who was fully co-operative once Lewis had explained the unusual and delicate nature of his enquiries. The Manager would ring back, he promised, within half an hour.

Lewis picked up the previous day's copy of the *Daily Mirror*, and sat puzzling for a few minutes over whether the answer to 1 across – 'River (3)' – was CAM, DEE, EXE, FAL, and so on through the alphabet; finally deciding on CAM, when he saw that it would fit neatly enough with COD, the fairly obvious answer to 1 down – 'Fish (3)'. He had made a firm start. But thereafter he had proceeded little, since the combination which had found favour with the setter of the crossword (EXE/EEL) had wholly eluded him. His minor hypothesis, like Morse's earlier major one, was sadly undone.

But he had no time to return (quite literally) to square one, since the phone rang. It had taken the Manager only fifteen minutes to assemble his fairly comprehensive information . . .

Mr and Mrs J. Storrs had checked into the hotel at 4 p.m. the previous afternoon, Saturday, 2 March: just the one night, at the special weekend-break tariff of £125 for a double room. The purpose of the Storrs' visit (almost certainly) had been to hear the Bath Festival Choir, since one of the reception staff had ordered a taxi for them at

7 p.m. to go along to the Abbey, where the Fauré *Requiem* was the centrepiece of the evening concert. The couple had been back in the hotel by about half past nine, when they had immediately gone into the restaurant for a late, pre-booked dinner, the only extra being a bottle of the house red wine.

If the sergeant would like to see the itemized bill . . . ?

No one, it appeared, had seen the couple after about 11 p.m., when they had been the last to leave the restaurant. Before retiring, however, Mr Storrs had rung through to room service to order breakfast for the two of them, in their room, at 7.45 a.m.: a full English for himself, a Continental one for his wife.

Again, the itemized order was available if the sergeant . . .

Latest check-out from the hotel (as officially specified in the brochure) was noon. But the Storrs had left a good while before then. As with the other details (the Manager explained) some of the times given were just a little vague, since service personnel had changed. But things could very soon be checked. The account had been settled by Mr Storrs himself on a Lloyds Bank Gold Card (the receptionist recalled this clearly), and one of the porters had driven the Storrs' BMW round to the front of the hotel from the rear garage – being tipped (it appeared) quite liberally for his services.

So that was that.

Or *almost* so – since Lewis was very much aware that Morse would hardly be overjoyed with such findings; and he now asked a few further key questions.

'I know it's an odd thing to ask, sir, but are you

completely sure that these people *were* Mr and Mrs Storrs?'

'Well, I . . .' The Manager hesitated long enough for Lewis to jam a metaphoric foot inside the door.

'You knew them – know them – *personally*?'

'I've only been Manager here for a couple of years. But, yes – they were here twelve months or so ago.'

'People change, though, don't they? *He* might have changed quite a bit, Mr Storrs, if he'd been ill or . . . or something?'

'Oh, it was *him* all right. I'm sure of that. Well, *almost* sure. And he signed the credit-card bill, didn't he? It should be quite easy to check up on that.'

'And you're quite sure it was *her*, sir? Mrs Storrs? Is there any possibility at all that he was spending the night with someone else?'

The laugh at the other end of the line was full of relief and conviction.

'Not – a – chance! You can be one hundred per cent certain of that. I think everybody here remembers her. She's, you know, she's a bit sharp, if you follow my meaning. Nothing unpleasant – don't get me wrong! But a little bit, well, *severe*. She dressed that way, too: white trouser-suit, hair drawn back high over the ears, beauty-parlour face. Quite the lady, really.'

Lewis drew on his salient reminiscence of Angela Storrs:

'It's not always easy to recognize someone who's wearing sunglasses, though.'

'But she wasn't wearing sunglasses. Not when I saw her, anyway. I just happened to be in reception when she booked in. And it was *she* recognized *me*! You see, the last time they'd been with us, *she* did the signing in, while Mr Storrs was sorting out the luggage and the parking. And I noticed the registration number of their BMW and I mentioned the coincidence that we were both "188J". She reminded me of it yesterday. She said they'd still got the same car.'

'You can swear to all this?'

'Certainly. We had quite a little chat. She told me they'd spent their honeymoon in the hotel – in the Sarah Siddons suite.'

Oh.

So that was that.

An alibi – for both of them.

Lewis thanked the Manager. 'But please do keep all this to yourself, sir. It's always a tricky business when we're trying to eliminate suspects in a case. Not *suspects*, though, just . . . just people.'

A few minutes later Lewis again rang the Storrs' residence in Polstead Road; again listening to Mrs Storrs on the answerphone: 'If the caller will please speak clearly after the long tone . . .' The voice was a little – what had the Manager said? – a little 'severe', yes. And quite certainly (Lewis thought) it was a voice likely to intimidate a few of the students if she became the new Master's wife. But after waiting for the 'long tone', Lewis put down the phone without leaving any message. He always felt awkward and tongue-tied at such moments; and he suddenly realized that he hadn't got a message to leave in any case.

Chapter Forty-Three

Horse-sense is something a horse has that prevents him from betting on people

(Father Mathew)

Morse was still seated at the kitchen table in Number 15 when Lewis rang through.

'So it looks,' concluded Lewis, 'as if they're in the clear.'

'Ye-es. How far is it from Oxford to Bath?'

'Seventy, seventy-five miles?'

'Sunday morning. No traffic. Do it in an hour and a half – no problem. Three hours there and back.'

'There's a murder to commit in the middle, though.'

Morse conceded the point. 'Three and a half.'

'Well, whatever happened, he didn't use his *own* car. That was in the hotel garage – keys with the porter.'

'Haven't you heard of a *duplicate* set of car-keys, Lewis?'

'What if he was locked in – or blocked in?'

'He *un*locked himself, and *un*blocked himself, all right?'

'He must have left about four o'clock this morning then, because he was back in bed having breakfast with his missus before eight.'

'Ye-es.'

'I just wonder what Owens was doing, sir – up and about and dressed and ready to let the murderer in at half past five or so.'

'Perhaps he couldn't sleep.'

'You're not taking all this seriously, are you?'

'All right. Let's cross 'em both off the list, I agree.'

'Have we *got* a list?'

Morse nodded. 'Not too many on it, I know. But I'd like to see our other runner in the Lonsdale Stakes.'

'Do you want *me* to see him?'

'No. You get back here and look after the shop till the SOCOs have left – they're nearly through.'

With which, Morse put down the phone, got to his feet, and looked cautiously through into the hallway; then walked to the front door, where a uniformed PC stood on guard.

'Has the Super gone?' asked Morse.

'Yes, sir. Five minutes ago.'

Morse walked back to the kitchen and opened the door of the refrigerator. The usual items: two pints of Co-op milk, Flora margarine, a packet of unsmoked bacon rashers, five eggs, a carton of grapefruit juice, two cans of Courage's bitter . . .

Morse found a glass in the cupboard above the draining-board, and poured himself a beer. The liquid was cool and sharp on his dry throat; and very soon he had opened the second can, his fingers almost sensuously feeling the cellophane-wrapped cigarettes in his pocket, still unopened.

By the time the SOCOs were ready to move into the kitchen, the glass had been dried and replaced on its shelf.

'Can we kick you out a little while, sir?' It was Andrews, the senior man.

'You've finished everywhere else?'

'Pretty well.'

Morse got to his feet.

'Ah! Two cans of beer!' observed Andrews. 'Think they may have had a drink together before . . . ?'

'Not at that time of the morning, no.'

'I dunno. I used to have a friend who drank a pint of Guinness for breakfast every morning.'

'Sounds a civilized sort of fellow.'

'Dead. Cirrhosis of the liver.'

Morse nodded morosely.

'Anyway, we'll give the cans a dusting over, just in case.'

'I shouldn't bother,' said Morse.

'Won't do any harm, surely?'

'I said, I shouldn't *bother*,' snapped Morse.

And suddenly Andrews understood.

Upstairs there was little to detain Morse. In the front room the bed was still unmade, a pair of pyjamas neatly folded on the top pillow. The wardrobe appeared exactly as he'd viewed it earlier. Only one picture on the walls: Monet's miserable-looking version of a haystack.

The 'study' (Morse's second visit there too!) was in considerable disarray, for the desk-drawers, now liberally dusted with fingerprint powder, had been taken out, their contents strewn across the floor, including the book which had stimulated some interest on Morse's previous visit. The central drawer likewise had been removed, and Morse assumed that after discovering the theft of the manila file Owens had seen no reason to repair the damaged lock.

Nothing much else of interest upstairs, as far as Morse could see; just that one, easy conclusion to be drawn: that the murderer had been looking for something – some documents, some papers, some evidence which could have constituted a basis for blackmail.

Exactly what Morse had been looking for.

Exactly what Morse had found.

He smiled sadly to himself as he looked down at the wreckage of the room. Already he had made a few minor blunders in the investigations; and one major, tragic blunder, of course. But how fortunate that he'd been able to avail himself of JJ's criminal expertise, since otherwise the crucial evidence found in the manila file would have vanished now for ever.

Downstairs, Morse had only the living-room to consider. The kitchen he'd already seen; and the nominal 'dining-room' was clearly a room where Owens had seldom, if ever, dined – an area thick with dust and crowded with the sorts of items most householders regularly relegate to their lofts and garden sheds: an old electric fire, a coal scuttle, a box of plugs and wires, a traffic cone, an ancient Bakelite wireless, a glass case containing a stuffed owl, a black plastic lavatory-seat, six chairs packed together in the soixante-neuf position – and a dog-collar with the name 'Archie' inscribed on its disc.

Perhaps, after all, there had been some little goodness somewhere in the man?

Morse had already given permission for the body to be removed, and now for the second time he ventured into the living-room. Not quite so dust-bestrewn here, certainly; but manifestly Owens had never been a house-proud man. Surfaces all around were dusted with powder, and chalk-marks outlined the body's former configuration on the settee. But the room was dominated by blood – the stains, the smell of blood; and Morse, as was his wont, turned his back on such things, and viewed the contents of the room.

He stood enviously in front of the black, three-decked Revox CD-cassette player which stood on a broad shelf in the alcove to the left of the front window, with dozens of CDs and cassettes below it, including, Morse noted with appreciation, much Gustav Mahler. And indeed, as he pressed the 'Play' panel, he immediately recognized *Das Lied von der Erde.*

No man is wholly bad, perhaps . . .

On the shelf beneath was an extended row of videos: *Fawlty Towers, Morecambe and Wise Christmas Shows, Porridge,* and several other TV classics. And two (fairly obviously) pornographic videos: *Grub Screws,* its crudely lurid, technicolor cover-poses hardly promising a course in carpentry with the Open University; and the plain-covered, yet succinctly entitled *Sux and Fux*, which seemed to speak quite unequivocally for itself. Morse himself had no video mechanism on his rented TV set; but he was in the process of thinking about the benefits of such a facility when Lewis came in, the latter immediately instructed to have a look around.

Morse's attention now turned to the single row of books in the opposite alcove. Mostly paperbacks: P. D. James, Jack Higgins, Ruth Rendell, Wilbur Smith, Minette Walters . . . *RAC Handbook*, *World Atlas*, *Chambers Dictionary*, *Pevsner's Oxfordshire* . . .

'See this?' Lewis suddenly raised aloft the *Grub Screws*. 'The statutory porn video, sir. Good one, that! Sergeant Dixon had it on at his stag-night.'

'You'd like to see it again, you mean?'

'*Again?* Not for me, sir. Those things get ever so boring after a while. But don't let me stop you if . . .'

'What? Me? I've got more important things to do than watch that sort of thing. High time I saw Cornford, for a start. Fix something up, Lewis. The sooner the quicker.'

After Lewis had gone, Morse felt unwilling to face the chorus of correspondents and the battery of cameras which awaited those periodically emerging from the front of Number 15. So he sat down, yet again, in the now empty kitchen; and pondered.

Always in his life, he had wanted to know the *answers* to things. In Sunday School he had once asked a question concerning the topographical position of Heaven, only to be admonished by an unimaginative middle-aged spinster for being so very silly. And he had been similarly discouraged when as a young grammar-school boy he had asked his Divinity master who it was, if God had created the Universe, who in turn had created God. And after receiving no satisfactory answer from his Physics master about what sort of thing could possibly exist out there at the end of the world, when space had run out, Morse had been compelled to lower his sights a little, thereafter satisfying his intellectual craving for answers by finding the values of 'x' and 'y' in (ever more complicated) algebraic equations, and by deciphering the meaning of (ever more complicated) chunks of choruses from the Greek tragedies.

Later, from his mid-twenties onwards, his need to *know* had transferred itself to the field of crossword puzzles, where he had so often awaited with almost paranoiac impatience the following day's answer to any clue he'd been unable to solve the day before. And now, as he sat in Bloxham Drive on that overcast, chilly Sunday afternoon in early March, he was aware that there *was* an answer to this present puzzle: probably a fairly simple answer to the question of what exactly had taken place earlier that morning. For a sequence of events *had* taken place, perhaps about 7.30. Someone had knocked on the door; had gained entry; had shot Owens twice; had gone upstairs to try to find something; had left via the kitchen door; had gone away, on foot, on a bike, in a car.

Who?

Who, Morse? For it was *someone* – someone with a human face and with a human motive. If only he could put together all the clues, *he would know.* And even as he sat there some pattern would begin to clarify itself in his mind, presenting a logical sequence of events, a causative chain of reactions. But then that same pattern would begin to blur and fade, since there was destined to be no flash of genuine insight on that afternoon.

Furthermore, Morse was beginning to feel increasingly worried about his present failure – like some hitherto highly acclaimed novelist with a score of bestsellers behind him who is suddenly assailed by a nightmarish doubt about his ability to write that one further winner; by a fear that he has come to the end of his creative output, and must face the possibility of defeat.

Lewis came back into the kitchen once more.

Dr Cornford would be happy to meet Morse whenever it suited. Five o'clock that afternoon? Before Chapel? In his rooms in Lonsdale?

Morse nodded.

'And I rang the Storrs again, sir. They're back in Oxford. Seems they had a bit of lunch in Burford on the way. Do you want me to go round?'

Morse looked up in some puzzlement.

'What the hell for, Lewis?'

Chapter Forty-Four

The bells would ring to call her
In valleys miles away:
'Come all to church, good people;
Good people, come and pray.'
But here my love would stay
(A. E. Housman,
A Shropshire Lad XXI)

MORSE ENQUIRED AT the Lodge, then turned left and walked along the side of the quad to the Old Staircase, where on the first floor he saw, above the door to his right, the Gothic-style white lettering on its black background: DR D. J. CORNFORD.

'I suppose it's a bit early to offer you a drink, Chief Inspector?'

Morse looked at his wristwatch.

'Is it?'

'Scotch? Gin? Vodka?'

'Scotch, please.'

Cornford began to pour an ever increasingly liberal tot of Glenmorangie into a tumbler.

'Say "when"!'

It seemed that the Chief Inspector may have had some difficulty in enunciating the monosyllable, for Cornford paused when the tumbler was half filled with the pale-golden malt.

'When!' said Morse.

'No ice here, I'm afraid. But I'm sure you wouldn't want to adulterate it, anyway.'

'Yes, I would, if you don't mind. Same amount of water, please. We've all got to look after our livers.'

Two doors led off the high-ceilinged, oak-panelled, book-lined room; and Cornford opened the one that led to a small kitchen, coming back with a jug of cold water.

'I would have joined you normally – without the water! – but I'm reading the Second Lesson in Chapel tonight' (it was Cornford's turn to consult his wristwatch) 'so we mustn't be all that long. It's that bit from the Epistle to the Romans, Chapter thirteen – the bit about drunkenness. Do you know it?'

'Er, just remind me, sir.'

Clearly Cornford needed no copy of the text in front of him, for he immediately recited the key verse, with appropriately ecclesiastical intonation:

> Let us walk honestly, as in the day; not in rioting and drunkenness, not in chambering and wantonness, not in strife and envying . . .

'You'll be reading from the King James version, then?'

'Absolutely! I'm an agnostic myself; but what a tragedy that so many of our Christian brethren have opted for these new-fangled versions! "Boozing and Bonking", I should think they translate it.'

Morse sat sipping his Scotch contentedly. He could have suggested 'Fux and Sux'; but decided against it.

Cornford smiled. 'What do you want to see me about?'

'Well, in a way it's about that last bit of your text: the "strife and envying" bit. You see, I know you're standing for the Mastership here . . .'

'Yes?'

Morse took a deep breath, took a further deepish draught, and then told Cornford of the murder that morning of Geoffrey Owens; told him that various documents from the Owens household pointed to a systematic campaign of blackmail on Owens' part; informed him that there was reason to believe that he, Cornford, might have been – almost certainly *would* have been – one of the potential victims.

Cornford nodded quietly. 'Are you sure of this?'

'No, not sure at all, sir. But—'

'But you've got your job to do.'

'You haven't received any blackmail letters yourself?'

'No.'

'I'll be quite blunt, if I may, sir. Is there anything you can think of in the recent past, or distant past, that could have been used to compromise you in some way? Compromise your candidature, say?'

Cornford considered the question. 'I've done a few things I'm not very proud of – haven't we all? – but I'm fairly sure I got away with them. That was in another country, anyway . . .'

Morse finished the quotation for him: '... and, besides, the wench is dead.'

Cornford's pale grey eyes looked across at Morse with almost childlike innocence.

'Yes.'

'Do you want to tell me about them?'

'No. But only because it would be an embarrassment for me and a waste of time for you.'

'You're a married man, I understand.'

'Yes. And before someone else tells you, my wife is American, about half my age, and extremely attractive.' The voice was still pleasantly relaxed, yet Morse sensed a tone of quiet, underlying strength.

'*She* hasn't been troubled by letters, anonymous letters, anything like that?'

'She hasn't told me of anything.'

'*Would* she tell you?'

Did Morse sense a hint of uneasy hesitation in Cornford's reply?

'She would, I think, yes. But you'd have to ask *her*.'

Morse nodded. 'I know it's a bit of a bother – but I *shall* have to do that, I'm afraid. She's, er, she's not around?'

Cornford again looked at his wristwatch.

'She'll be coming over to Chapel very shortly.'

'Has there been much feeling – much tension – between you and the, er, other candidate?'

'The atmosphere on High Table has been a little, let's say, uncomfortable once or twice, yes. To be expected, though, isn't it?'

'But you don't throw insults at each other like those boxers before a big fight?'

'No, we just *think* them.'

'No whispers? No rumours?'

'Not as far as I'm aware, no.'

'And you get on reasonably well with Mr Storrs?'

Cornford got to his feet and smiled again, his head slightly to one side.

'I've never got to know Julian all that well, really.'

The Chapel bell had begun to ring – a series of monotonous notes, melancholy, ominous almost, like a curfew.

Ten minutes to go.

'Come ye to church, good people,
Good people, come and pray,'

quoted Cornford.

Morse nodded, as he ventured one final question:

'Do you mind me asking you when you got up this morning, sir?'

'Early. I went out jogging – just before seven.'

'Just you?'

Cornford nodded vaguely.

'You didn't go out after that – for a paper? In the car, perhaps?'

'I don't have a car, myself. My wife does, but it's garaged out in New Road.'

'Quite a way away.'

'Yes,' repeated Cornford slowly, 'quite a way away.'

As Morse walked down the stairs, he thought he'd

recognized Cornford for exactly what he was: a civilized, courteous, clever man; a man of quiet yet unmistakable resolve, who would probably make a splendid new Master of Lonsdale.

Just two things worried him, the first of them only slightly: if Cornford was going to quote Housman, he jolly well ought to do it accurately.

And he might be wholly wrong about the second . . .

The bedroom door opened a few moments after Morse had reached the bottom of the creaking wooden staircase.

'And what do you think all *that* was about?'

'Couldn't you hear?'

'Most of it,' she admitted.

She wore a high-necked, low-skirted black dress, with an oval amethyst pinned to the bodice – suitably ensembled for a seat next to her husband in the Fellows' pews.

'His hair is whiter than yours, Denis. I saw him when he walked out.'

The bell still tolled.

Five minutes to go.

Cornford pulled on his gown and threw his hood back over his shoulders with practised precision; then repeated Housman (again inaccurately) as he put his arms around his wife and looked unblinkingly into her eyes.

'Have you got anything to pray for? Anything that's worrying you?'

Shelly Cornford smiled sweetly, trusting that such

deep dissimulation would mask her growing, now almost desperate, sense of guilt.

'I'm going to pray for you, Denis – for you to become Master of Lonsdale. That's what I want more than anything else in the world' (her voice very quiet now) 'and that's not for me, my darling – it's for you.'

'Nothing else to pray for?'

She moved away from him, smoothing the dress over her energetic hips.

'Such as what?'

'Some people pray for forgiveness, that sort of thing, sometimes,' said Denis Cornford softly.

Morse had walked to the Lodge, where he stood in the shadows for a couple of minutes, reading the various notices about the College's sporting fifteens, and elevens, and eights; and hoping that his presence there was unobserved – when he saw them. An academically accoutred Cornford, accompanied by a woman in black, had emerged from the foot of the Old Staircase, and now turned away from him towards the Chapel in the inner quad.

The bell had stopped ringing.

And Morse walked out into Radcliffe Square; thence across into the King's Arms in Broad Street, where he ordered a pint of bitter, and sat down in the back bar, considering so many things – including a wholly unprecedented sense of gratitude to the Tory Government for its reform of the Sunday licensing laws.

CHAPTER FORTY-FIVE

I'd seen myself a don,
Reading old poets in the library,
Attending chapel in an MA gown
And sipping vintage port by candlelight
(John Betjeman,
Summoned by Bells)

IN THE HILARY Term, in Lonsdale College, on Sunday evenings only, it had become a tradition for the electric lighting to be switched off, and for candles in their sconces to provide the only means of illumination in the Great Hall. Such a procedure was popular with the students, almost all of whom had never experienced the romance of candlelight except during power-cuts, and particularly enjoyable for those on the dais whereon the High Table stood, constantly aware as they were of flickering candles reflected in the polished silver of salt-cellars and tureens, and the glitter of the cutlery laid out with geometrical precision at every place.

On such evenings, no particular table-plan was provided, although it was the regular custom for the visiting preacher (on this occasion a black bishop from Central

Africa) to sit on the right side of the Master, with the College Chaplain on the left. The other occupants of High Table (which was usually fully booked on Sunday evenings) were regularly those who had earlier attended the Chapel service, often with their wives or with a guest; and in recent years, one student invited by each of the Fellows in rotation.

That evening the student in question was Antony Plummer, the new organ scholar, who had been invited by Julian Storrs for the very good reason that the two of them had attended the same school, the Services School, Dartmouth, to which establishment some members of the armed forces were wont to send their sons whilst they themselves were being shunted from one posting to another around the world – in former colonies, protectorates, mandated territories, and the few remaining overseas possessions.

Plummer had never previously been so honoured, and from his new perspective, seated between Mr and Mrs Storrs, he looked around him lovingly at the gilded, dimly illuminated portraits of the famous alumni – the poets and the politicians, the soldiers and the scientists – who figured so largely in the lineage of Lonsdale. The rafted timbers of the ceiling were lost in darkness, and the shadows were deep on the sombre panelling of the walls, as deftly and deferentially the scouts poured wine into the sparkling glasses.

Storrs, just a little late in the proceedings perhaps, decided it was time to play the expansive host.

'Where *is* your father now, Plummer?'

'Last I heard he was running some NATO exercise in Belgium.'

'Colonel now, isn't he?'

'Brigadier.'

'My goodness!'

'You were with him in India, I think.'

Storrs nodded: 'Only a captain, though! I followed my father into the Royal Artillery there, and spent a couple of years trying to teach the natives how to shoot. Not much good at it, I'm afraid.'

'Who – the natives?'

Storrs laughed good-naturedly. 'No – *me*. Most of 'em could have taught me a few things, and I wasn't really cut out for service life anyway. So I opted for a gentler life and applied for a Fellowship here.'

Angela Storrs had finished the bisque soup, and now complimented Plummer on the anthem through which he had conducted his largely female choir during the Chapel service.

'You enjoyed it, Mrs Storrs?'

'Er, yes. But to be quite truthful, I prefer boy sopranos.'

'Can you say why that is?'

'Oh, yes! One just *feels* it, that's all. We heard the Fauré *Requiem* yesterday evening. Absolutely wonderful – especially the "In Paradisum", wasn't it, Julian?'

'Very fine, yes.'

'And you see,' continued Angela, 'I would have *known* they were boys, even with my eyes shut. But don't ask me *why*. One just *feels* that sort of thing, as I said. Don't you agree? One shouldn't try to *rationalize* everything.'

Three places lower down the table, one of the other dons whispered into his neighbour's ear:

'If that woman gets into the Lodge, I'll go and piss all over her primroses!'

By coincidence, colonialism was a topic at the far end of the table, too, where Denis Cornford, his wife beside him, was listening rather abstractedly to a visiting History Professor from Yale.

'No. Don't be too hard on yourselves. The Brits didn't treat the natives all that badly, really. Wouldn't you agree, Denis?'

'No, I wouldn't, I'm afraid,' replied Cornford simply. 'I haven't made any particular study of the subject, but my impression is that the British treated most of their colonials quite abominably.'

Shelly slipped her left hand beneath the starched white tablecloth, and gently moved it along his thigh. But she could feel no perceptible response.

At the head of the splendid oak plank that constituted the High Table at Lonsdale, over the roast lamb, served with St Julien 93, Sir Clixby had been seeking to mollify the bishop's bitter condemnation of the English Examination Boards for expecting Rwandan refugees to study the Wars of the Roses. And soon after the profiteroles, the atmosphere seemed markedly improved.

All the conversation which had been criss-crossing the

evening – amusing, interesting, pompous, spiteful – ceased abruptly as the Master banged his gavel, and the assembled company rose to its feet.

Benedictus benedicatur.

The words came easily and suavely, from lips that were slightly over-red, slightly over-full, in a face so smooth one might assume that it seldom had need of the razor.

Those who wished, and that was most of them, now repaired to the SCR where coffee and port were being served (though wholly informally) and where the Master and Julian Storrs stood side-by-side, buttocks turned towards the remarkably realistic gas fire.

'Bishop on his way back to the railway station then?' queried Storrs.

'On his way back to *Africa*, I hope!' said the Master with a grin. 'Bloody taxi *would* have to be late tonight, wouldn't it? And none of you lot with a car here.'

'It's this drink-driving business, Master. I'm all in favour of it. In fact, I'd vote for random checks myself.'

'And Denis there – hullo, Denis! – he was no help either.'

Cornford had followed their conversation and now edged towards them, sipping his coffee.

'I sold my old Metro just before Christmas. And if you recall, Master, I only live three hundred yards away.'

The words could have sounded light-hearted, yet somehow they didn't.

'Shelly's got a car, though?'

Cornford nodded cautiously. 'Parked a mile away.'

The Master smiled. 'Ah, yes. I remember now.'

Half an hour later, as they walked across the cobbles of Radcliffe Square towards Holywell Street, Shelly Cornford put her arm through her husband's and squeezed it. But, as before, she could feel no perceptible response.

Chapter Forty-Six

But she went on pleading in her distraction; and perhaps said things that would have been better left to silence.

'Angel! – Angel! I was a child – a child when it happened! I knew nothing of men.'

'You were more sinned against than sinning, that I admit.'

'Then you will not forgive me?'

'I do forgive you, but forgiveness is not all.'

'And love me?'

To this question he did not answer

(Thomas Hardy, *Tess of the d'Urbervilles*)

'COFFEE?' SHE suggested, as Cornford was hanging up his overcoat in the entrance hall.

'I've just had some.'

'I'll put the kettle on.'

'No! Leave it a while. I want to talk to you.'

They sat together, if opposite is together, in the lounge.

'What did you do when the Chaplain invited us all to confess our manifold sins and wickedness?'

The measured, civilized tone of Cornford's voice had

shifted to a slightly higher, yet strangely quieter key; and the eyes, normally so kindly, seemed to concentrate ever narrowingly upon her, like an ornithologist focusing binoculars on an interesting species.

'Parrdon?'

'"In thought, word, and deed" – wasn't that the formula?'

She shook her head in apparent puzzlement. 'I haven't the faintest—'

But his words cut sharply across her protestation. 'Why are you lying to me?'

'What—?'

'Shut up!' The voice had lost its control. 'You've been unfaithful to me! *I* know that. *You* know that. Let's start from there!'

'But I haven't—'

'Don't lie to me! I've put up with your infidelity, but I can't put up with your *lies*!'

The last word was hissed, like a whiplash across his wife's face.

'Only once, really,' she whispered.

'Recently?'

She nodded, in helpless misery.

'Who with?'

In great gouts, the tears were falling now. 'Why do you have to know? Why do you have to torture yourself? It didn't mean anything, Denis! It didn't *mean anything*.'

'Hah!' He laughed bitterly. 'Didn't you think it might mean something to *me*?'

'He just wanted—'

'Who was it?'

She closed her eyes, cheeks curtained with mascara'd tears, unable to answer him.

'*Who was it?*'

But still she made no answer to the piercing question.

'Shall I tell *you*?'

He knew – she realized he knew. And now, her eyes still firmly shut, she spoke the name of the adulterer.

'He didn't come here? You went over to the Master's Lodge?'

'Yes.'

'And you went to his bedroom?'

'Yes.'

'And you undressed for him?'

'Yes.'

'You stripped naked for him?'

'Yes.'

'And you got between the sheets with him?'

'Yes.'

'And you had sex? The pair of you had sex together?'

'Yes.'

'How many times?'

'Only once.'

'*And you enjoyed it!*'

Cornford got to his feet and walked back into the entrance hall. He felt stunned, like someone who has just been kicked in the teeth by a recalcitrant shire-horse.

'Denis!' Shelly had followed him, standing beside him now as he pulled on his overcoat.

'You know *why* I did it, Denis? I did it for *you*. You *must* know that!'

He said nothing.

'How did you know?' Her voice was virtually inaudible.

'It's not what people say, is it? It's the *way* they say it. But I knew. I knew tonight . . . I knew before tonight.'

'How *could* you have known? Tell me! Please!'

Cornford turned up the catch on the Yale lock, and for a few moments stood there, the half-opened door admitting a draught of air that felt bitterly cold.

'I *didn't* know! Don't you see? I just hoped you'd deny everything – even if it meant you had to lie to me. But you hadn't even got the guts to *lie* to me! You didn't even want to spare me all this pain.'

The door banged shut behind him; and Shelly Cornford walked back into the lounge where she poured herself a vast gin with minimal tonic.

And wished that she were dead.

Chapter Forty-Seven

Virgil G. Perkins, author of international bestseller *Enjoying Jogging* (Crown Publications NY, 1992) collapsed and died whilst jogging with a group of fellow enthusiasts in St Paul yesterday. Mr Perkins, aged 26, leaves behind his wife, Beverley, their daughter, Alexis, and seven other children by previous marriages

(*Minnesota Clarion*, 23 December 1995)

In the King's Arms, that square, cream-painted hostelry on the corner of Parks Road and Holywell Street, Morse had been remarkably abstemious that evening. After his first pint, he had noticed on the door the pub's recommendation in the *Egon Ronay Guide* (1995); and after visiting the loo to inject himself, he had ordered a spinach-and-mushroom lasagne with garlic bread and salad. The individual constituents of this particular offering had never much appealed to him; yet the hospital dietitian (as he recalled) had been particularly enthusiastic about such fare. And, let it be said, the meal had been marginally enjoyed.

It was 7.45 p.m.

A cigarette would have been a paradisal plus; and yet

somehow he managed to desist. But as he looked around him, at the college crests, the coloured prints, the photographs of distinguished local patrons, he was debating whether to take a few more calories in liquid form when the landlord was suddenly beside him.

'Inspector! I hadn't seen you come in. This is for you – it's been here a couple of weeks.'

Morse took the printed card:

> Let me tell you of a moving experience – very moving! The furniture van is fetching my effects from London to Oxford at last. And on March 18th I'll be celebrating my south-facing patio with a shower of champagne at 53 Morris Villas, Cowley. Come and join me!
> RSVP (at above address)
>
> Deborah Crawford

Across the bottom was a handwritten note: 'Make it, Morse! DC.'

Morse remembered her well . . . a slim, unmarried blonde who'd once invited him to stay overnight in her north London flat, following a comparatively sober Metropolitan Police party; when he'd said that after such a brief acquaintance such an accommodation might perhaps be inappropriate.

Yes, that was the word he'd used: 'inappropriate'.

Pompous idiot!

But he'd given her his address, which she'd vowed she'd never forget.

Which clearly she had.

'She was ever so anxious for you to get it,' began the landlord – but even as he spoke the door that led to Holywell Street had opened, and he turned his attention to the newcomer.

'Denis! I didn't expect to see you in tonight. No good us both running six miles on a Sunday morning if we're going to put all the weight back on on a Sunday night.'

Morse looked up, his face puzzled.

'You mean – you went jogging – together – this morning? What time was that?'

'Far too early, wasn't it, David!'

The landlord smiled. 'Stupid, really. On a Sunday morning, too.'

'What time?' repeated Morse.

'Quarter to seven. We met outside the pub here.'

'And where did the pair of you run?'

'*Five* of us actually, wasn't it, Denis? We ran up to the Plain, up the Iffley Road, across Donnington Bridge, along the Abingdon Road up to Carfax, then through Cornmarket and St Giles' up to the Woodstock Road as far as North Parade, then across to the Banbury, South Parks, and we got back here . . .'

'Just before eight,' added Cornford, pointing to Morse's empty glass.

'What's it to be?'

'No, it's my round—'

'Nonsense!'

'Well, if you insist.'

In fact, however, it was the landlord who insisted, and who now walked to the bar as Cornford seated himself.

'You told me earlier' (Morse was anxious to get things

straight) 'you'd been on your own when you went out jogging.'

'No. If I did, you misunderstood me. You said, I think, "Just you?" And when I said yes, I'd assumed that you were asking if both of us had gone – Shelly and me.'

'And she didn't go?'

'No. She never does.'

'She just stayed in bed?'

'Where else?'

Morse made no suggestion.

'Do you ever go jogging, Inspector?' The question was wearily mechanical.

'Me? No. I walk a bit, though. I sometimes walk down to Summertown for a newspaper. Just to keep fit.'

Cornford almost grinned. 'If you're going to be Master of Lonsdale, you're supposed to be fit. It's in the Statutes somewhere.'

'Makes you wonder how Sir Clixby ever managed it!'

Cornford's answer was unexpected.

'You know, as you get older it's difficult for young people to imagine you were ever young yourself – good at games, that sort of thing. Don't you agree?'

'Fair point, yes.'

'And the Master was a very fine hockey player – had an England trial, I understand.'

The landlord came back with two pints of bitter; then returned to his bar-tending duties.

Cornford was uneasy, Morse felt sure of that. Something regarding his wife, perhaps? Had *she* had anything to do with the murder of Geoffrey Owens? Unlikely, surely. One thing looked an odds-on certainty, though:

if Denis Cornford had ever figured on the suspect list, he figured there no longer.

Very soon, after a few desultory passages of conversation, Morse had finished his beer, and was taking his leave, putting Deborah's card into the inside pocket of his jacket, and forgetting it.

Forgetting it only temporarily, though; for later that same evening he was to look at it again – more carefully. And with a sudden, strange enlightenment.

CHAPTER FORTY-EIGHT

Is it nothing to you, all ye that pass by? Behold and see if there be any sorrow like unto my sorrow, which is done unto me, wherewith the Lord hath afflicted me in the day of his fierce anger

(*Lamentations*, ch. 1, v. 12)

FEELING A WONDERFUL sense of relief, Shelly Cornford heard the scratch of the key in the front door at twenty-five past eleven. For over two hours she had been sitting upright against the pillows, a white bed-jacket over her pyjamas, her mind tormented with the terrifying fear that her husband had disappeared into the dark night, never to return: to throw himself over Magdalen Bridge, perhaps; to lay himself across the railway lines; to slash his wrists; to leap from some high tower. And it was to little avail that she'd listened to any logic that her tortured mind could muster: that the water was hardly deep enough, perhaps; that the railway lines were inaccessible; that he had no razor in his pocket; that Carfax Tower, St Mary's, St Michael's – all were now long shut . . .

Come back to me, Denis! I don't care what happens

to *me*; but come back tonight! Oh, God – *please*, God – let him come back safely. Oh, God, put an end to this, my overwhelming misery!

His words before he'd slammed the door had pierced their way into her heart. 'You hadn't even got the guts to lie to me . . . You didn't even want to spare me all this pain.'

Yet how wrong he'd been, with both his accusations!

Her mother had never ceased recalling that Junior High School report: 'She's such a gutsy little girl.' And the simple, desperately simple, truth was that she loved her husband far more than anything or anyone she'd ever loved before. And yet . . . and yet she remembered so painfully clearly her assertion earlier that same evening: that more than anything in the world she wanted Denis to be Master.

And now? The centre of her life had fallen apart. Her heart was broken. There was no one to whom she could turn.

Except, perhaps . . .

And again and again she recalled that terrible conversation:

'Clixby?'

'Shelly!'

'Are you alone?'

'Yes. What a lovely surprise. Come over!'

'Denis knows all about us!'

'What?'

'Denis knows all about us!'

'"All" about us? What d'you mean? There's nothing for him *to* know – not really.'

'*Nothing?* Was it nothing to you?'

'You sound like the book of *Proverbs* – or is it *Ecclesiastes*?'

'It *didn't* mean anything to you, did it?'

'It was only the *once*, properly, my dear. For heaven's sake!'

'You just don't understand, do you?'

'How did he find out?'

'He didn't.'

'I don't follow you.'

'He just guessed. He was talking to you tonight—'

'After Hall, you mean? Of course he was. You were there.'

'Did you say anything? Please, tell me!'

'What? Have you taken leave of your senses?'

'Why did he say he *knew*, then?'

'He was just guessing – you just said so yourself.'

'He must have had some reason.'

'Didn't you deny it?'

'But it was true!'

'What the hell's that got to do with it? Don't you see? All you'd got to do was to deny it.'

'That's exactly what Denis said.'

'Bloody intelligent man, Denis. I just hope you appreciate him. He was right, wasn't he? All you'd got to do was to deny it.'

'And that's what you wanted me to do?'

'*You're* not really being very intelligent, are you?'

'I just can't believe what you're saying.'

'It would have been far kinder.'

'Kinder to *you*, you mean?'

'To me, to you, to Denis – to everybody.'

'God! You're a shit, aren't you?'

'Just hold your horses, girl!'

'What are you going to do about it?'

'What do you mean – "do" about it? What d'you expect me to do?'

'I don't know. I've no one to talk to. That's why I rang you.'

'Well, if there's anything—'

'But there is! I want help. This is the worst thing that's ever happened to me.'

'But don't you see, Shelly? This is something you and Denis have got to work out for yourselves. Nobody else—'

'God! You *are* a shit, aren't you! Shit with a capital "S".'

'Look! Is Denis there?'

'Of course he's not, you fool.'

'Please don't call me a fool, Shelly! Get a hold on yourself and put things in perspective – and just remember who you're talking to!'

'Denis!'

'You get back to bed. I'll sleep in the spare room.'

'No. *I'll* sleep in there—'

'I don't give a sod who sleeps where. We're just not sleeping in the same room, that's all.'

His eyes were still full of anger and anguish, though his voice was curiously calm. 'We've got to talk about this. For a start, you'd better find out the rights and wrongs and the rest of it about people involved in divorce on the grounds of adultery. Not tonight, though.'

'Denis! Please let's talk *now* – please! – just for a little while.'

'What the hell about? About *me*? You know all about me, for Christ's sake. I'm half-pissed – and soon I'm going to be fully pissed – and as well as that I'm stupid – and hurt – and jealous – and possessive – and old-fashioned – and faithful . . . You following me? I've watched most of your antics, but I've never been too worried. You know why? Because I knew you *loved* me. Deep down I knew there was a bedrock of love underneath our marriage. Or I *thought* I knew.'

In silence, in abject despair, Shelly Cornford listened, and the tears ran in furrows down her cheeks.

'We're finished. The two of us are finished, Shelly – do you know, I can hardly bring myself to call you by your name? Our marriage is over and done with – make no mistake about that. You can feel free to do what you want now. I just don't care. You're a born flirt! You're a born prick-teaser! And I just can't live with you any longer. I just can't live with the picture of you lying there naked and opening your legs to another man. Can you try to get that into your thick skull?'

She shook her head in utter anguish.

'You said' (Cornford continued) 'you'd have given anything in life to see me become Master. Well, *I* wouldn't – do you understand that? But I'd have given anything in life for you to be faithful to me – whatever the prize.'

He turned away from her, and she heard the door of the spare bedroom close; then open again.

'When was it? Tell me that. *When?*'

'This morning.'

'You mean when I was out jogging?'

'Yes,' she whispered.

He turned away once more; and she beheld and could see no sorrow like unto her own sorrow.

The keys to her car lay on the mantelshelf.

CHAPTER FORTY-NINE

Monday, 4 March

I work all day, and get half-drunk at night.
Waking at four to soundless dark, I stare.
In time the curtain-edges will grow light.
Till then I see what's really always there:
Unresting death, a whole day nearer now,
Making all thought impossible but how
And where and when I shall myself die

(Philip Larkin, *Aubade*)

NEVER, IN HIS lifetime of muted laughter and occasional tears, had Morse spent such a horrifying night. Amid fitful bouts of semi-slumber – head weighted with pain, ears throbbing, stomach in spasms, gullet afire with bile and acidity – he'd imagined himself on the verge of fainting, of vomiting, of having a stroke, of entering cardiac arrest. One of Ovid's lovers had once besought the Horses of the Night to slacken their pace and delay thereby the onset of the Dawn. But as he lay turning in his bed, Morse longed for a sign of the brightening sky through his window. During that seemingly unending night, he had consumed several glasses of cold water, Alka-Seltzer tablets, cups of black coffee, and the equivalent of a weekly dosage of Nurofen Plus.

No alcohol, though. Not one drop of alcohol.

At last Morse had decided to abandon alcohol.

Lewis looked into Morse's bedroom at 7.30 a.m. (Lewis was the only person who had a key to Morse's flat.)

In the prestigious area of North Oxford, most householders had long since fitted their homes with anti-burglar devices, with neighbours holding the keys to the alarm mechanism. But Morse had little need of such a device, for the only saleable, stealable items in his flat were the CDs of all the operas of the man he regarded as a towering genius, Richard Wagner; and his earnestly assembled collection of first editions of the greatest hero in his life, the pessimistic poet A. E. Housman, who, like Morse, had left St John's College, Oxford, without obtaining a degree.

But not even North Oxford burglars had tastes that were quite so esoteric.

And in any case, Morse seldom spoke to either of his immediate neighbours.

'You look awful, sir.'

'Oh, for Christ's sake, Lewis! Don't you know if somebody says you *look* awful, you *feel* awful?'

'Didn't you feel awful *before* I said it?'

Morse nodded a miserable agreement.

'Shall I get you a bit of breakfast?'

'No.'

'Well, I reckon we can eliminate the Storrs – both of

'em. I've checked with the hotel as far as possible. And unless they hired a helicopter . . .'

'We can cross off the Cornfords, too – *him*, anyway. He's got four witnesses to testify he was running around Oxford pretending to be Roger Bannister.'

'What about *her*?'

'I can't really see why . . . or how.'

'Owens could have been blackmailing her?'

Morse fingered his stubbled chin. 'I don't think so somehow. But there's *something* there . . . something Cornford didn't want to tell me about.'

'What d'you think?'

But Morse appeared unable to answer, as he swung his legs out of bed and sat for a while, alternately turning his torso to left and right.

'Just easing the lumbago, Lewis. Don't *you* ever get it?'

'No.'

'Just nip and get me a glass of orange juice from the fridge. The *unsweetened* orange juice.'

As he walked into the kitchen, Lewis heard the post slither through the letter-box.

So did Morse.

'Lewis! Did you find out what time the postman usually calls in Polstead Road?'

'I've already told you. You were right.'

'About the only bloody thing I *have* been right about.'

'Arrghh! Cheer up, sir!'

'Just turn out those pockets, will you?' Morse pointed to the suit and shirt thrown carelessly over the only chair in the bedroom. 'Time I had a change of clothes – maybe bring me a change of luck.'

'Who's your new girlfriend?' Lewis held up the invitation card. '"Make it, Morse! DC."'

'That card is wholly private and—'

But Morse got no further.

He felt the old familiar tingling across the shoulders, the hairs on his lower arms standing up, as if a conductor had invited his orchestra to arise after a concert.

'Christ!' whispered Morse irreverently. 'Do you know what, Lewis? I think you've done it again!'

Chapter Fifty

Monday–Tuesday, 4–5 March

> The four-barrelled Lancaster Howdah pistol is of .577 in calibre. Its name derived from the story that it was carried by tiger hunters who travelled by elephant and who kept the pistol as a defence against any tiger that might leap on to the elephant's back
>
> (*Encyclopedia of Rifles and Handguns*, ed. SEAN CONNOLLY)

FOR THE RELATIVES, for the statement-takers and the form-fillers, for the boffins at ballistics and forensics, the murder of Geoffrey Owens would be a serious business. No less than for the detectives. Yet for Morse himself the remainder of that Monday had been unproductive and anti-climactic, with a morning of euphoria followed by an afternoon of blood-trouble.

Hospital instructions had been for him to take four daily readings of his blood sugar level, using a slim, pen-like appliance into which he inserted a test-strip duly smeared with a drop of his blood, with each result appearing, after only thirty seconds, in a small window on the side of the pen. Whilst the average blood sugar level of the healthy person is about 4.5, the pen is calibrated from 1 to 25, since the levels of diabetic patients often vary very considerably. Any level higher than 25 is registered as 'HI'.

Now thus far readings had been roughly what Morse had been led to expect (the highest 15.5): it would take some little while – and then only if he promised to do as he was told – to achieve that 'balance' which is the aim of every diabetic. More than disappointing to him therefore had been the 'HI' registered at lunchtime that day. In fact, more of a surprise than a disappointment, since momentarily he was misled into believing that 'HI' was analogous to the greeting from a fruit-machine: 'Hello And Welcome!'

But it wasn't; and Morse was rather worried about himself; and returned to his flat, where he took two further Nurofen Plus for his persisting headache, sat back in his armchair, decided he lacked the energy to do *The Times* crossword or even to turn on the CD player – and fairly soon fell fast asleep.

At six o'clock he rang Lewis to say he would be doing nothing more that day. Just before seven o'clock he measured his blood sugar once again; and finding it somewhat dramatically reduced, to 14.3, had decided to celebrate with a small glass of Glenfiddich before he listened to *The Archers*.

The following morning, feeling much refreshed, feeling eager to get on with things, Morse had been at his desk in Police HQ for half an hour before Lewis entered, holding a report.

'Ballistics, sir. Came in last night.'

Morse could no more follow the technical terminology of ballistics reports than he could understand a paragraph of Structural Linguistics or recall the configuration of the most recent map of Bosnia. To be sure he had a few vague notions about 'barrels' and 'grooves' and 'cylinders' and 'calibres'; but his knowledge went no further, and his interest not quite so far as that. Cursorily glancing therefore through the complex data assembled in the first five pages, he acquainted himself with the short, simply written summary on page six:

> Rachel James was fatally shot by a single bullet fired from a range of c. 45 cms; Geoffrey Owens was fatally shot by two bullets fired from a range of c. 100 cms. The pistol used in each case, of .577 in. calibre, was of the type frequently used by HM Forces. Quite certainly the same pistol was used in each killing.
>
> ASH: 4.iii.96

Morse sat back in the black-leather armchair and looked mildly satisfied with life.

'Ye-es. I think I'm beginning to wake up at last in this case, Lewis. You know, it's high time we got together, you and me. We've been doing our own little things so far, haven't we? *You've* gone off to see somebody – *I've* gone off to see somebody – and we've not got very far, have we? It's the same as always, Lewis. We need to do things together from now on.'

'No time like the present.'

'Pardon?'

Lewis pointed to the ballistics report. 'What do you think?'

'Very interesting. Same revolver.'

'*Pistol*, sir.'

'Same difference.'

'I think most of us had assumed it was the same, anyway.'

'Really?'

'Well, it's what most of the lads think.'

Morse's smile was irritatingly benign. 'Same revolver – same murderer. Is that what, er, most of the lads think as well?'

'I suppose so.'

'Do you?'

Lewis considered the question. It either was – or it wasn't. Fifty-fifty chance of getting it right, Lewis. Go for it!

'Yes!'

'Fair enough. Now let's consider a few possibilities. Rachel was shot through the kitchen window when she was standing at the sink. The blind was old and made of thinnish material and the silhouette was pretty clear, perhaps; but the murderer was taking a risk. Revolvers' (Lewis had given up) 'are notoriously inaccurate even at close range, and the bullet's got to penetrate a reasonably substantial pane of glass – enough perhaps to knock the aim off course a bit and hit her in the neck instead of the head. Agreed?'

Lewis nodded at what he saw as an analysis not particularly profound. And Morse continued:

'Now the shooting of Owens took place *inside* the house – from a bit further away; but no glass this time, and a very clear target to aim at. And Owens is shot in the chest, not in the head. A *modus operandi* quite different from the first.'

Lewis smiled. 'So we've got two *moduses operandi.*'

'Modi, Lewis! So it *could* be that we've two murderers. But that would seem on the face of it highly improbable, because it's not difficult to guess the reason for the difference . . . Is it?'

'Well, as I see things, sir, Owens was probably murdered by somebody he knew. He probably invited whoever it was in. Perhaps they'd arranged to meet anyway. Owens was dressed and—' Lewis stopped a moment. 'He hadn't shaved though, had he?'

'He was the sort of fellow who always looked as if he needed a shave.'

'Perhaps we should have checked more closely.'

'You don't expect *me* to check that sort of thing, do you? I'm a necrophobe – you've known me long enough, surely.'

'Well, that's it then, really. But *Rachel* probably didn't know him.'

'Or *her.*'

'She must have been really scared if she heard a tap on the window that morning and went to open the blind—'

'You're still assuming that both murders were committed by the same person, Lewis.'

'And *you* don't think so?'

Morse shrugged. 'Could have been two lovers or partners or husband and wife – or two completely separate people.'

Lewis was beginning to sound somewhat exasperated. 'You know, I shall be much happier when we've got a bit more of the routine work done, sir. It's all been a bit ad hoc so far, hasn't it?' (Morse raised his eyebrows at the Latinism.) 'Can't we leave a few of the ideas until we've given ourselves a chance to check everything a bit?'

'Lewis! You are preaching to the converted. That's exactly what we've got to do. Go back to the beginning. "In our beginning is our end," somebody said – Eliot, wasn't it? Or is it "In our end is our beginning"?'

'Where do you suggest we begin then, sir?'

Morse considered the question.

'What about you fetching me a cup of coffee? No sugar.'

Chapter Fifty-One

Tuesday, 5 March

The overworked man who agrees to any division of labour always gets the worst share

(Hungarian proverb)

'WHERE DO YOU suggest we begin then?' repeated Lewis, as Morse distastefully sipped his unsweetened coffee.

'When we *do* start again, we'll probably find that we've been looking at things from the wrong angle. We've been assuming – *I* have, anyway – that it was Owens who was pulling all the strings. As a journalist, he'd often been in a privileged position with regard to a few juicy stories; and as a man he pretty clearly gloried in the hold he could have on other people: blackmail. And from what we learned, I thought it was likely that the two candidates for the Mastership at Lonsdale were being blackmailed; I thought that they'd have as good a motive, certainly Storrs, as anybody for wishing Owens out of the way. But I never dreamed that Owens was in danger of being murdered, as you know . . .

'There's just the one trouble about following up that particular hypothesis though, isn't there? It's now clear that neither of those two, neither Storrs nor Cornford – nor their wives for that matter – could have been responsible for *both* murders. And increasingly unlikely, perhaps, that any of them could have been responsible even for *one* of the murders. So where does this all leave us? It's a bit like a crossword clue you sometimes get stuck with. You think one bit of the clue's the definition, and the other bit's a build-up of the letters. Then suddenly you realize you've got things *the wrong way round*. And perhaps I'm reading the clue the wrong way round here, Lewis. What if someone was blackmailing *Owens* – the exact opposite of our hypothesis? What if – we've spoken about it before – what if Rachel James came to discover something that would upset his carefully loaded apple-cart? And blackmailed *him*?'

'Trying to climb aboard the gravy-train herself?'

'Exactly. Money! You said right at the start that we needed a *motive* for Rachel's murder; and I suspect she'd somehow got to know about his own blackmailing activities and was threatening to expose him.'

Lewis was looking decidedly impatient.

'Sir! Could we *please* get along to Owens' office first, and get a few simple *facts* established?'

'Just what I was about to suggest. We shall have to get down there and find out everything we can about him. See the editor, the sub-editor, his colleagues, that personnel fellow – especially him! Go through his desk and his drawers. Get hold of his original application, if we can. Try to learn something about his men-friends, his girlfriends, his enemies, his habits, what he liked to eat and drink, his salary, any clubs he belonged to, his political leanings – '

'We know he voted Conservative, sir.'

' – the newspaper he took, where he usually parked his car, what his job prospects were – yes, plenty to be going on with there.'

'Quite a list. Good job there's two of us, sir.'

'Pardon?'

'Hefty agenda – that's all I'm saying.'

'Not all that much really. Far easier than it sounds. And if you get off straightaway . . .' Morse looked at his wristwatch: 10.45 a.m.

Lewis frowned. 'You mean you're not joining me?'

'Not today, no.'

'But you just said—'

'One or two important things I've got to do after lunch.'

'Such as?'

'Well, to be truthful, I've been told to take things a bit more gently. And I suppose I'd better take a bit of notice of my medical advisers.'

'Of course.'

'Don't get me wrong, mind! I'm feeling fine. But I think a little siesta this afternoon . . .'

'*Siesta?* That's what they have in Spain in the middle of the summer when the temperature's up in the nineties – but we're in England in the middle of winter and it's freezing outside.'

Morse looked down at his desk, a little sheepishly, and Lewis knew that he was lying.

'Come on, sir! It's something to do with that invite you had, isn't it? Deborah Crawford?'

'In a way.'

'Why are you being so secretive about it? You wouldn't tell me yesterday either.'

'Only because it needs a bit more thinking about, that's all.'

'"You and me together" – isn't that what you said?'

Morse fingered the still-cellophaned cigarettes, almost desperately.

'Si' down then, Lewis.'

Chapter Fifty-Two

It is the nature of an hypothesis, when once a man has conceived it, that it assimilates every thing to itself as proper nourishment, and, from the first moment of your begetting it, it generally grows the stronger by every thing you see, hear, read, or understand

(Laurence Sterne, *Tristram Shandy*)

'IT WASN'T DEBORAH Crawford, Lewis – it was her initials, "DC". When we found that list in the manila file, I jumped the gun. I automatically assumed that "JS" was Julian Storrs – I think I was right about that – and I assumed that "DC" was Denis Cornford – and I think I was *wrong* about that. As things have turned out I don't believe Owens ever knew Cornford at all, *or* his missus, for that matter. But he knew another "DC": the woman at Number 1 Bloxham Close – Adèle Beatrice Cecil – the ABC lass Owens knew well enough to call by her nickname, "Della". "DC". And the more I think about *her*, the more attractive a proposition I find it.'

'Well, most men would, sir. Lovely looker!'

Ignoring the pleasantry, Morse continued: 'Just consider for a minute what an important figure she is in the case. She's the prime witness, really. *She's* the one who sees Owens leave for work about sevenish on the morning Rachel was murdered; *she's* the one who rings Owens an hour or so later to tell him the police are in Bloxham Close' (again Lewis let it go) 'and gives him a headstart on all the other newshounds. That's what she says, isn't it? But she might not be telling the truth!'

Lewis sat in silence.

'Now, as I recall it, your objection to Owens himself ever being a suspect was the time-factor. You argued that he couldn't have gone to work that morning, parked his car, been seen in the newspaper offices, got in his car again, driven back to Kidlington, murdered Rachel, driven back to Osney Mead *again*, taken the phone-call from Della Cecil, driven back to Kidlington *again*, to be on hand with his mobile and his notebook while the rest of the press are pulling their socks on. He could *never* have done all that in such a short space of time, you said. Impossible! And of course you were right – '

'Thank you, sir.'

' – in one way; and quite wrong in another. Let's stick to our original idea that the list of initials we found was a blackmail list, and that *she's* on it – Della Cecil. He's got something on her, too. So when he asks her to help him in his plan to get Rachel out of the way, she's little option but to co-operate.'

'Have you any idea what this "plan" was, sir?'

'That's the trouble. I've got far too many ideas.'

'Want to try me?'

'All right. They're all the same sort of plan, really – any plan to cut down that *time* business you're so worried about. Let me just outline a possible plan, and see what you think of it. Ready? Owens drives out to work, at ten to seven, let's say – and *she follows him*, in her own car. When he's parked the car, when his entry's recorded, he goes into the building, makes sure he's seen by somebody – doesn't matter who it is – then immediately leaves via a side door and gets into *her* car, parked along the street in front of the offices. Back in Kidlington, he murders Rachel James, about half past seven, *and doesn't return to work at all*. He's got a key and he goes into *Della*'s house – and waits. At the appropriate time, when the police arrive, a call is made to his own office – he knows there'll be no one there! – and a message is left *or isn't left* on the answerphone. All that matters is that a telephonic communication is established, and gets recorded on those BT lists we all get, between *her* phone and Owens' phone in his office. Then all he's got to do is to emerge amid all the excitement once the murder's reported – the police, the local people, the Press, the TV . . . Well?'

'You make it up as you go along, sir.'

Morse's face betrayed some irritation. 'Of *course* I bloody do! That's what I'm here for. I just told you. If once we accept there could be *two* people involved – *two* cars – there are *dozens* of possibilities. It's like permutating your selection on the National Lottery. I've just given you *one* possibility, that's all.'

'But it just couldn't—'

'What's wrong with it? Come on! Tell me!'

'Well, let's start with the car—'

'*Cars*, plural.'

'All right. When he's parked his car—'

'I didn't say that. I deliberately said parked *the* car, if you'd been listening. It could have been his – it could have been hers: it's the *card* number that's recorded there, not the *car* number. She could have driven his car – he could have driven hers – and at any point they could have swapped. Not much risk. Very few people around there at seven. Or eight, for that matter.'

'Is it my turn now?' asked Lewis quietly.

'Go on!'

'I'm talking about Owens' car, all right? That was parked in Bloxham Drive – "Drive" *please*, sir – when Owens was there that morning. The street was cordoned off, but the lads let him in – because he told them he lived there. And I saw the car myself.'

'So? He could have left it – or she could have left it – in a nearby street. Anywhere. Up on the main road behind the terrace, say. That's where JJ—'

But Morse broke off.

'It *still* couldn't have happened like you say, sir!'

'No?'

'No! He was seen in his office, Owens was, remember? Just at the time when Rachel was being murdered! Seen by the Personnel Manager there.'

'We haven't got a statement from him yet, though.'

'He's been away, you know that.'

'Yes, I *do* know that, Lewis. But you spoke to him.'

Lewis nodded.

'On the phone?'

'On the phone.'

'You did it through the operator, I suppose?'

Lewis nodded again.

'Do you know who she probably put you through to?' asked Morse slowly.

The light dawned in Lewis's eyes. 'You mean . . . she could have put me through to Owens himself?'

Morse shrugged his shoulders. 'That's what we've got to find out, isn't it? Owens was *deputy* Personnel Manager, we know that. He was on a management course only last weekend.'

'Do you really think that's what happened?'

'I dunno. I know one thing, though: it *could* have happened that way.'

'But it's all so – so airy-fairy, isn't it? And you said we were going to get some *facts* straight first.'

'Exactly.'

Lewis gave up the struggle. 'I'll tell you something that *would* be useful: some idea where the gun is.'

'The "pistol", do you mean?'

'Sorry. But if only we knew where *that* was . . .'

'Oh, I think I know where we're likely to find the pistol, Lewis.'

PART FIVE

Chapter Fifty-Three

Wednesday, 6 March

A good working definition of Hell on Earth is a forced attendance for a couple of days or even a couple of hours at a Young Conservatives' Convention

(Cassandra, in the *Daily Mirror*, June 1952)

MISS ADÈLE CECIL (she much preferred 'Miss' to 'Ms' and 'Adèle' to 'Della') had spent the previous evening and night in London, where she had attended, and addressed, a meeting of the chairmen, chairwomen and chairpersons of the Essex Young Conservative Association. Thirty-eight such personages had assembled at Durrants, in George Street, a traditional English hotel just behind Oxford Street, with good facilities, tasteful cuisine, and comfortable beds. Proceedings had been businesslike, and the majority of delegates (it appeared) had ended up in the rooms originally allocated to them.

It was at a comparatively early breakfast in the restaurant that over her fresh grapefruit, with Full English to follow, the head-waiter had informed Adèle of the telephone message, which she had taken in one of the hooded booths just outside the breakfast-room.

'How did you know I was here?'

'Don't you remember me? I'm a detective.'

Yes, she remembered him – the white-haired, supercilious, sarcastic police officer she didn't want to meet again.

'I shan't be back in Oxford till lunchtime.'

'The Trout? Half past twelve?'

As she started on her eggs, bacon, mushrooms, and sausages, she accepted the good-natured twitting of her three breakfast companions, all male:

'Boyfriend?'

'Couldn't he wait?'

'What's *he* got . . . ?'

During her comparatively young life, Adèle had been companionably attached to a couple of dozen or so men, of varying ages, with many of whom she had slept – though seldom more than once or twice, and never without some satisfactory reassurance about the availability and reliability of condoms, and a relatively recent check-up for AIDS.

They were all the same, men. Well, most of them. Fingers fumbling for hooks at the backs of bras, or at the front these days. So why was she looking forward just a little to her lunchtime rendezvous? She wasn't really, she told herself, as she parked the Rover, crossed the narrow road just below the bridge, and entered the bar.

'What'll you have?'

'Orange juice and lemonade, please.'

They sat facing each other at a low wooden table, and Morse was immediately (and again) aware of her attractiveness. She wore a slimly tailored dark-grey outfit, with a high-necked Oxford blue blouse, her ash-blonde hair palely gleaming.

Morse looked down at his replenished pint of London Pride.

'Good time at the Conference?'

'I had a lovely time,' she lied.

'I'm glad it went well,' he lied.

'Do you mind?' She waved an unlit cigarette in the air.

'Go ahead, please.'

She offered the packet across.

'Er, not for the minute, thank you.'

'Well?'

'Just one or two questions.'

She smiled attractively: 'Go ahead.'

Morse experienced a sense of paramnesia. *Déjà vu.* 'You've already signed a statement – about the morning Rachel was murdered?'

'You know that, surely?'

'And it was the truth?' asked Morse, starkly. 'You couldn't have been wrong?'

'Of course not!'

'You told me you "had a heart-to-heart" with Rachel once in a while. I think those were your words?'

'So?'

'Does that mean you spoke about boyfriends – men-friends?'

'And clothes, and money, and work—'

'Did you know she was having an affair with Julian Storrs?'

She nodded slowly.

'Did you mention this to Mr Owens?' Morse's eyes, blue and unblinking, looked fiercely into hers.

And her eyes were suddenly fierce, too, as they held his. 'What the hell do you think I'd do that for?'

Morse made no direct answer as he looked down at the old flagstones there. And when he resumed, his voice was very quiet.

'Did *you* ever have an affair with Julian Storrs?'

She thought he looked sad, as if he hadn't really wanted to ask the question at all; and suddenly she knew why she'd been looking forward to seeing him. So many hours of her life had she spent seeking to discover what lay beneath the physical looks, the sexual prowess, the masculine charms of some of her lovers; and so often had she discovered the selfsame answer – virtually nothing.

She looked long into the blazing log-fire before finally answering:

'I spent one night with him – in Blackpool – at one of the Party Conferences.'

She spoke so softly that Morse could hardly hear the words, or perhaps it was he didn't wish to hear the words. For a while he said nothing. Then he resumed his questioning:

'You told me that when you were at Roedean there were quite a few daughters of service personnel there, apart from yourself?'

'Quite a few, yes.'

'Your own father served in the Army in India?'

'How did you know that?'

'He's in *Who's Who.* Or he was. He died two years ago. Your mother died of cancer twelve years ago. You were the only child of the marriage.'

'Orphan Annie, yeah!' The sophisticated, upper-crust veneer was beginning to crack.

'You inherited his estate?'

'*Estate?* Hah!' She laughed bitterly. 'He left all his money to the bookmakers.'

'No heirlooms, no mementoes – that sort of thing?'

She appeared puzzled. '*What* sort of thing?'

'A pistol, possibly? A service pistol?'

'Look! You don't seriously think *I* had anything to do with—'

'My job's to ask the questions—'

'Well, the answer's "no",' she snapped. 'Any more questions?'

One or two clearly:

'Where were you on Sunday morning – last Sunday morning?'

'At home. In bed. Asleep – until the police woke me up.'

'And *then?*'

'Then I was frightened. And you want me to tell you the truth? Well, I'm *still* bloody frightened!'

Morse looked at her again: so attractive; so vulnerable; and now just a little nervous, perhaps? Not frightened though, surely.

Was she hiding something?

'Is there anything more,' he asked gently 'anything at all, you can tell me about this terrible business?'

And immediately he sensed that she could.

'Only one thing, and perhaps it's got nothing ... Julian asked me to a Guest Night at Lonsdale last November, and in the SCR after dinner I sat next to a Fellow there called Denis Cornford. I only met him that once – but he was really nice – lovely man, really – the sort of man I wish I'd met in life.'

'Bit old, surely?'

'About your age.'

Morse's fingers folded round the cellophane, and he sought to stop his voice from trembling.

'What about him?'

'I saw him in the Drive, that's all. On Thursday night. About eight. He didn't see me. I'd just driven in and he was walking in front of me – no car. He kept walking along a bit, and then he turned into Number 15 and rang the bell. Geoff Owens opened the front door – and let him in.'

'You're quite sure it was him?'

'Oh, yes,' replied Adèle.

Chapter Fifty-Four

He looked into her limpid eyes: 'I will turn this Mozart off, if you don't mind, my love. You see, I can never concentrate on two beautiful things at the same time'

(Passage quoted by Terence Benczik in *The Good and the Bad in Mills and Boon*)

WITH SUSPICIOUSLY extravagant caution Morse drove the Jaguar up towards Kidlington HQ, again conscious of seeing the name-plate of that particular railway station flashing, still unrecognizably, across his mind. At the Woodstock Road roundabout he waited patiently for a gap in the Ring-Road traffic; rather too patiently for a regularly hooting hooligan somewhere behind him.

Whether he believed what his ABC girl had told him, he wasn't really sure. And suddenly he realized he'd forgotten to ask her whether indeed it was *she* who occasionally extended her literary talents beyond her humdrum political pamphlets into the fields of (doubtless more profitable) pornography.

But it was only for a few brief minutes that Morse considered the official confiscation of the titillatingly titled novel, since his car-phone had been ringing as he finally crossed into Five Mile Drive. He pulled over to the side of the road, since seldom had he been able to discharge two simultaneous duties at all satisfactorily.

It was Lewis on the line – an excited Lewis.

Calling from the newspaper offices.

'I just spoke to the Personnel Manager, sir. It was him!'

'Lew-is! Your pronouns! *What* exactly was *who*?'

'It wasn't Owens I spoke to on the phone. It was the Personnel Manager himself!'

Morse replied only after a pause, affecting a tone of appropriate humility: 'I wonder why I don't take more notice of you in the first place.'

'You don't sound all that surprised?'

'Little in life surprises me any longer. The big thing is that we're getting things straight at last. Well done!'

'So your girl *wasn't* involved.'

'I don't think so.'

'Did she tell you anything important?'

'I'm not sure. We know Owens had got something on Storrs, and perhaps . . . it might be he had something on Cornford as well.'

'Cornford? How does he come into things?'

'She tells me, our Tory lass, that she saw him going into Owens' house last Thursday.'

'Phew!'

'I'm just going back to HQ, and then I'll be off to see our friends the Cornfords – both of 'em – if I can park.'

'Last time you parked on the pavement in front of the Clarendon Building.'

'Ah, yes. Thank you, Lewis. I'd almost forgotten that.'

'Not forgotten your injection, I hope?'

'Oh no. That's now become an automatic part of my lifestyle,' said Morse, who had forgotten all about his lunchtime jab.

The phone was ringing when Morse opened the door of his office.

'Saw you coming in,' explained Strange.

'Yes, sir?'

'It's all these forms I've got to fill in – retirement forms. They give me a headache.'

'They give *me* a headache.'

'At least you know how to fill 'em in.'

'Can we leave it just a little while, sir? I don't seem able to cope with two things at once these days, and I've got to get down to Oxford.'

'Let it wait! Just don't forget *you*'ll be filling in the same forms pretty soon.'

Bloxham Drive was still cordoned off, the police presence still pervasively evident. But Adèle Beatrice Cecil – alias Ann Berkeley Cox, author of *Topless in Torremolinos* – was waved through by a sentinel PC, just as Geoffrey Owens had been waved through over a fortnight earlier, on the morning that Rachel James had been murdered.

As she let herself into Number 1, she was immediately aware that the house was (literally) almost freezing. Why hadn't she left the heating on? How good to have been able to jump straight into a hot bath; or into an electric-blanketed bed; or into a lover's arms . . .

For several minutes she thought of Morse, and of what he had asked her. What on earth had he suspected? And suddenly, alone again now, in her cold house, she found herself shivering.

Chapter Fifty-Five

> To an outsider it may appear that the average Oxbridge don works but twenty-four weeks out of the annual fifty-two. If therefore at any point in the academic year it is difficult to locate the whereabouts of such an individual, most assuredly this circumstance may not constitute any adequate cause for universal alarm
>
> (*A Workload Analysis of University Teachers*, ed. Harry Judge)

Just after 4 p.m. that same day, Morse rang the bell beside the red-painted front door of an elegant, ashlared house just across from the Holywell Music Room. It was the right house, he knew that, with the Lonsdale Crest fixed halfway between the neatly paned windows of the middle and upper storeys.

There was no answer.

There were no answers.

Morse retraced his steps up to Broad Street and crossed the cobbles of Radcliffe Square to the Porters' Lodge at Lonsdale.

'Do you know if Dr Cornford's in College?'

The duty porter rang a number; then shook his head.

'Doesn't seem to be in his rooms, sir.'

'Has he been in today?'

'He was in this morning. Called for his mail – what, ten? Quarter past?'

'You've no idea where he is?'

The porter shook his head. 'Doesn't come in much of a Wednesday, Dr Cornford. Usually has his Faculty Meeting Wednesdays.'

'Can you try him for me there? It's important.'

The porter rang a second number; spoke for a while; put down the phone.

'They've not seen him today, sir. Seems he didn't turn up for the two o'clock meeting.'

'Have you got his home number?'

'He's ex-directory, sir. I can't—'

'So am *I* ex-directory. You know who I am, don't you?'

The young porter looked as hopefully as he could into Morse's face.

'No, sir.'

'Forget it!' snapped Morse.

He walked back up to Holywell Street, along to the red door, and rang the bell.

There was no answer.

There were no answers.

An over-lipsticked middle-aged traffic-warden stood beside the Jaguar.

'Is this your vehicle, sir?'

'Yes, madam. I'm just waiting for the Chief Constable. He's' (Morse pointed vaguely towards the Sheldonian) 'nearly finished in there. At any rate, I hope he bloody has! And if he hasn't, put the bill to 'im, love – not to me!'

'Sorry!'

Morse wandered across to the green-shuttered Blackwell's, and browsed awhile; finally purchasing the first volume of Sir Steven Runciman's *History of the Crusades*.

He wasn't quite sure why.

Then, for the third time, he walked up to the red door in Holywell Street and rang the bell.

Morse heard the news back in HQ.

From Lewis.

A body had been found in a car, in a narrow lane off New Road, in a garage rented under the name of Dr Cornford.

For a while Morse sat silent.

'I only met him the once you know, Lewis. Well, the twice, really. He was a good man, I think. I liked him.'

'It isn't Dr Cornford though, sir. It's his wife.'

Chapter Fifty-Six

Thursday, 7 March

> Is it sin
> To rush into the secret house of death
> Ere death dare come to us?
> (Shakespeare, *Antony and Cleopatra*)

'TELL ME ABOUT it,' said Morse.

Seated opposite him, in the first-floor office in St Aldates Police Station, Detective Chief Inspector Peter Warner told the story sadly and economically.

Mrs Shelly Cornford had been found in the driving-seat of her own car, reclining back, with a hosepipe through the window. The garage had been bolted on the inside. There could be little doubt that the immediate cause of death was carbon-monoxide poisoning from exhaust fumes. A brief handwritten note had been left on the passenger seat: 'I'm so sorry, Denis, I can't forgive myself for what I did. I never loved anyone else but you, my darling – S.' No marks of violence; 97 mg blood alcohol – the equivalent (Warner suggested) of two or three stiffish gins. Still a few unanswered questions, of course: about her previous whereabouts that day; about the purchase of the green hosepipe and the connector, both new. But suspicion of foul play? None.

'I wonder where she had a drink?' asked Morse.

'Well, if she'd walked up from Holywell Street, there'd be the King's Arms, the White Horse, The Randolph . . . But you're the expert.'

Morse asked no more questions; but sat thinking of the questionnaire he had set for the *Police Gazette* (it seemed so long ago): 'If you could gladden your final days with one of the following . . .' Yes, without a doubt, if he'd been honest, Morse would have applauded Shelly Cornford's choice. And what the hell did it matter *where* she'd had those few last glasses of alcohol – few last 'units' rather – the measurements into which the dietitian had advised him to convert his old familiar gills and pints and quarts.

'Do you want to see her?'

Morse shook his head.

'You'd better see *him*, though.'

Morse nodded wearily. 'Is he all right?'

'We-ell. His GP's been in – but he refuses to take any medication. He's in the canteen with one of the sergeants. We've finished with him, really.'

'Tell me about it,' urged Morse.

Denis Cornford's voice was flat, almost mechanical, as he replied:

'On Sunday just before I met you in the pub she told me she'd been to bed with another man that morning. I hardly spoke to her after that. I slept in the spare room the last three nights.'

'The note?' asked Morse gently. 'Is that what she was referring to?'

'Yes.'

'Nothing to do with anything else?'

'No.'

'She was there, in your rooms, just before Chapel on Sunday, wasn't she?'

Cornford evinced no surprise.

'We'd had a few harsh words. She didn't want to see you.'

'Do you know who the other man was?'

'Yes. Clixby Bream.'

'*She* told you that, sir?'

'Yes.'

'So – so she couldn't have had anything to do with the Owens murder?'

'No. Nor could the Master.'

'Did *you* have anything to do with it?'

'No.'

'Why did you go to see Owens last Thursday?'

'I knew Owens a bit through various things I did for his newspaper. That night I had to go to Kidlington – I went on the bus – the Kidlington History Society – held at the school – "Effects of the Enclosure Acts in Oxfordshire" – seven o'clock to eight. He lived fairly near – five minutes' walk away. I'd done a three-part article for him on Mediaeval Oxford – Owens said it needed shortening a bit – we discussed some changes – no problems. I got a bus back to Oxford – about nine.'

'Why didn't you tell me you knew Owens?'

'I didn't want to get involved.'

'What will you do now?'

'I left a note for the Master about the election.' The voice was still monotonous; the mouth dry. 'I've withdrawn my nomination.'

'I'm so sorry about everything,' said Morse very quietly.

'Yes, I think you are, aren't you?'

Morse left the pale, bespectacled historian staring vaguely into a cup of cold tea, like a man who is temporarily anaesthetized against some overwhelming pain.

'It's a terrible business – terrible!'

The Master poured himself a single-malt Scotch.

'Drink, Chief Inspector?'

Morse shook his head.

'Won't you sit down?'

'No. I've only called to say that Dr Cornford has just told me everything – about you and his wife.'

'Mmm.'

'We shall have to get a statement from you.'

'Why is that?'

'The *time* chiefly, I suppose.'

'Is it really necessary?'

'There *was* a murder on that Sunday morning.'

'Mmm. Was she one of your suspects?'

Morse made no direct answer. 'She couldn't have been making love to you and murdering someone else at the same time.'

'No.' The bland features betrayed no emotion; yet

Morse was distastefully aware that the Master was hardly displeased with such a succinct, such an unequivocal assertion of Shelly Cornford's innocence, since by implication it was an assertion of his own.

'I understand that Dr Cornford has written to you, sir.'

'Exited from the lists, poor Denis, yes. That just leaves Julian Storrs. Good man though, Julian!'

Morse slowly walked to the door.

'What do you think about suicide, Sir Clixby?'

'In general?' The Master drained his tumbler, and thoughtfully considered the question. 'Aristotle, you know, thought suicide a form of cowardice – running away from troubles oneself and leaving all the heartache to everybody else. What do *you* think?'

Morse was conscious of a deep loathing for this smooth and odious man.

'I don't know what your particular heartache is, sir. You see I never met Mrs Cornford myself. But I'd be surprised if she was a coward. In fact, I've got the feeling she was a bit of a gutsy girl.' Morse stood beside the study door, his face drawn, his nostrils distended. 'And I'll tell you something else. She probably had far more guts in her little finger than you've ever had in the whole of your body!'

Lewis was waiting in the Jaguar outside the Porters' Lodge; and Morse quickly climbed into the passenger seat. His voice was still vicious:

'Get – me – out – of – here, Lewis!'

Chapter Fifty-Seven

Friday, 8 March

Those who are absent, by its means become present: correspondence is the consolation of life

(Voltaire, *Philosophical Dictionary*)

SERGEANT LEWIS had himself only just entered Morse's office when Jane came through with the post: six official-looking letters, opened, with appropriate previous correspondence paper-clipped behind them; one square white envelope, unopened, marked 'Private', and post-marked Oxford; and an airmail letter, also unopened, marked 'Personal', and postmarked 'Washington'.

Jane smiled radiantly at her boss.

'Why are you looking so cheerful?' queried Morse.

'Just nice to have you back, sir, that's all.'

Inside the white envelope was a card, the front showing an auburn-haired woman, in a white dress, reading a book; and Morse read the brief message inside:

Geoffrey Harris Ward
Radcliffe Infirmary
7 March 96

We all miss your miserable presence in the ward. If you haven't finished smoking, we shall never meet for that G&T you promised me. Look after yourself!

Affectionately
Janet (McQueen)

P.S. I looked through your old hospital records from <u>many</u> years ago. Know something? I found your Christian name!

'Why are *you* looking so cheerful?' asked Lewis.

But Morse made no answer, and indeed appeared to be reading the message again and again. Then he opened the letter from America.

Washington
4 March

Dear Morse,

Just read your thing in the Police Gazette. How did I know it was yours? Ah, I too was a detective! I'd have had the champagne myself. And I think the Fauré Requiem's a bit lightweight compared with the Verdi – in spite of the imprimatur of the Papacy. I know you've always wept to Wagner but I've alvays vept to Verdi myself – and the best Xmas present I had was the Karajan recording of Don Carlos.

I know you're frightened of flying, but a visit here – especially in the spring, they say – is something not to be missed in life. We'll get together again for a jar on my return (April) and don't leave it too long before you take your pension.

As aye,
Peter (Imbert)

Morse handed the letter across to Lewis.

'The old Metropolitan Commissioner!'

Morse nodded, rather proudly.

'Washington DC, that'll be, sir.'

'Where else?'

'Washington CD – County Durham, near enough.'

'Oh.'

'What's your programme today, sir?'

'Well, we've done most of the spadework—'

'Except the Harvey Clinic side of things.'

'And that's in hand, you say?'

'Seeing the woman this morning. She's just back from a few day's holiday.'

'Who's she again? Remind me.'

'I told you about her: Dawn Charles.'

'Mrs or Miss or Ms?'

'Not sure. But she's the main receptionist there. They say if anybody's likely to know what's going on, she is.'

'What time are you seeing her?'

'Ten o'clock. She's got a little flat out at Bicester on the Charles Church Estate. You joining me?'

'No, I don't think so. Something tells me I ought to see Storrs again.'

Lovingly Morse put the 'Girl Reading' (Perugini,

1878) back into her envelope, then looked through Sir Peter's letter once again.

Don Carlos.

The two words stood out and stared at him, at the beginning of a line as they were, at the end of a paragraph. Not an opera Morse knew well, *Don Carlos.* Another 'DC', though. It was amazing how many DCs had cropped up in their enquiries – and still another one just now in the District of Columbia. And suddenly in Morse's mind the name of the Verdi opera merged with a name he'd just heard: the 'Don' chiming in with the 'Dawn', and the 'Carlos' with the 'Charles'.

Was it *Dawn Charles* (Mrs or Miss or Ms) who held the key to the mystery? Did they belong to *her*, that pair of initials in the manila file?

Morse's eyes gleamed with excitement.

'I think,' he said slowly, 'Mr Julian Storrs will have to wait a little while. I shall be coming with you, Lewis – to Bicester.'

PART SIX

Chapter Fifty-Eight

The best liar is he who makes the smallest amount of lying go the longest way

(Samuel Butler, *Truth and Convenience*)

DAWN CHARLES looked nervous when she opened the door of her flat in Woodpecker Way and let the two detectives through into the grey-carpeted lounge, where the elder of the two, the white-haired one, was already complimenting her on such an attractive residence.

'Bit unlucky though, really. I bought it at the top of the property boom for fifty-eight thousand. Only worth thirty-four now.'

'Oh dear!'

The man made her feel uneasy. And her mind went back to the previous summer when on returning from France she'd put the Green Channel sticker on the windscreen – only to be diverted into the Red Channel; where pleasantly, far too pleasantly, she'd been questioned about her time abroad, about the weather, about anything and everything – except those extra thousand cigarettes in the back of the boot. It had been as if they were just stringing her along; knowing the truth all the time.

But these men couldn't possibly know the truth, that's what she was telling herself now; and she thought she could handle things. On Radio Oxford just before Christmas she'd heard P. D. James's advice to criminal suspects: 'Keep it short! Keep it simple! Don't change a single word unless you have to!'

'Please sit down. Coffee? I've only got instant, I'm afraid.'

'We both prefer instant, don't we, Sergeant?'

'Lovely,' said Lewis, who would much have preferred tea.

Two minutes later, Dawn held a jug suspended over the steaming cups.

'Milk?'

'Please,' from Lewis.

'Thank you,' from Morse.

'Sugar?'

'Just the one teaspoonful,' from Lewis.

But a shake of the head from Morse; a slight raising of the eyebrows as she stirred two heaped teaspoonfuls into her own coffee; and an obsequious comment which caused Lewis to squirm inwardly: 'How on earth do you manage to keep such a beautiful figure – with all that sugar?'

She coloured slightly. 'Something to do with the metabolic rate, so they tell me at the clinic.'

'Ah, yes! The clinic. I'd almost forgotten.'

Again he was sounding too much like the Customs man, and Dawn was glad it was the sergeant who now took over the questioning.

A little awkwardly, a little ineptly (certainly as Morse saw things) Lewis asked about her training, her past experience, her present position, her relationships with employers, colleagues, clients . . .

The scene was almost set.

She knew Storrs (she claimed) only as a patient; she'd known Turnbull (she claimed) only as a consultant; she knew Owens (she claimed) not at all.

Lewis produced the letter stating Julian Storrs' prognosis.

'Do you think this photocopy was made at the clinic?'

'I didn't copy it.'

'Someone must have done.'

'I didn't copy it.'

'Any idea who might have done?'

'*I* didn't copy it.'

It was hardly a convincing performance, and she was aware that both men knew she was lying. And quietly – amid a few tears, certainly, but with no hysteria – the truth came out.

Owens she had met when the Press had come along for the clinic's 25th anniversary – he must have seen something, heard something that night, about Mr Storrs. After Mr Turnbull had died, Owens had telephoned her – they'd met in the Bird and Baby in St Giles' – he'd asked her if she could copy a letter for him – yes, *that* letter – he'd offered her £500 – and she'd agreed – copied the letter – been paid in cash. That was it – that was all – a complete betrayal of trust, she knew that – something she'd never done before – would never have done in the normal course of events. It was just the money – nothing else – she'd desperately needed the money . . .

Morse had been silent throughout the interrogation, his attention focused, it seemed, on the long, black-stockinged legs.

'Where does that leave me – leave us?' she asked miserably.

'We shall have to ask you to come in to make an official statement,' said Lewis.

'Now, you mean?'

'That'll be best, yes.'

'Perhaps not,' intervened Morse. 'It's not *all* that urgent, Miss Charles. We'll be in touch fairly soon.'

At the door, Morse thanked her for the coffee: 'Not the best homecoming, I'm afraid.'

'Only myself to blame,' she said, her voice tight as she looked across at the Visitors' parking lots, where the Jaguar stood.

'Where did you go?' asked Morse.

'I didn't go anywhere.'

'You stayed here – in your flat?'

'I didn't go anywhere.'

'What was that about?' asked Lewis as he drove back along the A34 to Oxford. 'About her statement?'

'I want you to be with me when we see Storrs this afternoon.'

'What did you think of her?'

'Not a very good liar.'

'Lovely figure, though. Legs right up to her armpits! She'd have got a job in the chorus line at the Windmill.'

Morse was silent, his eyes gleaming again as Lewis continued:

'I read somewhere that they all had to be the same height and the same build – in the chorus line there.'

'Perhaps I'll take you along when the case is over.'

'No good, sir. It's been shut for ages.'

Dawn Charles closed the door behind her and walked thoughtfully back to the lounge, the suspicion of a smile about her lips.

Chapter Fifty-Nine

Everything in life is somewhere else, and you get there in a car

(E. B. White, *One Man's Meat*)

Lewis had backed into the first available space in Polstead Road, the tree-lined thoroughfare that leads westward from Woodstock Road into Jericho; and now stood waiting whilst Morse arose laboriously from the low passenger seat of the Jaguar.

'Seen *that* before, sir?' Lewis pointed to the circular blue plaque on the wall opposite: 'This house was the home of T. E. Lawrence (Lawrence of Arabia) from 1896–1921.'

Morse grunted as he straightened up his aching back, mumbling of lumbago.

'What about a plaque for Mr Storrs, sir? "This was the home of Julian Something Storrs, Master of Lonsdale, 1996 to . . . 1997?"'

Morse shrugged indifferently:

'Perhaps just 1996.'

The two men walked a little way along the short road. The houses here were of a pattern: gabled, red-bricked, three-storeyed properties, with ashlared, mullioned windows, the frames universally painted white; interesting and amply proportioned houses built towards the end of the nineteenth century.

'Wouldn't mind living here,' volunteered Lewis.

Morse nodded. 'Very civilized. Small large houses, these, Lewis, as opposed to large small houses.'

'What's the difference?'

'Something to do with the number of bathrooms, I think.'

'Not much to do with the number of garages!'

'No.'

Clearly nothing whatever to do with the number of garages, since the reason for the continuum of cars on either side of the road was becoming increasingly obvious: there *were* no garages here, nor indeed any room for such additions. To compensate for the inconvenience, the front areas of almost all the properties had been cemented, cobbled, gravelled, or paved, in order to accommodate the parking of motor cars; including the front of the Storrs' residence, where on the gravel alongside the front window stood a small, pale grey, D-registration Citroën, a thin pink stripe around its bodywork.

'Someone's in?' ventured Morse.

'Mrs Storrs, perhaps – he's got a BMW. A woman's car, that, anyway.'

'Really?'

Morse was still peering through the Citroën's front window (perhaps for some more eloquent token of femininity) when Lewis returned from his ineffectual ringing.

'No one in. No answer, anyway.'

'On another weekend break?'

'I could ring the Porters' Lodge.'

'You do that small thing, Lewis. I'll be . . .' Morse pointed vaguely towards the hostelry at the far end of the road.

It was at the Anchor, a few minutes later, as Morse sat behind a pint of John Smith's Tadcaster bitter, that Lewis came in to report on the Storrs: away again, for the weekend, the pair of them, this time though their whereabouts not vouchsafed to the Lodge.

Morse received the news without comment, appearing preoccupied; *thinking* no doubt, supposed Lewis, as he paid for his orange juice. Thinking and drinking . . . drinking and thinking . . . the twin activities which in Morse's view were ever and necessarily concomitant.

Not wholly preoccupied, however.

'I'll have a refill while you're at the bar, Lewis. Smith's please.'

After a period of silence, Morse asked the question:

'If somebody came to you with a letter – a photocopied letter, say – claiming your missus was having a passionate affair with the milkman – '

Lewis grinned. 'I'd be dead worried. We've got a woman on the milk-float.'

' – what would you do?'

'Read it, obviously. See who'd written it.'

'Show it to the missus?'

'Only if it was a joke.'

'How would you know that?'

'Well, you wouldn't really, would you? Not for a start. You'd try to find out if it was genuine.'

'Exactly. So when Storrs got a copy of that letter, a letter he'd pretty certainly not seen before—'

'Unless Turnbull showed it to him?'

'Doubt it. A death certificate, wasn't it? He'd want to let Storrs down a bit more gently than that.'

'You mean, if Storrs tried to find out if it *was* genuine, he'd probably go along to the clinic . . .'

Morse nodded, like some benevolent schoolmaster encouraging a promising pupil.

'And show it to . . . Dawn Charles?'

'Who else? She's the sort of Practice Manager there, if anybody is. And let's be honest about things. You're not exactly an expert in the Socratic skills yourself, are you? But how long did it take *you* to get the truth out of her? Three or four minutes?'

'You think Storrs did it as well?'

'Pretty certainly, I'd say. He's nobody's fool; and he's not going to give in to blackmail just on somebody's vague say-so. He's an academic; and if you're an academic you're trained to *check* – check your sources, check your references, check your evidence.'

'So perhaps Storrs has been a few steps in front of us all the time.'

Morse nodded. 'He probably rumbled our receptionist straightaway. Not *many* suspects there at the clinic.'

Slowly Lewis sipped his customary orange juice, his earlier euphoria fading.

'We're not exactly galloping towards the finishing-post, are we?'

Morse looked up, his blue eyes betraying some considerable surprise.

'Why do you say that, Lewis? That's exactly what we *are* doing.'

Chapter Sixty

Saturday, 9 March

Hombre apercebido medio combatido
(A man well prepared has already half fought the battle)
(Cervantes, *Don Quixote*)

SOMEWHAT CONCERNED about the adequacy of the Jaguar's petrol allowance, Morse had requisitioned an unmarked police car, which just before 10 a.m. was heading south along the A34, with Sergeant Lewis at the wheel. As they approached Abingdon, Morse asked Lewis to turn on Classic FM; and almost immediately asked him to turn it off, as he recognized the Brandenburg Concerto No. 2.

'Somebody once said, Lewis, that it was not impossible to get bored even in the presence of a mistress, and I'm sorry to say I sometimes get a little bored even in the company of Johann Sebastian Bach.'

'Really. I thought it was rather nice.'

'Lew-is! He may be terrific; he may be terrible – but he's never *nice*. Not Bach!'

Lewis concentrated on the busy road ahead as Morse sank back into his seat and, as was ever his wont in a car, said virtually nothing for the rest of the journey.

And yet Morse had said so many things – things upon

which Lewis's mind intermittently focused again, as far too quickly he drove down to the Chieveley junction with the M4 . . .

Once back from Polstead Road, Friday afternoon had been very busy and, for Lewis, very interesting. It had begun with Morse asking about their present journey.

'If you had a posh car, which way would you go to Bath?'

'A34, M4, A46 – probably the best; the quickest, certainly.'

'What if you had an old banger?'

'Still go the same way, I think.'

'What's wrong with the Burford–Cirencester way?'

'Nothing at all, if you like a bit of scenery. Or if you don't like motorway-driving.'

Then another question:

'How do we find out which bank the Storrs use?'

'Could be they have different banks, sir. Shouldn't be too difficult, though: Lloyds, Barclays, NatWest, Midland . . . Shall I ring around?'

Morse nodded. 'And try to find out how they've been spending their money recently – if it's possible.'

'May take a bit of time, but I don't see why not. Let me find out anyway.'

Lewis turned to go, but Morse had a further request.

'Before you do, bring me the notes you made about the Storrs' stay in Bath last weekend. I'm assuming you've typed 'em up by now?'

'All done. Maybe a few spelling mistakes – a few grammatical lapses – beautifully typed, though.'

It had taken Lewis only ten minutes to discover that Mr Julian Storrs and Mrs Angela Storrs both banked at Lloyds. But there had been far greater difficulty in dealing with Morse's supplementary request.

The Manager of Lloyds (Headington Branch) had been fully co-operative but of only limited assistance. It was very unusual of course, but not in cases such as this *unethical*, for confidential material concerning clients to be disclosed. But Lewis would have to contact Lloyds Inspection Department in Bristol.

Which Lewis had promptly done, again receiving every co-operation; also, however, receiving the disappointing news that the information required was unlikely as yet to be fully ready. With credit-card facilities now almost universally available, the volume of transactions was ever growing; and with receipt-items sometimes irregularly forwarded from retail outlets, and with a few inevitable checks and delays in processing and clearance – well, it would take a little time.

'Later this afternoon?' Lewis had queried hopefully.

'No chance of that, I'm afraid.'

'Tomorrow morning?'

Lewis heard a deep sigh at the other end of the line. 'We don't usually . . . It *is* very urgent, you say?'

*

The phone had been ringing in Morse's office (an office minus Morse) and Lewis had taken the brief call. The post-mortem on Shelly Cornford confirmed death from carbon-monoxide poisoning, and completely ruled out any suspicion of foul play.

A note on yellow paper was Sellotaped to the desk:

> Lewis!
> – Just off to the Diab. Centre (3.45)
> – Yr notes on Bath most helpful, but try to get Sarah Siddons right – two d's, please.
> – Good job we're getting a few facts straight before jumping too far ahead. Reculer pour mieux sauter!
> – We'll be jumping tomorrow a.m. tho' – to Bath. Royal Crescent informs me the Storrs – Herr und Frau – are staying there again!
> – I need yr notes on Julian Storrs.
> – Ring me at home – after the Archers.
>
> M

And on the side of the desk, a letter from the Thame and District Diabetic Association addressed to Det. Chief Inspector Morse:

Dear sir,

Welcome to the Club! Sorry to be so quick off the mark but news travels fast in diabetic circles.

We meet on the first Thursday of each month 7.30–9 p.m. in the Town Hall in Thame and we shall be delighted if you can come to speak to us. We can offer no fee but we can offer a warm-hearted and grateful audience.

During this last year we have been fortunate to welcome several very well-known people. For example our last six speakers have been Dr David Matthews, Lesley Hallett, Professor Harry Keane, Angela Storrs, Dr Robert Turner, and Willie Rushton.

Please try to support us if you can. For our 1996/7 programme we are still looking for speakers for October '96 and February '97. Any hope of you filling one of these slots?

I enclose SAE and thank you for your kind consideration . . .

But Lewis read only the first few lines, for never, except in the course of a criminal investigation, had he wittingly read a letter meant for the eyes of another person . . .

From the passenger seat Morse had still said nothing until Lewis, after turning off the M4 at Junction 18 on to the A46, was within a few miles of Bath.

'Lewis! If you had a mistress – '

'Not the milk-lady, sir. She's far too fat for me.'

' – and, say, you were having a weekend away together and you told your missus that you were catching the train but in fact this woman was going to pick you up in her car somewhere – The Randolph, say . . .'

'Yes, sir?' (Was Morse getting lost?)

'Would you still *go* to the railway station? Would you

make sure she picked you up *at* the railway station – not The Randolph?'

'Dunno, sir. I've never—'

'I know you haven't,' snapped Morse. 'Just *think*, man!'

So Lewis thought. And *thought* he saw what Morse was getting at.

'You mean it might make you feel a bit better in your own mind – feel a bit less guilty, like – if you did what you *said* you'd be doing – before you went?' (Was Lewis getting lost?)

'Something like that,' said Morse unenthusiastically as a sign welcomed the two detectives to the Roman City of Bath.

As soon as Lewis had stopped outside the Royal Crescent Hotel, Morse rang through on the mobile phone to the Deputy Manager, as had been agreed. No problem, it appeared. The Storrs had gone off somewhere an hour or so earlier in the BMW. The coast was clear; and Morse got out of the car and walked round to the driver's window.

'Good luck in Bristol!'

Lewis raised two crossed fingers of his right hand, like the logo of the National Lottery, as Morse continued:

'If you find what I *hope* you're going to find, the battle's half won. And it's mostly thanks to you.'

'No! It was you who figured it all out.'

'Wouldn't have done, though, without all those visits of yours to Soho.'

'Pardon, sir?'

'To see the chorus line, Lewis! The chorus line at the Windmill.'

'But I've never—'

'"Legs right up to her armpits," you said, right? And that was the *second* time you'd used those words, Lewis. Remember?'

CHAPTER SIXTY-ONE

Life, within doors, has few pleasanter prospects than a neatly arranged and well-provisioned breakfast table
(Nathaniel Hawthorne, *The House of the Seven Gables*)

MORSE STOOD FOR some while on the huge slabs that form the wide pavement stretching along the whole extent of the great 500-foot curve of cinnamon-coloured stone, with its identical façades of double Ionic columns, which comprise Bath's Royal Crescent. It seemed to him a breathtaking architectural masterpiece, with the four-star hotel exactly at its centre: Number 16.

He walked between the black spiked railings, through the white double-doors, into the black-and-white floor-tiled, high-ceilinged entrance hall, and then to reception, where he was immediately ushered into the beige-carpeted, pine-furnished office of the Deputy Manager, just beyond.

Sara Hickman was from Leicestershire, a tall, slimly attractive woman in her mid-thirties, with green eyes (just like Sister McQueen) and dark curly hair. She was dressed in a business-like suit; she spoke in a business-like manner; and so very clearly was she part of an extremely business-like hotel, since manifold awards – RAC Blue Ribbons, AA Rosettes, Egon Ronay Stars – vied with each other for space around the walls.

After hesitating, finally capitulating, over the offer of coffee, Morse soon found himself listening very carefully.

Sara had (she told him) been able to re-interview almost all of the service personnel who had been on duty the previous weekend, most of whom, as it happened, were performing similar duties that present weekend. But there seemed little to add, at least in general terms, to the details earlier communicated by the Manager himself to the Thames Valley Police. One minor correction: the room the Storrs had slept in was a Standard Twin, not a Standard Double; and in fact the couple had asked for the same room again, if it was available. Which, by some strange coincidence, it was: the only Standard Twin still available in the hotel that weekend. Registration? She passed to Morse the card dated the previous Saturday, 2.3.96: Guest's Name; Address; Telephone No.; Arrival Date; Departure Date; Nationality; Payment Type; Passport No.; Signature; Car Reg. No. – and more. All filled in with a neat, feminine, slightly forward-leaning script, in black Biro; and signed 'Angela Storrs'. It would be comparatively easy to check, of course; but Morse had little or no doubt that the signature was genuine.

'The Manager told my sergeant, when he rang about last weekend, that we might be able to see some itemized bills?'

Sara Hickman smiled.

'I thought somehow you might ask for them,' she said, and now read aloud from a small sheaf of bills in front of her.

'Last Saturday night they ate at Table twenty-six, in the far corner of the restaurant. He had the Carpaccio of Beef, Truffled Noodles, and Parmesan, for his starter; for his main course, the Seabass served with Creamed Celeriac and Fennel Liqueur; Passion Fruit Mousse for sweet. *She* wasn't quite so adventurous, I'm afraid: Consommé; with Baked Plaice and Green Salad for her main course; and then cream-crackers and Edam – the waiter particularly remembers her asking for the Edam.'

'Good low-fat cheese they tell me,' mumbled Morse, recalling his own hard-nosed dietitian's homily in the Geoffrey Harris Ward. And he was smiling vaguely to himself as the Deputy Manager continued:

'Now, Sunday morning. Mr Storrs had ordered breakfasts for the two of them over the phone the previous night – at about eleven, half past – can't be sure. He said he thought he was probably too late with the form, but he obviously had it in front of him – the night-porter remembers that. He said he'd have a Full English for himself, no kidney though, with the tomato well grilled, and two fried eggs. Said his wife would go for a Continental: said she'd like cereal, Ricicles, if we'd got some – Chief Inspector, we've got a bigger selection of cereals than Sainsbury's! – some brown toast and honey, the fresh-fruit compôte, and orange juice. Oh, yes' (Sara checked the form again) 'and hot chocolate.'

'The time?' asked Morse.

'It would have been between seven-thirty and eight. We don't serve Full English until after seven-thirty – and both breakfasts went up together.'

'And last night for dinner?'

'They didn't eat here.'

'This morning?'

'They had breakfast in their room again. This time they filled in the form early, and left it on the door-knob outside the room. Same as before for Mr Storrs—'

'How do you know it wasn't for *her*?'

'Well, it's exactly what he ordered before. Here, look for yourself.'

She passed the room-service order across the desk; and Morse saw the instructions: 'Well grilled' against 'Tomato'; no tick against 'Kidney'; the figure '2' against 'Eggs (fried)'.

'I see what you mean,' admitted Morse. 'Not even married couples have exactly the same tastes, I suppose.'

'*Especially* married couples,' said Sara Hickman quietly.

Morse's eyes continued down the form, to the Continental section, and saw the ticks against 'Weetabix' ('semi-skimmed milk' written beside it), 'Natural Yoghurt', 'Toast (brown)', 'Coffee (decaffeinated)'. The black-Biro'd writing was the same as that on the registration form. Angela Storrs' writing. Certainly.

'I shall have to have copies of these forms,' said Morse.

'Of course.' Sara got to her feet. 'I'll see that's done straightaway. Shall we go over to the bar?'

The day was brightening.

But for Morse the day had already been wonderfully bright; had been for the past hour or so, ever since the Deputy Manager had been speaking with him.

And indeed was very shortly to be brighter still.

Chapter Sixty-Two

Queen Elizabeth the First Slept Here
(Notice which according to the British Tourist Board
is to be observed in approximately 2400 residences
in the United Kingdom)

THEY WALKED ACROSS the splendidly tended garden area behind the main complex to the Dower House, an elegant annexe wherein were situated most of the hotel's suites and bedrooms, as well as the restaurant, the main lounge – and the bar.

Immediately inside the entrance, Morse saw the plaque (virtually a statutory requirement in Bath) commemorating a particularly eminent royal personage:

George IV
1820–1830
Resided here
1799
as
Prince of Wales

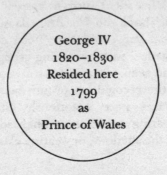

In the lounge, Morse sat down amid the unashamedly luxurious surroundings of elaborate wall-lights, marble busts – and courteously prompt service, for a uniformed waitress was already standing beside them.

'What would you like to drink, sir?'

Lovely question.

As he waited for his beer, Morse looked around him; and in particular at the portrait above the fireplace there: 'Lord Ellmore, 1765–1817', the inscription read, a fat-cheeked, smooth-faced man, with a protruding lower lip, who reminded Morse unhappily of Sir Clixby Bream.

Then he walked through to the Gents in the corridor just off the lounge where the two loos stood side by side, the Men's and the Ladies' logos quite unequivocally distinct on their adjacent doors.

It would have been difficult even for the myopic Mrs Adams to confuse the two, thought Morse, as he smiled and mouthed a few silent words to himself:

'Thank you! Thank you, Mrs Arabella Adams!'

It wasn't that she could have been certain – from some little distance? with her failing eyesight? – that the person she had seen was a man or a woman. Certainly not so far as the recognition of any facial features was concerned. Faces were notoriously difficult to distinguish, appearing so different when seen in profile, perhaps, or in the shadows, or wearing glasses. No! It was just that old Mrs Adams had always known what men looked like, and what women looked like, since habitually the men wore trousers and the women wore skirts. But of course if someone wore trousers, that certainly didn't prove that the wearer was a man, now did it, Morse? In fact it proved one thing and one thing *only*: that the person in question was wearing trousers!

Ten minutes later, as he worked his way with diminishing enthusiasm through an over-generous plateful of smoked-salmon sandwiches, Morse saw Sergeant Lewis appear in the doorway – a Lewis looking almost as self-satisfied as the oily Lord Ellmore himself – and raise his right thumb, before being introduced to Sara Hickman.

'Something to drink, Sergeant?'

'Thank you. Orange juice, please.'

'Something to eat?'

'What have you got?'

She smiled happily. 'Anything. Anything you like. Our Head Chef is at your command.'

'Can he rustle up some eggs and chips?'

She said she was sure – well, almost sure – that he could, and departed to investigate.

'Lew-is! This is a cordon bleu establishment.'

'Should taste good then, sir.'

The buoyant Lewis passed a note to Morse, simultaneously (and much to Morse's relief) helping himself to a couple of sandwiches.

'You don't mind, sir? I'm half starving.'

*

At 2.30 p.m. Marilyn Hudson, a small, fair-complexioned young woman, was called into Sara's office. Marilyn had been a chamber-cum-kitchenmaid at the hotel for almost three years; and it was soon clear that she knew as much as anyone was likely to know about the day-to-day – and night-by-night – activities there.

Morse now questioned her closely about the morning of the previous Sunday, 3 March.

'You took them breakfast?'

'Yes, sir. About quarter to eight.'

'You knocked on the door?'

'Like I always do, yes. I heard somebody say "Come in" so I—'

'You had a key?'

'I've got a master-key. So I took the tray in and put it on the dressing-table.'

'Were they in bed together?'

'No. Twin beds it is there. She was on the far side. Difficult to miss her, though.'

'Why do you say that?'

'Well, it was her *pyjamas* – yellow an' black an' green stripes – up an' down.'

'Vertical stripes, you mean?'

'I'm not sure about that, sir. Just up an' down, like I said. An' she's got the same pair now. I took their breakfast again this morning. Same room – thirty-six.' Marilyn gave a nervous little giggle. 'Perhaps it's time she changed them.'

'She may have got two pairs,' interposed Lewis – not particularly helpfully, judging from the scowl on Morse's face.

'Do you think it *could* have been anybody else – except Mrs Storrs?'

'No, sir. Like I say, she was there in the bed. But . . .'

'But what?'

'Well, I saw *her* all right. But I didn't really see *him*. He was in the bathroom having a shave – electric razor it was – and the door was open a bit and I saw he was still in his pyjamas and he said thank you but . . .'

'Would you have recognized him if he'd turned his head?'

For the first time Marilyn Hudson seemed unsure of herself.

'Well, I'd seen them earlier in the hotel, but I didn't notice him as much as her really. She was, you know, ever so dressy and smart – dark glasses she wore – and a white trouser-suit. Same thing as she's got on today.'

Morse turned to Lewis. 'Do you think she's got *two* white trouser-suits, Sergeant?'

'Always a possibility, sir.'

'So' (if Morse was experiencing some disappointment, he gave no indication of it) 'what you're telling us is that you're pretty sure it was her, but not quite so sure it was *him*?'

Marilyn considered the question a while before replying:

'No. I'm *pretty* sure it was both of them, sir.'

'Good girl, our Marilyn,' confided Sara, 'even if her vocabulary's a bit limited.'

Morse looked across at her quizzically:

'Vertical and horizontal, you mean? I shouldn't worry about that. I've always had trouble with east and west myself.'

'Lots of people have trouble with right and left,' began Lewis – but Morse was already making a further request:

'You've still got the details of who was staying here last Saturday?'

'Of course. Just a minute.'

She returned shortly with a sheaf of registration cards; and Morse was looking through, flicking them over one at a time – when suddenly he stopped, the familiar tingling of excitement across his shoulders.

He handed the card to Lewis.

And Lewis whistled softly, incredulously, as he read the name.

Morse turned again to Sara. 'Can you let us have a copy of the bill – account, whatever you call it – for Room fifteen?'

'You were right then, sir!' whispered Lewis excitedly. 'You always said it was "DC"!'

Sarah came back and laid the account in front of Morse.

'Single room – number fifteen. Just the one night. Paid by credit card.'

Morse looked through the items.

'No evening meal?'

'No.'

'No breakfast either?'

'No.'

'Look! Can we use your phone from here?'

'Of course you can. Shall I leave you?'

'Yes, I think so,' said Morse, 'if you don't mind.'

Morse and Lewis emerged from the office some twenty minutes later; and were walking behind reception when one of the guests came through from the entrance hall and asked for the key to Room 36.

Then he saw Morse.

'Good God! What are *you* doing here?' asked Julian Storrs.

'I was just going to ask you exactly the same question,' replied Morse, with a curiously confident smile.

CHAPTER SIXTY-THREE

'Why did you murder those workmen in 1893?'
'It wasn't in 1893. It was in '92.'
(Quoted by H. H. Asquith)

'DO YOU WANT my wife to be here as well? I dropped her in the city centre to do a bit of shopping. But she shouldn't be long – if that's what you want?'

'We'd rather talk to you alone, sir.'

'What's this bloody "sir" got to do with things?'

The three of them – Storrs, Morse, Lewis – were seated in Room 36, a pleasingly spacious room, whose windows overlooked the hotel's pool and the sodden-looking croquet-green.

'What's all this about anyway?' Storrs' voice was already sounding a little weary, increasingly tetchy. 'Can we get on with it?'

So Morse got on with it, quickly sketching in the background to the two murders under investigation:

Storrs had been having an affair with Rachel James – and Rachel James had been murdered.

Storrs had been blackmailed by Owens – and Owens had been murdered.

The grounds for this blackmail were three-fold: his extramarital relationship with Ms James; his dishonest concealment of his medical prognosis; and his wife's earlier career as striptease dancer and Soho call-girl. For these reasons, it would surely have been very strange had Storrs not figured somewhere near the top of the suspect list.

As far as the first murder was concerned, Storrs – both the Storrs – had an alibi: they had been in bed with each other. How did one break that sort of alibi?

As far as the second murder was concerned, Storrs – again *both* Storrs – had their alibis: but this time not only were they in the same bedroom together, but also eighty-odd miles away from the scene of the crime. In fact, in the very room where they were now. But alibis could be fabricated; and if so, they could be broken. Sometimes they *were* broken.

(Storrs was listening in silence.)

Means? Forensic tests had established that both murders had been committed with the same weapon – a pistol known as the Howdah, often used by senior ranks in the armed forces, especially in India, where Storrs had served until returning to Oxford. He had acquired such a pistol; probably still had it, unless he had got rid of it recently – *very* recently.

The predominant cause – the Prime Mover – for the whole tragic sequence of events had been his obsessive, overweening ambition to gain the ultimate honour during what was left to him of his lifetime – the Mastership of Lonsdale, with the virtually inevitable accolade of a knighthood.

Motive, then? Yes.

Means? Yes.

Opportunity, though?

For the first murder, transport from Polstead Road to Kidlington was easy enough – there were *two* cars. But the target had not been quite so easy. In fact, it might well have been that Rachel James was murdered mistakenly, because of a mix-up over house-numbers and a pony-tailed silhouette.

But for the second murder, planning had to be far more complicated – and clever. Perhaps the 'in-bed-together' alibi might sound a little thin the second time. But not if he was in a bed in some distant place; not if he was openly *observed* in that distant place at the time the murder must have been committed. No one had ever been in two places at the same time: that would be an affront to the rules by which the Almighty had established the universe. But the distance from Oxford to Bath was only eighty-odd miles. And in a powerful car, along the motorway, on a Sunday morning, early . . . An hour, say? Pushing it, perhaps? An hour and a quarter, then – two and a half hours on the road. Then there was a murder to be committed, of course. Round it up to three hours, say.

During the last few minutes of Morse's exposition, Storrs had walked across to the window, where he stood looking out over the garden. The afternoon had clouded, with the occasional spatter of rain across the panes. Storrs was humming quietly to himself; and Morse recognized the tune of "September', one of Richard Strauss's *Four Last Songs*:

> *Der Garten trauert*
> *Kühl sinkt in die Blumen der Regen . . .*

Then, abruptly, Storrs turned round.

'You do realize what you're saying?' he asked quietly.

'I think I do,' replied Morse.

'Well, let's get a few things straight, shall we? Last Sunday my wife Angela and I had breakfast here, in this room, at about a quarter to eight. The same young girl brought us breakfast this morning, as it happens. She'll remember.'

Morse nodded. 'She's not quite sure it was *you*, though, last Sunday. She says you were shaving at the time, in the bathroom.'

'Who the hell *was* it then? If it wasn't me?'

'Perhaps you'd got back by then.'

'Back? Back from Oxford? How did I manage that? Three hours, you say? I must have left at half past four!'

'You had a car—'

'Have you checked all this? You see, my car was in the hotel garage – and God knows where *that* is. I left it outside when we booked in, and gave the keys to one of the porters. That's the sort of thing you pay for in places like this – didn't you know that?'

Again Morse nodded. 'You're right. The garage wasn't opened up that morning until ten minutes to nine.'

'So?' Storrs looked puzzled.

'You could have driven someone else's car.'

'Whose, pray?'

'Your wife's, perhaps?'

Storrs snorted. 'Which just *happened* to be standing outside the hotel – is that it? A helicopter-lift from Polstead Road?'

'I don't know,' admitted Morse.

'All right. Angela's car's there waiting for me, yes? How did I get out of the hotel? There's only the one exit, so I must have slipped unnoticed past a sleeping night-porter—' He stopped. 'Have you checked up whether the front doors are locked after midnight?'

'Yes, we've checked.'

'And are they?'

'They are.'

'So?' Again Storrs appeared puzzled.

'So the only explanation is that you weren't in the hotel that night at all,' said Morse slowly.

'Really? And who signed the bloody bill on Sunday – what – ten o'clock? Quarter past?'

'Twenty past. We've tried to check everything. You signed the bill, sir, using your own Lloyds Visa Card.'

Suddenly Storrs turned his back and stared out of the rain-flecked window once more:

'Look! You must forgive me. I've been leading you up the garden path, I'm afraid. But it was extremely interesting hearing your story. Outside, just to the left – we can't quite see it from here – is what the splendid brochure calls its "outdoor heated exercise plunge pool". I was there that morning. I was there just after breakfast – about half past eight. Not just me, either. There was a rich American couple who were staying in the Beau Nash suite. They came from North Carolina, as I recall, and we must have been there together for twenty minutes or so. Want to know what we were talking about? Bosnia. Bloody Bosnia! Are you satisfied? You say you've tried to check everything. Well, just – check – that! And now, if you don't mind, my dear wife appears to be back. I just hope she's not spent— Good God! She's bought herself *another* coat!'

Lewis, who had himself remained silent throughout the interview, walked across to the rain-flecked window, and saw Mrs Storrs standing beneath the porchway across the garden, wearing a headscarf, dark glasses, and a long expensive-looking white mackintosh. She appeared to be having some little difficulty unfurling one of the large gaudy umbrellas which the benevolent management left in clumps around the buildings for guests to use when needed – needed as now, for the rain had come on more heavily.

Morse, too, got to his feet and joined Lewis at the window, where Storrs was quietly humming that tune again.

Der Garten trauert . . .

The garden is mourning . . .

'Would you and your good lady like to join me for a drink, sir? In the bar downstairs?'

Chapter Sixty-Four

Hypoglycaemia (n): abnormal reduction of sugar content of the blood – for Diabetes sufferers a condition more difficult to spell than to spot

(*Small's Enlarged English Dictionary*, 17th Edition)

'WHAT DO YOU think they're talking about up there, sir?'

'He's probably telling her what to say.'

Morse and Lewis were seated side-by-side in the Dower House lounge – this time with their backs turned on Lord Ellmore, since two dark-suited men sat drinking coffee in front of the fireplace.

Julian Storrs and a black-tied waiter appeared almost simultaneously.

'Angela'll be down in a minute. Just changing. Got a bit wet shopping.'

'*Before* she bought the coat, I hope, sir,' said Lewis.

Storrs gave a wry smile, and the waiter took their order.

'Large Glenfiddich for me,' said Storrs. 'Two pieces of ice.'

Morse clearly approved. 'Same for me. What'll you have, Lewis?'

'Does the budget run to an orange juice?'

'And' (Morse turned to Storrs) 'what can we get for your wife?'

'Large gin and slim-line tonic. And put 'em all on my bill, waiter. Room thirty-six.'

Morse made no protestation; and Lewis smiled quietly to himself. It was his lucky day.

'Ah! "Slim-line tonic",' repeated Morse. 'Cuts out the sugar, I believe.'

Storrs made no comment, and Morse continued:

'I know your wife's diabetic, sir. We checked up. We even checked up on what you both had to eat last weekend.'

'Well done!'

'Only one thing puzzles me really: your wife's breakfast on Sunday morning.' He gestured to Lewis, the latter now reading from his notebook:

'Ricicles – that's sort of sugar-frosted toasted rice – my kids used to love 'em, sir – toast and honey, a fruit cocktail, orange juice, and then some hot chocolate.'

'Not, perhaps,' added Morse, 'the kind of breakfast a diabetic would normally order, is it? All that sugar? Everything else she ate here was out of the latest diabetic cook-book.'

'Do you know anything *about* diabetes, Chief Inspector?'

It was a new voice, sharp and rather harsh – for Angela Storrs, dressed in the inevitable trouser-suit (lime-green, this time), but most unusually minus the dark glasses, had obviously caught some (most?) of the previous conversation.

'Not much,' admitted Morse as he sought to rise from his deep, low chair. 'I've only been diagnosed a week.'

'Please don't get up!' It sounded more an order than a request.

She took a seat next to her husband on the sofa. 'I've had diabetes for ten years myself. But you'll learn soon enough. You see, one of the biggest dangers for insulin-dependent diabetics is not, as you might expect, excessively high levels of blood sugar, but excessively *low* levels: hypoglycaemia, it's called. Are you on insulin yourself?'

'Yes, and they did try to tell me something about—'

'You're asking about last weekend. Let me tell you. On Saturday evening my blood sugar was low – *very* low; and when Julian asked me about breakfast I decided to play things safe. I did have some glucose with me; but I was still low on Sunday morning. And if it's of any interest, I thoroughly enjoyed my sugary breakfast. A rare treat!'

The drinks had arrived.

'Look!' she continued, once the waiter had asked for her husband's signature on the bill. 'Let me be honest with you. Julian has just told me why you're here. He'd already told me about everything else anyway: about his ridiculous affair with that young Rachel woman; about that slimy specimen Owens.'

'Did you hate him enough to murder him?'

'*I* did,' interrupted Storrs vehemently. 'God rot his soul!'

'And about this Mastership business?' Morse looked from one to the other. 'You were in that together?'

It was Julian Storrs who answered. 'Yes, we were. I told Angela the truth immediately, about my illness, and we agreed to cover it all up. You see' (suddenly he was looking very tired) 'I wanted it so much. I wanted it more than anything – didn't I, Angela?'

She smiled, and gently laid her own hand over his. 'And *I* did too, Julian.'

Morse drained his whisky, and thirsted for another.

'Mrs Storrs, I'm going to ask you a very blunt question – and you must forgive me, because that's my job. What would you say if I told you that you didn't sleep with your husband last Saturday night – that you slept with another man?'

She smiled again; and for a few moments the angularity of her face had softened into the lineaments of a much younger woman.

'I'd just hope he was a good lover.'

'But you'd deny it?'

'A childish accusation like that? It's hardly worth denying!'

Morse turned to Storrs. 'And you, sir? What would you say if I told you that *you* didn't sleep with your wife last Saturday night – that you slept with another woman?'

'I'd just hope *she* was a good lover, I suppose.'

'But you'd deny it, too?'

'Of course.'

'Anything *else* you want to check?' asked Angela Storrs.

'Well, just the one thing really, because I'm still not quite sure that I've got it right.' Morse took a deep breath, and exhaled rather noisily. 'You say you came here with your husband in his BMW, latish last Saturday afternoon – stayed here together overnight – then drove straight back to Oxford together the next morning. Is that right, Mrs Storrs?'

'Not quite, no. We drove back via Cirencester and Burford. In fact, we had a bite of lunch at a pub in Burford and we had a look in two or three antiques shops there. I nearly bought a silver toast-rack, but Julian thought it was grossly overpriced.'

'I see . . . I see . . . In that case, it's about time we told you something else,' said Morse slowly. 'Don't you think so, Sergeant Lewis?'

Chapter Sixty-Five

'Is this a question?'
(from an Oxford entrance examination)

'If it is, this could be an answer.'
(one candidate's reply)

APART FROM themselves and the two men still drinking coffee, the large lounge was now empty.

'Perhaps we could all do with another drink?' It was Morse's suggestion.

'Not for me,' said Angela Storrs.

'I'm all right, thank you,' said Julian Storrs.

'Still finishing this one,' said Lewis.

Morse felt for the cellophaned packet; and almost fell. He stared for a while out of the windows: heavy rain now, through which a hotel guest occasionally scuttled across to the Dower House, head and face wholly indistinguishable beneath one of the gay umbrellas. How easy it was to hide when it was raining!

Almost reluctantly, it seemed, Morse made the penultimate revelation:

'There was someone else staying here last Saturday

night, someone I think both of you know. She was staying – yes, it was a woman! – in the main part of the hotel, across there in Room fifteen. That woman was Dawn Charles, the receptionist at the Harvey Clinic in Banbury Road.'

Storrs turned to his wife. 'Good heavens! Did you realize that, darling?'

'Don't be silly! I don't even *know* the woman.'

'It's an extraordinarily odd coincidence, though,' persisted Morse. 'Don't you think so?'

'Of course it's odd,' replied Angela Storrs. '*All* coincidences are odd – by definition! But life's full of coincidences.'

(Lewis smiled inwardly. How often had he heard those selfsame words from Morse.)

'But this *wasn't* a coincidence, Mrs Storrs.'

It was Julian Storrs who broke the awkward, ominous silence that had fallen on the group.

'I don't know what that's supposed to mean. All I'm saying is that *I* didn't see her. Perhaps she's a Fauré fan herself and came for the Abbey concert like we did. You'll have to ask *her*, surely?'

'If we do,' said Morse simply, confidently, 'it won't be long before we learn the truth. She's not such a competent liar as you are, sir – as the *pair* of you are!'

The atmosphere had become almost dangerously tense as Storrs got to his feet. 'I am *not* going to sit here one minute longer and listen—'

'Sit down!' said his wife, with an authority so assertive that one of the coffee-drinkers turned his head briefly in her direction as Morse continued:

'You both deny seeing Miss Charles whilst she was here?'

'Yes.'

'Yes.'

'Thank you. Sergeant? Please?'

Lewis re-opened his notebook, and addressed Mrs Storrs directly:

'So it couldn't possibly have been you, madam, who filled a car with petrol at Burford on that Saturday afternoon?'

'*Last* Saturday? Certainly not!' She almost spat the words at her new interlocutor.

But Lewis appeared completely unabashed. 'Have you lost your credit card recently?'

'Why do you ask that?'

'Because someone made a good job of signing your name, that's all. For twelve pounds of Unleaded Premium at the Burford Garage on the A40 at about three o'clock last Saturday.'

'What exactly are you suggesting?' The voice sounded menacingly calm.

'I'm suggesting that you drove here to Bath that day in your own car, madam—'

But she had risen to her feet herself now.

'You were right, Julian. We are *not* going to sit here a second longer. Come along!'

But she got no further than the exit, where two men stood barring her way: two dark-suited men who had been sitting for so long beneath the portrait of the bland Lord Ellmore.

She turned round, her nostrils flaring, her wide naked

eyes now blazing with fury; and perhaps (as Morse saw them) with hatred, too, and despair.

But she said nothing further, as Lewis walked quietly towards her.

'Angela Miriam Storrs, it is my duty as a police officer to arrest you on the charge of murder. The murder of Geoffrey Gordon Owens, on Sunday, the third of March 1996. It is also my duty to warn you that anything you now say may be taken down in writing and used in evidence at any future hearing.'

She stood where she was; and still said nothing.

Chief Inspector Morse, too, stood where *he* was, wondering whether his sergeant had got the wording quite right, as Detective Inspector Briggs and Detective Constable Bott, both of the Avon CID, led Angela Miriam Storrs away.

PART SEVEN

Chapter Sixty-Six

Twas the first and last time that I'd iver known women to use the pistol. They fear the shot as a rule, but Di'monds-an'-Pearls she did not – she did not

(Rudyard Kipling, *Love-o'-Women*)

(Being the tape-recorded statement made by Angela Storrs at Thames Valley Police HQ, Kidlington, Oxon, on the morning of 11 March, 1996; transcribed by Detective Sergeant Lewis; and subsequently amended – for minor orthographic and punctuational vagaries – by Detective Chief Inspector Morse.)

I murdered both of them, Rachel James and Geoffrey Owens. I'm a bit sorry about Rachel.

I was seventeen when I first started working as a stripper in Soho and then as a prostitute and in some porno flicks. Julian Storrs came along several times to the club where I was performing seven or eight times a night, and he arranged to see me, and we had sex a few times in the West End. He was a selfish sod as I knew from the start, especially in those early days, as far as I was concerned. Which was fine by me. He was obsessively jealous about other men and this was something I wasn't used to. He wanted me body and soul, he said, and soon he asked me to marry him. Which was fine by me too.

I came from no family at all to speak of, but Julian came from a posh family and he had plenty of money. And he was a don at Oxford University and my mum was proud of me. She just wanted me to be somebody important like she'd never been.

I was unfaithful a few times after a few years, especially with some of the other dons who were about as pathetic as the old boys in the Soho basement who used to stick the odd fiver up your panties.

I enjoyed life at Oxford. But nobody took to me all that much. I wasn't quite in the same bracket as the others and I used to feel awkward when they asked me about where I'd been to university and all that jazz, because I couldn't even pretend I was one of them. I wanted to be one of them, though – God knows why! Ours wasn't a tight marriage even from the start. It wasn't too long before Julian was off with other women, and soon, as I say, I was off with other men. Including the Master. He needs his sheets changing every day, that man, like they do in the posh hotels. But he was going at last and that started things really, or is it finished things? Julian desperately wanted to be Master and only one person wanted that more than he did. Me!

In London I'd lived a dodgy, dangerous sort of life

like any woman on the sex-circuit does. I'd been mauled about quite a few times, and raped twice, once by a white and once by a black, so I can't be accused of racial prejudice. One of the other girls had a water-pistol that fired gentian-blue dye over anybody trying it on. I don't know why it was that colour but I always remember it from the paint-box I had when I was a little girl, next to burnt Siena and crimson Lake. But Julian had something far better than that. He'd kept a pistol from his Army days and after I had a bit of trouble late one Saturday night in Cornmarket with some football thugs, he said he didn't mind me carrying it around sometimes if it made me feel better. Which it did. I had a new-found sense of confidence, and one weekend Julian took me with some of his TA friends out to the shooting-range on Otmoor and for the first time ever I actually fired a pistol. I was surprised how difficult it was, with the way it jerked back and upwards, but I managed it and I loved it. After that I got used to carrying it around with me – loaded! – when I was out alone late at night. I felt a great sense of power when I held it.

Then came our big opportunity. Julian was always going to be a good bet for the Master's job, and we only had Cornford to beat. I always quite liked Denis but he never liked me, and to make up for it I detested his American wife. But this one thing that stood in the way suddenly became two things, because we learned that Julian would probably be dead within a year or so although we agreed never to say anything about it to anyone. Then there was that third thing – that bloody man Owens.

He'd written to Julian not to me, and he'd done his homework properly. He knew I'd been a call-girl (sounds better, doesn't it?). He knew about Julian's latest floozie. And he knew about Julian's illness and guessed he was hiding it from the College. He said he'd be ringing and he did, and they met in the Chapters' Bar at The Randolph. All Owens wanted was money, it seems, and Julian's never been short of that. But Julian played it cool and he went back to the bar later on and had a bit of luck because one of the barmaids knew who Owens was because he'd covered quite a few functions there for the newspapers. We didn't need to hire a detective to find his address because it was in the phone-book!

I knew what I was doing that morning because I'd already driven round the area twice and I'd done my homework too. I parked on the main road above the terrace and got through a gap in the fence down to the back. I don't think I meant to shoot him but just frighten him to death if I could and let him know that he'd never be able to feel safe in life again if he kept on with his blackmail. Then I saw him behind the kitchen blind, and I suddenly realized how ridiculously easy it would be to solve all our problems. It wouldn't take more than a single second. I knew he lived alone, and I knew this must be him. His head was only a couple of feet away and I saw the pony-tail that Julian had told me about. I'd planned to knock on the door and go in and sort things out. But I didn't. I just fired point-blank and that was that. There was a huge thud and a splintering noise and lots of smoke, but only for a second it seemed. Next thing I remember I was sitting in the car trembling all over and expecting to see people rushing around and police sirens and all that. But there was nothing. A few cars drove by and a paper-boy rode past on his bicycle.

It was all a bit like a nightmare I've often had – standing on top of some high building with no rail in front of me and knowing it would be so easy to jump off, and if I did jump off, that would be the end of everything. In the nightmare I was always just about going to jump off when I woke up sweating and terrified. It was the same sort of thing at that window. It was like somebody saying 'Do it!' And I did it. Julian knew what happened but he didn't have anything to do with it.

We planned the second murder together, though. Nothing to lose, was there?

Julian knew someone must have shopped him down at the clinic and he soon found out it was Dawn Charles. So we had the hold on her now and it wasn't difficult to get her to co-operate. She'd got money problems and Julian promised to help if she did what we wanted. Which wasn't much really.

Things went as we planned them. Julian drove down to Bath in the BMW and I followed in my car. He went M4. I went Burford way. He booked in and left his car in the hotel garage. I left my car in one of the side-streets behind the hotel. Dawn Charles went by train to Bath changing at Didcot, so Julian told me. She booked into the hotel as herself of course. After we got back from the Abbey, Julian and I had dinner together, and then I left. Julian rang Dawn Charles on the internal phone system and all she had to do was to walk across the garden. I drove back to Oxford and then up to Bicester where I'd got the key to Dawn's flat. It would have been far too risky to go back to Polstead Road.

Unless Julian persuaded her to sleep in the raw Dawn wore my pyjamas, and the hotel-girl took them breakfast in bed the next morning. Mistake about all that sugar, I agree! Dawn Charles is my sort of height and shape, so Julian tells me, and if she wore something that was obviously mine there wouldn't be much of a problem. The whole thing was very neat really. It didn't matter if she was seen round the hotel or if I was, because both of us were staying there officially.

I'd phoned Owens to arrange everything and last Sunday morning I drove round to Bloxham Drive again. Probably he'd have been more wary if I'd been a man instead of a woman but I told him I'd have the money with me. So he said he'd meet me and have a signed letter ready promising he wouldn't try any more blackmail. I went down the slope at the back like before and knocked on the right door this time. It was about a quarter past seven when he let me in and we went through to his front room. I don't think either of us spoke. He was standing there in front of the settee and I took the pistol out of my shopping bag and shot him twice and left him there for dead.

Angela Storrs
11.3.1996

(As it happened, Lewis was not to read this final version. Had he done so, he might have felt rather surprised – and a little superior? – to notice that his own 'burnt sienna' had been amended to 'burnt Siena', since he had taken the trouble to look up that colour in *Chambers*, and had spelt it accordingly.)

Chapter Sixty-Seven

Belbroughton Road is bonny, and pinkly burst the spray
Of prunus and forsythia across the public way,
For a full spring-tide of blossom seethed and departed hence,
Leaving land-locked pools of jonquils by a sunny garden fence
(John Betjeman, *May-Day Song for North Oxford*)

SPRING WAS particularly beautiful, if late, in North Oxford that year, and even Morse, whose only potential for floral exhibitionism was a small window-box, much enjoyed the full-belled daffodils and the short-lived violets, though not the crocuses.

Sir Clixby Bream received a letter from Julian Storrs on Tuesday, 12 March. Both contestants had now withdrawn from the Mastership Stakes. At an Extraordinary General Meeting held the next day in the Stamper Room, the Fellows of Lonsdale had little option but to extend yet again the term of the incumbent Master; and by a majority vote to call in the 'Visitor', that splendidly titled dignitary (usually an archbishop) whose right and duty it was, and is, periodically to inspect and to report on

College matters, and to advise and to intervene in any such disputatious circumstances as Lonsdale, *omnium consensu*, now found itself. An outside appointment seemed a certainty. But Sir Clixby accepted the situation philosophically, as was his wont ... and the College lawns were beginning to look immaculate again. Life had to go on, even if Denis Cornford was now a broken man, with Julian Storrs awaiting new developments – and death.

Adèle Beatrice Cecil had recently learned that the membership of the Young Conservatives had fallen from 500,000 twenty years earlier to 5,000 in January 1996; and anyway she had for several weeks been contemplating a change in her lifestyle. Morse may have been right in one way, she thought – *only* one way, though – in suggesting that it was the personnel rather than the policies which were letting the Party down. Yes, it might be time for a change; and on Wednesday, 13 March, she posted off her resignation to Conservative Central Office. She did so with deep regret, yet she knew she was never destined to be idle. She could write English competently, she knew that; as indeed did Morse; as did also her publishers, Erotica Press, who had recently requested an equally sexy sequel to *Topless in Torremolinos*. And already a nice little idea was burgeoning in her brain almost as vigorously as the wall-flowers she'd planted the previous autumn: an idea about an older man – well, say a whitish-haired man who wasn't *quite* so old as he looked – and a woman who was considerably younger, about her own age, say. Age difference, in heterosexual encounters, was ever a guaranteed 'turn-on', so her editor confided.

One man was to continue his officially unemployed status for the remainder of the spring; and probably indefinitely thereafter, although he was a little troubled by the rumour that the Social Security system was likely to be less sympathetic in the future. For the moment, however, he appeared to be adequately funded, judging from his virtually permanent presence in the local pubs and betting-shops. It was always going to be difficult for any official down in the Job Centre to refute his claim that the remuneration offered for some of their 'employment opportunities' could never compensate for his customary lifestyle: he was a recognized artist; and if anyone doubted his word, there was a man living in North Oxford who would always be willing to give him a reference . . .

On the mantelpiece in his bedroom, the little ormolu clock ticked on, keeping excellent time.

In the immediate aftermath of Mrs Storrs' arrest, Sergeant Lewis found himself extremely busy, happily i/c the team of companionable DCs assigned to him. So many enquiries remained to be made; so many statements to be taken down and duly typed; so many places to be visited and revisited: Soho, Bloxham Drive, the newspaper offices, the Harvey Clinic, Polstead Road, Lonsdale College, Woodpecker Way, The Randolph, the

Royal Crescent Hotel . . . He had met Morse for lunch on the Wednesday and had listened patiently as a rather self-congratulatory Chief Inspector remembered a few of the more crucial moments in the case: when, for example, he had associated that photograph of the young Soho stripper with that of the don's wife at Lonsdale; when the elegantly leggy Banbury Road receptionist had so easily slipped alongside that same don's wife in a chorus line at the Windmill. That lunchtime, however, Lewis's own crucial contributions to such dramatic developments were never even mentioned, let alone singled out for special praise.

Late on Thursday evening, Morse was walking home from the Cotswold House after a generous measure of Irish whiskey (with an 'e', as the proprietor ever insisted) when a car slowed down beside him, the front passenger window electronically lowered.

'Can I give you a lift anywhere?'

'*Hello!* No, thank you. I only live . . .' Morse gestured vaguely up towards the A40 roundabout.

'Everything OK with you?'

'Will be – if you'd like to come along and inspect my penthouse suite.'

'I thought you said it was a flat.'

Though clearly surprised to find Morse in his office over the Friday lunch-period, Strange refrained from his usual raillery.

'Can you nip in to see me a bit later this afternoon about these retirement forms?'

'Let's do it now, sir.'

'What's the rush?'

'I'm off this afternoon.'

'Official, is that?'

'Yes, sir.'

Strange eyed Morse shrewdly. 'Why are you looking so bloody cheerful?'

'Well, another case solved . . . ?'

'Mm. Where's Lewis, by the way?'

'There's still an awful lot of work to do.'

'Why aren't you helping him then?'

'Like I say, sir, I'm off for the weekend.'

'You're lucky, matey. The wife's booked *me* for the lawn-mower.'

'I've just got the window-box myself.'

'Anything in it?'

Morse shook his head, perhaps a little sadly.

'You, er, going anywhere special?' asked Chief Superintendent Strange.

Chapter Sixty-Eight

They fuck you up, your mum and dad.
They may not mean to, but they do.
They fill you with the faults they had
And add some extra, just for you
(Philip Larkin, *This Be the Verse*)

For several seconds after she opened her eyes, Janet McQueen had no idea whatsoever about where she was or what she'd been doing. Then, as she lay there in the green sheets, gradually it flooded back . . .

'Ah! Can I perhaps begin to guess our destination?' she'd asked, as the car turned left at Junction 18 and headed south along the A46. 'B&B in Bath – is that what it's going to be?'

'You'll see.'

As she *had* seen, for soon the Jaguar turned into the Circus, into Brock Street, and finally straight across a cobbled road, where it stopped beside a large magnolia tree. She looked at the hotel, and her green eyes widened as she brought her ringless, manicured fingers together in a semblance of prayer.

'Beautiful!'

Morse had turned towards her then, as she sat beside him in her navy pin-striped suit; sat beside him in her V-necked emerald-silk blouse.

'You're beautiful, too, Janet,' he said simply, and quietly.

'You've booked rooms for us *here*?'

Morse nodded. 'Bit over the top, I know – but, yes, I've booked the Sarah Siddons suite for myself.'

'What have you booked for me?'

'That's also called the Sarah Siddons suite.'

She was smiling contentedly as the Concierge opened the passenger-seat door.

'Welcome to the Royal Crescent Hotel, madam!'

She'd felt important then.

And she'd loved it.

Morse was already up – dressed, washed, shaved – and sitting only a few feet from her, reading *The Times*.

'Hello!' she said, softly.

He leaned over and kissed her lightly on the mouth. 'Headache?'

'Bit of one!'

'You know your trouble? You drink too much champagne.'

She smiled (she would always be smiling that weekend) as she recalled the happiness of their night together. And throwing back the duvet, she got out of bed and stood beside him for several seconds, her cheek resting on the top of his head.

'Shan't be long. Must have a shower.'

'No rush.'

'Why don't you see if you can finish the crossword before I'm dressed? Let's make it a race!'

But Morse said nothing – for he had already finished the crossword, and was thinking of the Philip Larkin line that for so many years had been a kind of mantra for him:

Waiting for breakfast while she brushed her hair.

*

It was late morning, as they were walking arm-in-arm down to the city centre, following the signs to the Roman Baths, that she asked him the question:

'Shall I just keep calling you "Morse"?'

'I'd prefer that, yes.'

'Whatever you say, sir!'

'You sound like Lewis. He always calls me "sir".'

'What do you call him?'

'"Lewis".'

'Does *he* know your Christian name?'

'No.'

'How come you got lumbered with it?'

Morse was silent awhile before answering:

'They both had to leave school early, my parents – and they never had much of a chance in life themselves. That's partly the reason, I suppose. They used to keep on to me all the time about trying as hard as I could in life. They wanted me to do that. They expected me to do that. Sort of emotional blackmail, really – when you come to think of it.'

'Did you love them?'

Morse nodded. 'Especially my father. He drank and gambled far too much . . . but I loved him, yes. He knew nothing really – except two things: he could recite all of Macaulay's *Lays of Ancient Rome* by heart; and he'd read everything ever written about his greatest hero in life, Captain Cook – "Captain James Cook, 1728 to 1779", as he always used to call him.'

'And your mother?'

'She was a gentle soul. She was a Quaker.'

'It all adds up then, really?' said Janet slowly.

'I suppose so,' said Morse.

'Do you want to go straight to the Roman Baths?'

'What are you thinking of?'

'Would you like a pint of beer first?'

'I'm a diabetic, you know.'

'I'll give you your injection,' she promised. 'But only if you do me one big favour . . . I shan't be a minute.'

Morse watched her as she disappeared into a souvenir shop alongside; watched the shapely straight legs above the high-heeled shoes, and the dark, wavy hair piled high at the back of her head. He thought he could grant her almost any favour that was asked of him.

She produced the postcard as Morse returned from the bar.

'What's that for?' he asked.

'*Who's* that for, you mean. That's for Sergeant Lewis . . . He means a lot to you, doesn't he?'

'What? Lewis? Nonsense!'

'He means a lot to you, doesn't he?' she repeated.

Morse averted his eyes from her penetrating, knowing gaze; looked down at the frothy head on his beer; and nodded.

'Christ knows why!'

'I want you to send him this card.'

'What for? We're back at work together on Monday!'

'I want you to send him this card,' she repeated. 'You can send it to his home address. You see, I think he deserves to know your Christian name. Don't you?'

Envoi

Monday, 18 March

This list is not for every Tom, Dick, and Harry. It's been compiled by Everett Williams, director of the Florida Bureau of Vital Statistics, and on it are the 150 most unusual names he's encountered in 34 years with the bureau. Examples are: Tootsie Roll, Curlee Bush, Emancipation Proclamation Cogshell, Candy Box, Starlight Cauliflower Shaw, and Determination Davenport. But he never encountered a fourth quadruplet called Mo! Williams figures that some parents have a sense of humor – or else a grudge against their offspring

(*Gainesville Gazette*, 16 February 1971)

ON THE FOLLOWING Monday evening, Mrs Lewis handed the card to her husband:

'This is for you – from Inspector Morse.'

'You mean, you've read it?'

'Course I 'ave, boy!'

Smelling the chips, Lewis made no protestation as he looked at the front of the card: an aerial view of Bath, showing the Royal Crescent and the Circus. Then, turning over the card, he read Morse's small, neat handwriting on the back. What he read moved him deeply; and when Mrs Lewis shouted through from the kitchen that the eggs were ready, he took a handkerchief from his pocket and pretended he was wiping his nose.

The card read as follows:

> For philistines like you, Lewis, as well as for classical scholars like me, this city with its baths, and temples must rank as one of the finest in Europe. You ought to bring the missus here some time.
>
> Did I ever get the chance to thank you for the few(!) contributions you made to our last case together? If I didn't, let me thank you now – let me thank you for everything, my dear old friend.
>
> Yours aye,
>
> Endeavour (Morse)

THE SECRET OF ANNEXE 3

for

Elizabeth, Anna, and Eve

Acknowledgements

The author and publishers wish to thank the following who have kindly given permission for the use of copyright material:

George Allen & Unwin (Publishers) Ltd, for a quotation by Bertrand Russell.

Curtis Brown Group Ltd, London, on behalf of the Estate of Ogden Nash for a quotation by him.

Peter Champkin for an extract from his book *The Waking Life of Aspern Williams.*

Faber and Faber Ltd, for an extract from 'La Figlia Che Piange' in *Collected Poems* by T. S. Eliot.

A. M. Heath & Company Ltd, on behalf of the Estate of the late Sonia Brownell Orwell for an extract from *Shooting an Elephant* by George Orwell, published by Secker & Warburg Ltd.

Henry Holt & Company Inc, for a quotation by Robert Frost.

A. D. Peters & Company and Jonathan Cape Ltd, on behalf of the Executors of the Estate of C. Day Lewis, for an extract from 'Departure in the Dark' in *Collected Poems,* 1954, published by the Hogarth Press.

The Society of Authors on behalf of the Bernard Shaw Estate for a quotation by Bernard Shaw.

A. P. Watt Ltd, on behalf of *The National Trust for*

Places of Historic Interest or Natural Beauty, for an extract by Rudyard Kipling from *The Thousandth Man.*

Every effort has been made to trace all the copyright holders but if any have been inadvertently overlooked the publishers will be pleased to make the necessary arrangement at the first opportunity.

Chapter One

November

The pomp of funerals has more regard to the vanity of the living than to the honour of the dead.

(LA ROCHEFOUCAULD, *Maxims*)

WHEN THE OLD man died, there was probably no great joy in heaven; and quite certainly little if any real grief in Charlbury Drive, the pleasantly unpretentious cul-de-sac of semi-detached houses to which he had retired. Yet a few of the neighbours, especially the womenfolk, had struck up some sort of distanced acquaintance with him as they pushed prams or shopping trolleys past his neatly kept front lawn; and two of these women (on learning that things were fixed for a Saturday) had decided to be present at the statutory obsequies. Margaret Bowman was one of them.

'Do I look all right?' she asked.

'Fine!' His eyes had not left the racing page of the tabloid newspaper, but he knew well enough that his wife would always be an odds-on favourite for looking all right: a tall, smart woman upon whom clothes invariably hung well, whether for dances, weddings, dinners – or even funerals.

'Well? Have a *look* then! Yes?'

So he looked up at her and nodded vaguely as he surveyed the black ensemble. She *did* look fine. What else was there to say? 'You look fine,' he said.

With a gaiety wholly inappropriate she twirled round on the points of her newly purchased black leather court shoes, fully aware, just as he was, that she did look rather attractive. Her hips had filled out somewhat alarmingly since that disappointing day when as a willowy lass of twenty (a year before marrying Tom Bowman) her application to become an air hostess had proved unsuccessful; and now, sixteen years later, she would have more than a little trouble (she knew it!) in negotiating the central aisle of a Boeing 737. Yet her calves and ankles were almost as slender as when she had slipped her nightgowned body between the stiff white sheets of their honeymoon bed in a Torquay hotel; it was only her feet, with a line of whitish nodules across the middle joints of her slightly ugly toes, that now presaged the gradual approach of middle age. Well, no. It wasn't *only* that – if she were being really honest with herself. There was that hebdomadal visit to the expensive clinic in Oxford . . . But she cast that particular thought from her mind. ('Hebdomadal' was a word she'd become rather proud of, having come across it so often in her job in Oxford with the University Examining Board.)

'Yes?' she repeated.

He looked at her again, more carefully this time. 'You're going to change your shoes, aren't you?'

'What?' Her hazel eyes, with their markedly flecked

irises, took on a puzzled, appealingly vulnerable aspect. Involuntarily her left hand went up to the back of her freshly brushed and recently dyed blonde hair, whilst the fingers of her right hand began to pluck fecklessly at some non-existent speck that threatened to jeopardize her immaculate, expensive nigritude.

'It's bucketing down – hadn't you noticed?' he said.

Little rivulets were trickling down the outside of the lounge window, and even as he spoke a few slanted splashes of rain re-emphasized the ugly temper of the windswept sky.

She looked down at the specially purchased black leather shoes – so classy-looking, so beautifully comfortable. But before she could reply he was reinforcing his line of argument.

'They're going to inter the poor sod, didn't you say?'

For a few moments the word 'inter' failed to register adequately in her brain, sounding like one of those strangely unfamiliar words that had to be sought out in a dictionary. But then she remembered: it meant they wouldn't be cremating the body; they would be digging a deep, vertically sided hole in the orange-coloured earth and lowering the body down on straps. She'd seen the sort of thing on TV and at the cinema; and usually it had been raining then, too.

She looked out of the window, frowning and disappointed.

'You'll get your feet drenched – that's all I'm trying to say.' He turned to the centre pages of his newspaper and began reading about the extraordinary sexual prowess of a world-famous snooker player.

For a couple of minutes or so at that point the course of events in the Bowman household could perhaps have continued to drift along in its normal, unremarkable neutral gear. But it was not to be.

The last thing Margaret wanted to do was ruin the lovely shoes she'd bought. All right. She'd bought them *for* the funeral; but it was ridiculous to go and waste more than £50. It wasn't necessary to go and trample all over the muddy churchyard of course; but even going out in them in this weather was pretty foolish. She looked down again at her expensively sheathed feet, and then at the clock on the mantelpiece. Not much time. But she *would* change them, she decided. Most things went reasonably well with black, and that pair of grey shoes with the cushioned soles would be a sensible choice. But if she was going to be all in black apart from just her shoes, wouldn't it be nicely fashionable to change her handbag as well? Yes! There was that grey leather handbag that would match the shoes almost perfectly.

She tripped up the stairs hurriedly.

And fatefully.

It was no more than a minute or so after this decision – not a decision that would strike anyone as being particularly momentous – that Thomas Bowman put down his newspaper and answered the confidently repeated stridencies at the front door, where in friendly fashion he nodded to a drably clad young woman standing at the porch in the pouring rain under a garishly multicoloured golf umbrella, and wearing knee-length boots of bright yellow plastic that took his thoughts back to the Technicolor broadcasts of the first manned landing on the moon. Some of the women on the estate, quite clearly, were considerably less fashion-conscious than his wife.

'She's nearly ready,' he said. 'Just putting on her ballet shoes for your conducted tour across the ploughed fields.'

'Sorry I'm a bit late.'

'You coming in?'

'Better not. We're a bit pushed for time. Hello Margaret!'

The chicly clad feet which moments ago had flitted lightly up the stairs were now descending more sombrely in a pair of grey, thickish-soled walking shoes. A grey-gloved hand hurriedly pushed a white handkerchief into the grey handbag – and Margaret Bowman was ready, at last, for a funeral.

Chapter Two

November

'Nobody ever notices postmen, somehow,' said he thoughtfully; 'yet they have passions like other men.'

(G.K. CHESTERTON, *The Invisible Man*)

IT WAS A little while after the front door had closed behind the two women that he allowed himself an oblique glance across the soggy lawn that stretched between the wide lounge window and the road. He had told Margaret that she could have the car if she wanted it, since he had no plans for going anywhere himself. But clearly they had gone off in the other woman's since the maroon Metro still stood there on the steepish slope that led down to the garage. Charlbury Drive might just as well have been uninhabited, and the rain poured steadily down.

He walked upstairs and went into the spare bedroom, where he opened the right-hand leaf of the cumbrous, dark mahogany wardrobe that served to store the overflow of his wife's and his own clothing. Behind this leaf, stacked up against the right-hand side of the wardrobe, stood eight white shoe boxes, one atop the other; and from this stack he carefully withdrew the third box from the bottom. Inside lay a bottle of malt whisky about two-thirds empty – or about one-third full, as a man who is thirsting for a drink would probably have described it. The box was an old one, and had been the secret little hiding place for two things since his marriage to Margaret. For a week, in the days when he was still playing football, it had hidden a set of crudely pornographic photographs which had circulated from the veteran goalkeeper to the fourteen-year-old outside-left. And now (and with increasing frequency) it had become the storage space for the whisky of which he was getting, as he knew, rather dangerously over-fond. Guilty secrets both, assuredly; yet hardly sins of cosmic proportions. In fact, he had slowly grown towards the view that the lovely if somewhat overweight Margaret would perhaps have forgiven him readily for the photographs; though not for the whisky, perhaps. Or *would* she have forgiven him for the whisky? He had sensed fairly early on in their married life together that she would probably always have preferred unfaithful sobriety to intoxicated fidelity. But had she changed? Changed recently? She must have smelled the stuff on his breath more than once, although their intimacy over the past few months had been unromantic, intermittent, and wholly unremarkable. Not that any such considerations were bothering his mind very much, if at all, at this particular juncture. He took out the bottle, put the box back, and was just pushing two of his old suits back into place along the rail when he caught sight of it – standing on the floor immediately behind the left-hand leaf of the wardrobe, a leaf which in his own experience was virtually never opened: it was the black handbag which his wife had at the very last minute decided to leave behind.

At first this purely chance discovery failed to register in his mind as an incident that should occasion any interest or surprise; but after a few moments he frowned a little – and then he frowned a lot. Why had she put the handbag behind the door of the wardrobe? He had never noticed any of her accessories there before. Normally she would keep her handbag on the table beside the twin bed that stood nearer the window – her bed. So why . . .? Still frowning, he walked across the landing into their bedroom and looked down at the two black leather shoes, one toppled on to its side, which had been so hurriedly taken off and carelessly left at the foot of her bed.

Back in the spare bedroom he picked up the handbag. An incurious man who had seldom felt any fascination for prying into others' affairs, he would never have thought of opening one of his wife's letters – or opening one of her handbags. Not in normal circumstances. But why had she tried to conceal her handbag? And the answer to that question now seemed very obvious indeed. There was something, perhaps more than one thing, *inside* the handbag that she didn't want him to see; and in her rush she hadn't had the time to transfer all its contents to the other one. The catch opened easily and he found the letter, four pages of it, almost immediately.

You are a selfish thankless bitch and if you think you can just back out of things when *you* like you'd better realize that you've got another big thick headaching think coming because it could be that I've got some ideas about what *I* like. You'd better understand what I'm saying. If you can act like a bitch you'd better know I can be a bit of a sod too. You were glad enough to get what you wanted from me and just because I wanted to give it to you you think that we can just drop everything and go back to square one. Well this letter is to tell you we can't and like I say you'd better understand what I'm telling you. You can be sure I'll get my own back on you...

His throat was dry as he rapidly skimmed the rest of the letter: it had no salutation on page one, no subscription on page four. But there was no doubt about the message of the letter – a message that screamed so loudly at him that even some under-achieving idiot would require no prompting about its import: *his wife was being unfaithful to him* – probably had been for a period of several months.

A sharp pain throbbed in the centre of his forehead, the blood was pounding in his ears, and for several minutes his thought processes were utterly incapable of any sharp tuning. Yet curiously enough he appeared to be adequately in control of the rest of his body, for his hands trembled not the merest millimetre as he filled the shabby little cylindrical glass he always used for the whisky. Sometimes he added a little cold tap water; sometimes not. Now he sipped the whisky neat: first just a small sip; then a large sip; then two large gulps of the burning liquor, and the glass was empty. He refilled his glass and soon had drained that, too. The last drops from the bottle just filled the third glass to the brim and this he sipped more slowly, feeling as he did so the familiar surge of warmth that slowly suffused his brain. And now it happened, paradoxically and totally unexpectedly, that instead of the vicious jealousy which a few minutes ago had threatened to swamp his foundering senses he was gradually becoming ever more conscious of the love he felt for his wife. This renewed consciousness reminded him vividly of the day when, under-prepared and over-confident, she had failed her first driving test; and when, as she sadly and quietly explained to him where she thought she had gone wrong, he had felt an overwhelming surge of sympathy for her. Indeed such had been his awareness of her vulnerability that day, so fierce his determination to protect her whenever possible from future disappointment, that he would willingly have shot the examiner who had been allotted the unavoidable task of reporting adversely on his wife's incompetence.

The glass was empty – the bottle was empty; and Thomas Bowman walked slowly but steadily down the stairs, the empty bottle in his left hand, the letter in his right. The car keys were on the kitchen table, and he picked them up and put on his mackintosh. Before getting into the Metro, he inserted the bottle beneath the four or five bundles of kitchen refuse which almost filled the larger of the two dustbins standing beside the garden shed. Then he drove off: there was one very simple little job he would do immediately.

It was only a mile or so to his place of work in

Chipping Norton, and as he drove he was conscious of the surprisingly clear-cut logicality of what he was proposing to do. It was only when he'd returned some fifteen minutes later to Charlbury Drive and replaced the letter in the handbag that he became fully aware of the blazing hatred he was feeling against the man, whoever he was, who had robbed him of his wife's affection and fidelity; a man who hadn't even got the guts to sign his name.

The woman with the grey handbag stood at the graveside, the purplish-yellow clay sucking and clinging to her sensible shoes. The rain had now almost stopped, and the fresh-faced young vicar intoned the interment rites with unrushed and edifying dignity. From the snatches of conversation she had heard, Margaret Bowman learned that the old fellow had been with the Allied spearhead on the Normandy beaches and that he had fought right through to VE Day. And when one of his old colleagues from the British Legion had thrown a Remembrance Day poppy down on to the top of the coffin lid, she had felt the tears welling up at the back of her eyes; and before she could turn her head away (though no one noticed it) a great blobby tear had splashed down on her gloves.

'That's it, then!' said the woman in the yellow boots. 'No port and ham sandwiches today, I'm afraid.'

'Do they usually have that after funerals?'

'Well, you need something to cheer you up. Specially on a day like this.'

Margaret was silent, and remained so until she got into the car.

'Would you like to nip along to the pub?' asked her companion.

'No. I'd better not. I'd better get home I think.'

'You're not going to cook him a meal, are you?'

'I said I'd get us a snack when I got in,' she said, rather weakly.

The yellow-booted driver made no further attempt to influence the course of events: it would be sensible, she knew, to get her nervous-looking passenger home as quickly as possible and then go and join some of the others at the local.

Margaret Bowman wiped her shoes on the front door mat and slid her latchkey into the Yale lock.

'I'm ho-ome,' she called.

But she received no reply. She looked quickly into the kitchen, the lounge, the bedroom – and then the spare room: but he wasn't there, and she was glad. The Metro hadn't been in the drive when she had come in; but he might of course have driven it into the garage out of the rain. More likely though he'd driven down to the local for a drink – and if he had, she was glad about that, too. In the spare room she opened the door of the wardrobe, picked up her handbag, and looked inside it: obviously she needn't have worried at all, and she began to wish she'd agreed to join her fellow mourners for a consolatory gin at the Black Horse. But that didn't really matter. The pile of shoe boxes on the right looked rather precariously askew and she squared them into a neater stack. In all, it was a great relief, and she promised herself that she would be far more careful in the future.

She reheated the leftovers from the chicken risotto she'd cooked the previous evening, but the few mouthfuls she managed to swallow tasted like the Dead Sea apples. What a mess she was in! What an unholy, desperate mess she'd landed herself in! She sat in the lounge and listened to the one o'clock news, and learned that the pound had perked up a little overnight on the Tokyo Stock Exchange. Unlike her heart. She turned on the television and watched the first two races from Newbury without having any recollection whatsoever of which horses had been first past the post. It was only after the third race had similarly bypassed her consciousness that she heard the squeak of the Metro's brakes on the drive. He kissed her lightly on the cheek, and his voice sounded surprisingly sober as he asked a few perfunctory questions about the funeral. But he had been drinking heavily, she could tell that; and she was not one whit surprised when he declared that he would have a lie-down for the remainder of the afternoon.

But Thomas Bowman rested little that Saturday afternoon, for a plan of action had already begun to form in his mind. The room at the post office housing the Xerox machine had been empty; and after copying the letter he had stood there looking out at the fleet of postal vans in the rear park. A small post office van (he had never quite seen things this way before) was as anonymous as any vehicle could be: no passer-by was interested in the identity of its driver, hemmed in as the latter was (from all but a directly frontal encounter) by the closed side of the secretive little red van that could creep along unobtrusively from one parking point to the next, immune from the tickets of the predatory traffic wardens who prowled the busier streets of Oxford. In the letter, the man who was making such a misery of Margaret's life had begged her to meet him at ten minutes to one on Monday outside the Summertown Library in South Parade – and yes! he, Tom Bowman, would be there too. There would be no real problem about borrowing one of the vans; he could fix that. Furthermore, he had often picked up Margaret, before she had passed her test, along exactly that same road, and he remembered perfectly clearly that there was a little post office right on the corner of South Parade and Middle Way, with a post-box just outside. There could hardly have been a more suitable spot . . .

Suddenly the thought struck him: how long had the letter been in her bag? There was no date on the letter – no way at all of telling which particular Monday was meant. Had it been *last* Monday? There was no way he could be certain about things; and yet he had the strong conviction that the letter, presumably addressed to her at work, had been received only a day or so previously. Equally, he felt almost certain that Margaret was going to do exactly what the man had asked her. On both counts, Thomas Bowman was correct.

*

In the wing-mirror at ten minutes to one the following Monday he could see Margaret walking towards him and he leaned backwards as she passed, no more than two or three yards away. A minute later a Maestro stopped very briefly just ahead of him, outside the Summertown Library, the driver leaning over to open the passenger door, and then to accelerate away with Margaret Bowman seated beside him.

The post office van was three cars behind when the Maestro came to the T-junction at the Woodstock Road, and at that moment a train of events was set in motion which would result in murder – a murder planned with slow subtlety and executed with swift ferocity.

Chapter Three

December

'I have finished another year,' said God,
'In grey, green, white, and brown;
I have strewn the leaf upon the sod,
Sealed up the worm within the clod,
And let the last sun down.'

(THOMAS HARDY, *New Year's Eve*)

THE TREE-LINED BOULEVARD of St Giles' is marked at three or four points by heavy cast-iron street-plaques (the latter painted white on a black background) that were wrought at Lucy's foundry in nearby Jericho. And Oxford being reckoned a scholarly city, the proper apostrophe appears after the final 's': indeed, if a majority vote were to be taken in the English Faculty, future signwriters would be exhorted to go for an extra 's', and print 'St Giles's'. But few of the leading characters who figure in the following chronicle were familiar with Fowler's advice over the difficulties surrounding the possessive case, for they were people who, in the crude distinction so often drawn in the city, would be immediately – and correctly – designated as 'Town' rather than 'Gown'.

At the northern end of St Giles', where in a triangle of grass a stone memorial pays tribute to the dead of two world wars, the way divides into the Woodstock Road, to the left, and the Banbury Road, to the right. Taking the second of these two roads (the road, incidentally, in which Chief Inspector Morse has lived these many years) the present-day visitor will find, after he has walked a few hundred yards, that he is viewing a fairly homogeneous stretch of buildings – buildings which may properly be called 'Venetian Gothic' in style: the houses have pointed arches over their doorways, and pointed arches over their clustered windows which are themselves vertically bisected or trisected by small columns of marble. It is as though Ruskin had been looking over the shoulders of the architects as they ruled and compassed their designs in the 1870s. Most of these houses (with their yellowish-beige bricks and the purple-blue slates of their roofs) may perhaps appear to the modern eye as rather severe and humourless. But such an assessment would be misleading: attractive bands of orange brick serve to soften the ecclesiastical discipline of many of these great houses, and over the arches the pointed contours are re-emphasized by patterns of orange and purple, as though the old harlot of the Mediterranean had painted on her eye-shadow a little too thickly.

This whole scene changes as the visitor walks further northwards past Park Town, for soon he finds houses built of a cheerful orange-red brick that gives an immediate impression of warmth and good fellowship after the slightly forbidding façades of the Venetian wedge. Now the roofs are of red tile, and the paintwork around the stone-plinthed windows of an almost uniform white. The architects, some fifteen years older now, and no longer haunted by the ghost of Ruskin, drew the tops of their windows, sensibly and simply, in a straight horizontal. And thus it is that the housing for about half a mile or so north of St Giles' exhibits the influences of its times – times in which the first batches of College Fellows left the cloisters and the quads to marry and multiply, and to employ cohorts of maids and under-maids and tweeny maids in the spacious suburban properties that slowly spread northward along the Banbury and Woodstock Roads in the last decades of the nineteenth century – their annual progress leaving its record no less surely than the annular tracings of a sawn-through tree of mighty girth.

Betwixt the two rings sketched briefly above, and partaking something of each, stands the Haworth Hotel. It will not be necessary to describe this building – or, rather, these buildings – in any great detail at this point, but a few things should be mentioned immediately. When (ten years since) the house had been put on the market, the successful purchaser had been one John Binyon, an erstwhile factory-hand from Leeds who had one day invested a £1 Treble Chance stake on the Pools, and who (to the incredulity of the rest of the nation) had thought fit to presume, in an early round of the FA Cup, that the current leaders of the First Division would be unable to defeat a lowly bunch of non-league part-time no-hopers from the Potteries –

Binyon's reward for such effrontery being a jackpot prize of £450,000 from Littlewoods. The large detached residence (first named the Three Swans Guest House and then the Haworth Hotel) had been his initial purchase – a building that paid tribute both to the staid Venetian planner of the 1880s and to his gayer rosy-fingered colleague of the 1890s. Yellow-bricked, red-roofed, the tops of doors and windows now compromised to gentle curves, the house openly proclaimed its divided loyalties in a quietly genteel manner, standing back from the road some ten yards or so with a slightly apologetic air, as if awaiting with only partial confidence the advent of social acceptability. After a few disappointing months, trade began to pick up for Binyon, and then to prosper most satisfactorily; after two years of a glorified B & B provision, the establishment was promoted to the hotel league, boasting now a fully licensed restaurant, colour-TV'd and showered or bathroomed accommodation, and a small exercise room for fitness fanatics; and four years after this, the proprietor had been able to stand under his own front porch and to look up with pride at the yellow sign which proclaimed that the AA had deemed it appropriate to award the Haworth Hotel one of its stars. Thereafter such was mine host's continued success that he was soon deciding to expand his operations – in two separate directions. First, he was able to purchase the premises immediately adjacent on the south side, in order to provide (in due course and after considerable renovation) a readily accessible annexe for the increasingly large number of tourists during the spring and summer seasons. Second, he began to implement his growing conviction that much of the comparatively slack period (especially weekends and holidays) from October to March could be revitalized by a series of tastefully organized special-rate functions. And it was for this reason that a half-page advertisement for the Haworth Hotel appeared (now for the third year running) in the 'Winter Breaks with Christmas and New Year Bonanzas' brochures which were to be seen on the racks of many a travel agent in the autumn of the year in which our story begins. And in order that the reader may get the flavour of the special features which attracted those men and women we are to meet in the following pages we reproduce below the prospectus in which the hotel was willing to offer 'at prices decidedly too difficult to resist' for a three-day break over the New Year.

TUESDAY

NEW YEAR'S EVE

12.30 p.m. Sherry reception! John and Catherine Binyon extend a happy welcome to as many of their guests as can make this early get-together.

1.00 p.m. Buffet lunch: a good time for more introductions – or reunions.

The afternoon will give you the opportunity for strolling down – only ten minutes' walk to Carfax! – into the centre of our beautiful University City. For those who prefer a little lively competition to keep them busy and amused, tournaments are arranged for anyone fancying his (her!) skills at darts, snooker, table-tennis, Scrabble, and video games. Prizes!

5.00 p.m. Tea and biscuits: nothing – but nothing! – else will be available. Please keep a keen edge on your appetite for . . .

7.30 p.m. OUR GRAND FANCY DRESS DINNER PARTY.

It will be huge fun if everyone – yes, everyone! – comes to the dinner in fancy dress. But *please* don't think that we shall be any less liberal with the pre-prandial cocktails if you can't. This year's theme is 'The Mystery of the East', and for those who prefer to improvise their costumes our own Rag Bag will be available in the games room throughout the afternoon.

10.00 p.m. Fancy Dress Judging: Prizes!! – continuing with live Cabaret and Dancing to keep you in wonderful spirits until . . .

Midnight – 1.00 a.m. Champagne! Auld Lang Syne! Bed!!!

WEDNESDAY

NEW YEAR'S DAY

8.30– 10.30 a.m. Continental Breakfast (quietly please, for the benefit of any of us – all of us! – with a mild hangover).

10.45 a.m. CAR TREASURE-HUNT, with clues scattered round a care-free, car-free (as we hope) Oxford. There are plenty of simple instructions, so you'll never get lost. Be adventurous! And get out for a breath of fresh air! (Approximately one and a half hours to complete.) Prizes!!

1.00 p.m. English Roast Beef Luncheon.

2.00 p.m. TOURNAMENTS once more for those who have the stamina; and the chance of an afternoon nap for those who haven't.

4.30 p.m. Devonshire Cream Tea.

6.30 p.m. Your pantomime coach awaits to take you to *Aladdin* at the Apollo Theatre.

There will be a full buffet awaiting you on your return, and you can dance away the rest of the evening at the DISCO (live music from Paper Lemon) until the energy (though not the bar!) runs out.

THURSDAY

9.00 a.m. Full English Breakfast – available until 10.30 a.m. The last chance to say your farewells to your old friends and your new ones, and to promise to repeat the whole enjoyable process again next year!

Of course (it is agreed) such a prospectus would not automatically appeal to every sort and condition of humankind. Indeed, the idea of spending New Year's

Eve being semi-forcibly cajoled into participating in a darts match, or dressing up as one of the Samurai, or even of being expected *de rigueur* to wallow in the company of their fellow men, would drive some solid citizens into a state of semi-panic. And yet, for the past two years, many a couple had been pleasingly surprised to discover how much, after the gentlest nudge of persuasion, they had enjoyed the group activities that the Binyons so brashly presented. Several couples were now repeating the visit for a second time; and one couple for a third – although it is only fair to add that neither member of this unattractive duo would ever have dreamed of donning a single item of fancy dress, delighting themselves only, as they had done, in witnessing what they saw as the rather juvenile imbecilities of their fellow guests. For the simple truth was that almost all the guests required surprisingly little, if any, persuasion to dress up for the New Year's Eve party – not a few of them with brilliant, if bizarre effect. And such (as we shall see) was to be the case this year, with several of the guests so subtly disguised, so cleverly bedecked in alien clothing, that even long-standing acquaintances would have recognized them only with the greatest difficulty.

Especially the man who was to win the first prize that evening.

Yes, especially him.

Chapter Four

December 30th/31st

> The feeling of sleepiness when you are not in bed, and can't get there, is the meanest feeling in the world.
>
> (E.W. HOWE, *Country Town Sayings*)

WHENEVER SHE FELT tired – and that was usually in the early hours of the evening – the almost comically large spherical spectacles which framed the roundly luminous eyes of Miss Sarah Jonstone would slowly slip further and further down her small and neatly geometrical nose. At such times her voice would (in truth) sound only perfunctorily polite as she spoke into whichever of the two ultramodern phones happened to be purring for her expert attention; at such times, too, some of the belated travellers who stood waiting to sign the register at the Haworth Hotel would perhaps find her expression of welcome a thing of somewhat mechanical formality. But in the eyes of John Binyon, this same slightly fading woman of some forty summers could do little, if anything, wrong. He had appointed her five years previously: first purely as a glorified receptionist; subsequently (knowing a real treasure when he spotted one) as his unofficial 'manageress' –

although his wife Catherine (an awkward, graceless woman) had still insisted upon her own name appearing in that senior-sounding capacity on the hotel's general literature, as well as in the brochures announcing bargain breaks for special occasions.

Like Easter, for example.

Or Whitsun.

Or Christmas.

Or, as we have seen, like New Year.

With Christmas now over, Sarah Jonstone was looking forward to her official week's holiday – a whole week off from everything, and especially from the New Year festivities – the latter, for some reason, never having enthused her with rapture unconfined.

The Christmas venture was again likely to be oversubscribed, and this fact had been the main reason – though not quite the only reason – why John Binyon had strained every nerve to bring part of the recently purchased, if only partially developed, annexe into premature use. He had originally applied for planning permission for a single-storey linking corridor between the Haworth Hotel and this adjoining freehold property. But although the physical distance in question was only some twenty yards, so bewilderingly complex had proved the concomitant problems of potential subsidence, ground levels, drains, fire exits, goods access and gas mains, that he had abandoned his earlier notions of a formal merger and had settled for a self-standing addendum physically separated from the parent hotel. Yet even such a limited ambition was proving (as Binyon saw it) grotesquely expensive; and a long-term token of such expenditure was the towering yellow crane which stood like some enormous capital Greek Gamma in what had earlier been the chrysanthemumed and foxgloved garden at the rear of the newly acquired property. From late August, the dust ever filtering down from the planked scaffolding had vied, in degrees of irritation, with the daytime continuum of a revolving cement mixer and the clanks and hammerings which punctuated all the waking and working hours. But as winter had drawn on – and especially during the record rainfall of November – such inconveniences had begun to appear, in retrospect, as little more than the mildest irritancies. For now the area in which the builders worked day by day was becoming a morass of thick-clinging, darkish-orange mud, reminiscent of pictures of Passchendaele. The mud was getting everywhere: it caked the tyres of the workmen's wheelbarrows; it plastered the surfaces of the planks and the duckboards which lined the site and linked its drier spots; and (perhaps most annoying of all) it left the main entrance to the hotel, as well as the subsidiary entrance to the embryo annexe, resembling the approaches to a milking parlour in the Vale of the Great Dairies. A compromise was clearly called for over the hotel tariffs, and Binyon promptly amended the Christmas and New Year brochures to advertise the never-to-be-repeated bargain of 15 per cent off rates for the rooms in the main hotel, and 25 per cent (no less!) off the rates for the three double rooms and the one single room now available on the ground floor of the semi-completed annexe. And indeed it *was* a bargain: no workmen; no noise; no real inconvenience whatsoever over these holiday periods – except for that omnipresent mud . . .

The net result of these difficulties, and of further foul weather in early December, had been that, in spite of daily Hooverings and daily scrapings, many rugs and carpets and stretches of linoleum were so sadly in need of a more general shampoo after the departure of the Christmas guests that it was decided to put into operation a full-scale clean-up on the 30th in readiness for the arrival of the New Year contingent – or the majority of it – at lunchtime on the 31st. But there were problems. It was difficult enough at the best of times to hire waitresses and bedders and charladies. But when, as now, extra help was most urgently required; and when, as now, two of the regular cleaning women were stricken with influenza, there was only one thing for it: Binyon himself, his reluctant spouse Catherine, Sarah Jonstone, and Sarah's young assistant-receptionist, Caroline, had been called to the colours early on the 30th; and (armed with their dusters, brushes, squeegees, and Hoovers) had mounted their attack upon the blighted premises to such good effect that by the mid-evening of the same day all the rooms and the corridors in both the main body of the hotel and in the annexe were completely cleansed of the quaggy, mire-caked traces left behind by the Christmas revellers, and indeed by their predecessors. When all was done, Sarah herself had seldom felt so tired, although such unwonted physical labour had not – far from it! – been wholly unpleasant for her. True, she ached in a great many areas of her body which she had forgotten were still potentially operative, especially the spaces below her ribs and the muscles just behind her knees. But such physical activity served to enhance the delightful prospect of her imminent holiday; and to show the world that she could live it up with the rest and the best of them, she had wallowed in a long 'Fab-Foam' bath before ringing her only genuine friend, Jenny, to say that she had changed her mind, was feeling fine and raring to go, and would after all be delighted to come to the party that same evening at Jenny's North Oxford flat (only a stone's throw, as it happened, from Morse's own small bachelor property). Jenny's acquaintances, dubiously moral though they were, were also (almost invariably) quite undoubtedly interesting; and it was at 1.20 a.m. precisely the following morning that a paunchy, middle-aged German with a tediously repeated passion for the works of Thomas Mann had suddenly asked a semi-intoxicated Sarah (yes, just like that!) if she would like to go to bed with him. And in spite of her very brief acquaintance with the man, it had been only semi-unwillingly that she had been dragged off to Jenny's spare room where she had made equally brief love with the hirsute lawyer from Bergisch Gladbach. She could not remember too clearly how she had finally reached her own flat in Middle Way – a road (as the careful reader will remember) which stretches down into South Parade, and at the bottom of which stands a post office.

At nine o'clock the same morning, the morning of the 31st, she was awakened by the insistent ringing of her doorbell; and drawing her dressing gown round her hips, she opened the door to find John Binyon on the doorstep: Caroline's mother (Sarah learned) had just rung to say that her daughter had the flu, and would certainly not be getting out of bed that day – let alone getting out of the house; the Haworth Hotel was in one almighty fix; could Sarah? would Sarah? it would be well worth it – very much so – if Sarah could put in a couple of extra days, please! And stay the night, of course – as Caroline had arranged to do, in the nice little spare room at the side, the one overlooking the annexe.

Yes. If she could help out, of course she would! The only thing she *couldn't* definitely promise was to stay awake. Her eyelids threatened every second to close down permanently over the tired eyes, and she was only half aware, amidst his profuse thanks, of the palms of his hands on her bottom as he leaned forward and kissed her gently on the cheek. He was, she knew, an inveterate womanizer; but curiously enough she found herself unable positively to dislike him; and on the few occasions he had tested the temperature of the water with her he had accepted without rancour or bitterness her fairly firm assurance that for the moment it was little if anything above freezing point. As she closed the door behind Binyon and went back to her bedroom, she felt a growing sense of guilt about her early morning escapade. It had been those wretched (beautiful!) gins and Campari that had temporarily loosened the girdle round her robe of honour. But her sense of guilt was, she knew, not occasioned just by the lapse itself, but by the anonymous, mechanical nature of that lapse. Jenny had been utterly delighted, if wholly flabbergasted, by the unprecedented incident; but Sarah herself had felt immediately saddened and diminished in her own self-estimation. And when finally she had returned to her flat, her sleep had been fitful and unrefreshing, the eiderdown perpetually slipping off her single bed as she had tossed and turned and tried to tell herself it didn't matter.

Now she took two Disprin, in the hope of dispelling her persistent headache, washed and dressed, drank two cups of piping hot black coffee, packed her toilet bag and night-clothes, and left the flat. It was only some twelve minutes' walk down to the hotel, and she decided that the walk would do her nothing but good. The weather was perceptibly colder than the previous day: heavy clouds (the forecasters said) were moving down over the country from the north, and some moderate falls of snow were expected to reach the Midlands by the early afternoon. During the previous week the bookmakers had made a great deal of money after the tenth consecutive non-white Christmas; but they must surely have stopped taking any more bets on a white New Year, since such an eventuality was now beginning to look like a gilt-edged certainty.

Not that Sarah Jonstone had ever thought of laying a bet with any bookmaker, in spite of the proximity of the Ladbrokes office in Summertown which she passed almost daily on her way to work. Passed it, indeed, again now, and stared (surely, far too obviously!) at the man who had just emerged, eyes downcast, from one of the swing-doors folding a pink, oblong betting slip into his wallet. How extraordinarily strange life could become on occasions! It was just like meeting a word in the English language for the very first time, and then – lo and behold! – meeting exactly the same word for the *second* time almost immediately thereafter. She had seen this same man, for the first time, the previous evening as she had walked up to Jenny's flat at about 9.30 p.m.: middle-aged; greyish-headed; balding; a man who once might have been slim, but who was now apparently running to the sort of fat which strained the buttons on his shabby-looking beige raincoat. *Why* had she looked at him so hard on that former occasion? *Why* had she recorded certain details about him so carefully in her mind? She couldn't tell. But she did know that this man, in his turn, had looked at *her*, however briefly, with a look of intensity which had been slightly (if pleasurably) disturbing.

Yet the man's cursory glance had been little more than a gesture of approbation for the high cheekbones that had thrown the rest of her face into a slightly mysterious shadow under the orange glare of the street lamp which illuminated the stretch of road immediately outside his bachelor flat. And after only a few yards, he had virtually forgotten the woman as he stepped out with a purpose in his stride towards his nightly assignation at the Friar.

Chapter Five

Tuesday, December 31st

> Serious sport has nothing to do with fair play. It is bound up with hatred, jealousy, boastfulness, and disregard of all the rules.
>
> (GEORGE ORWELL, *Shooting an Elephant*)

IN VIEW OF the events described in the previous chapter, it is not surprising that from the start of subsequent police investigations Sarah Jonstone's memories should have resembled a disorderly card index, with times and people and sequences sometimes hopelessly confused. Interview with one interrogator had been followed by interview with another, and the truth was that her recollection of some periods of December 31st had grown as unreliable as a false and faithless lover.

Until about 11.30 a.m. she spent some time in the games room: brushing down the green baize on the snooker table; putting up the ping-pong net; repolishing the push-penny board; checking up on the Monopoly, Scrabble and Cluedo sets; and putting into their appropriate niches such items as cues, dice, bats, balls, chalk, darts, cards, and scoring pads. She spent some time, too, in the restaurant; and was in fact helping to set up the trestles and spread the tablecloths for the buffet lunch when the first two guests arrived – guests signed in, as it happened, by a rather poorly and high-temperatured Mrs Binyon herself in order to allow Sarah to nip upstairs to her temporary bedroom and change into regulation long-sleeved cream-coloured blouse, close-buttoned to the chin, and regulation mid-calf, tightly fitting black skirt which (Sarah would have been the first to admit) considerably flattered waist, hips, thighs and calves alike.

From about noon onwards, guests began to arrive regularly, and there was little time, and little inclination, for needless pleasantries. The short-handed staff may have been a little short-tempered here and there – particularly with each other; but the frenetic to-ings and fro-ings were strangely satisfying to Sarah Jonstone that day. Mrs Binyon kept out of the way for the most part, confining her questionable skills to restaurant and kitchen before finally retiring to bed; whilst Mr Binyon, in between lugging suitcases along corridors and up stairs, had already repaired one squirting radiator, one flickering TV and one noisily dripping bath tap, before discovering in early afternoon that some of the disco equipment was malfunctioning, and spending the next hour seeking to beg, cajole and bribe anyone with the slightest knowledge of circuits and switches to save his hotel from imminent disaster. Such (not uncommon) crises meant that Sarah was called upon to divide her attention mainly between Reception – a few guests had rung to say that the bad weather might delay their arrival – and the games room.

Oh dear – the games room!

The darts (Sarah soon saw) was not going to be one of the afternoon's greater successes. An ex-publican from East Croydon, a large man with the facility of lobbing his darts into the treble-twenty with a sort of languid regularity, had only two potential challengers for the championship title; and one of these could hardly be said to pose a major threat – a small, ageing charlady from somewhere in the Chilterns who shrieked with juvenile delight whenever one of her darts actually managed to stick in the board instead of the wooden surround. On the other hand, the Cluedo players appeared to be settling down quite nicely – until one of the four children booked in for the festivities reported a 'Colonel Mustard' so badly dog-eared and a 'Conservatory' so sadly creased that each of the two cards was just as easily recognizable from the back as from the front. Fortunately the knock-out Scrabble competition, which was being keenly and cleanly played by a good many of the guests, had reached the final before any real dissension arose, and that over both the spelling and the admissibility of 'Caribbean'. (What an unpropitious omen *that* had been!) But these minor worries could hardly compare with the consternation caused on the Monopoly front by a swift-fingered checker-out from a Bedford supermarket whose palm was so extraordinarily speedy in the recovery of the two dice thrown from the cylindrical cup that her opponents had little option but to accept, without ever seeing the slightest evidence, her instantaneously enunciated score, and then to watch helplessly as this sharp-faced woman moved her little counter along the board to whichever square seemed of the greatest potential profit to her entrepreneurial designs. No complaint was openly voiced at the time; but the speed with which she bankrupted her real-estate rivals was later a matter of some general dissatisfaction – if also of considerable amusement. Her prize, though, was to be only a bottle of cheap, medium-sweet sherry; and since she did not look the sort of woman who would ever own a real-life hotel in Park Lane or Mayfair, Sarah had said nothing, and done nothing, about it. The snooker and the table-tennis tournaments were happily free from any major controversy; and a friendly cheer in mid-afternoon proclaimed that the ageing charlady from the Chilterns (who appeared to be getting on very nicely thank-you with the ex-publican from East Croydon) had at last managed to hit the dartboard with three consecutive throws.

Arbiter, consultant, referee, umpire – Sarah Jonstone was acquitting herself well, she thought, as she emulated the impartiality of Solomon that raw but not unhappy afternoon. Especially so since she had been performing, indeed was still performing, a contemporaneous role at the reception desk.

In its main building, the Haworth Hotel boasted sixteen bedrooms for guests – two family rooms, ten double rooms and four single rooms – with the now partially opened annexe offering a further three double rooms and one single room. The guest-list for the New

Year festivities amounted to thirty-nine, including four children; and by latish afternoon all but two couples and one single person had registered at the desk, just to the right of the main entrance, where Sarah's large spectacles had been slowly slipping further and further down her nose. She'd had one glass of dry sherry, she remembered that; and one sausage roll and one glass of red wine – between half-past one and two o'clock, that had been. But thereafter she'd begun to lose track of time almost completely (or so it appeared to those who questioned her so closely afterwards). Snow had been falling in soft, fat flakes since just before midday, and by dusk the ground was thickly covered, with the white crystalline symbols of the TV weatherman portending further heavy falls over the whole of central and southern England. And this was probably the reason why very few of the guests – none, so far as Sarah was aware – had ventured out into Oxford that afternoon, although (as she later told her interrogators) it would have been perfectly possible for any of the guests to have gone out (or for others to have come in) without her noticing the fact, engaged as she would have been for a fair proportion of the time with form-filling, hotel documentation, directions to bedrooms, general queries, and the rest. Two new plumbing faults had further exercised the DIY skills of the proprietor himself that afternoon; yet when he came to stand beside her for a while after the penultimate couple had signed in, he looked reasonably satisfied.

'Not a bad start, eh, Sarah?'

'Not bad, Mr Binyon,' she replied quietly.

She had never taken kindly to *too* much familiarity over Christian names, and 'John' would never have fallen easily from those lips of hers – lips which were slightly fuller than any strict physiognomical proportion would allow; but lips which to John Binyon always looked softly warm and eminently kissable.

The phone rang as he stood there, and she was a little surprised to note how quickly he pounced upon the receiver.

'Mr Binyon?' It was a distanced female voice, but Sarah could hear no more: the proprietor clamped the receiver tight against his ear, turning away from Sarah as he did so.

'But you're not as sorry as I am!' he'd said . . .

'No – no chance,' he'd said . . .

'Look, can I ring you back?' he'd said. 'We're a bit busy here at the minute and I could, er, I could look it up and let you know . . .'

Sarah thought little about the incident.

It was mostly the *names* of the people, and the association of those names with the *faces*, that she couldn't really get fixed in her mind with any certitude. Some had been easy to remember: Miss Fisher, for example – the embryo property tycoon from Bedford; Mr Dods, too ('Ornly t'one "d" in t'middle, lass!') – she remembered *his* face very clearly; Fred Andrews – the mournful-visaged snooker king from Swindon; Mr and Mrs J. Smith from Gloucester – a marital appellation not unfamiliar to anyone who has sat at a hotel reception desk for more than a few hours. But the others? It really was very difficult for her to match the names with the faces. The Ballards from Chipping Norton? *Could* she remember the Ballards from Chipping Norton? They must, judging from the register, have been the very last couple to sign in, and Sarah *thought* she could remember Mrs Ballard, shivering and stamping her snow-caked boots in front of Reception, looking not unlike an Eskimo determined to ward off frostbite. Names and faces . . . faces and names . . . names which were to echo again and again in her ears as first Sergeant Phillips, then Sergeant Lewis, and finally a distinctly brusque and hostile Chief Inspector Morse, had sought to reactivate a memory torpid with shock and far-spent with weariness. Arkwright, Ballard, Palmer, Smith . . . Smith, Palmer, Ballard, Arkwright.

It was funny about names, thought Sarah. You could often tell what a person was like from a name. Take the Arkwright woman, for instance, who had cancelled her room, Annexe 4 – the drifting snow south of Solihull making motoring a perilous folly, it appeared. Doris Arkwright! With a name like that, she just had to be a suspicious, carefully calculating old crab-crumpet! And she wasn't coming – Binyon had just brought the message to her.

Minus one: and the number of guests was down to thirty-eight.

Oddly enough, one of the things very much on Sarah Jonstone's mind early that evening was the decision she had made (so authoritatively!) to allow 'Caribbean' in the Scrabble final. And she could hardly forget the matter, in view of a most strange coincidence. Later on in the evening, the judge for the fancy-dress competition would be asking whether another 'Caribbean' should be allowed, since one of the male entrants had gaily bedecked himself in a finely authentic Rastafarian outfit. 'The Mystery of the East' (the judge suggested) could hardly accommodate such an obviously West Indian interpretation? Yet (as one of the guests quietly pointed out) it wasn't really 'West Indian' at all – it was 'Ethiopian'; and Ethiopia had to be East in anyone's atlas – well, Middle East, anyway. Didn't it all depend, too (as another of the guests argued with some force), on exactly what this 'East' business meant, anyway: didn't it depend on exactly whereabouts on the globe one happened to be standing at any particular time? The upshot of this difference of opinion was that 'Caribbean' was accepted for a second time in the Haworth Hotel that New Year's Eve.

It would be a good many hours into New Year's Day itself before anyone discovered that the number of guests was down to thirty-seven.

Chapter Six

December 31st/January 1st

Beware of all enterprises that require fancy clothes.

(THOREAU)

DURING THE TIMES in which these events are set, there occurred a quite spectacular renaissance in fancy-dress occasions of all types. In pubs, in clubs, in ballrooms, at discos, at dinner parties – it was as if a collective mania would settle upon men and women wherever they congregated, demanding that at fairly regular intervals each of them should be given an opportunity to bedeck the body in borrowed plumes and for a few hours to assume an entirely alien personality. Two years previously (the Haworth's first such venture) the New Year's party had taken 'What we were wearing when the ship went down' as its theme, with the emphasis very much upon the degree of imagination, humour and improvisation that could be achieved with a very minimum of props. The theme for the following New Year's Eve had been 'This Sporting Life'; and since this theme had been announced in the brochure, some of the guests had taken the challenge most seriously, had turned their backs on improvisation, and had brought appropriate costumes with them. This year, in accord with the temper of the times, participants had been given even wider scope than before, with ample time and opportunity to hire their chosen outfits and to acquire suitable make-up and accessories – in short, to take the whole thing far too seriously. The hotel's 'Rag Bag' still stood in the games room, but only one or two had rummaged through its contents that afternoon. After all, the current theme had been likewise pre-announced, and all the guests knew exactly what was coming; and, to be fair, in many cases the fancy-dress evening was one of the chief reasons for them choosing the Haworth Hotel in the first place. On such occasions, the greatest triumph would be registered when a person went through the first part of the evening – sometimes a good deal longer – totally unrecognized even by close acquaintances: a feat which Binyon himself had accomplished the previous year when only by a process of elimination had even his hotel colleagues finally recognized the face of their proprietor behind the bushy beard and beneath the Gloucestershire cricket-cap of Dr W.G. Grace.

This year the enthusiasm of the guests was such – all but six had presented themselves in various guises – that even Sarah, not by nature one of the world's obvious have-a-go extroverts, found herself wishing that she were one of the happy band drinking red or blue cocktails in the restaurant-cum-ballroom on the ground floor at the back of the hotel, where everything was now almost ready. The whole of the area was surprisingly warm, the radiators round the walls turned up to their maximum readings, and a log fire burning brightly in a large old grate that was simultaneously the delight of guests and the despair of management. But tonight the fire was dancing smokelessly and merrily, and the older folk there spoke of the times when their shadows had passed gigantic round the walls of their childhood, and when in the late hours of the night the logs had collapsed of a sudden in a firework of sparks. Abetting this fire, in a double illumination, were tall red candles, two on each of the tables, and all already lit, with the haloes that formed around them creating little pools of warm light amid the darkling, twinkling dining room, and reflecting their elongated yellow flames in the gleaming cutlery.

It would have been easiest to divide the original guest-list into three tables of thirteen; but in deference to inevitable superstition Binyon had settled for two tables of fourteen and one of eleven, with each place set only for two courses. At each place, a small white card denoted the seating arrangements for these first two courses, spouse duly positioned next to spouse; but each of these cards also had two numbers printed on it, denoting a different table for the third and fourth courses, and a different table again for the fifth and sixth. This system had been tried out the previous year; and although on that occasion one or two of the couples had failed to follow instructions too carefully, the social mix effected thereby had proved a huge success. The only real problem attendant upon such a system was the awkwardness of transferring side plates from one seat to another, but this had been solved by the supremely simple expedient of dispensing with rolls and butter altogether.

It was at about a quarter to eight (eating would begin at eight o'clock) when the nasty little episode occurred: Sarah could vouch for the time with reasonable confidence. One of the women guests from the annexe, one dressed in the black garb of a female adherent of the Ayatollah, informed Sarah in a voice muffled by the double veil of her yashmak that there was something rather unpleasant written on the wall of the Ladies' lavatory, and Sarah had accompanied this woman to inspect the offending graffito. And, yes, she agreed with the voice behind the veils that it was not really very nice at all: 'I'm nuts' had been daubed on the wall over one of the washbasins in a black felt pen; and underneath had been added 'So are Binyon's B—'. Oh dear! But it had taken only a few minutes with sponge and detergent to expunge these most distressing words – certainly to the point of illegibility.

The cocktails turned out to be a huge success, for even the most weirdly bedizened strangers were already beginning to mix together happily. Binyon himself, gaudily garbed as the Lord High Executioner, was making no attempt this year to cloak his identity, and in a kindly way (so Sarah thought, as she looked in briefly) was making a successful fuss of one of the children, a small-boned nervous little girl dressed up prettily in Japanese costume. The mystical lure of the Orient had clearly provoked a colourful response, and there were one or two immediate hits – the most stunning being a woman with a lissomly sinuous figure, whose Turkish belly-dancer's outfit (what little there was of it) was causing several pairs of eyes (besides Binyon's) to sparkle widely with fornicatory intent. There was, as far as Sarah could see, only one real embarrassment amongst the whole lot, and that in the form of the gaunt-faced snooker king from Swindon, who had turned up as a rather too convincing version of Gandhi – a Gandhi, moreover, clearly in the latter stages of one of his emaciating fasts. But even he appeared happy enough, holding a cocktail in one hand, and ever hitching up his loin-cloth with the other.

It would not be long now before the guests began to drift to their places, to start on the Fresh Grapefruit Cerisette – already laid out (to be followed by the Consommé au Riz); and Sarah picked up a Tequila Sunrise and walked back through to Reception, where she locked the front door of the hotel. Her head was aching slightly, and the last thing she wanted was a six-course meal. An early night was all she really craved for; and that (she told herself) was what she *would* have, after giving a hand (as she'd promised) with the Grilled Trout with Almonds and then with the Pork Chop Normandy. (The Strawberry Gâteau, the cheese and biscuits and the coffee, Binyon had assured her, would be no problem.) She had never herself been a big eater, and for this reason she was always a little vexed that she could put on weight so easily; and unlike the Mahatma, perhaps, she most certainly did not wish to face the new year with a little extra poundage.

The cocktail tasted good; and with ten or fifteen

minutes to spare before the grapefruit plates would need to be cleared Sarah lit one of the half-dozen cigarettes she allowed herself each day, enjoying the sensation as she sat back in her chair and inhaled deeply.

Ten minutes to eight.

It could have been only some two or three minutes later that she heard the noise, fairly near her. And suddenly, illogically – with the stillness of the half-lit, empty entrance hall somehow emphasized by the happy voices heard from the dining room – she experienced a sense of fear that prickled the roots of her honey-coloured hair. And then, equally suddenly, everything was normal once again. From the door of the Gents' lavatory there emerged a gaily accoutred personage who on any normal evening might justifiably have been the cause of some misgiving on her part; but upon whom she now bestowed a knowingly appreciative smile. It must have taken the man some considerable time to effect such a convincing transformation into a coffee-coloured, dreadlocked Rastafarian; and perhaps he hadn't quite finished yet, for even as he walked across to the dining room he was still dabbing his brown-stained hands with a white handkerchief that was now more chocolate than vanilla.

Sarah drank some more of the liberally poured cocktail – and began to feel good. She looked down at the only letter that had found its way into her tray that morning: it was from a Cheltenham lady thanking the hotel for the fact that her booking of a room had been answered with 'laudable expedition' ('very quickly', translated Sarah), but at the same time deploring the etiquette of these degenerate days that could allow the 'Dear Madam' of the salutation to be complemented by the 'Yours sincerely' of the valediction. Again, Sarah smiled to herself – the lady would probably turn out to be a wonderful old girl – and looked up to find the Lord High Executioner smiling down, in turn, at her.

'Another?' he suggested, nodding to the cocktail.

'Mm – that would be nice,' she heard herself say.

What had she remembered then? She could recall, quite certainly, clearing away after the soup course; picking up the supernumerary spoons and forks that marked the place of that pusillanimous spirit from Solihull, Doris Arkwright; standing by in the kitchen as a Pork Chop Normandy had slithered off its plate to the floor, to be replaced thither after a perfunctory wipe; drinking a third cocktail; dancing with the Lord High Executioner; eating two helpings of the gâteau in the kitchen; dancing, in the dim light of the ballroom, a sort of chiaroscuro cha-cha-cha with the mysterious 'Rastafarian' – the latter having been adjudged the winner of the men's fancy-dress prize; telling Binyon not to be so silly when he'd broached the proposition of a brief dive beneath the duvet in her temporary quarters; drinking a fourth cocktail, the colour of which she could no longer recall; feeling slightly sick; walking up the stairs to her bedroom before the singing of 'Auld Lang Syne'; feeling *very* sick; and finally finding herself in bed. Those were the pretty definite events of a crowded evening. ('But there must have been so many other little things, Miss Jonstone?') And there *were* other things, yes. She remembered, for example, the banging of so many doors once the music and the singing had finally ended – half-past midnight, it must have been – when standing by her window (alone!) she had seen the guests from the annexe walking back to their rooms: two of the women, their light-coloured raincoats wrapped around them, with the prize-winning Rastafarian between them, a hand on either shoulder; and behind that trio, another trio – the yashmak'd, graffiti-conscious woman, with a Samurai on one side and Lawrence of Arabia on the other; and bringing up the rear the Lord High Executioner, with a heavy, dark coat over his eastern robes. Yes! And she remembered quite clearly seeing all of them, including Binyon, go *into* the annexe, and then Binyon, fairly shortly afterwards, coming *out*, and fiddling for a moment or two with the Yale lock on the side door of the annexe – presumably to secure the inmates against any potential intruders.

It was just before 7 a.m. when Sarah woke, for a few seconds finding some difficulty in recalling exactly where she was. Then, it had been with a wholly childlike delight that on opening her curtains she saw the canopy of snow that enveloped everything – four or five inches of it on the ledge outside her window, and lodging heavily along the branches of the trees. The world outside looked so bitterly chill. But she was happily conscious of the square little radiator, now boiling hot, that made her room under the eaves so snugly warm; and through the frost-whorled window-panes she looked out once more at the deep carpet of snow: it was as if the Almighty had taken his brush, after the last few hours of the death-struck year, and painted the earth in a dazzling Dulux Super-White. Sarah wondered about slipping back into bed for a brief while, but decided against it. Her head was beginning to ache a little, and she knew there were some aspirin in the kitchen. In any case she'd promised to help with the breakfasts. Much better to get up – even to go out and walk profanely across the virgin snow. As far as could be seen, there were no footprints, no indentations whatsoever, in the smooth surface of snow that surrounded the strangely still hotel, and a line from a poem she'd always loved came suddenly to mind: 'All bloodless lay the untrodden snow . . .'

The water in the washbasin became very hot indeed after only ten or fifteen seconds, and she was taking her flannel from her washing bag when she noticed a creosote-looking stain on the palm of her right hand; and then noticed the same sort of stain on one of the fluffy white towels she must have used before going to bed. And, of course, she knew immediately where *that* had come from. Had that wretched Rastafarian stained her blouse as well, when his left hand had circled her waist (perhaps a fraction too intimately) above her black tight-fitting skirt? Yes! He had! Blast it! For a few minutes as her headache became gradually worse she moistened the offending patch on her cream blouse and cleaned off the stain as best she could. No one would notice it, anyway.

It was seven forty-five when she walked into the kitchen. Seemingly, she was the only person stirring in the whole hotel. And, had Sarah Jonstone known it at that time, there was a person in the same hotel who never would be seen to stir again. For in the room designated, on the key-hook board behind Reception, as 'Annexe 3', a man lay stiffly dead – the window of his ground-floor room thrust open, the radiator switched completely off, and the temperature around the body as icily frigid as an igloo's.

The end of the year had fallen cold; and the body that lay across the top of the coverlet on one of the twin beds in Annexe 3 was very, very cold indeed.

Chapter Seven

Wednesday, January 1st: p.m.

> But if he finds you and you find him,
> The rest of the world don't matter;
> For the Thousandth Man will sink or swim
> With you in any water.
>
> (RUDYARD KIPLING, *The Thousandth Man*)

FOR THE CHIEF Constable of Oxfordshire, a man internationally renowned for his handling of terrorist sieges, the new year dawned upon fewer problems than had been anticipated. With the much-publicized CND march from Carfax to Greenham Common badly hit by the weather, and with the First Division game between Oxford United and Everton inevitably postponed, many of the extra police drafted in for special duties in both the city and the county had not been required. There had been, it was true, a whole string of minor accidents along the A40, but no serious injuries and no serious hold-ups. Indeed, it had been a very gentle New Year's Day; and at 6.30 p.m. the Chief Constable was just about to leave his office on the second floor of the Kidlington Police HQ when Superintendent Bell rang from the City Police HQ in St

Aldates to ask whether among extra personnel available that day there happened to be any spare inspectors from the CID division.

The phone had been ringing for a good while before the sole occupant of the bachelor flat at the top of the Banbury Road in North Oxford turned down the mighty volume of the finale of *Die Walküre* and answered it.

'Morse!' he said curtly.

'Ah, Morse!' (The Chief Constable expected his voice to be instantly recognized, and it almost always was.) 'I suppose you've just staggered out of bed all ready for another night of debauchery?'

'A Happy New Year to you, too, sir!'

'Looks like being a pretty good new year for the crime rate, Morse: we've got a murder down at the bottom of your road. I'm assuming you had nothing to do with it, of course.'

'I'm on furlough, sir.'

'Well, never mind! You can make up the days later in January.'

'Or February,' mumbled Morse.

'Or February!' admitted the Chief Constable.

'Not tonight, I'm afraid, sir. I'm taking part in the final of the pub quiz round at the Friar.'

'I'm glad to hear others have got such confidence in your brains.'

'I'm quite good, really – apart from Sport and Pop Music.'

'Oh, I know that, Morse!' The Chief Constable was speaking very slowly now. 'And *I* have every confidence in your brains, as well.'

Morse sighed audibly into the phone and held his peace as the Chief Constable continued: 'We've got dozens of men here if you need 'em.'

'Is Sergeant Lewis on duty?' asked a Morse now fully resigned.

'Lewis? Ah yes! As a matter of fact he's on his way to pick you up now. I thought, you know, that er . . .'

'You're very kind, sir.'

Morse put down the phone and walked to the window where he looked down on the strangely quiet, muffled road. The Corporation lorries had gritted for a second time late that afternoon, but only a few carefully driven cars were intermittently crawling past along the icy surfaces. Lewis wouldn't mind coming out, though. In fact, thought Morse, he'd probably be only too glad to escape the first night of the new year television.

And what of Morse himself? There was perhaps just a hint of grim delight to be observed on his features as he saw the police car pull into the gutter in a spurt of deep slush, and waved to the man who got out of it – a thick-set, slightly awkward-looking man, for whom the only blemishes on a life of unexciting virtuousness were a gluttonous partiality for egg and chips, and a passion for fast driving.

Sergeant Lewis looked up to the window of the flat, and acknowledged Morse's gesture of recognition. And had Lewis been able to observe more closely at that moment he might have seen that in the deep shadows of Morse's rather cold blue eyes there floated some reminiscences of an almost joyful satisfaction.

Chapter Eight

Wednesday, January 1st: p.m.

I therefore come before you armed with the delusions of adequacy with which so many of us equip ourselves.

(AIR VICE-MARSHAL A. D. BUTTON)

LEWIS PULLED IN behind the two other police cars outside the Haworth Hotel, where a uniformed constable in a black-and-white chequered hat stood outside the main entrance, with one of his colleagues, similarly attired, guarding the front door of the adjacent property further down the Banbury Road.

'Who's in charge?' asked Morse, of the first constable, as he passed through into the foyer, stamping the snow from his shoes on the doormat.

'Inspector Morse, sir.'

'Know where he is?' asked Morse.

'Not sure, sir. I've only just got here.'

'Know him by sight, do you?'

'I don't know him at all.'

Morse went on in, but Lewis tapped the constable on the shoulder and whispered in his ear: 'When you meet this Morse fellow, he's a *chief* inspector – all right? – and a nasty one at that! So watch your step, lad!'

'Famous pair, we are!' murmured Morse as the two of them stood at Reception, where in a small room at the back of the desk Sergeant Phillips of the City CID (Morse recognized him) stood talking to a pale-faced, worried-looking man who was introduced as Mr John Binyon, the hotel proprietor. And very soon Morse and Lewis knew as much – or as little – as anyone about the tragedy so recently discovered in his own hotel by the proprietor himself.

The two Anderson children had been putting the finishing touches to their snowman just as it was getting dark that afternoon when they were joined by their father, Mr Gerald Anderson. And it had been he who had observed that one of the rear windows on the ground floor of the annexe was open; and who had been vaguely uneasy about this observation, since the weather was raw, with a cutting wind sweeping down from the north. He had finally walked closer and seen the half-drawn curtains flapping in the icy draught – although he had not gone all the way up to the window, under which (as he'd noticed) the snow was still completely undisturbed. He had mentioned this fact to his wife once he was back in the hotel, and it was at her instigation that he reported his disquiet to the proprietor himself – at about 5 p.m., that was; with the result that the pair of them, Anderson and Binyon, had walked across to the annexe and along the newly carpeted corridor to the second bedroom on the right, where over the doorknob was hooked a notice, written in English, French, and German, instructing potential intruders that the incumbent was not to be disturbed.

After repeated knockings, Binyon had opened the door with his master-key, and had immediately discovered why the man they found there had been incapable (for some considerable time, it seemed) of responding to any knocking from within or to any icy blast from without.

For the man on the bed was dead and the room was cold as the grave.

The news of the murder was known almost immediately to everyone in the hotel; and despite Binyon's frenetic protestations, some few of the guests (including, it appeared, *everyone* from the annexe) had taken the law into their own hands, packed their belongings, strapped up their cases (and in one case not paid any part of the bill), and disappeared from the Haworth Hotel before Sergeant Phillips from St Aldates had arrived at about 5.40 p.m.

'You *what*?' bellowed Morse as Phillips explained how he'd allowed four more of the guests to leave the hotel when full names and addresses had been checked.

'Well, it was a very difficult situation, sir, and I thought—'

'Christ man! Didn't someone ever tell you that if you've got a few suspicious circumstances you're expected to hold on to a few of the *suspects*? And what do *you* do, Sergeant? You tell 'em all to bugger off!'

'I got all the details—'

'Bloody marvellous!' snapped Morse.

Binyon, who had been standing by in some embarrassment as Morse (not, it must be admitted, without just cause) lashed the luckless Phillips, decided to come to the rescue.

'It really was a very difficult situation, Inspector, and we thought—'

'*Thought?*' Morse's instantaneous repetition of the monosyllable sounded like a whiplashed retaliation for such impertinence, and it was becoming abundantly clear that he had taken an instant dislike to the hotel proprietor. 'Mr Binyon! They don't pay you, do they, for having any thoughts about this case? No? But they *do* pay *me*! They even pay Sergeant Phillips here; and if I was angry with him just now it was only because I basically respect what *he* thought and what he tried to do. But I shall be obliged if *you* will kindly keep your thoughts out of things until I ask for them – all right?'

In the latter part of this little homily, Morse's voice was as cool and as level as the snow upon which Sarah Jonstone had looked out early that same morning; and she herself as she sat silently at Reception was more than a little alarmed by this new arrival; more than a little upset by his harsh words. But gossip had it that the corpse found in the room called Annexe 3 had been horridly mutilated about the face; and she was relieved that the police seemed at least to have matched the gravity of the crime by sending a man from the higher echelons of its detective branch. But he was disturbingly strange, this man with the hard-staring, startling eyes – eyes that had at first reminded her of the more fanatical politicians, like Benn or Joseph or Powell, as she'd watched them on TV; eyes that seemed uncommunicative and unseeing, eyes fixed, it seemed, upon some distanced, spiritual shore. And yet that wasn't true, and she knew it; for after his initial ill-temper he had looked so directly and so daringly into her eyes that for a second or two she could have sworn that he was about to wink at her.

A man she'd seen three times now in three days!

Another man had come in – the humpbacked man she'd seen earlier – and he, too, was in Sarah's eyes one of the more unusual specimens of humankind. With a cigarette hanging down at forty-five degrees from a thin-lipped, mournful mouth, and with the few remaining strands of his lank, black hair plastered in parallels across a yellowish dome of a skull, anyone could perhaps be forgiven for supposing his profession to be that of a moderately unsuccessful undertaker. (Oddly enough, over the fifteen years they had known – and respected – each other, Morse had invariably addressed this police surgeon by his Christian name, whilst the surgeon had never addressed Morse by anything other than his surname.)

'I was here an hour ago,' began the surgeon.

'You want me to give you a medal or something?' said Morse.

'You in charge?'

'Yes.'

'Well, go and have a look at things. I'll be ready when you want me.'

Following closely behind Binyon and Phillips and Lewis, Morse was walking over to the annexe when he stopped halfway and gazed up at the giant crane, its arm outstretched some hundred and twenty feet above the ground as if in benediction, or perhaps in bane, upon one or other of the two blocks of buildings between which it was positioned.

'Not a job they'd get me on, Lewis,' he said, as his eyes went up towards the precarious-looking box at the top of the structure, in which, presumably, some operator would normally sit.

'No need, sir. You can operate those things from the bottom.' Lewis pointed to a platform, only some six feet above the ground, on which a series of knobbed levers stuck up at various angles through the iron floor. Morse nodded; and averted his eyes from the crane's nest atop the criss-crossed iron girders that stood out black against the heavy, darkened sky.

Through the side door of the annexe they proceeded, where Morse looked along the newly carpeted passage that stretched some ten to twelve yards in front of him, its terminus marked by pieces of boarding, nailed (not too professionally) across an aperture which would, in due course, lead through to the front entrance hall of the annexe. Morse strode to the far end of the corridor and looked through the temporary slats to the foyer beyond, where rickety-looking planks, resting on pairs of red bricks, were set across the recently cemented floor. Dust from such activities had filtered through, and was now lying, albeit lightly, on the surfaces just a few feet inside the completed section of the ground-floor annexe, and it seemed clear that there had been no recent entrance, and no recent exit, from that particular point. Morse turned, and for a few seconds looked back up the short corridor down which they had walked; looked at the marks of many muddy shoes (including their own) on the purple carpeting – the latter seeming to Morse almost as distasteful as the reproduction of the late Renoir, 'Les nues dans l'herbe', which hung on the wall to his right.

As he stood there, still looking back up to the side entrance, he noted the simple geography of the annexe. Four doors led off the corridor: to his right were those numbered 2 and 1; immediately opposite 1 was 4; and then, set back behind a narrow, uncarpeted flight of stairs (temporarily blocked off but doubtless leading to the hitherto undeveloped first floor) a door numbered 3. From what he had already learned, Morse could see little hope of lifting any incriminatory fingerprints from the doorknob of this last room which had been twisted quite certainly by Binyon and probably by others. Yet he looked at the knob with some care, and at the trilingual notice that was still hooked over it.

'There should be an umlaut over the "o" in "Storen",' said Morse.

'*Ja! Das sagen mir alle,*' replied Binyon.

Morse, whose only knowledge of German stemmed from his addiction to the works of Richard Wagner and Richard Strauss, and who was therefore supremely unfitted to converse in the language, decided that it would be sensible to say no more on the point; decided, too, that Binyon was not perhaps quite the nonentity that his weak-chinned appearance might seem to signify.

Inside Annexe 3, a door immediately to the right

gave access to a small, rather cramped toilet area, with a washbasin, a WC, and a small bath with shower attachment. In the bedroom itself, the main items of furniture were twin beds, pulled close together, with matching white coverlets; a dressing table opposite them, a TV set in the corner; and just to the left of the main door a built-in wardrobe. Yet it was not the furniture which riveted the attention of Morse and Lewis as they stood momentarily in the doorway. Across the further of the two beds, the one that stood only some three or four feet from the opened window, lay the body of a dead man. Morse, as he invariably did, recoiled from an immediate inspection of the corpse; yet he knew that he had to look. And an extraordinary oddity it was upon which he looked: a man dressed in Rastafarian clothes lay on his side, his face towards them, his head lying in a great, coldly clotted pool of blood, like red wine poured across the snow. The dead man's left hand was trapped beneath the body; but the right hand was clearly visible below the long sleeve of a light blue shirt; and it was – without any doubt – the hand of a white man.

Morse, now averting his eyes from this scene of gory mutilation, looked long and hard at the window, then at the TV set, and finally put his head inside the small washroom.

'You've got a good fingerprint man coming?' he asked Phillips.

'He's on his way, sir.'

'Tell him to have a go at the radiator, the TV, and the lever on the WC.'

'Anything else, sir?'

Morse shrugged. 'Leave it to him. I've never had much faith in fingerprints myself.'

'Oh, I don't know, sir—' began Phillips.

But Morse lifted his hand like a priest about to pronounce a benediction, and cut off whatever Phillips had intended to say. 'I'm not here to argue, lad!' He looked around again, and seemed just on the point of leaving Annexe 3 when he stepped back inside the room and opened the one drawer, and then the other, of the chest below the TV set, peering carefully into the corners of each.

'Were you expecting to find something?' asked Lewis quietly as he and Morse walked back across to the Haworth Hotel.

Morse shook his head. 'Just habit, Lewis. I once found a ten-pound note in a hotel in Tenby, that's all.'

Chapter Nine

Wednesday, January 1st: p.m.

The great advantage of a hotel is that it's a refuge from home life.

(G. B. SHAW)

ON THEIR RETURN to the main building, Morse himself addressed the assembled guests in the ballroom area (not, as Lewis saw things, particularly impressively), telling everyone what had happened (they knew anyway), and asking everyone to be sure to tell the police if they had any information which might be of use (as if they wouldn't!).

None of those still remaining in the hotel appeared at all anxious to return home prematurely. Indeed, it soon became apparent to Lewis that the 'Annexe Murder' was, by several kilometres, the most exciting event of most lives hitherto; and that far from wishing to distance themselves physically from the scene of the crime, the majority of the folk left in the hotel were more than happy to stay where they were, flattered as they had been to be told that their own recollections of the previous evening's events might possibly furnish a key clue in solving the murder which had been committed. None of these guests appeared worried about the possibility of an indiscriminate killer being abroad in Oxford's semi-civilized acres – a worry which would, in fact, have been totally unfounded.

Whilst Lewis began the documentation of the hotel guests, Morse was to be seen sitting at the receipt of custom, with Sarah Jonstone to his right, looking through the correspondence concerned with those annexe guests whom (the duly chastened) Sergeant Phillips had earlier blessed or semi-blessed upon their homeward ways.

A pale Sarah Jonstone, a nerve visibly twitching at her left nostril, lit a cigarette, drew upon it deeply, and then exhaled the rarefied smoke. Morse, who the previous day (for the thousandth time) had rid himself of the odious habit, turned to her with distaste.

'Your breath must smell like an old ashtray,' he said.

'Yes?'

'Yes!'

'Who to?'

'"To whom?", do you mean?'

'Do you want me to help you or not?' said Sarah Jonstone, the skin around her cheekbones burning.

'Room 1?' asked Morse.

Sarah handed over the two sheets of paper, stapled together, the lower sheet reading as follows:

29A Chiswick Reach
London, W4
20 Dec

Dear Sir(s)

My wife and I would like to book a double room – preferably with double bed – for the New Year Offer your hotel is advertising. If a suitable room is available, we look forward to hearing from you.

Yours faithfully,
F. Palmer

On top of this originating handwritten letter was the typewritten reply (ref JB-SJ) to which Morse now briefly turned his attention:

Dear Mr Palmer,

Thank you for your letter of 20 Dec. Our New Year programme has been extremely popular, and we are now fully booked as far as the main hotel is concerned. But you may be interested in the Special Offer (please see last page of current brochure) of accommodation in one of the rooms of our newly equipped annexe at three-quarters of the normal tariff. In spite of a few minor inconveniences, these rooms are, we believe, wonderfully good value, and we very much hope that you and your wife will be able to take advantage of this offer.

Please be sure to let us know immediately – preferably by phone. The Christmas post is not likely to be 100 per cent reliable.

Yours sincerely,

There was no further correspondence; but across the top letter was a large tick in blue biro, with 'Accepted 23rd Dec' written beneath it.

'You remember them?' asked Morse.

'Not very well, I'm afraid.' She recalled (she thought) a darkly attractive woman of about thirty or so, and a smartly dressed, prosperous-looking man about ten years her senior, perhaps. But little else. And soon she found herself wondering whether the people she was thinking of were, in fact, the Palmer pair at all.

'Room 2?'

Here the documentary evidence Sarah produced was at an irreducible minimum: one sheet of hotel paper recorded the bare facts that a Mr Smith – a 'Mr J. Smith' – had rung on December 23rd and been told that there had been a late cancellation in the annexe, that a double room would now be available, and that written confirmation should be put in the post immediately.

'There's no confirmation here,' complained Morse.

'No. It was probably held up in the Christmas post.'

'But they came?'

'Yes.' Again, Sarah thought she remembered them – certainly *him*, a rather distinguished-looking man, hair prematurely grey, perhaps, with a good-humoured, twinkling sort of look about him.

'You get quite a few "John Smiths"?'

'Quite a few.'

'The management's not worried?'

'No! Nor me. Or would you prefer "Nor I"?'

"That'd be a little bit pedantic, wouldn't it, miss?'

Sarah felt the keen glance of his eyes upon her face, and again (maddeningly) she knew that her cheeks were a burning red.

'Room 3?'

Sarah, fully aware that Morse already knew far more about the situation in Room 3 than she did, handed over the correspondence without comment – this time a typewritten originating letter, stapled below a typewritten reply.

84 West Street
Chipping Norton
Oxon
30th Nov

Dear Proprietor,

Please book in my husband and myself for the Haworth Hotel's New Year Package as advertised. We would particularly wish to take advantage of the rates offered for the 'annexe rooms'. As I read your brochure, it seems that each of these rooms is on the ground floor and this is essential for our booking since my husband suffers from vertigo and is unable to climb stairs. We would prefer twin beds if possible but this is not essential. Please answer as a matter of urgency by return (s.a.e. enclosed) since we are most anxious to fix things up immediately and shall not be at our present address (see above) after the 7th December, since we shall be moving to Cheltenham.

Yours sincerely,
Ann Ballard (Mrs)

The prompt reply (dated 2nd December) was as follows:

Dear Mrs Ballard,

Thank you for your letter of 30th November. We are glad to be able to offer you a double room on the ground-floor annexe, with twin beds, for our New Year Package.

We look forward to your confirmation, either by letter or by phone.

We very much look forward to meeting you and your husband, and we are confident that you will both greatly enjoy your stay with us.

Yours sincerely,

In biro across this letter, too, the word 'Accepted' was written, with the date '3rd Dec'.

Morse looked down again at the letter from Mrs Ballard, and seemed (at least to Sarah Jonstone) to spend an inexplicably long time re-reading its meagre content. Finally he nodded very slowly to himself, put the two sheets of paper down, and looked up at her.

'What do you remember about that pair?'

It was the question Sarah had been afraid of, for her recollections were not so much vague as confused. She thought it had been *Mrs* Ballard who had collected the key from Reception; Mrs Ballard who had been nodded in the direction of the annexe at about 4 p.m. that New Year's afternoon; Mrs Ballard who had appeared in her Iranian outfit just before the evening festivities were due to begin and pointed out the distasteful graffito in the Ladies' loo. And it had been *Mr* Ballard, dressed in his distinctively Rastafarian outfit of light blue shirt, white trousers, baggy checked cap, and maroon knee-boots, who had emerged from the Gents' loo just before everyone was due to eat; Mr Ballard who in fact had eaten very little at all that evening (indeed Sarah herself had cleared away his first two courses virtually untouched); Mr Ballard who had kept very close to his wife throughout the evening, as if they were still in some lovey-dovey idyll of a recent infatuation; Mr Ballard who had asked her – Sarah! – to dance in the latter part of an evening which was becoming less and less of a distinct sequence of events the more she tried to call it back to mind . . .

All these things Sarah told a Morse intensely interested (it seemed) in the vaguest facts she was able to dredge up from the chaotic jumble of her memory.

'Was he drunk?'

'No. I don't think he drank much at all.'

'Did he try to kiss you?'

'No!' Sarah's face, she knew, was blushing again, and she cursed herself for such sensitivity, aware that Morse appeared amused by her discomfiture.

'No need to blush! Nobody'd blame a fellow for wanting to kiss someone like you after one of your boozy midnight parties, my love!'

'I'm not your "love"!' Her upper lip was trembling and she felt the tears beginning to brim behind her eyes.

But Morse was looking at her no more: he picked up the phone and dialled Directory Enquiries on 192.

'There's no Ballard at 84 West Street,' interrupted Sarah. 'Sergeant Phillips—'

'No, I know that,' said Morse quietly, 'but you don't mind if I just check up, do you?'

Sarah was silent as Morse spent a few minutes speaking to some supervisor somewhere, asking several questions about street names and street numbers. And whatever he'd learned, he registered no surprise, certainly no disappointment, as he put down the phone and grinned boyishly at her. 'Sergeant Phillips was right, Miss Jonstone. There isn't a Mr Ballard of 84 West Street, Chipping Norton. There isn't even a number 84! Which makes you think, doesn't it?' he asked, tapping the letter that Sarah herself had written to precisely that non-existent address.

'I'm past thinking!' said Sarah quietly.

'What about Room 4?'

Here, the initiating letter, addressed from 114 Worcester Road, Kidderminster, and dated 4th December, was a model of supremely economical, no-nonsense English, and written in a small, neat hand:

> Dear Sir,
> Single – cheapest available – room for your New Year Package. Confirm, please.
> Yours,
> Doris Arkwright

Such confirmation had been duly forthcoming in the form of an almost equally brief reply, this time signed by the proprietor himself, and dated 6th December. But across this letter was now pencilled 'Cancelled 31st Dec – snow.'

'Did she ring up?' asked Morse.

'Yes, she must have rung Mr Binyon, I think.'

'You don't ask for a deposit?'

She shook her head. 'Mr Binyon doesn't think it's good business practice.'

'You don't get many cancellations?'

'Very few.'

'Really? But you've had two out of the four rooms in the annexe!'

Yes, he was right. And he looked like the wretched sort of man who would *always* be right.

'Have you ever had this old biddy staying with you before?' continued Morse.

'What makes you think she's an "old biddy", Inspector?'

'With a name like Doris Arkwright? Straight out of the Lancashire mills, isn't it? Pushing a sprightly ninety, I shouldn't wonder, and drives an ancient Austin.'

Sarah opened her mouth, but closed it again. Morse (as she watched him) had perched a pair of NHS half-lenses on his Jewish-looking nose and looked again at the short letter from Doris Arkwright.

'Do you think she's got anything to do with the case?' asked Sarah.

'Do I think so?' He waited for a few pregnant seconds before taking off his spectacles and looking at her quizzically. 'No, I don't think she's got anything at all to do with the murder. Do *you,* Miss Jonstone?'

Chapter Ten

Wednesday, January 1st: p.m.

He was once a doctor but is now an undertaker; and what he does as an undertaker he used to do as a doctor.

(MARTIAL)

For Lewis, the next two hours of the evening of New Year's Day were hardly memorable. A good deal of the earlier excitement had dissipated, with even the novelty of murder worn thin; and the Haworth Hotel now looked an uninviting place, its high-ceilinged rooms harshly lit by neon strips, its guests standing or sitting in small groups, quiet and unsmiling – and waiting. Morse had asked him to check (factually) with Phillips all the names and addresses of those staying in the hotel, and briefly himself to interview as many vital witnesses as he could find – with Phillips to take on the rest; to try to form a picture (synoptically) of the scene at the hotel on the previous evening; and to keep his antennae attuned (almost metaphysically, it appeared) for any signals from an unsuspected psychopath or any posthumous transmissions from the newly dead. Festivities – all of them, including the pantomine – had been cancelled, and the hotel was now grimly still, with not even the quiet click of snooker balls from the games room to suggest that murder was anything but a deadly serious matter.

Lewis himself had never spent a Christmas or a New Year away from home since his marriage; and although he knew that family life was hardly prize-winning roses all along the way, he had never felt the urge to get away from his own modest semi-detached house up in Headington over such holiday periods. Yet now – most oddly, considering the circumstances – he began to see for the first time, some of the potential attractions: no frenetic last-minute purchases from supermarkets; no pre-feastday preparations of stuffings and sauces; no sticky saucepans to scour; no washing-up of plates and cutlery. Yes! Perhaps Lewis would mention the idea to the missus, for it seemed perfectly clear to him as he spoke to guest after guest that a wondrously good time was being had by all – until a man had been found murdered.

Exactly where Morse had been during the whole of this period, Lewis had little idea, although (Lewis had heard part of it) the chief inspector had interviewed the woman on Reception at some considerable length – a woman (as Lewis saw her) most pleasingly attractive, with a quiet, rather upper-class manner of speaking that contrasted favourably with the somewhat abrasive questioning she was being subjected to – with Morse obviously still in a tetchy frame of mind after his altercations with the luckless Phillips, and apparently quite unconcerned about venting his temporary ill-humour on anyone and everyone, including Sarah Jonstone.

It was just after 10 p.m. that the police surgeon came back into the main building again, the inevitable long-ashed cigarette dropping from his lips, his black bag in one hand, two sheets of A4 in the other.

'My God, you do pick 'em, Morse!' began the surgeon as the three of them, Max, Morse and Lewis, sat down together in the deserted games room.

'Get on with it, Max!' said Morse.

The surgeon looked quickly at his notes – then began.

'Onc – he's a wasp, Morse.'

'He's a *what*?'

'He's a WASP – a White Anglo-Saxon Protestant – though he could well be a Catholic, of course.'

'Of course.'

'Two – his age is about thirty to forty, though he could be twenty-nine or forty-one, for that matter.'

'Or forty-two,' said Morse.

The surgeon nodded. 'Or twenty-eight.'

'Get on with it!'

'Three – his height's five foot seven and a half inches. You want that in metres, Morse?'

'Not so long as it's accurate in inches.'

'Can't promise that.'

'Christ!'

'Four – he's dressed up as a Rastafarian.'

'Very perceptive!'

'Five – he's got a wig on: black, curlyish.'

'Something several of us could do with!'

'Six – he's got dreadlocks.'

'Which are?'

'Long, thin bits of hair, plaited into strands, with cylindrical beads at the end.'

'I saw them! It's just that I didn't know—'

'Seven – these strands of hair are stapled to the inside of the hat he's wearing.'

Morse nodded.

'Eight – this hat is a sort of baggy, felt "cap", with a big peak, a black-grey-white check pattern, filled out with folded toilet-paper. You want to know which brand?'

'No!'

'Nine – his face is darkened all over with what's known in theatrical circles as "stage-black".'

Again Morse nodded.

'Ten – this stage-black stretches down to the top of the shirt-level, just round his neck; the backs of the hands are similarly bedaubed, Morse, but not the palms.'

'Is that important?'

'Eleven' – the surgeon ignored the question – 'his light blue shirt has got six buttons down the front, all but the top one done up, long-sleeved, obviously very new and probably being worn for the first time.'

No comment from Morse.

'Twelve – his white trousers are made of some cheap summer-wear material, a bit worn here and there.'

'And nothing in the pockets,' said Morse; but it wasn't a question.

'Thirteen – he's got three longish chains round his neck: junk stuff that you'd find in a cheap second-hand shop.'

Morse was beginning to show the first signs of restlessness.

'Fourteen – there was a pair of sunglasses on the floor just between the two beds, the ear-hooks quite shallowly slanted.'

'As if they'd fall off his ears, you mean?'

'They *did* fall off his ears.'

'I see.'

'Fifteen – a false moustache, affixed with strong adhesive, still exactly in position across the upper lip.'

'Why do you say "affixed", instead of just plain "fixed"?'

'Sixteen – a pair of high-heeled, knee-level boots: highly polished, light maroon plastic.'

'You sure it's not a *woman* we've got there on the bed, Max?'

'Seventeen – time of death: difficult to judge.'

'As well we might have known!'

'About sixteen to twenty-four hours before the body was found – at a guess. But the room temperature is only just above freezing point – which could upset calculations either way.'

'So?'

For the first time, the surgeon seemed slightly less than happy with himself: 'As I say, Morse, it's very difficult.'

'But you *never* come up with a plain statement of when—'

'They pay me to report facts.'

'And they pay me to find out who killed the poor sod, Max.' But Morse, it seemed, was making little impression upon the mournful man who lit another cigarette before continuing.

'Eighteen – cause of death? A mighty whack, probably only one, across the front of the skull, with the bone smashed in from the top of the right eye across the nasal bridge to the left cheekbone.'

Morse was silent.

'Nineteen – he wasn't a navvie, judging from his fingernails.'

'Now you're getting down to things.'

'No I'm not, Morse. I've nearly finished.'

'You're going to tell me who he is, you mean?'

'Twenty – he had flat feet.'

'You mean he *has* flat feet?'

The surgeon permitted himself a bleak smile. 'Yes, Morse. When he was alive he had flat feet, and in death those feet were not unflattened.'

'What does that suggest, Max?'

'Perhaps he's a policeman, Morse.' The surgeon stood up, the cigarette ash dropping on to his black waistcoat. 'I'll let you have the written report as soon as I can. Not tonight though.' He looked at his watch. 'We've got half an hour if you want to nip up to the Gardeners'? I've got a car.'

For a moment or two, Lewis almost thought that Morse was going to resist the temptation.

Chapter Eleven

Wednesday, January 1st: p.m.

When I drink, I think; and when I think, I drink.

(Rabelais)

'Gin and Campari for me, Morse, and buy yourself one as well. My GP keeps on telling me it's sensible to keep off the spirits.'

Soon the two old friends were seated facing each other in the lounge bar, the surgeon resting his heavy-looking dolichocephalic skull upon his left hand.

'Time of death!' said Morse. 'Come on!'

'Nice drink this, Morse.'

'The science of thanatology hasn't advanced a millimetre in your time, has it?'

'Ah! Now you're taking advantage of my classical education.'

'But nowadays, Max, you can look down from one of those space-satellite things and see a house fly rubbing its hands over a slice of black pudding in a Harlem delicatessen – you know that? And yet *you* can't—'

'The room was as cold as a church, Morse. How do you expect—'

'You don't know anything about churches!'

'True enough.'

They sat silently for a while, Morse looking at the open fire where a log suddenly shifted on its foundations and sent a shower of red-glowing sparks against the back of the old grate, beside which was a stack of wood, chopped into quartered segments.

'Did you notice they'd chopped down a couple of trees at the back of the annexe, Max?'

'No.'

Morse sipped his gin. 'I could develop quite a taste for this.'

'You think it might have been the branch of a tree or something . . .? Could have been, I suppose. About two feet long, nice easy grip, couple of inches in diameter.'

'You didn't see any wood splinters?'

'No.'

'What about a bottle?'

'No broken glass on his face, either, as far as I could see.'

'Tough things, though. Some of these people who launch battleships have a hell of a job breaking champagne bottles.'

'We may find something, Morse.'

'When can you let me have a report?'

'Not tonight.'

'Much blood, would there have been?'

'Enough. No spurting though.'

'No good asking the guests if they saw a fellow walking around with blood all over his best shirt?'

'What about a *woman*, Morse? With blood all over her liberty bodice?'

'Perhaps, I suppose.'

The surgeon nodded non-committally and looked into the fire: 'Poor sod . . . Do *you* ever think of death? *Mors, mortis,* feminine – remember that?'

'Not likely to forget a word like that, am I? Just add on "e" to the end and . . .'

The surgeon smiled a sour acknowledgement of the point and drained his glass. 'We'll just have the other half. Then we'll get back, and show you round the scene of the crime again.'

'When the body's out of the way?'

'You don't like the sight of blood much, do you?'

'No. I should never have been a policeman.'

'Always turned me on, blood did – even as a boy.'

'Unnatural!'

'Same again?'

'Why not?'

'What turns *you* on?' asked the surgeon as he picked up the two glasses.

'Somebody from the *Oxford Times* asked me that last week, Max. Difficult, you know – just being asked out of the blue like that.'

'What did you say?'

'I said I was always turned on by the word "unbuttoning".'

'Clever!'

'Not really. It comes in one of Larkin's poems somewhere. It's just that you know nothing about the finer things in life . . .'

But the surgeon, apparently unhearing, was already standing at the bar and rattling an empty glass imperiously on the counter.

Chapter Twelve

Wednesday, January 1st: p.m.

Close up the casement, draw the blind,
Shut out that stealing moon.

(THOMAS HARDY)

UNDER THE SURGEON'S supervision, the frozen-footed ambulancemen had finally stretchered away the white-sheeted corpse to the morgue at the Old Radcliffe at 11.30 p.m., and Lewis was glad that the preliminaries of the case were now almost over. The two fingerprint men had departed just after eleven, followed ten minutes later by the spiky-haired young photographer, clutching the neck of his flash-bulb camera as if it were some poisonous serpent. The surgeon himself had driven off in his old black Ford at a quarter to midnight, and the hotel seemed strangely still as Lewis followed Morse across the slush and blackened snow to the room called Annexe 3, where the two men stood for the second time that evening, and where, each in his own way, they now took a more detailed mental inventory of what they saw.

Immediately to the left in the spacious room (about twenty feet by fourteen feet) stood a built-in wardrobe of white wood, in which nine plastic coat-hangers hung from the cross-rail; beyond it stood a dressing table, its drawers (as we have seen) quite empty, with a brochure of the hotel lying on its top, next to a card with the handwritten message: 'Welcome – your room has been personally prepared by Mandy'; a colour TV set stood in the corner; and, between it and the dressing table, a ledge some four feet from the floor held a kettle, a small teapot, two cups and two saucers, and a rectangular plastic tray, on which, in separate compartments, were small cellophaned packets of biscuits, sachets of Nescafé, sachets of sugar, teabags, and little squat tubs of Eden Vale milk.

Along the far wall was a long low radiator, and just above its top the sill of an equally long window, the latter a triptych of panes, the centre one fixed, but the left and right panes still opened outwards to the elements at an angle of forty-five degrees, and the darkish-green curtains drawn only half across. Liberally sprinkled fingerprint powder was observable all round the window, where a few daubs of unpromising-looking blotches had been circled with a black felt pen.

'Perhaps,' said Morse, a shiver running down his vertebrae, 'we should take our first positive moves in this case, Lewis, eh? Let's close those bloody windows! And turn on the radiator!'

'You're not worried about the prints, sir?'

'It's not going to help us to arrest anybody if we land up in some intensive-care unit with bronchial pneumonia.'

(Lewis, at that moment, felt quite unconscionably happy.)

The twin beds occupied most of the area in the rest of the room, their tops close against the wall to the right, beneath a long headboard panel of beige plastic, set into which were the controls for TV and radio, loudspeakers, various light switches, and an early-morning-alarm unit with what seemed to Lewis instructions that were completely incomprehensible. On a small table between the beds was a white digital telephone; and on a shelf beneath that, the Holy Bible, as placed by the ever-persevering Gideons. The walls and ceiling were painted in a very pale shade of apple green, and the floor was carpeted wall to wall in a grey-green chequered pattern.

All very neat, very clean, and very tidy – apart from the obscene blotch of dried blood across the further bed.

Completing the circuit of this accommodation, the two men came to the tiny bathroom, only some seven feet by five feet, whose door stood a few feet inside and to the right of the main entrance to Annexe 3. Immediately facing was the WC, a unit of the usual white enamel, the bowl a sparkling tribute to the ministrations of the conscientious Mandy; on the left was a washbasin by which stood two tumblers and a diminutive bar of soap (unopened) in a pink paper wrapping bearing the name 'Haworth'; to the right was a bath, fairly small, with shower attachment, and a ledge let into the wall containing a second bar of soap (also unopened); finally, on the wall opposite, to the left of the WC, were racks for a whole assortment of fluffy white towels (all seemingly unused), and fixtures for toilet paper and Kleenex tissues. The walls were tiled in a light olive-green, with the vinyl flooring of a slightly darker, matching green.

'They don't look, whoever they were, as if they made much use of the facilities, sir.'

'No-o.' Morse walked back into the main part of the room and stood there nodding to himself. 'Good point! I wonder if . . .' He fiddled with some of the buttons and switches which appeared to determine the reception of a TV programme; but with no effect.

'Shall I plug it in, sir?'

'You mean . . .?' Again Morse appeared deep in thought as an indeterminate blur dramatically developed into a clearly delineated picture, and a late-night newsreader announced that in Beirut the Shi'ite and the Christian Militias had begun the new year with exactly the same implacable hatred as they had finished the old one.

'Funny, you know, Lewis – turn that thing off! – you'd have thought they would have made *some* use of the facilities, wouldn't you?' Morse carefully drew back the coverings on the bed nearer the window; but the sheets appeared quite virgin, apart from the indentations caused by the superimposition of a corpse. With the other bed, too, the evidence seemed very much the same: someone might well have sat on the side, perhaps, but it seemed reasonably clear that neither bed had been the scene of any frolicsome coition.

It was Lewis, emerging from the bathroom, who had found the only tangible trace of the room's most recent tenants: a screwed-up brown-stained Kleenex tissue, which had been the only item in the waste-bin.

'Looks like this is the only thing they left behind, sir.'

'Not blood is it?'

'It's the stage-black for the make-up, I think.'

'Well, at least we've got *one* clue, Lewis!'

Before leaving, Morse once more slid open the door of the wardrobe along its smooth runners and took another look inside.

'Doesn't look as if your fingerprint lads did much dusting here.'

Lewis looked at the powder marks that covered several points on the white outer-door: 'I wouldn't say that, sir. It looks as if—'

'I meant *inside*,' said Morse quietly.

It was midnight before Sarah Jonstone got to bed that night, and way into the early hours before she finally dropped off into a restless slumber. Her mind was reverting continually to the strangely disturbing chief inspector – a man she was growing to dislike intensely – and to what he had asked, and asked, and asked her. Occasionally, as he had listened to her answers, he had seemed to promote a simple, honest confession of ignorance or forgetfulness on her part to the status of an almost unforgivable sin. And above all her mind reverted to his repeated insistence that she must try to recall anything unusual: anything *unusual*; *anything* unusual ... The words had re-echoed round the walls of her brain – being all the more disturbing precisely because there *had*, she thought, been something unusual ... Yet this 'something' continued to elude her: almost, on several occasions, she had it in her grasp – and then it had slithered away like a slippery bar of soap along the bottom of the bath.

Chapter Thirteen

Thursday, January 2nd: a.m.

> Snow is all right while it is snowing: it is like inebriation, because it is very pleasing when it is coming, but very unpleasing when it is going.
>
> (OGDEN NASH)

MORSE HAD DECIDED that it was needful, at least for a couple of days, to set up a temporary Murder HQ *in situ*; and from the comparatively early hours of the next morning, the room at the rear of the annexe building, a broad-windowed area that looked as if it would make an excellent classroom, was taken over by Lewis and Morse as an official 'Operations Room'.

An innocently deep night's sleep, an early-morning shower and a fried breakfast of high cholesterol risk had launched a zestful Lewis on his way to the Haworth Hotel at 6.30 a.m., where an ill-rested, unshowered, unbreakfasted Morse had joined him twenty minutes later.

At half-past seven it was John Binyon, the hotel proprietor, who was the first of many that day to sit opposite the two detectives at a rickety trestle table.

'It's a terrible thing,' said Binyon. 'Terrible! Just when we'd started getting things going nicely, too.'

'Never mind, sir,' said Morse, calling upon all his powers of self-control to force the last of these three words through the barrier of his teeth. 'Perhaps you'll have a long queue of people waiting to sleep in the famous room.'

'Would you queue for it, Inspector?'

'Certainly not!' said Morse.

The talk turned to the subject of guests in general, and Binyon admitted that things had changed a good deal, even during his own limited experience. 'They don't even pretend these days, some of them – don't even put a ring on, some of the women. Mind you, we turn one or two away – well, you know, make out we're full up.'

'Do you think you could always spot them – if they weren't married?'

Binyon gave the question serious thought. 'No! No – I wouldn't say that. But I think I'd know if they were staying together for the first time.'

'How so?'

'Lots of things. The way they act, I suppose – and they always pay by cash – and they often get addresses wrong. For example, we had a fellow last month who came with his girlfriend, and he put down his address as Slough, *Berks*!'

'What did you do?' asked Morse, frowning.

'Nothing. I wasn't on the desk when he signed in; but I was when he booked out, and I told him straight that the next hotel he went to it might be valuable to know that Slough was in Bucks.'

'What did *he* say?' asked Morse, frowning more than ever.

'He just grinned – as if he hadn't heard me.'

'But Slough *is* in Berks!' said Morse.

The proprietor's general grasp of hotel procedures was clearly considerably in advance of his knowledge of geography, and Morse found himself not unfavourably impressed by his succinct account of current practice at the Haworth Hotel. Normally, between 80 per cent and 90 per cent of the guests contacted the hotel, in the first instance, by phone. Often, there would be insufficient time to seek or to obtain confirmation by letter. Most usually, a credit-card number was sufficient warranty from the hotel's point of view to establish a *bona fides*; but for something so specifically pre-planned and widely advertised as a Christmas or a New Year function, obviously the great majority of guests had *some* correspondence with the hotel. As far as actual registration was concerned, the pattern was (the two detectives learned) exactly what any seasoned traveller would expect at any established hostelry: 'Name?' would be the first question; and, when this was checked against the booking list, a card would be handed over which asked for surname, forename(s), company, company address, home address, method of settling account, nationality, car registration, passport number, and finally signature. Such a fairly straightforward task completed, the guest (or guests) would be given a card showing details of room number, tariff, type of breakfast, type of room, and the like. With a room key handed over from one of the hooks behind Reception, 'registration' was now appropriately effected, with only a final negotiation remaining about the choice of a morning newspaper. And that was that. In such a comparatively small hotel, no porter was employed to carry cases, although the management was of course always on the lookout to ensure suitable assistance for any ageing couples who appeared at risk from cardiac arrest at the prospect of lugging their belongings to the first-floor landing.

At eight fifteen, confirmation was received from Chipping Norton that none of the five Ballard couples on the local Electoral Register had a wifely component answering to the name Ann; and that the town's official archivist, after delving as far back towards Domesday as local records allowed, was prepared to state quite categorically that there was not, nor ever had been, a number 84 along the thoroughfare now known, and always known, as West Street, Chipping Norton.

At eight forty-five, Superintendent Bell rang through from St Aldates to ask if Morse required any further men to help him. But Morse declined the offer; for the moment he could think of nothing he could profitably effect with a posse of policemen, except perhaps to conduct some inevitably futile house-to-house inquiries in and around Chipping Norton to ascertain whether anyone had knowledge of a man of indeterminate age, partner to a pseudonymous Ann Ballard, with neither a club-foot, nor a withered arm, nor a swastika tattooed on his forehead to assist any possible identification. Further, it became quite clear from the guests interviewed later that morning that none of them would with any certitude be able to recognize Mr Ballard again. Such diffidence (as Morse saw things) was hardly surprising: the only time the other guests had met Ballard was during that one evening; up until then he had been a complete stranger to them; and he had spent most of the evening closely shielded and chaperoned by what others had taken to be a jealously possessive wife. Indeed the only reason that many could recall him at all was the extremely obvious one: he had won first prize in the men's fancy-dress competition, dressed in the consummately skilful disguise of a West Indian reggae musician. The only new fact of any substance to emerge was that he had, certainly in the later part of the evening, drunk more than one glass of whisky – Bell's, according to Mandy, the stand-in barmaid. But there was also general agreement, fully corroborating Sarah Jonstone's earlier evidence, that Ballard had eaten very little indeed. Several witnesses had a clear recollection of him dancing with his yashmak'd companion (lover? mistress? wife?), and only with her, for most of the evening; but Mr Dods ('With t'one "d"') was almost prepared to swear on Geoffrey Boycott's batting average that Ballard had also danced, towards midnight, with an animated youngish woman named Mrs Palmer – 'Philippa' or 'Pippa' Palmer, as he recalled – as well as with the hotel receptionist ('A little tipsy, Inspector, if ah mair sair sor!'). And that was about that. And towards the end of the morning it was becoming increasingly obvious to both Morse and Lewis that the only firm and valuable testimony they were going to get was that given the previous evening by Sarah (tipsy or not!) Jonstone, who had claimed in her statement to Lewis that she had peeped out of her window at about 1 a.m. and seen at that late, flake-falling, whitely covered hour, the prize-winning Rastafarian walking back across to the annexe with an arm around each of the women on either side of him. It seemed good to Morse, therefore, to summon the fair Miss Jonstone once again.

She sat there, her legs crossed, looking tired, every few moments pushing her spectacles up to the top of her nose with the middle finger of her ringless left hand – and thereby irritating Morse to a quite disproportionate extent – as he himself hooked his half-lenses behind his ears and trusted that he projected an appropriate degree of investigative acumen.

'After the annexe lot left the party, the others finished too – is that right?'

'I think so.'

'You don't *know* so?'

'No.'

'You say Ballard had his arms round these two women?'

'No, he had one arm round one woman and one—'

'Which two women?'

'Mrs Palmer was one – I'm fairly sure of that.'

'And the other one?'

'I think it was . . . Mrs Smith.'

'You'd had quite a lot to drink, hadn't you!'

Sarah Jonstone's pale face coloured deeply; and yet perhaps it was, that morning, more from anger than from shame. 'Oh yes!' she said, in a firm, quiet voice. 'I don't think you'll find a single person in the hotel who would disagree with that.'

'But you saw the women fairly clearly?' (Morse was beginning to appreciate Miss Jonstone more and more.)

'I saw them clearly from the back, yes.'

'It was snowing, wasn't it?'

'Yes.'

'So they had their coats on?'

'Yes. Both of them had light-coloured winter macs on.'

'And you say' – Morse referred to her statement – 'that the other three members of the annexe sextet were just behind them?'

Sarah nodded.

'So, if you're right about the first three, that leaves us with Mrs Ballard, Mr Palmer and Mr . . . Smith – yes?'

Sarah hesitated – and then said 'Yes!' – then pushed her spectacles up once more towards her luminous eyes.

'And behind them all came Mr Binyon?'

'Yes – I think he was going to make sure that the side door to the annexe was locked up after them.'

'That's what *he* says, too.'

'So it might be true, Inspector.'

But Morse appeared not to have heard her. 'After Mr Binyon had locked up the annexe, no one else could have got *in* there?'

'Not unless he had a key.'

'Or *she* had a key!'

'Or she had a key, yes.'

'But anyone could have got *out* of the annexe later on?'

Again Sarah hesitated before answering. 'Yes, I suppose so. I hadn't really thought of it, but – yes. The lock's an ordinary Yale one, and any of the guests could have got out, if they'd wanted to.'

It was Lewis who, at this point, made an unexpected intervention.

'Are you absolutely *sure* it was snowing then, Miss Jonstone?'

Sarah turned towards the sergeant, feeling relieved to look into a pair of friendly eyes and to hear a friendly voice. And she *wasn't* quite sure, now she came to think of it. The wind had been blowing and lifting up the settled snow in a drifting whirl around her window; and whether it *had* been snowing, at that particular moment, she wasn't really prepared to assert with any dogmatism.

'No,' she said simply. 'I'm *not* absolutely sure.'

'It's just,' continued Lewis, 'that according to the weatherman on Radio Oxford the snow in this area had virtually stopped falling just about midnight. There may have been the odd flurry or two; but it had pretty well finished by then – so they say.'

'What are you trying to get at, Sergeant? I'm not . . . quite sure . . .'

'It's just that if it *had* stopped snowing, and if someone had left the annexe that night, there would have been some footprints, wouldn't there? Wouldn't such a person have to make his way across to the main road?'

Sarah was thinking back, thinking back so very hard. There had been *no* prints the next morning leading from the annexe across to the Banbury Road. None! She could almost swear to that. But *had* it been snowing when she looked out that fateful evening? Yes, it had!

Thus it was that she answered Lewis simply and quietly. 'No, there were no footprints from the annexe to be seen that morning – yesterday morning. But yes, it *was* snowing when I looked out – I'm sure of it.'

'You mean that the weatherman at Radio Oxford has got things all wrong, miss?'

'Yes, I do, Sergeant.'

Lewis felt a little taken aback by such strong, and such conflicting evidence, and he turned to Morse for some kind of arbitration. But as he did so, he noticed (as he had so often in the past) that the chief inspector's eyes were growing brighter and brighter by the second, in some sort of slow incandescence, as though a low-powered filament had been switched on somewhere at the back of his brain. But Morse said nothing for the moment, and Lewis tried to rediscover his bearings.

'So from what you say, you think that Mr Ballard

must have been murdered by one of those five other people there?'

'Well, yes! Don't you? I think he was murdered by Mr or Mrs Palmer, or by Mr or Mrs Smith, or by Mrs Ballard – whoever *she* is!'

'I see.'

During these exchanges, Morse himself had been watching the unshadowed, unrouged, unlipsticked blonde with considerable interest; but no longer. He stood up and thanked her, and then seemed relieved that she had left them.

'Some shrewd questioning there, Lewis!'

'You really think so, sir?'

But Morse made no direct answer. 'It's time we had some refreshment,' he said.

Lewis, who was well aware that Morse invariably took his lunchtime calories in liquid form, was himself perfectly ready for a pint and a sandwich; but he was a little displeased about Morse's apparently total lack of interest in the weather conditions at the time of the murder.

'About the snow, sir—' he began.

'The snow? The snow, my old friend, is a complete white herring,' said Morse, already pulling on his greatcoat.

In the back bar of the Eagle and Child in St Giles', the two men sat and drank their beer, and Lewis found himself reading and reading again the writing on the wooden plaque fixed to the wall behind Morse's head:

> C.S. LEWIS, his brother, W.H. Lewis, J.R.R. Tolkien, Charles Williams, and other friends met every Tuesday morning, between the years 1939–1962 in the back room of this their favourite pub. These men, popularly known as the 'Inklings', met here to drink beer and to discuss, among other things, the books they were writing.

And strangely enough it was Sergeant Lewis's mind, after (for him) a rather liberal intake of alcohol, which was waxing the more imaginative as he pictured a series of fundamental emendations to this received text; 'CHIEF INSPECTOR MORSE, with his friend and colleague Sergeant Lewis, sat in this back room one Thursday, in order to solve . . .'

Chapter Fourteen

Thursday, January 2nd: p.m.

'Is there anybody there?' he said.

(WALTER DE LA MARE, *The Listeners*)

IF, AS NOW seemed most probable, the Haworth Hotel murderer was to be sought amongst the fellow guests who had been housed in the annexe on New Year's Eve, it was high time to look more carefully into the details of the Palmers and the Smiths, the guests (now vanished) who had been staying in Annexe 1 and Annexe 2 respectively; and Lewis looked at the registration forms he had in front of him, each of them fully filled in; each of them, on the face of it, innocent enough.

The Palmers' address, the same on the registration form as on the earlier correspondence, was given as 29A Chiswick Reach; and the telephone operator confirmed that there was indeed such a property, and that it did indeed have a subscriber by the name of Palmer, P. (sex not stated) listed in the London Telephone Directory. Lewis saw Morse's eyebrows lift a little, as if he were more than a fraction surprised at this intelligence; but for his own part he refused to assume that everyone who had congregated quite fortuitously in the Haworth annexe was therefore an automatic criminal. He dialled the number and waited, letting the phone at the other end ring for about a minute before putting down the receiver.

'We could get someone round there, perhaps?'

'Not yet, Lewis. Give it a go every half-hour or so.'

Lewis nodded, and looked down at the Smiths' card.

'What's their address?' asked Morse.

'Posh sort of place, by the look of it, "*Aldbrickham*, 22 Spring Street, Gloucester".'

This time Lewis saw Morse's eyebrows lift a lot. 'Here! Let me look at that!' said Morse.

And as he did so, Lewis saw him shake his head slowly, a smile forming at the corners of his mouth.

'I'm prepared to bet you my bank-balance that there's no such address as that!'

'I'm not betting anything!'

'I know the place, Lewis. And so should you! It's the street where Jude and Sue Fawley lived!'

'Should I know them?'

'In *Jude the Obscure*, Lewis! And "Aldbrickham" is Hardy's name for Reading, as you'll remember.'

'Yes, I'd forgotten for the moment,' said Lewis.

'Clever!' Morse nodded again as though in approbation of the literary tastes of Mr and Mrs John Smith. 'There's no real point in trying but . . .' Lewis heard an audible sigh from the girl on 192 as she heard that Lewis wanted Smith, J.; and it took her a little while to discover there was no subscriber of that name with a

Spring Street address in Gloucester. A further call to the Gloucester Police established, too, that there was not a Spring Street in the city.

Lewis tried Chiswick again: no reply.

'Do you reckon we ought to try old Doris – Doris Arkwright?' asked Morse. 'Perhaps she's another crook.'

But before any such attempt could be made, a messenger from the pathology lab came in with the police surgeon's preliminary findings. The amateurishly typewritten report added little to what had already been known, or assumed, from the previous evening's examination: age thirty-five to forty-five; height five foot eight and a half ('He's grown an inch overnight!' said Morse); no fragments of wood or glass or steel in the considerable facial injury, caused likely enough by a single powerful blow; teeth – in exceptionally good condition for a male in the age group, with only three minor fillings in the left-hand side of the jaw, one of them very recent; stomach – a few mixed vegetables, but little recent intake by the look of things.

That, in essence, was all the report said. No further information about such key issues as the time of death; an array of medical terms, though, such as 'supra-orbital foramen' and 'infra-orbital fissure', which Morse was perfectly happy to ignore. But there was a personal note from the surgeon written in a spidery scrawl at the foot of this report. 'Morse: A major drawback to any immediate identification is going to be the very extensive laceration and contusion across the inferior nasal concha – this doesn't give us any easily recognizable lineaments for a photograph – and it makes the look of the face harrowing for relatives. In any case, people always look different when they're dead. As for the time of death, I've nothing to add to my definitive statement of yesterday. In short, your guess is as good as mine, although it would come as a profound shock to me if it was any better. Max.'

Morse glanced through the report as rapidly as he could, which was, to be truthful, not very rapidly at all. He had always been a slow reader, ever envying those of his colleagues whose eyes appeared to have the facility to descend swiftly through the centre of a page of writing, taking in as they went the landscape both to the left and to the right. But two points – two simple, major points – were firmly and disappointingly apparent: and Morse put them into words.

'They don't know who he is, Lewis; and they don't know when he died. Bloody typical!'

Lewis grinned: 'He's not a bad old boy, though.'

'He should be pensioned off! He's too old! He drinks too much! No – he's not a bad old boy, as you say; but he's on the downward slope, I'm afraid.'

'You once told me *you* were on the downward slope, sir!'

'We're *all* on the downward slope!'

'Shall we go and have a look at the other bedrooms?' Lewis spoke briskly, and stood up as if anxious to prod a lethargic-looking Morse into some more purposive line of inquiry.

'You mean they may have left their Barclaycards behind?'

'You never know, sir.' Lewis fingered the great bunch of keys that Binyon had given him, but Morse appeared reluctant to get moving.

'Shall I do it myself, sir?'

Morse got up at last. 'No! Let's go and have a look round the rooms – you're quite right. You take the Palmers' room.'

In the Smiths' room, Annexe 2, Morse looked around him with little enthusiasm (wouldn't the maid have tidied Annexe 1 and Annexe 2 during the day?), finally turning back the sheets on each of the twin beds, then opening the drawers of the dressing table, then looking inside the wardrobe. Nothing. In the bathroom, it was clear that one or both of the Smiths had taken a shower or a bath fairly recently, for the two large white towels were still slightly damp and the soap in the wall-niche had been used – as had the two squat tumblers that stood on the surface behind the washbasin. But there was nothing to learn here, Morse felt sure of that. No items left behind; no torn letters thrown into the waste-paper basket; only a few marks over the carpet, mostly just inside the door, left by shoes and boots that had tramped across the slush and snow. In any case, Morse felt fairly sure that the Smiths, whoever they were, had nothing at all to do with the crime, because he thought he knew just how and why the pair of them had come to the Haworth Hotel, booking *in* at the last possible moment, and getting *out* at the earliest possible moment after the murder of Ballard had been discovered.

'Smith, J.' (there was little doubt in Morse's mind) was an ageing rogue in middle management, drooling with lust over a new young secretary, who'd told his long-suffering spouse that he had to go to a business conference in the Midlands over the New Year. Such conduct was commonplace, Morse knew that; and perhaps there was little point in pursuing the matter further. Yet he would like to meet her, for she was, according to the other guests, a pleasingly attractive woman. He sat on one of the beds, and picked up the phone.

'Can I help you?' It was Sarah Jonstone.

'Do you know what's the first thing they tell you if you go on a course for receptionists?'

'Oh! It's you.'

'They tell you never to say "Can I help you?"'

'Can I hinder you, Inspector?'

'Did the Smiths make any telephone calls while they were here?'

'Not from the bedroom.'

'You'd have a record of it – on their bill, I mean – if they'd phoned anyone?'

'Ye-es. Yes we would.' Her voice sounded oddly hesitant, and Morse waited for her to continue. 'Any phone call gets recorded automatically.'

'That's it then.'

'Er – Inspector! We've – we've just been going through accounts and we shall have to check again but – we're almost sure that Mr and Mrs Smith didn't square up their account before they left.'

'Why the hell didn't you tell me before?' snapped Morse.

'Because – I – didn't – know,' Sarah replied, spacing the four words deliberately and quietly and only just resisting the impulse to slam the receiver down on him.

'How much did they owe?'

Again, there was a marked hesitation at the end of the line. 'They had some champagne taken to their room – expensive stuff—'

'Nobody's ever had a *cheap* bottle of champagne – in a hotel – have they?'

'And they had four bottles—'

'*Four?*' Morse whistled softly to himself. 'What exactly was this irresistible vintage?'

'It was Veuve Clicquot Ponsardin 1972.'

'It it good stuff?'

'As I say, it's expensive.'

'How expensive?'

'£29.75 a bottle.'

'It's *what?*' Again Morse whistled to himself, and his interest in the Smiths was obviously renascent. 'Four twenty-nines are . . . Phew!'

'Do you think it's important?' she asked.

'Who'd pick up the empties?'

'Mandy would – the girl who did the rooms.'

'And where would she put them?'

'We've got some crates at the back of the kitchen.'

'Did anyone else raid the champagne cellar?'

'I don't think so.'

'So you ought to have four empty bottles of '72 whatever-it-is out there?'

'Yes, I suppose so.'

'No "suppose" about it, is there?'

'No.'

'Well, check up – straight away, will you?'

'All right.'

Morse walked back into the bathroom, and without picking up the tumblers leaned over and sniffed them one by one. But he wasn't at all sure if either smelled of champagne, though one pretty certainly smelled of some peppermint-flavoured toothpaste. Back in the bedroom, he sat down once more on the bed, wondering if there was something *in* the room, or something *about* the room, that he had missed. Yet he could find nothing – not even the vaguest reason for his suspicions; and he was about to go when there was a soft knocking on the door and Sarah Jonstone came in.

'Inspector, I—' Her upper lip was shaking and it was immediately clear that she was on the verge of tears.

'I'm sorry I was a bit short with you—' began Morse.

'It's not that. It's just . . .'

He stood up and put his arm lightly round her shoulders. 'No need to tell me. It's that penny-pinching Binyon, isn't it? He's not only lost the Smiths' New Year contributions, he's an extra one hundred and nineteen pounds short – yes?'

She nodded, and as the eyes behind the large round lenses brimmed with glistening tears Morse lightly lifted off her spectacles and she leaned against his shoulder, the tears coursing freely down her cheeks. And finally, when she lifted her head and smiled feebly, and rubbed the backs of her hands against her tear-stained face, he took out his only handkerchief, originally white and now a dirty grey, and pushed it into her grateful hands. She was about to say something, but Morse spoke first.

'Now don't you worry, my girl, about Binyon, all right? Or about these Smiths, either! I'll make sure we catch up with 'em sooner or later.'

Sarah nodded. 'I'm sorry I was so silly.'

'Forget it!'

'You know the champagne bottles? Well, there are only *three* of them in the crate. They must have taken one away with them – it's not here.'

'Perhaps they didn't quite finish it.'

'It's not very easy to carry a half-full bottle of bubbly around.'

'No. You can't get the cork back in, can you?'

She smiled, feeling very much happier now, and found herself looking at Morse and wondering if he had a wife or a series of women-friends or whether he just wasn't interested: it was difficult to tell. She was conscious, too, that his mind hadn't seemed to be on her at all for the last few minutes. And indeed this was true.

'You feeling better?' she heard him say; but he appeared no longer to have any interest in her well-being, and he said no more as she turned and left him in the bedroom.

A few minutes later he poked his head round the door of Annexe 1 and found Lewis on his hands and knees beside the dressing table.

'Found anything?' he asked.

'Not yet, sir.'

*

Back in the temporary Operations Room, Morse rang the pathology lab and found the police surgeon there.

'Could it have been a bottle, Max?'

'Perhaps,' admitted that morose man. 'But if it was it didn't break.'

'You mean even you would have found a few lumps of glass sticking in the fellow's face?'

'Even me!'

'Do you think with a blow like that a bottle *would* have smashed?'

'*If* it was a bottle, you mean?'

'Yes, *if* it was a bottle.'

'Don't know.'

'Well, bloody guess, then!'

'Depends on the bottle.'

'A champagne bottle?'

'Many a day since I saw one, Morse!'

'Do you think whoever murdered Ballard was left-handed or right-handed?'

'If he was a right-handed tennis player it must have been a sort of backhand shot: if he was left-handed, it must have been a sort of smash.'

'You're not very often as forthcoming as that!'

'I try to help.'

'Do you think our tennis player was right-handed or left-handed?'

'Don't know,' said the surgeon.

Lewis came in a quarter of an hour later to report to his rather sour-looking superior that his exhaustive search of the Palmer suite had yielded absolutely nothing.

'Never mind, Lewis! Let's try the Palmer number again.'

But Morse could hear the repeated 'Brr-brrs' from where he sat, and sensed somehow that for the moment at least there would be no answer to the call. 'We're not having a great afternoon, one way or another, are we?' he said.

'Plenty of time yet, sir.'

'What about old Doris? Shall we give her a ring? We know *she's* at home – warming her corns on the radiator, like as not.'

'You want me to try?'

'Yes, I do!'

But there was no Arkwright of any initial listed in the Kidderminster area at 114 Worcester Road. But there *was* a subscriber at that address; and after some reassurance from Lewis about the nature of the inquiry the supervisor gave him the telephone number. Which he rang.

'Could I speak to Miss Doris Arkwright, please?'

'I think you've got the wrong number.'

'That *is* 114 Worcester Road?'

'Yes.'

'And you haven't got a Miss or a Mrs Arkwright there?'

'We've got a butcher's shop 'ere, mate.'

'Oh, I see. Sorry to have troubled you.'

'You're welcome.'

'I just don't believe it!' said Morse quietly.

CHAPTER FIFTEEN

Thursday, January 2nd: p.m.

Even in civilized mankind, faint traces of a monogamic instinct can sometimes be perceived.

(BERTRAND RUSSELL)

HELEN SMITH'S HUSBAND, John, had told her he would be back at about one o'clock, and Helen had the ingredients for a mushroom omelette all ready. Nothing for herself, though. She would have found it very difficult to swallow anything that lunchtime, for she was sick with worry.

The headlines on 'The World at One' had just finished when she heard the crunch of the BMW's wheels on the gravel outside – the same BMW which had spent the New Year anonymously enough in the large multi-storey car park in the Westgate shopping centre at Oxford. She didn't turn as she felt his light kiss on the back of her hair, busying herself with excessive fussiness over the bowl as she whisked the eggs, and looking down at the nails of her broad, rather stumpy fingers, now so beautifully manicured . . . and so very different from the time, five years ago, when she had first met John, and when he had mildly criticized her irritating habit of biting them down to the quicks ... Yes, he had smartened her up in more than one way in their years of marriage together. That was certain.

'Helen! I've got to go up to London this afternoon. I may be back later tonight; but if I'm not, don't worry. I've got a key.'

'Um!' For the moment, she hardly dared risk a more fully articulated utterance.

'Is the water hot?'

'Mm!'

'Will you leave the omelette till I've had a quick bath?'

She waited until he had gone into the bathroom; waited until she heard the splash of water; even then gave things a couple of minutes more, just in case ... before stepping out lightly and quietly across the drive and trying the front passenger door of the dark-blue BMW – almost whimpering with anticipation.

It was open.

Two hours after Mr John Smith had stretched himself out in his bath at Reading, Philippa Palmer lay looking up at the ceiling of her own bedroom in her tastefully furnished, recently redecorated, first-floor flat in Chiswick. The man who lay beside her she had spotted at 12.30 p.m. in the Cocktail Lounge of the Executive Hotel just off Park Lane – a tall, dark-suited, prematurely balding man, perhaps in his early forties. To Philippa, he looked like a man not short of a few pounds, although it was always difficult to be certain. The exorbitant tariffs at the Executive (her favourite hunting-ground) were almost invariably settled on business expense accounts, and bore no necessary correlation with the apparent affluence of the hotel's (largely male) clientèle. She'd been sitting at the bar, nylon-stockinged, legs crossed, split skirt falling above the knee; he'd said 'Hullo', pleasantly; she'd accepted his offer of a drink – gin and tonic; she'd asked him, wasting no time at all, whether he wanted to be 'naughty' – an epithet which, in her wide experience, was wonderfully efficacious in beguiling the vast majority of men; he had demurred, slightly; she had moved a little closer and shot a sensual thrill throughout his body as momentarily she splayed a carmine-fingered hand along his thigh. The 'How much?' and the 'When?' and the 'Where?' had been settled with a speed unknown in any other professional negotiating body; and now here she lay – a familiar occurrence! – in her own room, in her own bed, waiting with ineffable boredom for the two-hour contract (at £60 per hour) to run its seemingly interminable course. She'd gauged him pretty well correctly from the start: a man of rather passive, voyeuristic tendencies rather than one of the more thrusting operatives in the fornication field. Indeed, the aggregate time of his two (hitherto) perfunctory penetrations could hardly have exceeded a couple of minutes; and of that Philippa had been duly glad. He might, of course, 'after a few minutes' rest' as the man had put it, rise to more sustained feats of copulatory stamina; but blessedly (from Philippa's point of view) the few minutes' rest had extended itself to a prolonged period of stertorous slumber.

The phone had first rung at about 2.30 p.m., the importunate burring making the man quite disproportionately nervous as he'd undressed. But she had told him that it would only be her sister; and he had appeared to believe her, and to relax. And as she herself had begun unzipping her skirt, he had asked if she would wear a pair of pyjamas while they were in bed together – a request with which she was not unfamiliar, knowing as she did that more than a few of her clients were less obsessed with nudity than with *semi*-nudity, and that the slow unbuttoning of a blouse-type top, with its tantalizing lateral revelations, was a far more erotic experience for almost all men than the vertically functional hitch of a nightdress up and over the thighs.

It was 3.15 p.m. when the phone rang again, and Philippa felt the man's eyes feasting on her body as she leaned forward and picked up the receiver.

'Mrs Palmer? Mrs Philippa Palmer?' The voice was loud and clear, and she knew that the man at her side would be able to hear every word.

'Ye-es?'

'This is Sergeant Lewis here, Thames Valley Police. I'd like to have a word with you about—'

'Look, Sergeant. Can you ring me back in ten minutes? I'm just having a shower and—'

'All right. You'll make sure you're there, Mrs Palmer?'

'Of course! Why shouldn't I be?'

The man had been sitting on the edge of the bed pulling on his socks with precipitate haste from the words 'Sergeant Lewis' onwards, and Philippa was relieved that (as always) pecuniary matters had been fully settled before the start of the performance. Seldom had Philippa seen a man dress himself so quickly; and his hurried goodbye and immediate departure were a relief to her, although she knew he was probably quite a nice sort of man, really. She admitted to herself that his underclothes had been the cleanest she had seen in weeks; and he hadn't mentioned his wife, if he had one, once.

It was a different voice at the end of the line when the telephone rang again ten minutes later: an interesting, educated sort of voice that she told herself she rather liked the sound of, announcing itself as Chief Inspector Morse.

Morse insisted that it would be far more sensible for himself (not Lewis) to go to interview the woman finally found at the other end of a telephone line in Chiswick. He fully appreciated Lewis's offer to go, but he also emphasized the importance of someone (Lewis) staying at the hotel and continuing to 'sniff around'. Lewis, who had heard this sort of stuff many times, was smiling to himself as he drove Morse down to Oxford station to catch the 4.34 train to Paddington that afternoon.

Chapter Sixteen

Thursday, January 2nd: p.m.

And he that seeketh findeth.

(MATTHEW vii, 8)

ON HIS RETURN from Oxford railway station, Lewis was tempted to call it a day and get off home. He had been up since 5 a.m., and it was now just after 5 p.m. A long enough stretch for anybody. But he didn't call it a day; and in retrospect his decision was to prove a crucial one in solving the mystery surrounding Annexe 3.

He decided to have a last look round the rooms in the annexe before he went home, and for this purpose he left the Operations Room by the front door (the partition between the main annexe entrance and the four rooms in use had not been dismantled) and walked round the front of the building to the familiar side-entrance, where a uniformed constable still stood on duty.

'It's open, Sarge,' Lewis heard as he fumbled with his embarrassment of keys.

'Give it till seven, I reckon. Then you can get off,' said Lewis. 'I'll just have a last look round.'

First, Lewis had a quick look round the one room that no one had as yet bothered about, Annexe 4; and here he made one small find – alas, completely insignificant. On the top shelf of the built-in wardrobe he found a glossy magazine illustrated with lewdly pornographic photographs, and filled out with a minimum of text which (judging from a prevalence of ø-looking letters) Lewis took to be written in some Scandinavian tongue. If Morse had been there (Lewis knew it so well) he would have sat down on the bed forthwith and given the magazine his undivided attention; and it often puzzled Lewis a little to understand how an otherwise reasonably sensitive person such as Morse could simultaneously behave in so unworthily crude a fashion. Yet he knew that nothing was ever likely to change the melancholy, uncommitted Morse; and he put the magazine back on the shelf, deciding that his superior should know nothing of it.

In Annexe 3 itself, there were so many chalked marks, so many biro'd circles, so many dusted surfaces, so much shifted furniture, that it was impossible to believe any clue would now be found there that had not been found already; and Lewis turned off the light and closed the door, making sure it was locked behind him.

In Annexe 1, the Palmers' room, Lewis could find nothing that he had missed in his earlier examination, and he paused only for a moment before the window, seeing his own shadow in the oblong of yellow light that was thrown across the snow, before turning the light off there too, and closing the door behind him.

He would have a quick look at the last room, the Smiths' room, and then he really would call an end to his long, long day.

In this room, Annexe 2, he could find nothing of any import; and Morse (Lewis knew) would have looked over it with adequate, if less than exhaustive, care. In any case, Morse had a creative imagination that he himself could never hope to match, and often in the past there had been things – those oddly intangible things – which the careful Lewis himself had missed and which Morse had almost carelessly discovered. Yet it would do no harm to have one final eleventh-hour check before permission was given to Binyon (as soon it must be) for the rooms to be freed for hotel use once more.

It was five minutes later that Lewis made his exciting discovery.

Sarah Jonstone saw Lewis leave just before 6 p.m., his car headlights, as he turned in front of the annexe, sending revolving patches of yellow light across the walls and ceiling of her unlit room. Then the winter darkness was complete once more. She had never minded the dark, even as a little girl, when she'd always preferred the door of her bedroom shut and the light on the landing switched off; and now as she looked out she was again content to leave the light turned off. She was developing a slight headache and she had dropped two soluble Disprin into a glass of water and was slowly swishing the disintegrating tablets round. Mr Binyon had asked her to stay on another night, and in the circumstances it would have been unkind for her to refuse. But it was an oddly unsatisfactory, anticlimactic sort of time: the night was now still after so many comings and goings; the lights in the annexe all switched off, including the light in the large back room which Morse and Lewis had been using; the press, the police, the public – almost everyone seemed to have gone; gone, too, were all the New Year revellers, all of them gone back home again – all except one, of course, the one who would never see his home again. The only signs left of all the excitement were the beribboned ropes that still cordoned off the annexe area, and the single policeman in the flat, black-and-white checked hat who still stood at the side entrance of the annexe, his breath steaming in the cold air, stamping his feet occasionally, and pulling his greatcoat ever more closely around him. She was wondering if she ought to offer him something – when she heard Mandy, from just below her window, call across and ask him if he wanted a cup of tea.

She herself drank the cloudy, bitter-tasting mixture from the glass, switched on the light, washed the glass, smoothed the wrinkled coverlet on which she had earlier been lying, turned on the TV, and listened to the main items of the six o'clock news. The world that day, that second day of the brand-new year, was familiarly full of crashes, hijackings, riots and terrorism; yet somehow such cataclysmic, collective disasters seemed far less disturbing to her than the murder of that one man, only some twenty-odd yards from where she stood. She turned off the TV, and went over to the window to pull the curtains across; she would smarten herself up a bit before going down to have her evening meal with the Binyons.

Odd!

A light was on again in the annexe, and she wondered who it could be. Probably the constable, for he was no longer standing by the side door. It was almost certainly in Annexe 2 that the light was on, she thought, judging from the yellow square of snow in front of the building. Then the light was switched off; and standing there at her window, arms outspread, Sarah was just about to pull the curtains across when she saw a figure, just inside the annexe doorway, pressed against the left-hand wall. Her heart seemed to miss a beat, and she felt a constriction somewhere at the back of her throat as she stood there for a few seconds completely motionless, mesmerized by what she had seen. Then she acted. She threw open the door, scampered down the stairs, rushed through to the main entrance and then along to the side door of the main building, where the constable stood talking with Mandy over a cup of steaming tea.

'There's someone across there!' Sarah whispered hoarsely as she pointed over to the annexe block.

'Pardon, miss?'

'I just saw someone in the doorway!'

The man hurried across to the annexe, with Sarah and Mandy walking nervously a few steps behind. They saw him open the side door (it hadn't been locked, that much was clear) and then watched as the light flicked on in the corridor, and then flicked off.

'There's no one there now,' said the worried-looking constable, clearly conscious of some potentially disastrous dereliction of duty.

'There *was* someone,' persisted Sarah quietly. 'It was in Annexe 2 – I'm sure of it. I saw the light on the snow.'

'But the rooms are all locked up, miss.'

Sarah said nothing. There were only two sets of master-keys, and Binyon (Sarah knew) had given one of those sets to Sergeant Lewis. But Sergeant Lewis had gone. Had Binyon used the other set *himself*? Had the slim figure she had seen in the doorway been Binyon's? And if so, what on earth—?

It was Binyon himself, wearing a raincoat but no hat, who had startlingly materialized from somewhere, and who now stood behind them, insisting (once he had asked about the nature of the incident) that they should check up on the situation forthwith.

Sarah followed him and the constable into the annexe corridor, and it was immediately apparent that someone *had* stood – and that within the last few minutes or so – in front of the door to Annexe 2. The carpet just below the handle was muddied with the marks of slushy footwear, and little slivers of yet unmelted snow winked under the neon lighting of the corridor.

*

Back in her room, Sarah thought hard about what had just happened. The constable had refused to let the door of Annexe 2 be touched or opened, and had immediately tried to contact Lewis at the number he had been instructed to ring should anything untoward occur. But Lewis had not yet arrived home; and this fact tended to bolster the belief, expressed by both Binyon and the constable, that it had probably been Lewis who had called back for some unexpected though probably quite simple reason. But Sarah had kept her counsel. She knew quite certainly that the figure she had glimpsed in the annexe doorway could never have been the heavily built Sergeant Lewis. *Could* it have been Mr Binyon, though? Whilst not impossible, that too, thought Sarah, was wildly improbable. And, as it happened, her view of the matter was of considerably greater value than anyone else's. Not only was she the sole witness to the furtive figure seen in the doorway; she was also the only person, at least for the present, who knew a most significant fact: the fact that although there were only two sets of master-keys to the annexe rooms, it was perfectly possible for *someone else* to have entered the room that evening without forcing a door or breaking a window. *Two other people*, in fact. On the key-board behind Reception, the hook was still empty on which should have been hanging the black-plastic oblong tab, with 'Haworth' printed over it in white, and the room key to Annexe 2 attached to it. For Mr and Mrs John Smith had left behind their unsettled account, but their room key they had taken with them.

Chapter Seventeen

Thursday, January 2nd: p.m.

Aspern Williams wanted to touch the skin of the daughter, thinking her beautiful, by which I mean separate and to be joined.

(PETER CHAMPKIN, *The Waking Life of Aspern Williams*)

MORSE WALKED THROUGH the carpeted lounge of the Great Western Hotel where several couples, seemingly with little any longer to say to each other, were desultorily engaged in reading paperbacks, consulting timetables or turning over the pages of the London *Standard*. Time, apparently, was the chief item of importance here, where a video-screen gave travellers up-to-the-minute information about arrivals and departures, and where frequent glances were thrown towards the large clock above the Porters' Desk, at which stood two slightly supercilious-looking men in gold-braided green uniforms. It was 5.45 p.m.

Immediately in front of him, through the revolving door that gave access to Praed Street, Morse could see the white lettering of PADDINGTON on the blue Underground sign as he turned right and made his way towards the Brunel Bar. At its entrance, a board announced that 5.30 p.m. to 6.30 p.m. encompassed 'The Happy Hour', with any drink available at half-price – a prospect doubtless accounting for the throng of dark-suited black-briefcased businessmen who stood around the bar, anxious to get in as many drinks as possible before departing homewards to Slough or Reading or Didcot or Swindon or Oxford. Wall-seats, all in a deep maroon shade of velveteen nylon, lined the rectangular bar; and after finally managing to purchase his half-priced pint of beer, Morse sat down near the main entrance behind one of the free-standing, mahogany-veneered tables. The tripartite glass dish in front of him offered nuts, crisps, and cheese biscuits, into which he found himself dipping more and more nervously as the hands of the clock crept towards 6 p.m. Almost (he knew it!) he felt as excited as if he were a callow youth once more. It was exactly 6 p.m. when Philippa Palmer walked into the bar. For purposes of recognition, it had been agreed that she should carry her handbag in her left hand and a copy of the London *Standard* in her right. But the fact that she had got things the wrong way round was of little consequence to Morse; he himself was quite incapable of any instant and instinctive knowledge of east and west, and he would have spotted her immediately. Or so he told himself.

He stood up, and she walked over to him.

'Chief Inspector Morse?' Her face betrayed no emotion whatsoever: no signs of nervousness, embarrassment, co-operation, affability, humour – nothing.

'Let me get you a drink,' said Morse.

She took off her raincoat, and as Morse waited his turn again at the crowded bar he watched her from the corner of his eye: five foot five or six, or thereabouts, wearing a roll-necked turquoise-blue woollen dress which gently emphasized the rounded contours of her bottom but hardly did the rest of her figure much justice, perhaps. When he set the glass of red wine in front of her, she had crossed her nyloned legs, her slim-style high-heeled shoes accentuating the slightly excessive muscularity of her calves; and across the back of her right ankle Morse noticed a piece of Elastoplast, as though her expensive shoes probably combined the ultimate in elegance with a sorry degree of discomfiture.

'I tried to run a half-marathon – for charity,' she said, following his eyes, and his thoughts.

'For the Police Welfare Fund, I trust!' said Morse lightly.

Her eyes were on the brink of the faintest smile, and Morse looked closely at her face. It was undeniably an attractive face, framed by a head of luxuriant dark-brown hair glinting overall with hints of auburn; but it was the eyes above the high cheekbones – eyes of a deep brown – that were undoubtedly the woman's most striking feature. When she had spoken (with a slight Cockney accent) she had shown rather small regular teeth behind a mouth coated with only the thinnest smear of dark-red lipstick, and a great many men (Morse knew it) would find her a very attractive woman; and more than a few would find her necessary, too.

She had quite a lot to tell, but it took no great time to tell it. She was (she admitted) a high-class call-girl, who regularly encountered her clients in the cocktail bars of the expensive hotels along Park Lane and Mayfair. Occasionally, especially in recent years with wealthy Arabian gentlemen, she would dispense her favours on the site, as it were, in the luxury apartments and penthouse suites on the higher floors of the hotels themselves. But with the majority, the more usual routine was a trip back to Chiswick in a taxi, where her own discreet flat, on the eighth (and top) floor of a private, modern block, was ideal, served as it was by a very superior lift, and where no children, pets or hawkers (in that order) were allowed. This flat she shared with a happy-souled, feckless, mightily bosomed, blonde dancer who performed in the Striporama Revue Club off Great Windmill Street; but the two of them had agreed from the start that no men visitors should ever be invited to stay overnight, and the agreement had as yet remained unbreached. So that was her CV – not much else to say, really. 'Mr Palmer', a stockbroker from Gerrards Cross, she had met several times previously; and when the prospect cropped up of a New Year conference in Oxford – well, that's how this business had all started. They needed an address for correspondence, and she, Philippa, had written and booked the room from her Chiswick flat – perfectly above board. (An address *was* needed, she insisted; and Morse refrained from arguing the dubious point.) She herself had completed the documentation for both of them at lunchtime on the 31st, though not filling in the registration number of the Porsche which they had left in the British Rail car park. He'd had a good time, her client – she was quite sure of that until . . . And then, of course, there was every chance of him being found out – 'Just like being caught by the police in a raid on a Soho sex-joint!' – and he'd asked her to settle up immediately in cash, and then he'd got the pair of them out of there in double quick time, taking her with him to the station in a taxi and leaving her on the platform. From what he'd told her, he was going to book in at the Moat Hotel (at the top of the Woodstock Road) for the rest of the conference, and keep as big a distance as he possibly could between himself and the ill-fated annexe at the Haworth. Did the inspector *really* have to have his name? And in any case she hadn't the faintest idea of his address in Gerrards Cross. Quite certainly, in her view, he could have had nothing whatsoever to do with the killing of Ballard, because when she'd gone back to her room after the party she'd actually walked across to the annexe *with Ballard*, and then gone immediately into her own room with her, well, her sleeping companion, and she could vouch for the fact that he hadn't left the room that night – or left the bed for that matter! Assuredly not!

Morse nodded, a little enviously, perhaps. 'He was a pretty rich man, then?'

'Rich enough.'

'But not rich enough to afford a room in the main hotel?'

'There weren't any rooms left. We had to take what was going.'

'I know, yes. I'm glad you're telling me the truth, Miss Palmer. I've seen your correspondence with the hotel.'

For a few seconds her dark eyes held his – eyes that seemed momentarily to have grown hard and calculating – and she continued in a somewhat casual tone: 'He gave me the cash – in £20 notes. He was happy for me to make all the arrangements.'

'You made a bit on the side, then?'

'Christ!' It seemed as if she were about to explode at such a banal accusation, and her eyes flashed darkly with anger. 'You think that I have to rely on fiddling a few quid like that to make a living?'

But Morse couldn't answer. He was furious with himself for his stupid, naïve, condescending question; and he was relieved when she agreed to a second glass of red wine.

The Happy Hour was over.

The New Year party itself? It had been good fun, really – and the food had been surprisingly good. She herself had dressed up – maybe the inspector preferred 'dressed down'? – as a Turkish belly-dancer; with her companion, to her surprise, entering into the party spirit with considerable zest and ingenuity, and fashioning for himself from the rag-bag provided by the hotel an outfit not unworthy of an Arabian sheik. Quite a success, too! Not half as good as Ballard's, of course; but then some people took these things too seriously, as *he* had done – coming along all prepared with the necessary gear and grease and everything. As far as Philippa could remember, the Ballards had come in a few minutes later than all the rest; but she wasn't really very clear about the point, or about a lot of other things that went on during that evening. There had been eating and drinking and dancing and no doubt a little bit of semi-licit smooching (yes! on her part, too – just a little) in the candle-lit ballroom, and perhaps later on still a bit of . . . Philippa appeared to have difficulty in finding the right words for what Morse took to be some incidence of *sub mensa* gropings. Ballard, she thought, hadn't really come to life until after the judging of the fancy dress, spending much of the earlier part of the evening looking into the eyes (about the only feature he could look into!) of his yashmak'd wife – or whatever was another word for 'wife'. For it had seemed pretty clear to Philippa that she was not the only one involved that evening in extra-conjugal infidelity.

Anything else? She didn't think so. She'd already mentioned that Ballard had walked back to the annexe with her? Yes, of course she had. One arm round her, and one arm round Helen Smith: yes, she remembered Helen Smith; *and* liked her. Liked her husband, John, too, if he *was* her – augh! What was the point? She didn't know what their relationship was, and she wasn't in the slightest degree concerned! The next day? New Year's Day? She'd had a terrible head – which only served her right; had nothing but coffee at breakfast; had missed the Treasure Hunt; had spent the hour pre-lunch in bed; had enjoyed the roast beef; had spent the hour post-lunch in bed; and had only begun to take any interest in hotel activities during the late afternoon when she'd played ping-pong with one of the young lads. Oddly enough, she had been looking forward a good deal to going to the pantomime until . . . No, she hadn't seen anything at all of Mrs Ballard all that day, not so far as she could remember; and, of course, quite certainly nothing of Mr Ballard, either . . .

Morse got another drink for each of them, conscious that he was beginning to make up questions just for the sake of things. But why not? She couldn't tell him anything of importance, he was *almost* sure of that; but she was a lovely girl to be with – he was *absolutely* sure of that! They were sitting close together now, and gently she moved her left leg against the roughish tweed of his trousers. And, just as gently, he responded, saying nothing and yet saying everything.

'Would you like to treat me to a night in the Great Western Hotel?' She asked the question confidently; and yet there had been (had Morse but known it) a vibrancy and gentleness in her voice that had seldom been heard by any other man. Morse semi-shook his head, but she knew from the slow, sad smile that played about his lips that such an immediate reaction was more the mark of sad bewilderment than of considered refusal.

'I don't snore!' said Philippa softly against his ear.

'I don't know whether I do or not,' replied Morse. He was suddenly desperately aware that the time for a decision had come; but he was conscious, too, of the need (he had drunk four pints of beer already) to relieve himself, and he left her for a while.

On his return from the ground-floor Gents', he

walked over to Reception and asked the girl there whether there was a room available for the night.

'Just for yourself, is it, sir?'

'Er, no. A double room – for myself and my wife.'

'Just a second . . . No, I'm awfully sorry, sir, we've no rooms left at all this evening. But we may get a cancellation – we often get one or two about this time. Will you be in the hotel for a while, sir?'

'Yes – just for a while. I'll be in the bar.'

'Well, I'll let you know if I hear of anything. Your name, sir?'

'Er, Palmer. Mr Palmer.'

'All right, Mr Palmer.'

It was ten minutes later that the Muzak was switched off and a pleasantly clear female voice made the announcement to everyone in the Great Western Hotel, in the lounge, in the restaurant, and in the bar: 'Would Chief Inspector Morse please come to Reception immediately. Chief Inspector Morse, to Reception, please.'

He helped her on with her mackintosh, an off-white expensive creation that would have made almost any woman look adequately glamorous; and he watched her as she pulled the belt tight and evened out the folds around her slim waist.

'Been nice meeting you, Inspector.'

Morse nodded. 'We shall probably need some sort of statement.'

'I'd rather not – if you can arrange it.'

'I'll see.'

As she turned to leave, Morse noticed the grubby brown stain on the left shoulder of her otherwise immaculate raincoat: 'Were you wearing that when you left the party?' he asked.

'Yes.' She squinted down at the offending mark. 'You can't walk around semi-nude in the snow, can you?'

'I suppose not.'

'Pity, though. Cost a fiver at least to get it cleaned, that will. You'd 'a'thought, wouldn't you, if you dress up as a wog you might keep your 'ands off . . .'

The voice had slipped, and the mask had slipped; and Morse felt a saddened man. She could have been a lovely girl, but somehow, somewhere, she was flawed. A man had been savagely murdered – a man (who knows? with maybe just a little gentleness in his heart) who after a party one night had put his left hand, sweatily stained with dark-brown stage make-up, on to a woman's shoulder; and she was angry because it would possibly cost a few pounds to get rid of a stain that might detract from her appearance. They said farewell, and Morse sought to hide his two-fold disappointment behind the mask that he, too, invariably wore for most occasions before his fellow men. Perhaps – the thought suddenly struck him – it was the masks that were the reality, and the faces beneath them that were the pretence. So many of the people in the Haworth that fatal evening had been wearing some sort of disguise –

a change of dress, a change of make-up, a change of attitude, a change of partner, a change of life almost; and the man who had died had been the most consummate artist of them all.

After she had left, Morse walked back through the lounge to Reception (it *must* be Lewis who had rung for him – Lewis was the only person who had any idea where he was) and prayed that it would be a different young girl on duty. But it wasn't. Furthermore she was a girl who obviously possessed a fairly retentive memory.

'I'm afraid we haven't had any cancellations yet, Mr Palmer.'

'Oh, Christ!' muttered Morse under his breath.

Chapter Eighteen

Thursday, January 2nd: p.m.

Men seldom make passes
At girls who wear glasses.

(Dorothy Parker)

Mr John Smith returned home that evening, unexpectedly early, to find his wife Helen in a state of tear-stained distraction; and once he had persuaded her to start talking, it was impossible to stop her . . .

Helen had caught the 3.45 train from Reading that afternoon, and arrived in Oxford at 4.20. Apart from the key to Annexe 2 which she clasped tight in the pocket of her duffel coat, she carried little else: no handbag, no wallet, no umbrella – only the return ticket to Reading, two pound coins, and a few shillings in smaller change. A taxi from Oxford station might have been sensible, but it certainly wasn't necessary; and in any case she knew that the twenty-minute walk would do her no harm. As she began to make her way to the Haworth Hotel her heart was beating as nervously as when she had opened the front passenger door of the BMW, and had frantically felt all over the floor of the car, splayed her hands across and under and down and round the sides of seats and everywhere – *everywhere*! And found nothing: nothing except a two-pence piece, a white indigestion tablet, and a button from a lady's coat (not one of her own) . . .

She walked quickly past the vast glass-fronted Blackwells' building in Hythe Bridge Street, through Gloucester Green, and then along Beaumont Street into St Giles', where at the Martyrs' Memorial she crossed over to the right-hand side of the thoroughfare and, now more slowly, made her way northwards along the Banbury Road.

Opposite the Haworth Hotel she could see the two front windows of the annexe clearly – and so very near! There seemed to be some sort of light on at the back of the building somewhere; but each of the two rooms facing the street – and especially one of them, the one on the left as she watched and waited – was dark and almost certainly empty. A glass-sided bus shelter almost directly opposite the annexe protected her from the drizzle, if not from the wind, and gave her an ideal vantage point from which to keep watch without arousing suspicion. A bus came and picked up the two people waiting there, a very fat West Indian woman and a wiry little English woman, both about sixty, both (as Helen gathered) cleaners in a nearby hospice, who chatted together on such easy and intimate terms that it was tempting to be optimistic about future prospects for racial harmony. Helen stood aside – and continued to watch. Soon another bus was coming towards her, its headlights illuminating the silvery sleet; but she stood back inside the shelter, and the bus passed on without stopping. Then she saw something – something which seemed to make her heart lurch towards her mouth. A light had been turned on in the room on the right, Annexe 1: the window, its curtains undrawn, glared brightly in the darkness, and a figure was moving around inside. Then the light was switched off, and the light in the next room – *her* room – was switched on. A bus had stopped, the doors, folding inwards, inviting her to climb aboard; and she found herself apologizing and seeing the look on the driver's face as he tossed his head in contempt before leaning forward over the great steering-wheel and driving away. The light was still on in Annexe 2, and she saw a figure silhouetted against the window for a few seconds; and then that light too was switched off. A man came out of the side door, walked round to the front of the annexe, immediately opposite to her, and disappeared inside; and the two rooms facing the street were dark and empty once more. *But the policeman was still there at the side entrance.* He had been there all along, his black-and-white checkered cap conspicuous under the light that illuminated the path between the Haworth Hotel and the cordoned area of the annexe – the red, yellow, and white tabs on the ropes tilting back and forth in the keen wind.

If Helen Smith had ever been likely to despair, she would have done so at this point. And yet somehow she knew that she would *not* despair. It may have been the cold, the hopelessness, the futility of it all; it may have been her awareness that there could be nothing more for her to lose. She didn't know. She didn't want to know. But she sensed within herself a feeling of wild determination that she had never known before. Her whole being seemed polarized between the black-and-white hat across the road and the key still clutched so tightly and warmly in her right hand. There had to be *some* way of diverting the man's attention, so that she would have the chance to slip swiftly and silently through the side door. But it had been so much easier than that! He had just walked across to the main hotel, where he now stood drinking a cup of something from a white plastic beaker, and happily engrossed in conversation with a young woman from the hotel.

Helen was in the corridor almost before her courage had been called upon.

No problem! With shaking hand she inserted the key in the lock of Annexe 2, closed the door behind her, and stood stock-still for a moment or two in the dark. Then she felt her way across to the bed nearer the window, and ran her hands along the smooth sheets, and beneath and around the pillow, and along the headboard, and finally over the floor. They *had* been there: they *had* been underneath her pillow – she *knew* it. And an embryo sob escaped her lips as again her hands frantically, but fruitlessly, searched around. There were two switches on the headboard, and she turned on the one above the bed she had slept in: she *had* to make sure! For half a minute she searched again desperately in the lighted room; but to no avail. And now, for the first time, it was fear that clutched her heart as she switched off the light, left the room and edged her way noiselessly through the side door. Then she froze where she stood against the wall. Immediately opposite, at one of the windows on the first floor of the main hotel, a woman stood watching her – and then was gone. Helen felt quite certain that the woman had seen her, and an icy panic seized her. She could remember little of how she left the hotel; but fear had given its own winged sandals to her feet.

The next thing she knew, she was walking along the Banbury Road, a good way down from the Haworth Hotel, her heart thumping like a trip-hammer in an ironmaster's yard. She walked without looking back for a single second; she walked and walked like some revenant zombie, oblivious to her surroundings, still panic-stricken and trembling – yet safe, blessedly safe! At the railway station, with only ten minutes to wait, she bought herself a Scotch, and felt fractionally better. But as she sat in a deserted compartment in the slow train back to Reading, she knew that each of the wearisome stops, like the stations of the cross, was bringing her nearer and nearer to a final reckoning.

Morse had made no secret of the fact that he would be meeting Philippa Palmer at the Great Western Hotel, and had agreed that should Lewis think it necessary he might be reached there. The news *could* wait until the morning of course – Lewis knew that; and it probably wasn't crucially important in any case. Yet everyone is anxious to parade a success, and for Lewis it had been a successful evening. In Annexe 2, the room in which

Mr and Mrs John Smith had spent the night of December 31st, he had found, beneath the pillow of the bed nearer the window, in a brown imitation-leather case, a pair of spectacles: small, feminine, rather fussy little things. At first he had been disappointed, since the case bore no optician's name, no address, no signification of town or county – nothing. But inside the case, squashed down at the very bottom, he had found a small oblong of yellow material for use (as Lewis knew) in the cleaning of lenses; and printed on this material were the words 'G.W. Lloyd, Opticians, High Street, Reading'. Fortunately Mr Lloyd, a garrulous Welshman hailing from Mountain Ash, had still been on the premises when Lewis rang him, and had willingly agreed to remain so until Lewis arrived. If it had taken Lewis only forty minutes to reach Reading, it had taken Lloyd only four or five to discover the owner of the lost spectacles. In his neat records the resourceful Lloyd kept full information about all his clients: this defect, that defect; long sight, short sight; degrees of astigmatism; type of spectacle frames; private or NHS. And tracing the spectacles had been almost childishly easy. Quite an able fellow, Lewis decided, this little Welshman who had opted for ophthalmology.

'I found them under the pillow, sir,' said Lewis when he finally got through to Morse at Paddington.

'Did you?'

'I thought it wouldn't perhaps do any harm just to check up on things a bit.'

'Check up on me, you mean!'

'Well, we can all miss things.'

'You mean to say they were there when I looked over that room? Come off it, Lewis! You don't honestly think I'd have missed something like that, do you?'

The thought that the spectacles had been planted in Annexe 2 by some person or other *after* Morse had searched the room had not previously occurred to Lewis, and he was beginning to wonder about the implications of such a strange notion when Morse spoke again.

'I'm sorry.'

'Pardon, sir?'

'I said I'm sorry, that's all. I must have missed the bloody things! And there's something else I want to say. Well done! No wonder I sometimes find it useful having you around, my old friend.'

Lewis was looking very happy when, after giving Morse the Smiths' address, he put down the phone, thanked the optician, and drove straight back to Oxford. He and Morse had agreed not to try to see either of the mysterious Smith couple until the following day. And Lewis was glad of that since he was feeling very tired indeed.

Mrs Lewis could see that her husband was happy when he finally returned home just before 9 p.m. She cooked him egg and chips and once again marvelled at the way in which Chief Inspector Morse could, on occasions, have such a beneficent effect upon the man she'd married. But she was very happy herself, too; she was always happy when he was.

Deciding, after he had finished his telephone conversation with Lewis, that he might just as well stay on in London and then stop off at Reading the following morning on his return to Oxford, Morse approached the receptionist (the same one) for the third time, and asked her sweetly whether she could offer him a single room for the night. Which she could, for there had been a cancellation. The card which she gave him Morse completed in the name of Mr Philip Palmer, of Irish nationality, and handed it back to her. As she gave him his room key, the girl looked at him with puzzlement in her eyes, and Morse leaned over and spoke quietly to her. 'Just one little t'ing, miss. If Chief Inspector Morse happens to call, please send him up to see me immediately, will you?'

The receptionist, now utterly bewildered, looked at him with eyes that suggested that either he was quite mad, or she was. And when he walked off towards the main staircase, she wondered whether she should ring the duty manager and acquaint him with her growing suspicion that she might have just booked an IRA terrorist into the hotel. But she decided against it. If he had a bomb with him, it was quite certainly not in his suitcase, for he had no suitcase; had no luggage at all, in fact – not even a toothbrush by the look of things.

Chapter Nineteen

January 2nd/3rd

Love is strong as death; jealousy is cruel as the grave.
(SONG OF SOLOMON viii, 6)

THE WHOLE DESPERATE business had acquired a gathering momentum born of its own progress. It was, for Margaret Bowman, like driving a car whose brakes had failed down an ever more steeply inclined gradient – where the only thing to do was to try to steer the accelerating vehicle with the split-second reactions of a racing driver and to pray that it would reach the bottom without a fatal collision. To stop was utterly impossible.

It had been about a year ago when she had first become aware that her husband was showing unmistakable signs of becoming a semi-drunkard. There would be days when he would not touch a drop of alcohol; but there were other periods when two or three times a week she would return from work to find him in a sort of slow-thinking half-daze after what must clearly have been fairly prolonged bouts of drinking, about which her own occasional criticism had served merely to trigger off an underlying crude and cruel streak in his nature which had greatly frightened her. Had it been because of his drinking that (for the first time in their marriage) she had been unfaithful to him? She wasn't sure. Possibly – probably, even – she might in any case have drifted into some sort of illicit liaison with one or two of the men she had recently got to know at work. Everyone changed as the years went by, she knew that. But Tom, her husband, seemed to have undergone a fundamental change of character, and she had become increasingly terrified of him finding out about her affair, and deeply worried about what dreadful things he would do to her; and to *him*, and perhaps to himself, if he ever did find out. Her infidelity had spanned the late summer and most of the autumn before she began to realize that any affair was just as fraught with risk as marriage was. For the first few weeks, a single afternoon a week had sufficed: he, by regulating his varied weekend workings, was able to take a day off every week, and this was easily synchronized with her own afternoon off (on Thursdays) when the pair of them made love in the bedroom of an erstwhile council house in North Oxford which he now owned himself. That had been the early pattern; and for the first two or three months he had been interesting to be with, considerate, anxious to please. But as time went on, he too (just like her husband) had appeared to change: he became somewhat crude in one or two respects, more demanding, less talkative, with (quite clearly to Margaret Bowman) his own craving for sexual gratification dominating their post-meridian copulations. Progressively he'd wished to see her more often, ever badgering her to fabricate for her employers a series of visits to dentists, doctors, and terminally ill relatives; or to take home to her husband tales of overtime workings necessitated by imaginary backlogs. And while she despised the man to some degree for so obviously allowing all his professed love for her to degenerate into an undisguised lust, yet there was a physical side to her own nature, at once as crude and selfish and demanding as his, which welded them into an almost perfect partnership between the sheets. The simple truth was that the more he used and abused her, the more sexual satisfaction he managed to wring from her, and the more she was conscious of her pride in being the physical object of his apparently insatiable appetite for her body. Indeed, as the year moved into its last quarter, she began to suspect that she needed him almost as much as he needed her, although for a long time she refused to countenance, even to herself, the full implications of such a suspicion. But then she was forced to face them. He was soon making *too* many demands upon her, begging her to be with him even for an odd half-hour at lunchtimes when (truth to tell) she would more often than not have preferred a glass of red wine and a ham sandwich with her friend and colleague Gladys Taylor in the Dew Drop. And then had come the show-down, as perhaps she'd known would be inevitable. He'd asked her to leave her husband and come to live with him: it was about time, surely, that she left the man she didn't love and moved in with the one she did. And although coming within an ace of saying 'yes', she'd finally said 'no'.

Why Margaret Bowman had thus refused, she would

herself have found difficult to explain. Perhaps it was because (for the present at least) it was all far too much *bother*. The rather dull, the slightly overweight, the only semi-successful man who was her husband, was the man with whom she had shared so much for so many years now. And there were far too many other shared things to think of packing everything up just like that: payments on the car, life insurances, the house mortgage, family friends and relations, neighbours – even the disappointments and the quarrels and the boredoms, which all seemed to form a strangely binding sort of tie between them. Yet there was perhaps, too, one quite specific reason why she had refused. Gladys (Margaret had come to work in the same section as Gladys in the spring) had become a genuine friend; and one day in the Dew Drop she had told Margaret how she had been temporarily jilted by her husband, and how for many months after that she had felt so hurt and so belittled that she'd wondered whether she would ever be able to lift up her head in life again. 'Having had it done to me' (she'd confided) 'I couldn't ever think of doing it to anyone else.' It had been a simple little thing to say, and it had not been said with any great moral fervour; yet it had made its point with memorable effect . . .

That particular Thursday afternoon when she had finally said 'no' they'd had their first blazing row, and she had been alarmed by the look of potential violence in his eyes. Although he had finally calmed down, she found herself making excuses for the whole of the next week, including the hitherto sacrosanct p.m. period on Thursday. It had been a sad mistake, though, since the following fortnight had been a nightmare. He had rung her at work, where she had taken the message in front of all the other women in the section, their eyes glued on her as (nonchalantly, she hoped) she promised to get in touch. Which she *had* done, asking him sensibly, soberly, just to let things ride for a few weeks and see if they would sort themselves out. Then there had been the first letter, addressed to her at work – pleasantly, lovingly, imploring her to go back to the old pattern of their former meetings. And then, when she did not reply to the first letter, a second one, which was addressed to her home and which she'd picked up from the front-hall mat at eight o'clock on a wet and miserable November morning *when she was going to a funeral.* Tom was still in bed, and she'd hurriedly torn the envelope open and looked through the letter – the cruel, vindictive, frightening letter which she'd quickly stuck into the bottom of her handbag as she heard the creak at the top of the stairs.

When, that same morning, her husband sat opposite her at the kitchen table, she seemed engrossed in the half-dozen brochures she had picked up the previous lunchtime in Summertown Travel, giving details of trips ranging from gentle strolls round the hill-forts of Western England to lung-racking rambles in the Himalayan foothills. *Yet how fervently at that moment did she wish her lover dead!*

Tom Bowman had not told his wife about his discovery of the letter until the following Wednesday evening. It had been a harrowing occasion for her, but Tom had not flown into a rage or threatened her with physical violence. In retrospect, she almost wished he had done so; for far more frightening, and something that sent the four guardians scurrying from the portals of her sanity, was the change that seemed to have come over him: there was a hardness in his voice and in his eyes; an unsuspected deviousness about his thinking; a firmness of purpose about his frightening suggestions; and, underlying all (she suspected), a terrifyingly vicious and unforgiving jealousy against the man who had tried to rob him of his wife. What he said that evening was so fatuous really, so fanciful, so silly, that his words had not registered with her as forming any plausible or practicable plan of revenge. Yet slowly and inexorably the ideas which he had outlined to her that evening had set in motion a self-accelerating series of events which had culminated in murder.

Even now, right at the end of things, she was aware of the ambivalence of all her thoughts, her motives, her hopes – and her mind would give her no rest. After watching the late-night news on BBC2 she took four aspirin tablets and went to bed, where (wonderfully!) she fell easily enough into sleep. But by a quarter past one she was awake once more, and for the next four hours her darting eyes could not remain still for a second in their burning sockets as the whirligig of her brain sped round and round without any hint of slowing down, as if the fairground operator had pushed the lever forward on to 'Fast' and then fallen into an insensate stupor over the controls.

*

That same night, the night of January 2nd, Morse himself had a pleasantly refreshing sleep, with a mildly erotic dream (about a woman with a large Elastoplast over one ankle) thrown in for good measure. He told himself, on waking at 6.30 a.m., that if only there had been a double room available the night before . . . But he had never been a man to be unduly perturbed by the 'if onlys' of life, and he possessed a wholly enviable capacity for discounting most disappointments. Remembering a programme he had heard the previous week on cholesterol (a programme which the Lewis family had obviously missed), Morse decided to forgo the huge and rare treat of a fried breakfast in the restaurant, and caught the 9.10 train to Reading from platform 2. In the second-class compartment in which he made the journey were two other persons: in one corner, an (equally unshaven) Irishman who said nothing whatsoever after a polite 'Good morning, sorr!' but who thereafter smiled perpetually as though the day had dawned exceedingly bright; and in the other corner, a pretty young girl wearing (as Morse recognized it) a Lady Margaret Hall scarf, who scowled unceasingly as she studied a thick volume of anthropological essays, as though the world had soured and worsened overnight.

It seemed, to Morse, a metaphor.

Chapter Twenty

Friday, January 3rd: a.m.

There's a kind of release
And a kind of torment in every goodbye for every man.
(C. DAY LEWIS)

FOR MANY HOURS before Morse had woken, Helen Smith had been lying wide awake in bed, anticipating the worries that would doubtless beset her during the coming day. After her dreadful ordeal of the previous day, it had been wonderfully supportive of John to show such understanding and forgiveness; indeed, he had almost persuaded her that, even if she *had* left anything potentially incriminating behind, police resources were so overstretched in coping with major felonies that it was very doubtful whether anyone would find the time to pursue their own comparatively minor misdemeanours. And at that point, she had felt all the old love for him which she had known five years previously when they had met in Yugoslavia, her native country; and when after only two weeks' courtship she had agreed to marry him and go to live in England. He had given her the impression then – very much so! – of being a reasonably affluent businessman; and in any case she was more than glad to get away from a country in which her family lived under the shadow of a curiously equivocal incident from the past, in which her paternal grandfather, for some mysterious reason, had been shot by the Titoists outside Trieste. But from the earliest days in England she had become aware of her husband's strange life-style, of his dubious background, of his shady present, and of his far from glittering prospects for the future. Yet in her own quiet, gentle way, she had learned to love him, and to perform (without overmuch reluctance) the rôle that she was called upon to play.

At 7.30 a.m. they sat opposite each other over the pine-wood table in the small kitchen of their rented property, having a breakfast of grapefruit juice, toast and marmalade, and coffee. When they had finished, John Smith looked across at his wife and put his hand over hers. In his eyes she was still a most attractive woman – that at least was a point on which he had no need to lie. Her legs, for the purist, were perhaps a little too slim; and likewise her bust was considerably less bulging than the amply bosomed models who unfailingly featured on one of the earlier pages of their daily newspaper; her face had a pale, Slavonic cast, with a slightly pitted, rather muddy-looking skin; but the same face, albeit somewhat sullen in repose, was ever irradiated when she smiled, the intense, greenish eyes flashing into life, and the lips curling back over her regular teeth. She was smiling, though a little sadly, even now.

'Thank you!' she said.

*

At 8 a.m. John Smith told his wife that he wanted her to go up to the January sales in Oxford Street and buy herself a new winter coat. He gave her five £20 notes, and would countenance no refusal. He took her down to the station in the car, and waited on the platform with her until the 8.40 '125' pulled in to carry her off to the West End.

As her train drew into Paddington's platform 5 at 9.10 a.m., another '125' was just pulling out of platform 2 and soon gliding along the rails at a high, smooth speed towards Reading. In a second-class compartment (as we have already seen), rather towards the rear of this train, and with only two wholly uncommunicative fellow-passengers for company, sat Morse, reading the *Sun*. At home he invariably took *The Times*, though not because he much enjoyed it, or even read it (apart from the letters page and the crossword); much more because the lady local councillor who ran the newsagent's shop down in Summertown was fully aware of Morse's status, and had (to Morse's knowledge) more than once referred to him as 'a really civilized gentleman'; and he had no wish prematurely to destroy such a flattering illusion.

If the serious-minded undergraduette from Lady Margaret Hall had bothered to lift her eyes from her reading, she would have seen a man of medium height who had filled out into a somewhat barrel-shaped figure, with his waist and stomach measurements little altered from his earlier days and yet with his shirt now stretching tight around his chest. His unshaven jowls (the young student might have thought) suggested an age of nearer sixty than fifty (in fact, the man was fifty-four), and his face seemed cast in a slightly melancholy mould, not at all brightened that morning by the insistence of the young ticket-collector that he was obliged to pay a surcharge on the day-return ticket he had paid for the previous evening.

The taxi carrying its fare from Reading railway station to the Smiths' newly discovered address was told to pull up fifty yards into Eddleston Road, where Morse told the driver to wait as he walked across the road and rang the bell on the door of number 45.

When John Smith turned into the street, he immediately saw the taxi opposite his house, and stopped dead in his tracks at the corner shop where he appeared to take an inordinate interest in the hundred-and-one rectangular white notices which announced a multitude of wonderful bargains, from a pair of training shoes (hardly ever worn) to a collection of Elvis Presley records (hardly ever played). The taxi's exhaust was still running, sending a horizontal stream of vapour across the lean, cold air; and reflected in the corner-shop window Smith could see a man in an expensive-looking dark grey overcoat seemingly reluctant to believe that neither of the occupants of the house could be at home. Finally, slowly, the importunate caller walked away from the house, stood back to take a last look at the property, and then got back into the taxi, which was off immediately in a spurt of dirty slush.

*

John Smith entered the shop, purchased a packet of twenty Silk Cut, and stood for three or four minutes at the magazine rack leafing through *Wireless Weekly*, *Amateur Photographer*, and the *Angling Times*. But apparently he had decided that none of these periodicals was exactly indispensable, and he walked out empty-handed into the street. He had always prided himself on being able to sniff out danger a mile away. But he sensed there was none now; and he strolled down the street with exaggerated unconcern, and let himself into number 45.

He had a fastidiously tidy mind, and even now was tempted to wash up the few breakfast things that stood in the kitchen sink, particularly the two knives that looked almost obscenely sticky from the polyunsaturated Flora and Cooper's Thick Cut Oxford Marmalade. But the walls were closing in, he knew it. The BMW would have been the riskiest thing; and half an hour ago he had sold the three-year-old beauty at Reading Motors for a ridiculously low-pitched £6,000 in cash. Then he had gone along to the town-centre branch of Lloyds Bank, where he had withdrawn (again in cash) the £1,200 which stood in the joint account of John and Helen Smith.

Helen had spent a brief but successful time in Selfridges (she had bought herself a new white mackintosh) and was back in the house just after noon, when she immediately saw the note beside the telephone.

Helen, my love!

They are on to us, and there's little option for me but to get away. I never told you quite everything about myself but please believe that if they catch up with me now I shall be sent to prison for a few years – I can't face that. I thought they might perhaps confiscate the little savings we managed to put together, and so I cashed the lot and you'll find thirty £20 notes in your favourite little hiding place – that's a precaution just in case the police get here before you find this! If I ever loved anyone in the world, I loved you. Remember that! I'm sorry it's got to be like this.

Ever yours,
John

She read the brief letter without any sense of shock – almost with a sense of resigned relief. It couldn't have gone on for ever, that strange life she'd led with the oddly maverick confidence-man who had married her, and who had almost persuaded her at times that he loved her. Yes, that was the only really deep regret: if he had *stayed* – stayed with her and faced the music whatever tune they played – then life would indeed have been an undoubted triumph for the dark young lady from Yugoslavia.

She was upstairs in the front bedroom, changing her clothes, when she heard the front-door bell.

Chapter Twenty-one

Friday, January 3rd: mostly a.m.

As when heaved anew
Old ocean rolls a lengthened wave to shore
Down whose green back the short-lived foam, all hoar
Burst gradual, with a wayward indolence.

(John Keats)

Morse had felt tempted to ring Lewis to tell him not to bother with their original plan of meeting in Eddleston Road at 11 a.m. But he didn't so do. The prospect of more trains and more taxis was an intolerable one; and in any case he was now almost completely out of ready cash. At 10.50 he was again knocking on the door of the Smiths' house; once again without getting any reply. The road was part of a reasonably elegant residential quarter. But heading off from it, on the southern side, were smaller, meaner streets of Victorian two-storey red-brick terraced houses; and as Morse strolled through this area he began to feel pleasantly satisfied with life, a state of mind that may not have been unconnected with the fact that he was in unfamiliar circumstances, with nothing immediately or profitably to be performed, with a small public house on the next corner facing him and with his wrist-watch showing only a minute or so short of opening time.

The Peep of Dawn (as engagingly named a pub as Morse could remember) boasted only one bar, with wooden wall-seats, and after finding out from the landlord which bitter the locals drank he sat with his pint in the window alcove and supped contentedly. He wasn't quite sure whether his own oft-repeated insistence that he could always think more lucidly after an extra ration of alcohol was wholly true. He certainly *believed* it to be true, though; and quite certainly many a breakthrough in previous investigations had been made under such attendant circumstances. It was only in recent months that he had found himself querying his earlier assumption about such a *post hoc, ergo propter hoc* proposition; and it had occasionally occurred to him that fallacious logic was not infrequently the offspring of wishful thinking. Yet for Morse (and he quite simply accepted the fact) the world *did* invariably seem a much warmer, more manageable place after a few pints of beer; and quite certainly he knew that (for himself, at any rate) it was on such occasions that the imaginative processes usually *started*. It may have been something to do with the very *liquidity* of alcohol, for he had often seen these processes in terms of just such a metaphor. It was as if he were lulled and sitting idly on the sea-front, and watching, almost entranced, as some great Master of the Tides drew in the foam-fringed curtains of the waters towards his feet and then pulled them back in slow retreat to the creative sea.

But whatever the truth of the matter, he knew he would have to do some serious thinking very soon, and for the moment the problem that was uppermost in his mind was how a letter which had been written from a non-existent address had also been received at the very same non-existent address. It was easy of course to write anything *from* anywhere in the world – say from 'Buckingham Palace, Kidlington'; but how on earth, in turn, was it possible for a letter to be delivered *to* such improbably registered premises? Yet that is what *had* happened, or so it seemed. The man who had been murdered was, on the face of things, the husband of a woman who had booked a room from an address which did not exist; had booked the room by letter; and had received confirmation of the booking, also by letter – with the pair of them duly arriving on December 31st, taking part in the evening's festivities (incidentally, with outstanding success), and finally, after joining their fellow guests in wishing themselves, one and all, a happily prosperous new year, walking back to their room in the annexe. And then . . .

'You'd not forgotten me, had you?' said a voice above him.

'Lewis! You're a bit late aren't you?'

'We agreed to meet at the house, if you remember, sir!'

'I went there. There's no one at home.'

'I *know* that. Where do you think *I've* been?'

'What's the time now?'

'Twenty past eleven.'

'Oh dear! I am sorry! Get yourself a drink, Lewis – and a refill for me, please. I'm a bit short of cash, I'm afraid.'

'Bitter, was it?'

Morse nodded. 'How did you find me?'

'I'm a detective. Had you forgotten that, too?'

But it would have taken more than Morse's meanness with money, and more than Morse's cavalier notions of punctuality, to have dashed Lewis's good spirits that morning. He told Morse all about his encounter with the Welsh optician; and Morse, in turn, told Lewis (almost) all about his encounter with the fair Philippa at Paddington. At a quarter to twelve Lewis made another fruitless visit to Eddleston Road. But half an hour later, this time with Morse, it was immediately clear that someone had returned to number 45. It was the only house in the row whose occupants had dispensed with the need for keeping its front garden in any neat trim by the simple (albeit fairly drastic) expedient of covering the whole area with small beige pebbles, which crunched noisily as the two men walked up the sinking shingle to the door.

Chapter Twenty-Two

Friday, January 3rd: p.m.

You can fool too many of the people too much of the time.

(JAMES THURBER)

THROUGHOUT THE WHOLE of the last five years (admitted Helen Smith) the two of them had successfully contrived to defraud dozens of honourable institutions of their legitimate income. But neither her husband John nor herself had the means whereby to make any reparation even fractionally commensurate with such deceit. She, Helen, fully understood why society at large should expect some expiation for her sins; but (she stressed the point) if such compensation were to be index-linked to its £ s. d. equivalents, there was no prospect whatsoever of any settlement of the overdue account. She showed Lewis the note she had found on her return from London; and would be happy to show him, too, the little hidey-hole beneath the second floorboard from the left in the spare bedroom where she had duly found the £600 referred to – that is if Lewis wanted to see it. (Lewis didn't.) Unshakably, however, she refused to hazard any information about where her husband might have made for; and indeed her refusal was genuinely founded in total ignorance, both of his present whereabouts and of his future plans.

The pattern had seldom varied: ringing round half a dozen hotels at holiday periods; taking advantage of late cancellations (an almost inevitable occurrence); there and then accepting, by phone, any vacancy which so lately had arisen; promising a.s.a.p. a confirmatory letter (with both parties appreciating the unreliability of holiday-time postal services); staying only two nights where 'The Businessman's Break' was scheduled for three; or staying just the one night where it was scheduled for two. And that was about it. Easy enough. There were of course always a few little secrets about such professional deception: for example, it was advisable *always* to carry as little baggage as was consistent with reasonably civilized standards of hygiene; again, it was advisable *never* to park a car on the hotel premises, or to fill in the section on the registration form asking for car-licence numbers. Yet there was one principle above all that had to be understood, namely, that the more demands you made upon the establishment, the more enhanced would be your status *vis-à-vis* the management and staff of all hotels. Thus it was that the Smiths had learned *always* to select their meals from the higher echelons of the *à la carte* specialities of the chef, and wines and liqueurs from any over-valued vintage; to demand room-service facilities at the most improbable periods of day or night; and, finally, *never* to exchange too many friendly words with anyone in sight – from the manager down, through receptionist to waitress, porter or cleaner. Such (Helen testified) were the basic principles she and her husband had observed in their remarkably successful bid to extract courtesy and respect from some of the finest hotels across the length and breadth of the United Kingdom. The only thing then left to be staged was their disappearance, which was best effected during that period when no one normally booked out of hotels – mid-afternoon. And that had usually been the time when the Smiths had decided to take leave of their erstwhile benefactors – sans warning, sans farewell, sans payment, sans everything.

When Helen Smith came to court (inevitably so, as Lewis saw things) it seemed wholly probable that this darkly attractive, innocent-looking defendant would plead guilty to the charges brought against her, and would pretty certainly ask, too, for one-hundred-and-one other offences to be taken into consideration. But she hardly looked or sounded like a criminal, and her account of the time she had spent at the Haworth Hotel appeared honest and clear. Four (yes!) bottles of champagne had been ordered – they both liked the lovely stuff! – two on New Year's Eve and two on New Year's Day, with the last of the four still in the larder if Lewis wanted to see it. (Lewis did.) Yes, she remembered a few things about the Ballards, *and* about the Palmers; but her recollections of specific times and specific details were even hazier than Philippa Palmer's had been the previous evening. Like Philippa, though, she thought that the evening had been well organized – and great fun; and that the food and drink had been very good indeed. The Smiths, both of them, enjoyed fancy-dress parties; and that New Year's Eve they had appeared – an oddly uncomplementary pair! – as a seductive Cleopatra and as a swordless Samurai. Would Lewis like to see the costumes? (Lewis would.) Whether Ballard had eaten much or drunk much that evening, she couldn't remember with any certainty. But she did remember, most clearly, Ballard walking back with her through the snow (Oh yes! it had been snowing heavily then) to the hotel annexe, and ruining the right shoulder-lapel of her mackintosh, where his right hand had left a dirty dark-brown stain – which of course Lewis could see if he so desired. (As Lewis did.)

During the last part of this interview Morse had seemed only minimally interested in Lewis's interrogation, and had been leafing through an outsize volume entitled *The Landscape of Thomas Hardy*. But now, suddenly, he asked a question.

'Would you recognize *Mrs* Ballard if you saw her again?'

'I – I don't really know. She was in fancy dress and—'

'In a yashmak, wasn't she?'

Helen nodded, somewhat abashed by the brusqueness of his question.

'Didn't she *eat* anything?'

'Of course, yes.'

'But you can't eat anything in a yashmak!'

'No.'

'You must have *seen* her face, then?'

Helen knew that he was right; and suddenly, out of the blue, she *did* remember something. 'Yes,' she began slowly. 'Yes, I did see her face. Her top lip was a bit red, and there were red sort of pin-pricks – you know, sort of little red spots . . .'

But even as Helen spoke these words, her own upper lip was trembling uncontrollably, and it was clear that the hour of questioning had left her spirits very low indeed. The tears were suddenly springing copiously and she turned her head sharply away from the two policemen in total discomfiture.

In the car, Lewis ventured to ask whether it might not have been wiser to take Helen Smith back to Oxford there and then for further questioning. But Morse appeared unenthusiastic about any such immediate move, asserting that, compared with the likes of Marcinkus & Co. in the Vatican Bank, John and Helen Smith were sainted folk in white array.

It was just after they had turned on to the A34 that Morse mentioned the strange affair of the yashmak'd lady's upper lip.

'How did you guess, Lewis?' he asked.

'It's being married, sir – so I don't suppose you ought to blame yourself too much for missing it. You see, most women like to look their best when they go away, let's say for a holiday or a trip abroad or something similar; and the missus has a bit of trouble like that – you know, a few unsightly hairs growing just under the chin or a little fringe of hairs on the top lip. A lot of women have the same trouble especially if they've got darkish sort of hair—'

'But your missus has got *fair* hair!'

'All right; but it happens to everybody a bit as they get older. You get rather self-conscious and embarrassed about it if you're a woman, so you often go to one of the hair clinics like the *Tao* or something and they give you electrolysis and they put a needle sort of thing into the roots of the hairs and – well, sort of get rid of them. Costs a bit though, sir!'

'But being a rich man you can just about afford to let the missus go along to one of these beauty parlours?'

'Just about!'

Lewis suddenly put down his foot with a joyous thrust, turned on his right-hand flasher, took the police car up to 95 m.p.h., veered in a great swoop across the outside lane, and netted a dozen lorries and cars which had thoughtfully decelerated to the statutory speed limit as they'd noticed the white car looming up in their rear mirrors.

'The treatment they give you,' continued Lewis, 'makes the skin go a bit pinkish all over and they say if it's on the top lip it's very sensitive and you often get a histamine reaction – and a sort of tingling sensation . . .'

But Morse was no longer listening. His own body was tingling too; and there crossed his face a beatific smile as Lewis accelerated the police car faster still towards the City of Oxford.

*

Back in Kidlington HQ, Morse decided that they had spent quite long enough in the miserably cold and badly equipped room at the back of the Haworth annexe, and that they should now transfer things back home, as it were.

'Shall I go and get a few new box-files from the stores?' asked Lewis. Morse picked up two files which were heavily bulging with excess paper, and looked cursorily through their contents. 'These'll be OK. They're both OBE.'

'OBE, sir?'

Morse nodded: 'Overtaken By Events.'

The phone rang half an hour later and Morse heard Sarah Jonstone's voice at the other end. She'd remembered a little detail about Mrs Ballard; it might be silly of her to bother Morse with it, but she could almost swear that there had been a little red circular sticker – an RSPCA badge, she thought – on Mrs Ballard's coat when she had booked in at registration on New Year's Eve.

'Well,' said Morse, 'we've not done a bad job between us, Lewis. We've managed to find two of the three women we were after – and it's beginning to look as if it's not going to be very difficult to find the last one! Not tonight, though. I'm tired out – and I could do with a bath, and a good night's sleep.'

'*And* a shave, sir!'

Chapter Twenty-Three

Saturday, January 4th

> Arithmetic is where the answer is right and everything is nice and you can look out of the window and see the blue sky – or the answer is wrong and you have to start all over and try again and see how it comes out this time.
>
> (CARL SANDBURG, *Complete Poems*)

THE THAW CONTINUED overnight, and lawns that had been totally subniveal the day before were now resurfacing in patches of irregular green under a blue sky. The bad weather was breaking; the case, it seemed, was breaking too.

At Kidlington HQ Morse was going to be occupied (he'd said) with other matters for most of the morning; and Lewis, left to his own devices, was getting progressively more and more bogged down in a problem which at the outset had looked comparatively simple. The Yellow Pages had been his starting point, and under 'Beauty Salons and Consultants' he found seven or eight addresses in Oxford which advertised specialist treatment in what was variously called Waxing, Facials, or Electrolysis; with another five in Banbury; three more (a gloomier Lewis noticed) in Bicester; and a good many other establishments in individual places that could be reached without too much travelling by a woman living in Chipping Norton – if (and in Lewis's mind it was a biggish 'if') 'Mrs Ballard' *was* in fact a citizen of Chipping Norton.

But there were *two* quadratic equations, as it were, from which to work out the unknown 'x': and it was the second of these – the cross-check with the charity flag days – to which Lewis now directed his thinking. In recent years, the most usual sort of badge received from shakers of collection tins had come in the form of a little circular sticker that was pressed on to the lapel of the contributor's coat; and Lewis's experience was that such a sticker often fell off after a few minutes rather than stuck on for several days. And so Morse's view, Lewis agreed, was probably right: if Mrs Ballard was still wearing a sticker on New Year's Eve, she'd probably bought it the same day, or the day before at the very outside. But Lewis had considerable doubts about Morse's further confidently stated conviction that there must have been an RSPCA flag day in Oxford on the 30th or 31st, and that Mrs Ballard had bought a flag as she went into a beauty salon in the city centre. 'Beautifully simple!' Morse had said. 'We've got the time, we've got the place – and we've almost got the woman, agreed? Just a little phoning around and . . .'

But Lewis had got off to a bad start. His first call elicited the disappointing information that the last street-collection in Oxford for the RSPCA had been the previous July; and he had no option but to start making another list, and a very long list at that. First came the well-known medical charities, those dealing with multiple sclerosis, rheumatoid arthritis, heart diseases, cancer research, blindness, deafness, et cetera; then the major social charities, ranging from Christian Aid and Oxfam to War on Want and the Save the Children Fund, et cetera; next came specific societies that looked after ambulancemen, lifeboatmen and ex-servicemen, et cetera; finally were listed the local charities which funded hospices for the terminally ill, hostels for the criminally sick or the mentally unbalanced, et cetera. Lewis could have added scores of others – and he knew he was getting into an awful mess. He could even have added the National Association for the Care and Resettlement of Criminal Offenders. But he didn't.

Clearly some sort of selection was required, and he would have been more than glad to have Morse at his side at that moment. It was like being faced with a difficult maths problem at school: if you weren't careful, you got more and more ensnared in some increasingly complex equations – until the master showed you a beautifully economic short-cut that reduced the problem to a few simple little sums and produced a glittering (and correct) solution at the foot of the page. But his present master, Morse, was still apparently otherwise engaged, and so he decided to begin in earnest: on the second of the two equations.

Yet an hour later he had advanced his knowledge of charity collections in Oxford not one whit; and he was becoming increasingly irritated with telephone numbers which didn't answer when called, or which (if they did answer) appeared manned by voluntary envelopelickers, decorators, caretakers or idiots – or (worst of all!) by intimidating answering machines telling Lewis to start speaking 'now'. And after a further hour of telephoning, he hadn't found a single charitable organization which had held a flag day in Oxford – or anywhere else in the vicinity, for that matter – in the last few days of December.

He was getting, ridiculously, nowhere; and he said as much when Morse finally put in another appearance at 11 a.m. with a cup of coffee and a digestive biscuit, both of which (mistakenly) Lewis thought his superior officer had brought in for him.

'We need some of those men we've been promised, sir.'

'No, no, Lewis! We don't want to start explaining everything to a load of squaddies. Just have a go at the clinic angle if the other's no good. I'll come and give you a hand when I get the chance.'

So Lewis made another start – this time on those Oxford hair clinics which had bothered to take a few centimetres of advertising space in the Yellow Pages: only four of them, thank goodness! But once again the problem soon began to take on unexpectedly formidable dimensions – once he began to consider the sort of questions he could ask a clinic manageress – *if* she was on the premises. For what *could* he ask? He wanted to find out if a woman whose name he didn't know, whose appearance he could only very imperfectly describe, and of whose address he hadn't the faintest notion, except perhaps that it might just be in Chipping Norton – whether such a woman had been in for some unspecified treatment, but probably upper-lip depilation, at some unspecified time, though most probably on the morning of, let him say, any of the last few days of December. What a farce, thought Lewis; and what a fruitless farce it did in fact become. The first of the clinics firmly refused to answer questions, even to the police, about such 'strictly confidential' matters; the second was quite happy to inform him that it had no customers whatsoever on its books with an address in Chipping Norton; a recorded message informed him that the third would re-open after the New Year break on January 6th; and the fourth suggested, politely enough, that he must have misread the advertisement: that whilst it cut, trimmed, singed and dyed, the actual *removal* of hair was not included amongst its splendid services.

Lewis put down the phone – and capitulated. He went over to the canteen and found Morse – the only one there – drinking another cup of coffee and just completing *The Times* crossword puzzle.

'Ah, Lewis. Get yourself a coffee! Any luck yet?'

'No, I bloody haven't,' snapped Lewis – a man who swore, at the very outside, about once a fortnight. 'As I said, sir, I need some help: half a dozen DCs – that's what I need.'

'I don't think it's necessary, you know.'

'Well, I *do*!' said Lewis, looking as angry as Morse had ever seen him, and about to use up a whole month's ration of blasphemies. 'We're not even sure the bloody woman *does* come from Chipping Norton. She might just as well come from Chiswick – like the tart you met in Paddington!'

'Lew-is! Lew-is! Take it *easy*! I'm sure that neither the "Palmers" nor the Smiths had anything at all to do with the murder. And when I said just now it wasn't necessary to bring any more people in on the case, I didn't mean that you couldn't have as many as you like – if you really need them. But not for this particular job, Lewis, I don't think. I didn't want to disturb you, so I've been doing a bit of phoning from here; and I'm waiting for a call that ought to come through any minute. And if it tells me what I think it will, I reckon we know exactly who this "Mrs Ballard" is, and exactly where we should be able to find her. Her name's Mrs Bowman – Mrs Margaret Bowman. And do you know where she lives?'

'Chipping Norton?' suggested Lewis, in a rather wearily defeated tone.

Chapter Twenty-Four

Sunday, January 5th

A man is in general better pleased when he has a good dinner upon his table than when his wife talks Greek.

(SAMUEL JOHNSON)

MORSE HAD BEEN glad to accept Mrs Lewis's invitation to her traditional Sunday lunch of slightly undercooked beef, horseradish sauce, velvety-flat Yorkshire pudding, and roast potatoes; and the meal had been a success. In deference to the great man's presence, Lewis had bought a bottle of Beaujolais Nouveau; and as Morse leaned back in a deep-cushioned armchair and drank his coffee, he felt very much at his ease.

'I sometimes wish I'd taken a gentle little job in the Egyptian Civil Service, Lewis.'

'Fancy a drop of brandy, sir?'

'Why not?'

From the rattle and clatter coming from the kitchen, it was clear that Mrs Lewis had launched herself into the washing-up, but Morse kept his voice down as he spoke again. 'I know that a dirty weekend away with some wonderful woman sounds just like the thing for some jaded fellow getting on in age a bit – like you,

Lewis – but you'd be an idiot to leave that lovely cook you married—'

'I've never given it a thought, sir.'

'There are one or two people in this case, though, aren't there, who seem to have been doing a bit of double-dealing one way or another?'

Lewis nodded as he, too, leaned back in his armchair sipping his coffee, and letting his mind go back to the previous day's startling new development, and to Morse's explanation of how it had occurred . . .

'. . . If you ever decide to kick over the traces' (Morse had said) 'you've *got* to have an accommodation address – that's the vital point to bear in mind. All right, there are a few people, like the Smiths, who can get away without one; but don't forget they're professional swindlers and they know all the rules of the game backwards. In the normal course of events, though, you've got to get involved in some sort of correspondence. Now, if the princess you're going away with isn't married or if she's a divorcee or if she is just living on her own anyway, then there's no problem, is there? She can be your mistress *and* your missus for the weekend and *she* can deal with all the booking – just like Philippa Palmer did. She can use – she *must* use – her own address and, as I say, there are no problems. Now let's just recap for a minute about where we are with the third woman in this case, the woman who wrote to the hotel as "Mrs Ann Ballard" and who booked in as "Mrs Ann Ballard" from an address in Chipping Norton. Obviously, if we can find her, and find out from her what went on in Annexe 3 on New Year's Eve – or New Year's morning – well, we shall be home and dry, shan't we? And in fact we know a good deal about her. The key thing – or what I *thought* was the key thing – was that she'd probably gone to a hair clinic a day or so before turning up at the Haworth Hotel. I'm sorry, Lewis, that you've had such a disappointing time with that side of things. But there was this *other* side which I kept on thinking about – the address she wrote *from* and the address the hotel wrote *to*. Now you can't exchange correspondence with a phoney address – obviously you can't! And yet, you know, you *can*! You *must* be able to – because it *happened*, Lewis! And when you think about it you can do it pretty easily if you've got one particular advantage in life – just the one. And you know what that advantage is? *It's being a postman.* Now let's just take an example. Let's take the Banbury Road. The house numbers go up a long, long way, don't they? I'm not sure, but certainly to about four hundred and eighty or so. Now if the last house is, say, number 478, what exactly happens to a letter addressed to a non-existent 480? The sorters in the main post office are not going to be much concerned, are they? It's only *just* above the last house-number; and as likely as not – even if someone did spot it – he'd probably think a new house was being built there. But if it were addressed, say, to 580, then obviously a sorter is going to think that something's gone askew, and he probably won't put that letter into the appropriate pigeon-hole. In cases like that, Lewis, there's a tray for problem letters, and one of the higher-echelon post-office staff will try to sort them all out later. But whichever way things go, whether the letter would get into the postman's bag, or whether it would get put into the problem tray – it wouldn't matter! You see, the postman himself would be there on the premises while all this sorting was taking place! I know! I've had a long talk on the phone with the Chief Postmaster from Chipping Norton – splendid fellow! – and he said that the letter we saw from the Haworth Hotel, the one addressed to 84 West Street, would pretty certainly have gone straight into the West Street pigeon-hole, because it's only a couple over the last street-number; and even if it had been put in the problem tray, the postman waiting to get his sack over his shoulder would have every opportunity of seeing it, and taking it. And there were only two postmen who delivered to West Street in December: one was a youngish fellow who's spending the New Year with his girlfriend in the Canary Islands; and the other is this fellow called Tom Bowman, who lives at Charlbury Drive in Chipping Norton. But there's nobody there – neither him nor his wife – and none of the neighbours knows where they've gone, although Margaret Bowman was at her work in Summertown on Thursday and Friday last week: I've checked that. Anyway there's not much more we can do this weekend. Max says he'll have the body all sewn up and presentable again by Monday, and so we ought to know who he is pretty soon.'

It had been after Morse had finished that Lewis ventured the most important question of all: 'Do you think the murdered man is Tom Bowman, sir?' And

Morse had hesitated before replying. 'Do you know, Lewis, I've got a strange sort of feeling that *it isn't* . . .'

Morse had nodded off in his chair, and Lewis quietly left the room to help with the drying-up.

That same Sunday afternoon Sarah Jonstone at last got back to her flat. She knew that she would almost certainly never have such an amazing experience again in her life, and she had been reluctant to leave the hotel whilst police activity was continuously centred upon it. But even the ropes that had cordoned off the area were gone, and no policeman now stood by the side door of the annexe block. Mrs Binyon (who had not originally intended to stay at the Haworth for the New Year anyway, but who had been pressed into reluctant service because of the illnesses of so many staff) had at last, that morning, set off on her trip north to visit her parents in Leeds. Only half a dozen people were booked into the hotel that Sunday evening, although (perversely!) the staff who had been so ill were now almost fully recovered. Sarah was putting on her coat at 3.30 p.m. when the phone went in Reception and a young woman's voice, a quietly attractive one, asked if she could please speak to Mr Binyon if he was there. But when Sarah asked for the woman's name, the line went suddenly dead.

Sarah found herself recalling this little incident later in the evening as she sat watching TV. But it wasn't important, she told herself; probably just a line cut off by some technical trouble or other. *Could* it be important though? Chief Inspector Morse had begged her to dredge her memory to salvage *anything* that she could recall; and there *had* been that business about the sticker on Mrs Ballard's coat . . . But there was something else, she knew, if only her mind could get hold of it.

But, for the moment, it couldn't.

Chapter Twenty-five

Monday, January 6th: a.m.

> By working faithfully eight hours a day, you may eventually get to be a boss and work twelve hours a day.
>
> (ROBERT FROST)

GLADYS TAYLOR WOULD be very sorry to leave 'The University of Oxford Delegacy of Local Examinations'. It was all a bit of a mouthful when people asked her where she worked; but the Examination Board's premises, a large, beige-bricked, flat-roofed building in Summertown, had been her happy second home for nineteen and a half years now – and some neat streak within her wished it could have been the full twenty. But the 'Locals', as the Board was affectionately known, insisted that those women like herself – 'supernumeraries', they were called – had their contracts terminated in the session following their sixtieth birthday. These 'sessions', four or five of them every academic year, varied in duration from three or four weeks to nine or ten weeks; and the work involved in each session was almost as varied as its duration. For example, the current short session (and Gladys's last – for she had been sixty the previous November) involved three weeks of concentrated arithmetical checking of scripts – additions, scalings, transfers of marks – from the autumn GCE retake examinations. The entry was very much smaller than the massive summer one, comprising those candidates who had failed adequately to impress the examiners on the earlier occasion. But such young men and women (the 'returned empties', as some called them) were rather nearer Gladys Taylor's heart than many of the precious summer thoroughbreds (she knew a few of them!) who seemed to romp around the academic racecourses with almost arrogant facility. For, in her own eyes, Gladys had been a bit of a failure herself, leaving her secondary-modern school at the beginning of the war, at the age of fifteen, with nothing to show any prospective employer except a lukewarm testimonial to her perseverance and punctuality. Then, at the age of forty-one, following the premature death of a lorry-driver husband who, besides faltering in fidelity, had failed to father any offspring, she had applied to work at the Locals – and she had been accepted. During those first few months she had brought to her duties a care over detail that was almost pathological in its intensity, and she had often found herself waking up in the early hours and wondering if she had perpetrated some unforgivable error. But she had settled down; and thoroughly enjoyed the work. Her conscientiousness had been recognized by her supervisors and acknowledged by her fellow 'Supers'; and finally, over the last few years, she had been rewarded by a belated promotion to a post of some small responsibility, part of which involved working with inexperienced women who came to join the various teams; and for the past six months Gladys had been training a very much younger woman in the mysteries of the whole complex apparatus. This younger woman's name was Margaret Bowman.

For the past three sessions, the two of them had worked together, becoming firm friends in the process, and learning (as women sometimes do) a good many things about each other. At the start, Margaret had seemed almost as diffident and insecure as she herself, Gladys, had been; and it was – what was the word? – yes, such vulnerability that had endeared the younger woman to Gladys, and very soon made the older woman come to look upon Margaret more as a daughter than a colleague. Not that Margaret was ever *too* forthcoming about the more intimate details of her life with Tom, her husband; or (during the autumn) about the clandestine affair she was so obviously having with someone else (Gladys had never learned his name). How could anyone *not* have guessed? For the affair was engendering the sort of bloom on the cheek which (unbeknown to Gladys) Aristotle himself had once used in seeking to define his notion of pure happiness. Then, in the weeks of late autumn, there had occurred a change in Margaret: there were now moments of (hitherto) unsuspected irritability, of (hitherto) uncharacteristic carelessness, and (perhaps most disturbing of all) a sort of coarseness and selfishness. Yet the strangely close relationship between them had survived, and on two occasions Gladys had tried to ask, tried to help, tried to offer more than just a natural friendliness; but nothing had resulted from these overtures. And when on a Friday in mid-December the last session of the calendar year had finally come to its close, that was the last Gladys had seen of her colleague until the new-year resumption – on January 2nd, a day on which it hardly required the talents of a clairvoyant to see that there was something quite desperately wrong.

Smoking was banned from the room in which the Supers worked; but several of the women were moderately addicted to the weed, and each day they greatly looked forward to the morning coffee-breaks and afternoon tea-breaks, both taken in the Delegacy canteen, in which smoking *was* allowed. Hitherto – and invariably – during the time Gladys had known her, Margaret would sit patiently puffing her way through a single cigarette a.m.; a single cigarette p.m. But on that January 2nd, and again on the 3rd, Margaret had been getting through three cigarettes in each of the twenty-minute breaks, inhaling deeply and dramatically on each one.

Margaret's work, too, during the whole of her first day back, had been quite unprecedentedly slack: ten marks missed at one point in a simple addition; a wrong scaling, and a very obvious one at that, not spotted; and then (an error which would have made Gladys herself blanch with shame and mortification) an addition of 104 and 111 entered as 115 – a total which, but for Gladys's own rechecking, would probably have given some luckless candidate an 'E' grade instead of an 'A' grade.

At lunchtime on Friday, January 3rd, Gladys had

invited Margaret for a meal at the Chinese restaurant just across the Banbury Road from the Delegacy; and over the sweet-and-sour pork and the Lotus House Special chop suey, Margaret had confided to Gladys that her husband was away on a course over the New Year and that she herself had been feeling a bit low. And how enormously it had pleased Gladys when Margaret had accepted the invitation to spend the weekend with her – in Gladys's home on the Cutteslowe housing estate in North Oxford.

Mrs Mary Webster, the senior administrative assistant who kept a very firm (if not unfriendly) eye upon the forty or so women who sat each day in the large first-storey room overlooking the playing fields of Summerfields Preparatory School, had not returned to her accustomed chair after the coffee-break on the morning of January 6th. Most unusual! But it was the intelligence gleaned by Mrs Bannister (a woman somewhat handicapped in life by a bladder of minimal capacity, but whose regular trips to the downstairs toilet afforded, by way of compensation, a fascinating window on the world) that set the whole room a-buzzing.

'A police car!' she whispered (audibly) to half the assembled ladies.

'Two men! They're in the Secretary's room!'

'You mean the police are down there talking to *Mrs Webster*?' asked one of Mrs Bannister's incredulous colleagues.

But further commentary and interpretation was

immediately forestalled by Mrs Webster herself, who now suddenly entered the door at the top of the long room, and who began to walk down the central gangway between the desks and tables. The whole room was immediately still, and silent as a Trappist's cell. It was not until she reached Gladys's table, almost at the very bottom of the room, that she stopped.

'Mrs Bowman, can you come with me for a few minutes, please?'

Margaret Bowman said nothing as she walked down the wooden stairs, one step behind Mrs Webster, and then into the main corridor downstairs and directly to the room whose door of Swedish oak bore the formidable nameplate of 'The Secretary'.

Chapter Twenty-six

Monday, January 6th: a.m.

The cruellest lies are often told in silence.

(ROBERT LOUIS STEVENSON)

'THE SECRETARY' WAS one of those endearingly archaic titles in which the University of Oxford abounded. On the face of it, such a title seemed to point to a personage with Supreme (upper-case, as it were) Stenographic Skills. In fact, however, the Secretary of the Locals, Miss Gibson, was a poor typist, her distinction arising from her outstanding academic and administrative abilities which had led, ten years previously, to her appointment as the boss of the whole outfit. Grey-haired, tight-lipped, pale-faced, Miss Gibson sat behind her desk, in an upright red leather chair, awaiting the arrival of Mrs Margaret Bowman. Arranged in front of her desk were three further red leather chairs, of the same design: in the one to the Secretary's left sat a man of somewhat melancholy mien, the well-manicured fingers of his left hand occasionally stroking his thinning hair and who was at that moment (although Miss Gibson would never have guessed the fact) thinking what a very attractive woman the Secretary must have been in her earlier years; in the middle sat a slightly younger man – another policeman, and one also in plain clothes – but a man both thicker set, and kindlier faced. Miss Gibson introduced the two police officers after Margaret Bowman had knocked and entered and been bidden to the empty chair.

'You live in Chipping Norton?' asked Lewis.

'Yes.'

'At 6 Charlbury Drive, I think?'

'Yes.' Even with the two monosyllabic answers, Margaret knew that her tremulous upper lip was betraying signs of her nervousness, and she felt uncomfortably aware of the fierce blue-grey eyes of the other man upon her.

'And you work here?' continued Lewis.

'I've been here seven months.'

'You had quite a bit of time off over Christmas, I understand?'

'We had from Christmas Eve to last Thursday.'

'Last Thursday, let's see – that was January the second?'

'Yes.'

'The day after New Year's Day.'

Margaret Bowman said nothing, although clearly the man had expected – hoped? – that she would make some comment.

'You had plenty of things to occupy you, I suppose,' continued Lewis. 'Christmas shopping, cooking the mince pies, all that sort of thing?'

'Plenty of shopping, yes.'

'Summertown's getting a very good shopping centre, I hear.'

'Very good, yes.'

'And the Westgate down in the centre – they say that's very good, too.'

'Yes, it is.'

'Did you shop in Summertown here – or down in Oxford?'

'I did all my shopping at home.'

'You didn't come into Oxford at all, then?'

Why was she hesitating? Was she lying? Or was she just thinking back over things to make sure?

'No – I didn't.'

'You didn't go to the hairdressers'?'

Margaret Bowman's right hand went up to the top of her head, gently lifting a few strands of her not-so-recently-dyed-blonde hair, and she permitted herself a vague and tired-looking smile: 'Does it look like it?'

No, it doesn't, thought Lewis. 'Do you go to any beauty salons, beauty clinics, you know the sort of thing I mean?'

'No. Do you think I ought to?' Miraculously almost, she was feeling very much more at ease now, and she took a paper handkerchief from her black leather handbag and held it under her nose as she snuffled away some of the residual phlegm from a recent cold.

For his own part, Lewis was conscious that his questioning was not yet making much progress. 'Does your husband work in Oxford?'

'Look! Can you please give me some idea of why

you're asking me all these things? Am I supposed to have done something wrong?'

'We'll explain later, Mrs Bowman. We're trying to make all sorts of important inquiries all over the place, and we're very glad of your co-operation. So, please, if you don't mind, just answer the questions for the minute, will you?'

'He works in Chipping Norton.'

'What work does he do?'

'He's a postman.'

'Did he have the same time off as you over Christmas?'

'No. He was back at work on Boxing Day.'

'You spent Christmas Day together?'

'Yes.'

'And you celebrated the New Year together?'

The question had been put, and there was silence in the Secretary's office. Even Morse who had been watching a spider up in the far corner of the ceiling stopped tapping his lower teeth with a yellow pencil he had picked up, its point needle-sharp. *How long was the well-nigh unbearable silence going to last?*

It was the Secretary herself who suddenly spoke, in a quiet but firm voice: 'You must tell the police the truth, Margaret – it's far better that way. You didn't tell the truth just now – about being in Oxford, did you? We saw each other in the Westgate Car Park on New Year's Eve, you'll remember. We wished each other a Happy New Year.'

Margaret Bowman nodded. 'Oh yes! Yes, I do

remember now.' She turned to Lewis. 'I'm sorry, I'd forgotten. I did come in that Tuesday – I went to Sainsbury's.'

'And then you went back and you spent the New Year at home with your husband?'

'No!'

Morse, whose eyes had still been following the little spider as it seemed to practise its eight-finger exercises, suddenly shifted in his chair and turned round fully to face the woman.

'Where is your husband, Mrs Bowman?' They were the first six words he had spoken to her, and (as events were to work themselves out) they were to be the last six. But Margaret Bowman made no direct answer. Instead, she unfastened her bag, drew out a folded sheet of paper and handed it over to Lewis. It read as follows:

31st December

Dear Maggie

You've gone into Oxford and I'm here sitting at home. You will be upset and disappointed I know but please try and understand. I met another woman two months ago and I knew straightaway that I liked her a lot. I've just got to work things out that's all. Please give me that chance and don't think badly of me. I've decided that if we can go away for a few days or so we can sort things out. You are going to want to know if I love this woman and I don't know yet and she doesn't know either. She is not married and she is thirty one. We are going in her car up to Scotland if the roads are all right. Nobody else need know anything. I got a week off work quite officially though I didn't tell you. I know what you will feel like but it will be better for me to sort things out.

Tom

Lewis read through the letter quickly – and then looked at Mrs Bowman. Was there – did he notice – just a brief flash of triumph in her eyes? Or could it have been a glint of fear? He couldn't be sure, but the interview had obviously taken a totally unexpected turn, and he would have welcomed at that point a guiding hand from Morse. But the latter still appeared to be perusing the letter with inordinate interest.

'You found this note when you got back home?' asked Lewis.

She nodded. 'On the kitchen table.'

'Do you know this woman he mentions?'

'No.'

'You've not heard from your husband?'

'No.'

'He's taking a long time to, er "sort things out".'

'Has – has my husband had an accident – a car accident? Is that why—'

'Not so far as we know, Mrs Bowman.'

'Is that – is that all you want me for?'

'For the minute, perhaps. We shall have to keep the letter – I'm sure you'll understand why.'

'No, I *don't* understand why!'

'Well, it might not be from your husband at all – have you thought of that?' asked Lewis slowly.

'Course it's from him!' As she spoke these few words,

she sounded suddenly sharp and almost crude after her earlier quietly civilized manner, and Lewis found himself wondering several things about her.

'Can you be sure about that, Mrs Bowman?'

'I'd know his writing anywhere.'

'Have you got any more of his writing with you?'

'I've got the very first letter he wrote me – years ago.'

'Can you show it to us, please?'

From her handbag she brought out an envelope, much soiled, drew from it a letter, much creased, and handed it to Lewis, who cursorily compared the two samples of handwriting, and pushed them along the desk to Morse – the latter nodding slowly after a few moments: it seemed to him that by amateur and professional experts alike, the writing would pretty certainly be adjudged identical.

'Can I please go now?'

Lewis wasn't at all sure whether or not this oddly unsatisfactory interview should be temporarily terminated, and he turned to Morse – receiving only a non-committal shrug.

So it was that Margaret Bowman left the office, exhorted in a kindly way by the Secretary to get herself another cup of coffee from the canteen, and to be ready to come down again if the police needed her for further questioning.

'We're sorry to have taken so much of your time, Miss Gibson,' said Morse after Mrs Bowman had left. 'And if we could have a room for an hour or so we'd be most grateful.'

'You can stay here if you like, Inspector. There are a good many things I've got to see to round the office.'

'What do you make of all that, sir?' asked Lewis when they were alone.

'We haven't got a thing to charge her with, have we? We can't take her in just for forgetting she bought a pound of sausages from Sainsbury's.'

'We're not getting far, are we, sir? It's all a bit disappointing.'

'What? Disappointing? Far from it! We've just been looking at things from the wrong end, Lewis, that's all.'

'Really?'

'Oh yes. And we owe a lot to Mrs Bowman – it was about time somebody put me on the right track!'

'You think she was telling the truth?'

'Truth?' Morse shook his head. 'I didn't believe a word of her story, did you?'

'I don't know, sir. I feel very confused.'

'Confused? Surely not!' He turned to Lewis and put the yellow pencil down on the Secretary's desk. 'Do you want to know what happened in Annexe 3 on New Year's Eve?'

Chapter Twenty-Seven

Monday, January 6th: a.m.

It is a bad plan that admits of no modification.

(PUBLILIUS SYRUS)

'LET ME EXPLAIN one thing from the start. I just said we've been looking at things from the wrong end and I mean just that. Max gave us a big enough margin for the time of death, and instead of listening to him I kept trying to pin him down. Even now it's taken a woman's pack of lies to put me on the right track, because the most important thing about Mrs Bowman is that she was forced to show us the letter, supposedly from her husband, to give herself a reasonable alibi. It was the last shot in her locker; and she had no option but to use it, because we were getting – we *are* getting! – dangerously close to the truth. And I just said "supposedly from her husband" – but that's not the case: it *was* from her husband, you can be certain of that. Everything fits, you see, *once you turn the pattern upside down.* The man in Annexe 3 wasn't murdered after the party: he was murdered *before the party.* Let's just assume that Margaret Bowman has been unfaithful, and let's assume that she gets deeply involved with this lover of hers, and that he threatens to blackmail her in some way if she doesn't agree to see him again – threatens to tell her husband – to cut his own throat – to cut *her* throat – anything you like. Let's say, too, that the husband, Tom Bowman, deliverer of Her Majesty's mail at Chipping Norton, finds out about all this – let's say that he intercepts a letter; or, more likely, I think, she's desperate enough to tell him all about it – because there must have been some sort of reconciliation between them. Together, they decide that something has got to be done to get rid of the threat that now affects *both* of them; and at that point, as I see it, the plot was hatched. They book a double room for a New Year break at a hotel, using a non-existent accommodation address so that later on no one will be able to trace them; and Tom Bowman is exactly the person to cope with that problem – none better. So things really start moving. Margaret Bowman tells this dangerous and persistent lover of hers – let's call him Mr X – that *she can spend the New Year with him.* He's a single man; he's head over heels about her; and now he's over the moon, too! He thought she'd ditched him. But here she is offering to spend a couple of whole days with him. *She's* taken the initiative; *she's* fixed it all up; *she's* booked the hotel; *she* wants *him*! She's even told him – and she must have expected he'd agree – that *she'll* provide the fancy-dress costumes they're going to wear at the New Year party. She tells him to be ready, let's say, from four o'clock on the 31st. She herself probably books in under her false name and a false address an hour or so earlier, but a bit later than most of the other guests. She wants to be seen by as few of the others as possible, but she's still got to give herself plenty of time. She finds herself alone at the reception desk, she turns up her coat and pulls her scarf around her face, she signs the form, she takes the room key, she takes her suitcase over to Annexe 3 – and all is ready. She rings up X from the public phone-box just outside the hotel, tells him what their room number is, and he's on his way like a shot. And while the rest of the guests are playing Cluedo, he's spending the rest of that late afternoon and early evening with his bottom on the top sheet, as they say. Then, when most of the passion's spent itself, she tells him that they'd better start dressing up for the party; she shows him what she's brought for the pair of them to wear; and about 7 p.m. the pair of them are ready: she rubs a final bit of stage-black on his hands – makes some excuse about leaving her purse or her umbrella at Reception – says she'll be back in a minute – takes the key with her – pulls her mackintosh over her costume – and goes out bang on the stroke of seven. Tom Bowman, *himself dressed in exactly the same sort of outfit as X,* has been waiting for her, somewhere in the immediate vicinity of the hotel; and while Margaret Bowman spends the most nerve-racking few minutes of her life, probably in the bus shelter just across from the hotel, *Tom Bowman lets himself into Annexe 3.*

'Exactly what happened then, we don't know – and we may never know. But very soon the Bowmans are playing out the rest of the evening as best they can – pretending to eat, pretending to be lovey-dovey with each other, pretending to enjoy the festivities. There's little enough chance of them being recognized, anyway: she's hiding behind her yashmak, and he's hiding behind a coat of dark greasepaint. But they both want to be seen going into the annexe after the party's over, and in fact Tom Bowman performs his role with a bit of panache. He waits for the two other women he knows are lodged in the annexe, throws an arm across their shoulders – incidentally ruining their coats with his greasy hands – and gives the impression to all and sundry that he's about to hit the hay. As it happens, Binyon was bringing up the rear – pretty close behind them. But the lock on the side door is only a Yale; and after Binyon had made sure all was well, the Bowmans slipped out quietly into the winter's night. They went down and got their car from the Westgate – or wherever it was parked – and Tom Bowman dropped Margaret back to Charlbury Drive, where she'd left the lights on anyway so that the neighbours would assume she was celebrating the New Year. And then Bowman himself took off into the night somewhere so that if ever the need arose he could establish an alibi for himself up in Inverness or wherever he found himself the next morning, leaving Margaret the pre-planned note about his fictitious girlfriend. And that's about it, Lewis! That's about what happened, as far as I can make out.'

Lewis himself had listened with great interest, and without interruption, to what Morse had said. And although, apart from the *time* of the murder, it wasn't a particularly startling analysis, it was just the sort of self-consistent hypothesis that Lewis had come to expect from the chief inspector, bringing together, as it did, into one coherent scheme all the apparently inconsistent clues and puzzling testimony. But there were one or two weaknesses in Morse's argument: at least as Lewis saw things.

'You said they spent the afternoon in bed, sir. But we didn't, to be honest, find much sign of anything like that, did we?'

'Perhaps they performed on the floor – I don't know. I was just telling you what probably happened.'

'What about the maid, sir – Mandy, wasn't it? Doesn't someone usually come along about seven o'clock or so and turn down the counterpane—'

'Counterpane? Lewis! You're still living in the nineteenth century. And this wasn't the Waldorf Astoria, you know.'

'Bit of a risk, though, sir – somebody coming in and finding—'

'They were short-staffed, Lewis – you know that.'

'But the *Bowmans* didn't know that!'

Morse nodded. 'No-o. But they could have hung one of those "Do Not Disturb" signs on the door. In fact, they *did*.'

'Bit risky, though, hanging out a sign like that if you're supposed to be at a party.'

'Lewis! Don't you understand? They were taking risks the whole bloody time.'

As always when Morse blustered on in such fashion, Lewis knew that it was best not to push things overmuch. Obviously, what Morse had said was true; but Lewis felt that some of the explanations he was receiving were far from satisfactory.

'If, as you say, sir, Bowman was dressed up, all ready to go, in exactly the same sort of clothes as the other fellow, where was he—?'

'*Where*? I dunno. But I'm sure all he had to do was put a few finishing touches to things.'

'Do you think he did that in Annexe 3?'

'Possibly. Or he could have used the Gents' just off Reception.'

'Wouldn't Miss Jonstone have seen him?'

'How am I supposed to know? Shall we *ask* her, Lewis? Shall *I* ask her? Or what about *you* asking her – you're asking *me* enough bloody questions.'

'It's only because I can't quite understand things, that's all, sir.'

'You think I've got it all wrong, don't you?' said Morse quietly.

'No! I'm pretty sure you're on the right lines, sir, but it doesn't all *quite* hang together, does it?'

Chapter Twenty-Eight

Monday, January 6th: a.m.

What is the use of running when we are not on the right road?

(GERMAN PROVERB)

THERE WAS A knock on the door and Judith, the slimly attractive personal assistant to the Secretary, entered with a tray of coffee and biscuits.

'Miss Gibson thought you might like some refreshment.' She put the tray on the desk. 'If you want her, she's with the Deputy – the internal number's 208.'

'We don't get such VIP treatment up at HQ,' commented Lewis after she'd left.

'Well, they're a more civilized lot here, aren't they? Nice sort of people. Wouldn't harm a fly, most of them.'

'Perhaps *one* of them would!'

'I see what you mean,' said Morse, munching a ginger biscuit.

'Don't you think,' said Lewis, as they drank their coffee, 'that we're getting a bit too complex, sir?'

'Complex? Life *is* complex, Lewis. Not for *you*, perhaps. But for most of us it's a struggle to get through from breakfast to coffee-time, and then from coffee-time—'

There was a knock on the door and Miss Gibson herself re-entered. 'I saw Mrs Webster just now and she said that Mrs Bowman hadn't got back to her work yet. I thought perhaps she might be back here . . .'

The two detectives looked at each other.

'She's not in the canteen?' asked Morse.

'No.'

'She's not in the Ladies'?'

'No.'

'How many exits are there here, Miss Gibson?'

'Just the one. We've all been so worried about security recently—'

But Morse was already pulling on his greatcoat. He thanked the Secretary and with Lewis in his wake walked quickly along the wooden-floored corridor towards the exit. At the reception desk sat the Security Officer. Mr Prior, a thick-set, former prison officer, whose broad, intelligent face looked up from the Court Circular of the *Daily Telegraph* as Morse fired a salvo of questions at him.

'You know Mrs Bowman?'

'Yessir.'

'How long ago did she leave?'

'Three – four minutes.'

'By car?'

'Yessir. Maroon Metro – 1300 – A reg.'

'You don't know the number?'

'Not offhand.'

'Did she turn left or right at the Banbury Road?'

'Can't see from here.'

'She was wearing a coat?'

'Yessir. Black, fur-collared coat. But she hadn't changed her shoes.'

'What do you mean?'

'Most of 'em come in boots this weather – and then change into something lighter when they're here. She still had a pair of high heels on – black; black leather, I should think.'

Morse was impressed by Prior's powers of observation, said as much, and asked if he'd noticed anything else that was at all odd.

'Don't think so. Except perhaps when she said "Goodbye!"'

'Don't most people say "Goodbye" when they leave?'

Prior thought for a second before replying: 'No, they don't! They usually say "See you!" or "Cheers!" or something like that.'

Morse walked from the Locals, his eyes downcast, a deep frown on his forehead. The snow had been brushed away from the shallow steps that led down to the car park, and a watery-looking sun had almost dried the concrete. The forecast was for continued improvement in the weather, although in places there were still patches of hazardous ice.

'Where to?' asked Lewis as Morse got into the passenger seat of the police car.

'I'm – not – quite – sure,' replied Morse as they drove up to the black-and-yellow striped barrier that regulated the progress of unauthorized vehicles into Ewert Place, the narrow street that led down to the

Delegacy's private car park. Bob King, the courteous, blue-uniformed attendant, touched his peaked cap to them as he pressed the button to raise the barrier; but before going through, Morse beckoned him round to his window and asked him if he remembered a maroon Metro leaving a few minutes earlier; and if so whether it had turned left or right into the Banbury Road. But whilst the answer to the first question had been 'yes', the answer to the second question had been 'no'. And for the minute Morse asked Lewis to stop the car where it was: the Straw Hat Bakery ('Everything baked on the Premises') on the left; and, to the right (its immediate neighbour across the narrow road), the giant Allied Carpets shop, whose vast areas of glass frontage were perpetually plastered over with notices informing the inhabitants of Summertown that the current sale must undoubtedly rank as the biggest bargain in the annals of carpetry. Betwixt and between – there the car stood: left, down into Oxford; right, up and out of the city and, if need be, thence to Chipping Norton.

'Chipping Norton,' said Morse suddenly – 'quick as you can!'

Blue rooflight flashing, siren wailing, the white Ford raced up to the Banbury Road roundabout then across to the Woodstock Road roundabout, and was soon out on the A34, a happy-looking Lewis behind the wheel.

'Think she'll go back home straight away?'

'My God, I hope so!' said Morse with unwonted vehemence.

It was when the car had passed the Black Prince and was climbing the hill out of Woodstock that Morse spoke again. 'Going back to what you were saying about Annexe 3, Lewis, you *did* have a look at the bed-linen, didn't you?'

'Yes, sir. In both beds.'

'You don't think you missed anything?'

'Don't think so. Wouldn't matter much if I did, though. We've still got all the bedclothes – I sent everything along to the path lab.'

'You did?'

Lewis nodded. 'But if you want my opinion, nobody'd been sleeping in either of those two beds, sir.'

'Well, you couldn't tell with the one, could you? It was all soaked in blood.'

'No, it wasn't, sir. The blood had seeped through the counterpane or whatever you call it, and a bit through the blankets; but the sheets weren't marked at all.'

'And you don't think that they'd been having sex that afternoon or evening – in either of the beds.'

Lewis was an old hand in murder investigations, and some of the things he'd found in rooms, in cupboards, in wardrobes, in beds, under beds – he'd have been more than happy to be able to forget. But he knew what Morse was referring to, and he was more than confident of his answer. 'No. There were no marks of sexual emissions or anything like that.'

'You have an admirably delicate turn of phrase,' said Morse, as Lewis sped past an obligingly docile convoy of Long Vehicles. 'But it's a good point you made earlier, you know. If the old charpoy *wasn't* creaking all that afternoon . . .'

'As you said, though, sir – they might have made love on the carpet.'

'Have you ever made love on the carpet in mid-winter?'

'Well, no. But—'

'Central heating's one thing. But you get things like draughts under doors, don't you?'

'I haven't got much experience of that sort of thing myself.'

The car turned off left at the Chipping Norton/ Moreton-in-Marsh/Evesham sign; and a few minutes later Lewis brought it to a gentle stop outside 6 Charlbury Drive. He noticed the twitch of a lace curtain in the front window of number 5; but no one seemed to be about at all, and the little road lay quiet and still. No maroon Metro stood outside number 6, or in the steep drive that led down to the white-painted doors of the single garage.

'Go and have a look!' said Morse.

But there was no car in the garage, either; and the front-door bell seemed to Lewis to re-echo through a house that sounded ominously empty.

Chapter Twenty-Nine

Monday, January 6th: a.m.

The last pleasure in life is the sense of discharging our duty.

(William Hazlitt)

Where Morse decided to turn right past Allied Carpets, Margaret Bowman, some five minutes earlier, had decided to turn left past the Straw Hat, and had thence proceeded south towards the centre of the city. In St Giles', the stiff penalty recently introduced for any motorists outstaying their two-hour maximum (even by a minute or so) had resulted in the unprecedented sight of a few free rectangles of parking space almost invariably being available at any one time; and Margaret pulled into the one she spotted just in front of the Eagle and Child, and walked slowly across to the ticket machine, some twenty-odd yards away. For the whole of the time from when she had sat down in the Secretary's office until now, her mind had been numbed to the reality of her underlying situation, and far-distanced, in some strange way, from what (she knew) would be the disastrous inevitability of her fate. Her voice and her manner, as she had answered the policemen, had been much more controlled than she could have dared to hope. Not *quite* all the time; but anyone, even someone who was wholly innocent, would always be nervous in those circumstances. Had they believed her? But she knew now that the answer even to such a crucial question was perhaps no longer of any great importance. (She prodded her fingers into the corner of her handbag for the necessary change.) But to say that at that very moment Margaret Bowman had finally come to any conclusion about ending her life would be untrue. Such a possibility had certainly occurred to her – oh, so many times! – over the past few days of despair and the past few nights of hell. Academically, she had not been a successful pupil at the Chipping Norton Comprehensive School, and in O-level *Greek Literature in Translation* (Margaret had not been considered for the high fliers' Latin course) she had been 'Unclassified'. Yet she remembered something (in one of the books they were supposed to read) about Socrates, just before he took the hemlock: when he'd said that he would positively welcome death if it turned out to be just one long and dreamless sleep. And that's what Margaret longed for now – a long, a wakeless and a dreamless sleep. (She could not find the exact number of coins which the notice on the ticket machine so inexorably demanded.) And then she remembered her mother, dying of cancer in her early forties, when Margaret was only fourteen: and before dying saying how desperately tired she was and how she just wanted to be free from pain and never wake again . . .

Margaret had found five 10p coins – still one short –

and she looked around her with a childlike pleading in her eyes, as though she almost expected her very helplessness to work its own deliverance. A hundred or so yards away, just passing the Taylorian, and coming towards her, she saw a yellow-banded traffic warden, and suddenly a completely new and quite extraordinary thought came to her mind. Would it matter if she *were* caught? Didn't she *want* to be caught? Wasn't there, after all hope had been cruelly cancelled, a point when even total despair could hold no further terrors? A notice ('No Change Given') outside the Eagle and Child informed Margaret that she could expect little help from that establishment; but she walked in and ordered a glass of orange juice.

'Ice?'

'Pardon?'

'You want ice in it?'

'Oh – yes. Er – no. I'm sorry, I didn't quite hear . . .'

She felt the hard eyes of the well-coiffeured bar-lady on her as she handed over a £1 coin and received 60p in exchange: one 50p piece, and one 10p. Somehow she felt almost childishly pleased as she put her six 10p pieces together and held the little stack of coins in her left hand. She had no idea how long she stayed there, seated at a table just in front of the window. But when she noticed that the glass in front of her was empty, and when she felt the coins so warmly snug inside her palm, she walked out slowly into St Giles'. It occurred to her – so suddenly! – that there she was, in St Giles'; that she had just come down the Banbury Road; that she must have passed directly in front of the Haworth Hotel; and that *she hadn't even noticed it.* Was she beginning to lose control of her mind? Or had she got *two* minds now? The one which had pushed itself into auto-pilot in the driving seat of the Metro; and the other, logical and sober, which even now, as she walked towards the ticket machine, was seeking to keep her shoes (the ones she had bought for the funeral) out of the worst of crunching slush. She saw the celluloid-covered document under the near-side windscreen-wiper; and caught sight of the traffic warden, two cars further up, leaning back slightly to read a number plate before completing another incriminating ticket.

Margaret walked up to her, pointing to the maroon Metro.

'Have I committed an offence?'

'Is that your car?'

'Yes.'

'You were parked without a ticket.'

'Yes, I know. I've just been to get the right change.' Almost pathetically she opened her left palm and held the six warm coins to view as if they might just serve as some propitiatory offering.

'I'm sorry, madam. It tells you on the sign, doesn't it? If you haven't got the right change, you shouldn't park.'

For a moment or two the two women, so little different in age, eyed each other in potential hostility. But when Margaret Bowman spoke, her voice sounded flat, indifferent almost.

'Do you enjoy your work?'

'Not the point, is it?' replied the other. 'There's nothing *personal* in it. It's a job that's got to be done.'

Margaret Bowman turned and the traffic warden looked after her with a marked expression of puzzlement on her face. It was her experience that on finding a parking ticket virtually all of them got into their cars and drove angrily away. But not this tall, good-looking woman who was now walking away from her car, down past the Martyrs' Memorial; and then, almost out of sight now, but with the warden's last words still echoing in her mind, across into Cornmarket and up towards Carfax.

Chapter Thirty

Monday, January 6th: noon

Then the devil taketh him up into the holy city, and setteth him on a pinnacle of the temple.

(MATTHEW iv, 5)

MARGARET BOWMAN STOOD beneath Carfax Tower, a great, solid pile of pale-yellowish stone that stands on the corner of Queen Street and Cornmarket, and which looks down, at its east side, on to the High. White lettering on a background of Oxford blue told her that a splendid view of the city and the surrounding district was available from the top of the tower: admission 50p, Mondays to Saturdays, 10 a.m. to 6 p.m.; and her heart pounded as she stood there, her eyes ascending to the crenellated balustrade built four-square around the top. Not a high balustrade either; and often in the past she'd noticed people standing there, almost half their bodies visible as they gazed out over Oxford or waved to friends who stood a hundred feet below. She was not one of those acrophobes (as, for example, Morse was) who burst into a clammy sweat of vertiginous panic when forced to stand on the third or the fourth rung of a household ladder. But she was always terrified of being *pushed* – had been ever since one of the boys on a school party to Snowdon had *pretended* to push her, and when for a split second she had experienced a sense of imminent terror of falling over the precipitous drop that yawned almost immediately below her feet. People said you always thought of your childhood before you died, and she was conscious that twice already – no, three times – her mind had reverted to early memories. And now she was conscious of a fourth – of the words her father had so often used when she tried to put off writing a letter, or starting her homework: 'The longer you put things off, the harder they become, my girl!' Should she put things off now? Defer any fateful decision? No! She pushed the door to the tower. But it was clear that the tower was shut; and it was with a sense of despairing disappointment that she noticed the bottom line of the notice: '20th March – 31st October'.

The spire of St Mary the Virgin pointed promisingly skywards in front of her as she walked down the High, and into the Mitre.

'Large Scotch – Bell's, please – if you have it.' (How often had she heard her husband use those selfsame words!)

A young barmaid pushed a tumbler up against the bottom of an inverted bottle, and then pushed again.

'Ice?'

'Pardon?'

'Do you want ice?'

'Er – no. Er – yes – yes please! I'm sorry. I didn't quite hear . . .'

As she sipped the whisky, a hitherto dormant nerve

throbbing insistently along her left temple, the world seemed to her perhaps fractionally more bearable than it had done when she'd left the Delegacy. Like some half-remembered medicine – foul-tasting yet efficacious – the whisky seemed to do her good; and she bought another.

A few minutes later she was standing in Radcliffe Square; and as she looked up at the north side of St Mary's Church, a strange and fatal fascination seemed to grip her soul. Halfway up the soaring edifice, his head and shoulders visible over the tricuspid ornamentation that marked the intersection of tower and spire, Margaret could see a duffel-coated young man, binoculars to his eyes, gazing out across the northern parts of Oxford. The tower must be open, surely! She walked down the steps towards the main porch of the church and then, for a moment, turned round and gazed up at the dome of the Radcliffe Camera behind her; and noticed the inscription on the top step: *Dominus custodiat introitum tuum et exitum tuum.* But since she had no Latin, the potential irony of the words escaped her. TOWER OPEN was printed in large capitals on a noticeboard beside the entrance; and just inside, seated behind a table covered with postcards, guidebooks and assorted Christian literature, was a middle-aged woman who had already assumed that Margaret Bowman wished to ascend, for she held out a maroon-coloured ticket and asked for 60p. A few flights of wide wooden stairs led up to the first main landing, where a notice on a locked door to the left advised visitors that here was the Old Library – the very first one belonging to the University – where the few books amassed by the earliest scholars were so precious that they were chained to the walls. Margaret had seldom been interested in old churches, or old anythings for that matter; but she now found herself looking down at the leaflet the woman below had given her:

> when Mary became Queen and England reverted to Roman Catholicism, Archbishop Cranmer and two of his fellow bishops, Latimer and Ridley, were tried in St Mary's for heresy. Latimer and Ridley were burned at the stake. Cranmer himself, after officially recanting, was brought back to St Mary's and condemned to death. He was burned at the stake in the town ditch, outside Balliol College, holding his right hand (which had written his recantation) steadily in the flames . . .

Margaret looked at her own right hand – a couple of blue biro marks across the bottom of the thumb – and thought of the tortured atonement that Cranmer had sought, and welcomed, for his earlier weaknesses. A tear ran hurriedly down her cheek, and she took from her handbag a white paper handkerchief to dry her eyes.

The stairs – iron now, and no longer enclosed for the next two flights – led up and over the roof of the Lady Chapel, and she felt a sense of exhilaration in the cold air as she climbed higher still to the Bell Tower, where the man with the binoculars, his hair windswept, had just descended the stone spiral staircase that led to the top.

'Not much further!' he volunteered. 'Bit blowy up there, though. Bit slippery, too. Be careful!'

For several seconds as she emerged at the top of the tower, Margaret was conscious of a terrifying giddiness as her eyes glimpsed, just below her feet, the black iron ring that circled the golden-painted Roman numerals of the great clock adorning the north wall of the church. But the panic was soon gone, and she looked out across at the Radcliffe Camera; and then to the left of the Camera at the colleges along Broad Street; then the buildings of Balliol where Cranmer had redeemed his soul amid the burning brushwood; then she could see the leafless trees along St Giles', and the roads that led off from there into North Oxford; and then the giant yellow crane that stood at the Haworth Hotel in the Banbury Road. She took a few steps along the high-walk towards the north-western corner of the tower, and she suddenly felt a sense of elation, and the tears welled up again in her eyes as the wind blew back her hair, and as she held her head up to the elements with the same joyous carelessness she had shown as a young girl when the rain had showered down on her tip-tilted face . . .

At a point on the corner, her wholly inadequate and unsuitable shoes had slipped along the walkway, and a man standing below watched the black handbag as it plummeted to the earth and landed, neatly erect, in a drift of snow beneath the north-west angle of the tower.

Chapter Thirty-One

Monday, January 6th: p.m.

Everything comes to him who waits – among other things, death.

(F. H. BRADLEY)

MORSE WAS DISSATISFIED and restless – that much was obvious as they sat outside the Bowmans' house in Charlbury Drive. Ten minutes they waited, Morse just sitting there in the passenger seat, his safety-belt still on, staring out of the window. Then another ten minutes, with Morse occasionally clicking his tongue and taking sharp audible breaths of impatient frustration.

'Think she's coming back?' said Lewis.

'I dunno.'

'How long are we going to wait?'

'How do *I* know!'

'Just asked.'

'I tell you one thing, Lewis. I'm making one bloody marvellous mess of this case!'

'I don't know about that, sir.'

'Well you *should* know! We should never have let her out of our sight.'

Lewis nodded, but said nothing; and for a further ten minutes the pair of them sat in silence.

But there was no sign of Margaret Bowman.

'What do you suggest we do, Lewis?' asked Morse finally.

'I think we ought to go to the post office: see if we can find some of Bowman's handwriting – there must be something there; see if any of his mates know anything about where he is or where he's gone; that sort of thing.'

'And you'd like to get somebody from there to go and look at the body, wouldn't you? You think it *is* Bowman!'

'I'd just like to check, that's all. Check it *isn't* Bowman, if you like. But we haven't done anything at all yet, sir, about identification.'

'And you're telling me it's about bloody time we did!'

'Yessir.'

'All right. Let's do it your way. Waste of time but—' His voice was almost a snarl.

'Are you feeling all right, sir?'

'Course I'm not feeling all right! Can't you see I'm dying for a bloody cigarette, man?'

The visit to the post office produced little information that was not already known. Tom Bowman had worked on the Thursday, Friday and Saturday following Christmas Day, and then had taken a week's holiday. He should have been back at work that very day, the 6th; but as yet no one had seen or heard anything of him. It seemed he was a quiet, punctual, methodical sort of fellow, who had been working there for six years now. No one knew his wife Margaret very well, though it was common knowledge that she had a job in Oxford and took quite a bit of trouble over her clothes and her personal appearance. There were two handwritten letters from Bowman in the personnel file: one dating back to his first application to join the PO; the second concerning itself with his options under the PO pension provisions. Clearly there had been little or no calligraphic variance in Bowman's penmanship over the years, and here seemed further evidence – if any were required – that the letter Margaret Bowman had produced from her handbag that morning was genuinely in her husband's hand. Mr Jeacock, the co-operative and neatly competent postmaster, could tell them little more; but, yes, he was perfectly happy for one of Bowman's colleagues to follow the police officers down into Oxford to look at the unidentified body.

'Let's hope to God it's *not* Tom! he said as Morse and Lewis got up and left his small office.

'I honestly don't think you need to worry about that, sir,' said Morse.

As always, the cars coming up in the immediate rear had all decelerated to the statutory speed limit; and by the time the police car reached the dual carriageway just after Blenheim Palace, with Mr Frederick Norris, sorter of Her Majesty's mail in Chipping Norton, immediately behind, there was an enormous tailback of vehicles. Morse, who had told Lewis to take things quietly, sat silent throughout the return journey, and Lewis too held his peace. At the bottom of the Woodstock Road he turned right into a narrow road at the Radcliffe Infirmary and stopped on an 'Ambulances Only' parking lot outside the mortuary to which the body found in the Haworth annexe had now been transferred. Norris got out of the car that pulled up behind them.

'You coming, sir?' asked Lewis.

But Morse shook his head.

Fred Norris stood stock-still for a few seconds, and then – somewhat to Lewis's bewilderment – nodded slowly, his own pallor only a degree less ghastly than the skin that backed the livid bruising of the murdered man's features. No words were spoken; but as the mortuary attendant replaced the white sheet, Lewis put a kindly, understanding hand on Norris's shoulder, and then gently urged him out of the grim building into the bright January air.

An ambulance had pulled in just ahead of the police car, and Lewis, as he stood fixing a time with Norris for an official statement, saw the ambulance driver unhurriedly get out and speak to one of the porters at the Accident entrance. From the general lack of urgency, Lewis gathered that the man was probably delivering some fussy octogenarian for her weekly dose of physiotherapy. But the back doors were suddenly opened to reveal the body of a woman covered in a red blanket, with only the shoeless stockinged feet protruding.

Lewis's throat was dry as he walked past the police car, and saw Morse (the latter still unaware of the dramatic news that Lewis was about to impart) point to the back of the ambulance.

'Who is she?' asked Lewis as the two ambulancemen prepared to fix the runners for the stretcher.

'Are you . . .?' The driver jerked his thumb towards the police car.

'Chief Inspector Morse – him! Not me!'

'Accident. They found her—'

'How old?'

The man shrugged. 'Forty?'

'You know who she is?'

The man shook his head. 'No one knows yet. No purse. No handbag.'

Lewis drew back the blanket and looked at the woman's face, his heart pounding in anticipatory dread – for such an eventuality, as he well knew, was exactly what Morse had feared.

But the ambulance driver was right in suggesting that no one knew who she was: Lewis didn't know, either. For the dead woman in the back of the ambulance was certainly not Mrs Margaret Bowman.

That same lunch-hour, some fifty minutes before Norris had positively identified the man murdered at the Haworth Hotel as Mr Thomas Bowman, Ronald Armitage, an idle, dirty, feckless, cold, hungry, semi-drunken sixty-three-year-old layabout – unemployed and unemployable – experienced a remarkable piece of good fortune. He had spent the previous night huddled up on a bench in the passage that leads from Radcliffe Square to the High, and had spent most of the morning on the same bench, with an empty flagon of Bulmer's Cider at his numbed feet, and one dirty five-pound note and a few 10p coins in the pocket of the ankle-length greatcoat that for many years had been his most treasured possession. When he had first seen the black handbag as it plummeted to the ground, and came to rest in a cushion of deep snow at the corner of the church, his instinctive reaction was to look sharply and suspiciously around him. But for the moment the square was empty; and he quickly grabbed the handbag, putting it beneath the front of his coat, and walked hurriedly off over the snow-covered cobbles outside Brasenose into the lane on the left that led through to the Turl. Here – with none of his cronies in sight – like a wolf which grabs a great gobbet of meat from the kill and takes it away from the envious eyes of the rest of the pack, he examined his exciting discovery. Inside the handbag he found a lipstick, a powder compact, a comb, a cheap cigarette lighter, a packet of white paper handkerchiefs, a leaflet about St Mary the Virgin, a small pair of nail scissors, a bunch of car keys, two other keys – and a brown leather purse-cum-wallet. The plastic cards – Visa, Access, Lloyds – he ignored, but he quickly pocketed the two beautifully crisp ten-pound notes and the three one-pound coins he found therein.

In mid-afternoon, he wandered slowly up the High

to Carfax, and then turned left down past Christ Church and into St Aldates Police Station where he handed the bag over to Lost Property.

'Where did you find it?' asked the sergeant on duty.

'Someone must have dropped it—'

'You better leave your name—'

'Nah! Don't fink so.'

'Might be a reward!'

'Cheers, mate!'

Chapter Thirty-two

Monday, 6th January: p.m.

Wordsworth recalls in 'The Prelude' how he was soothed by the sound of the Derwent winding among grassy holms.

(*Literary Landscapes of the British Isles*)

It was seldom that Morse ever asked for more personnel. Indeed, it was his private view that the sight (as so often witnessed on TV) of a hundred or so uniformed policemen crawling in echelon across a tract of heathland often brought the force into something approaching derision. He himself had once taken part in such a massive sweep across a field in North Staffordshire, ending up, as he had done, with one empty packet of Featherlite Durex, one empty can of alcohol-free lager – and (the next morning) a troublesome bout of lumbago.

But he *did* ask for more personnel on the afternoon of January 6th; and Lewis, for one, was glad that much needed help (in the shape of Sergeant Phillips and two detective constables) had been summoned to follow up all inquiries regarding Margaret Bowman.

Oddly enough (yet almost everything about him was

odd, as Lewis knew) Morse had shown no great surprise on hearing the news that the murdered man was Thomas Bowman; indeed, the only emotion he showed – and that of immense relief – was after learning that the other corpse on view that lunchtime was *not* Margaret Bowman's. In fact, Morse suddenly seemed much more at peace with himself as he sat with Lewis in the Royal Oak, just opposite the hospital – a circumstance (as Lewis rightly guessed) not wholly unconnected with the fact that after his Herculean efforts over Christmas and the New Year he had finally surrendered and bought himself a packet of cigarettes. At two-thirty, they were once more on the A34 to Chipping Norton, this time with a much firmer mission – to investigate the property at 6 Charlbury Drive, which had now quite definitely become the focus of the murder inquiry.

'Shall we break one of the front windows or one of the back ones?' Morse asked as they stood in front of the property, faces at a good many windows in the quiet cul-de-sac now watching the activity with avid curiosity. But such forcible ingress proved unnecessary. Lewis it was who suggested that most people ('Well, the missus does') leave a key with the neighbours: and so it proved in this case, with the elderly woman in number 5 promptly producing both a back-door and a front-door key. Mrs Bowman, it appeared, had gone out on Friday evening, saying she wouldn't be back until Monday after work; hadn't been back, either – as far as the woman knew.

Finding nothing of immediate interest in the downstairs rooms, Lewis went upstairs where he found Morse in one of the two spare bedrooms looking into a cumbrous dark mahogany wardrobe which (apart from an old-fashioned armchair) was the only item of furniture there.

'Found anything, sir?'

Morse shook his head. 'Lots of shoes he had.'

'Not much help.'

'No help at all.'

'Can you smell anything, sir?'

'Such as?'

'Whisky?' suggested Lewis.

Morse's eyes lit up as he sniffed, and sniffed again.

'I reckon you're right, you know.'

There was a stack of white shoe boxes, and they found the half-full bottle of Bell's in the third box from the bottom.

'You think he was a secret drinker, sir?'

'What if he was? *I'm* a secret drinker – aren't you?'

'No, sir. And I wouldn't have got away with this. The missus cleans all my shoes.'

The other spare room upstairs (little more than a small boxroom) was similarly short on furniture, with three sheets of newspaper spread out across the bare floorboards on which ranks of large, green cooking apples were neatly arranged. 'They take the *Sun*,' observed Lewis, as his eye fell on a young lady leaning forward to maximize the measurements of a mighty bosom. 'You think he was a secret sex maniac?'

'*I'm* a secret—' But Morse broke off as he saw the

broad grin across his sergeant's face, and he found himself smiling in return.

The main bedroom, though furnished fully (even tastefully, as Morse saw it), seemed at first glance to offer little more of interest than the rest of the house. Twin beds, only a few inches apart, were neatly made, each covered with an olive-green quilt, each with a small bedside table – the feminine accoutrements on the one nearer the window clearly signifying 'hers'. On the right as one entered the room was a large white-wood wardrobe, again 'hers', and on the left a tallboy obviously 'his'. A composite piece of modern furniture, mirror in the middle, three shelves above (two of them full of books), with drawers below, stood just beyond the tallboy – at the bottom of Margaret Bowman's bed. Since there seemed about three times as much of her clothing as of his, Morse agreed that Lewis should concentrate on the former, he on the latter. But neither of them was able to come up with anything of value, and Morse soon found himself far more interested in the two shelves of books. The thick spines of four white paperbacks announced a sequence of the latest international best-sellers by Jackie Collins, and beside these stood two apparently unopened Penguins, *Brideshead Revisited* and *A Passage to India.* Then two large, lavishly illustrated books on the life and times of Marilyn Monroe; an ancient impression of the Concise Oxford Dictionary; and, a very recent purchase by the look of things, a book in the 'Hollywood Greats' series covering the career of Robert Redford (a star – unlike Miss

Monroe – who had yet to swim into Morse's ken). On the wall beside this top shelf of books were two colour photographs cut from sporting periodicals: one of Steve Cram, the great middle-distance runner; the other of Ian Terence Botham, his blond locks almost reaching the top of his England cricket sweater. The title *Sex Parties,* on the lower shelf, caught Morse's eye and he took it out and opened a page a random:

> Her hand slid across the gear-lever and touched his leg below the tennis shorts. 'Let's go to my place – quick!' she murmured in his ear.
>
> 'I shan't argue with that, my love!' he replied huskily as the powerful Maserati swerved across the street...
>
> As they lay there together the next morning –

Such anti-climactic pianissimo porn had no attraction whatever for Morse and he was putting the book back in its slot when he noticed that there was something stuck in the middle of the large volume next to it, a work entitled *The Complete Crochet Manual.* It was a holiday postcard from Derwentwater, addressed to Mrs M. Bowman, the date stamp showing July 29th, the brief message reading:

Greetings from Paradise
Regained – I wish
you were here
Edwina

Morse turned the card over and looked lovingly at the pale-green sweep of the hills before putting the card back in its place. An odd place, perhaps, his brain suggested gently. And not the sort of book, surely, that Tom Bowman would often dip into for amusement or instruction? Edwina was doubtless one of Margaret's friends – either a local woman or one of her colleagues at Oxford. For the moment, he thought no more about it.

Downstairs once more, Lewis collected up the pile of documents he'd already selected from the mass of letters and bills that appeared to have been stuffed haphazardly into the two drawers of the corner cabinet in the lounge – water, electricity, mortgage, HP, bank statements, car insurance. Morse, for his part, sat down in one of the two armchairs and lit a cigarette.

'They kept their accounts and things in one hell of a mess, sir!'

Morse nodded. 'Mm!'

'Looks almost as if someone has been looking through all this stuff pretty recently.'

Morse shot up in the armchair as if a silken-smooth car driver had suddenly, without warning, decided to practise an emergency stop. 'Lewis! You're a genius, my son! The paper! There's a pile of newspapers in the kitchen, and I glanced at them while you were in here. Do you know something? *I think today's copy's there!*'

Lewis felt the blood tingling in his own veins as he

followed Morse into the kitchen once more, where beneath a copy of the previous week's *Oxford Times* was the *Sun*, dated January 6th.

'She must have been here some time today, sir.'

Morse nodded. 'I think she came back here *after we saw her this morning*. She must have picked up the paper automatically from the doormat—'

'But surely somebody would have seen her?'

'Go and see if you can find out, Lewis.'

Two minutes later, whilst Morse had progressed no further than page three of the Bowmans' daily, Lewis came back: the woman still peeping at events from the window immediately opposite had seen Margaret Bowman get out of a taxi.

'A *taxi*?'

'That's what she said – and go into the house, about half-past one.'

'When we were on the way back to Oxford . . .'

'I wonder what she wanted, sir?'

'She probably wanted her building society book or something – get a bit of ready cash. I should think that's why those drawers are in such a mess.'

'We can check easily enough – at the building societies.'

'Like the beauty clinics, you mean?' Morse smiled. 'No! Let Phillips and his lads do that – tedious business, Lewis! I'm really more interested to know why she came in a taxi.'

'Shall we get Sergeant Phillips to check on the taxis, too?' grinned Lewis, as for the present the two men left

6 Charlbury Drive. The house had been icily cold, and they were glad to get away.

Margaret Bowman's Metro was located, parking ticket and all, in St Giles' at 4.45 p.m. that same day, and the news was immediately rung through to Kidlington. But a folding umbrella, a can of de-icing spray, and eight 'Scrabble' tokens from Esso garages did not appear to Morse to be of the slightest help in the murder inquiry.

It was not until ten thirty the following morning that Sergeant Vickers rang Kidlington from St Aldates with the quite extraordinary news that Margaret Bowman's handbag had been found. Morse himself, Vickers learned (not without a steady sinking of his heart), would be coming down immediately to view the prize exhibit.

Chapter Thirty-three

Tuesday, 7th January: a.m.

JACK (gravely): In a handbag.
LADY BRACKNELL: A handbag?

(OSCAR WILDE)

'WHAA—?'

Morse's inarticulate utterance sounded like the death agonies of a wounded banshee, and Lewis felt his sympathy going out to whichever of the officers in St Aldates had been responsible the previous day for the Lost Property inventory.

'We get a whole lot of lost property in every day, sir—'

'—and not all of it' (Morse completed the sentence with withering scorn) 'I would humbly suggest, Sergeant, a prime item of evidence in a murder inquiry – and if I may say so, *not* an inquiry of which this particular station is wholly ignorant. In fact, only yesterday afternoon your colleague Sergeant Phillips and two of your own detective constables were specifically seconded from their duties here to assist in that very inquiry. Remember? And do you know who asked for them – me! And do you know why I'm so anxious to show some interest in this inquiry? Because this bloody station *asked* me to!'

Palely, Sergeant Vickers nodded, and Morse continued.

'You! – and you'll do it straight away, Sergeant – you'll get hold of the bloody nincompoop who sat in that chair of yours yesterday and you'll tell him I want to see him immediately. Christ! I've never known anything like it. There are rules in this profession of ours, Sergeant – didn't you know that? – and they tell us to get names and addresses and occupations and times and details and all the rest of it – and here we are without a bloody clue who brought it in, where it was found, when it was found – nothing!'

A constable had come through in the midst of this shrill tirade, waiting until the peroration before quietly informing Morse there was a telephone call for him.

After Morse had gone, Lewis looked across at his old pal, Sergeant Vickers.

'Was it you, Sam?'

Vickers nodded.

'Don't worry! He's always flying off the handle.'

'He's right, though. I tell everybody else to fill in the forms and follow the rules but . . .'

'Do you remember who brought it in?'

'Vaguely. One of the winos. We've probably got him on the books for pinching a bottle of cider from a supermarket or something. Poor sod! But the last thing we can cope with is having the likes of him here! I suppose he nicked the money when he "found" the bag and then just brought it in to square his conscience. I didn't discover where he found it, though – or when – or what his name was. I just thought – well, never mind!'

'He can't shoot you, Sam.'

'It's not as if there's much in it to help, I don't think.'

Lewis opened the expensive-looking handbag and looked through its contents: as Vickers had said, there seemed little enough of obvious interest. He pulled out the small sheaf of cards from the front compartment of the wallet: the usual bank and credit cards, two library tickets, two creased first-class stamps, a small rectangular card advertising the merits of an Indian restaurant in Walton Street, Oxford, and an identity pass-card for the Locals, with a coloured photograph of Margaret Bowman on the left. One by one, Lewis picked them up and examined them, and was putting them back into the wallet when he noticed the few words written in red biro on the back of the white restaurant card:

M. I love you
darling. T.

Obviously, thought Lewis, a memory from happier days, probably their first meal together, when Tom and Margaret Bowman had sat looking dreamily at each other over a Bombay curry, holding hands and crunching popadums.

*

A brighter-looking Morse returned.

An intelligent and resourceful Phillips, it appeared, had discovered that Margaret Bowman had gone back – not in her own car, of course – to Chipping Norton the previous lunchtime, and had withdrawn £920 of her savings in the Oxfordshire Building Society there – leaving only a nominal £10 in the account.

'It's all beginning to fit together, Lewis,' said Morse. 'She was obviously looking for her pay-in book when she got a taxi back there. And this clinches things of course' – he gestured to the handbag. 'Car keys there, I'd like to bet. But she must have had an extra house key on her . . . Yes! Cheque card, I see, but I'd be surprised if she kept that *and* her chequebook together. Most people have more sense these days.'

Lewis, not overjoyed by the high praise bestowed upon his fellow sergeant, ventured his own comments on the one item in the handbag which had puzzled him – the (obviously very recently acquired) leaflet on St Mary the Virgin. 'I remember when I was a lad, sir, somebody jumped from the tower there, and I was wondering—'

'Nonsense, Lewis! You don't do that sort of thing these days. You take a couple of boxes of pills, don't you, Sergeant Vickers?'

The latter, so unexpectedly appealed to, decided to take this opportunity of putting the record straight. 'Er, about the handbag, sir. I wasn't exactly telling you the whole truth earlier—'

But Morse was not listening. His eyes were staring at the small oblong card which Lewis had just examined and which lay on top of the little pile of contents, the handwritten message uppermost.

'What's that?' he asked with such quietly massive authority in his voice that Vickers found the hairs rising up on his brawny forearms.

But neither of the two sergeants could answer, for neither knew what it was that the chief inspector had asked, nor why it was that his eyes were gleaming with such triumphant intensity.

Morse looked cursorily through the other items from the handbag, quickly deciding that nothing merited further attention. His face was still beaming as he clapped a hand on Lewis's shoulder. 'You are – not for the first time in your life – a bloody genius, Lewis! As for you, Vickers, we thank you for your help, my friend. Forget what I said about that idiot colleague of yours! Please, excuse us! We have work to do, have we not, Lewis?'

'The Indian restaurant, is it?' asked Lewis as they got into the car.

'You hungry, or something?'

'No, sir, but—'

'I wouldn't say no to a curry myself, but not just for the time being. Put your foot down, my son!'

'Er – where to, sir?'

'Chipping Norton! Where else?'

Lewis saw that the fascia clock showed a quarter past twelve as the car passed through Woodstock.

'Fancy a pint?' asked a cheerful Lewis.

Morse looked at him curiously. 'What's the matter with you this morning? I hope you're not becoming an alcoholic?'

Lewis shook his head lightly.

'You want to be like me, Lewis. I'm a dipsomaniac.'

'What's the difference?'

Morse pondered for a while. 'I think an alcoholic is always trying to *give up* drink.'

'Whereas such a thought has never crossed your mind, sir?'

'Well put!' said Morse, thereafter lapsing into the silence he habitually observed when being driven in a car.

As they neared the Chipping Norton turning off the A34, a woman driving a very ancient Ford Anglia passed them on her way down from Birmingham to spend a night at the Haworth Hotel.

Chapter Thirty-four

Tuesday, January 7th: p.m.

A certain document of the last importance has been purloined.

(EDGAR ALLAN POE)

'WELL, I'LL BE buggered!' Morse shook his head in bewildered disappointment as he stood, once again, in Margaret Bowman's bedroom – *The Complete Crochet Manual* in his hands. 'It's gone, Lewis!'

'*What's* gone?'

'The card I showed you – the card from the Lake District – the one signed "Edwina".'

'You never showed it to me,' protested Lewis.

'Of course I—. Perhaps I didn't. But the handwriting on that postcard was the same as the handwriting on the back of your whatsitsname Indian place in Walton Street. *Exactly the same!* I can swear to it! The postcard was from Ullswater or some place like that and' (Morse sought to bully his brain into a clearer remembrance) 'it said something like "It's Paradise Regained – I wish you were here". But, you know, it's a bit odd, on a postcard, to say "*I* wish you were here". Nineteen times out of twenty, people just say "*Wish* you were here", don't they? Do you see what I mean? That postcard *didn't* say "It's Paradise Regained" – then a dash – "I wish you were here"; it said "It's Paradise Regained *minus one.* Wish you were here". That card was from Margaret Bowman's lover, telling her there was only one thing missing from his Paradise – *her*!'

'Not much use if it's gone,' said Lewis dubiously.

'It *is* though! Don't you see? The very fact that Margaret Bowman came back a second time shows exactly *how* important it is. And I *think* I remember the postmark – it was August. All we've got to do is to find out who spent his holidays up in the Lake District last August!'

'It might have been the August before.'

'Don't be so pessimistic, man!' snapped Morse.

'But we *ought* to be pessimistic,' persisted Lewis, remembering his recent experience with the beauty clinics. 'Millions of people go up to the Lakes every summer. And who's this "Edwina"?'

'He's the lover-boy. Tom Bowman would have been very suspicious, wanting to know who the fellow was if he'd signed his own name. But the man we're dealing with, Lewis – *the man who almost certainly murdered Bowman* – is pretty clever: he changed his name – but he didn't change it too much! And that gives us a whacking great clue. The fellow signs himself "T" on the Indian thing – and then signs himself "Edwina" on the postcard. *So we've already got his Christian name, Lewis!* The "T" doesn't stand for Tom – it stands for Ted. And "Ted" is an abbreviation of "Edward"; and he signs himself in the feminine form of it – "Edwina"! QE bloody D, Lewis – as we used to say in the Lower Fourth! All right! You say there are a few millions every year who look forward to hearing the rain drumming on their caravan roofs in Grasmere. But not all that many of them were christened "Edward", and about half of *them* would be too old – or too young – to woo our fair Margaret. And, what's more, he'll pretty certainly live in Oxford, this fellow we're looking for – or not too far outside. And if he can afford to spend a holiday in the Lake District, he's probably in work, rather than on the dole, agreed?'

'But—'

'*And* – just let me finish! – not everybody's all that familiar with *Paradise Regained*. Mr Milton's not everybody's cup of tea in these degenerate days, and I'm going to hazard a guess that our man was a grammar-school boy!'

'But they're all comprehensives now, sir.'

'You know what I mean! He's in the top 25 per cent of the IQ range.'

'The case seems to be closed, then, sir!'

'Don't be so bloody sarcastic, Lewis!'

'I'm sorry, sir, but—'

'I've not finished! What was the colour of Bowman's hair?'

'Well – blondish, sort of.'

'Correct! And what have Robert Redford, Steve Cram and Ian Botham got in common?'

'All the girls go for them.'

'No! Physical appearance, Lewis.'

'You mean, they've all got blond hair?'

'Yes! And if Margaret Bowman's running to form, this new beau of hers has got fair hair, too! And if only about a quarter of Englishmen have got fair hair—'

'He could be a Swede, sir.'

'What? A Swede who's read *Paradise Regained*?'

For Lewis, the whole thing was becoming progressively more improbable; yet he found himself following Morse's deductive logic with reluctant admiration. If Morse were right there couldn't be all that many employed, fair-haired people christened Edward, in the twenty-five to forty-five age range, living in or just outside Oxford, who had spent their most recent summer holidays in the Lake District, could there? And Lewis appreciated the force of one point Morse had just made: Margaret Bowman had been willing to make *two* extraordinarily risky visits to her house in Charlbury Drive over the last twenty-four hours. If the *first* had been to fetch her building society book (or whatever) and to get some ready cash out, it couldn't really be seen as all that incriminating. But if the overriding purpose of the *second*, as Morse was now suggesting, had been to remove from the house any pieces of vital evidence that might have been hidden in the most improbable places . . .

Lewis was conscious, as he sat there in the Bowmans' bedroom that afternoon, that he had not yet even dared to mention to Morse the thought that had so obstinately lodged itself at the back of his mind. At the time, he had dismissed the idea as utterly fanciful – and yet it would not wholly go away.

'I know it's ridiculous, sir, but – but I can't help worrying about that crane at the back of the hotel.'

'Go on!' said Morse, not without a hint of interest in his voice.

'Those cranes can land the end of a girder on a sixpence: they *have* to – match up with the bolts and everything. So if you wanted to, you could pick up a box, let's say, and you could move it wherever you wanted – *outside a window, perhaps*? It's only a thought, sir, but could it just be that Bowman was murdered *in the main part of the hotel*? If the murderer wraps up the body, say, and hooks it on to the crane, he can pinpoint it to just outside Annexe 3, where he can get an accomplice in the room to pull the box gently in. The murderer himself wouldn't be under any suspicion at all, because he's never been *near* the annexe. And if it had been snowing – like the forecast said – there wouldn't be any footprints *going in*, would there? There's so much mess and mud outside the back of the hotel, though, that nobody's going to notice anything out of the ordinary there; and nobody's going to hear anything, either – not with all the racket of a disco going on. I know it may be a lot of nonsense, but it does bring all those people staying in the hotel back into the reckoning, doesn't it? And I think you'll agree, sir, we *are* getting a bit short of suspects.'

Morse, who had been listening with quiet attention, now shook his head with perplexed amusement. 'What you're suggesting, Lewis, is that *the murderer's a crane-driver*, is that it?'

'It was only a thought, sir.'

'Narrows things down, though. A fair-haired crane-driver called Ted who spent a week in Windermere or somewhere . . .' Morse laughed. 'You're getting worse than I am, Lewis!'

Morse rang HQ from the Bowmans' house, and two men, Lewis learned, would immediately be on their way to help him undertake an exhaustive search of the whole premises at 6 Charlbury Drive.

Morse himself took the car keys and drove back thoughtfully into Oxford.

Chapter Thirty-Five

Tuesday, January 7th: p.m.

No words beyond a murmured 'Good-evening' ever passed between Hardy and Louisa Harding.

(*The Early Life of Thomas Hardy*)

INSTEAD OF GOING straight back to Kidlington HQ, Morse drove down once more into Summertown and turned into Ewert Place where he drove up to the front steps and parked the police car. The Secretary, he learned, was in and would be able to see him almost immediately.

As he sat waiting on the long wall-seat in the foyer, Morse was favourably struck (as he had been on his previous visit) by the design and the furnishings of the Delegacy. The building was surely one of the (few) high spots of post-1950 architecture in Oxford, and he found himself trying to give it a date: 1960? 1970? But before he reached a verdict, he learned that the Secretary awaited him.

Morse leaned back in the red leather armchair once again. 'Lovely building, this!'

'We're very lucky, I agree.'

'When was it built?'

'Finished in 1965.'

'I was just comparing it to some of the hideous structures they've put up in Oxford since the war.'

'You mustn't think we don't have a few problems, though.'

'Really?'

'Oh, yes. We get floods in the basement fairly regularly. And then, of course, there's the flat roof: anyone who designs a building as big as this with a flat roof – in England! – hardly deserves the Queen's medal for architecture. Not in my book, anyway.'

The Secretary had spoken forcefully, and Morse found himself interested in her reaction. 'You've had trouble?'

'*Had?* Yes, we've had trouble, and we've got trouble now, and it'll be a great surprise if we don't have more trouble in the future. We've only just finished paying for a complete re-roofing repair – the *third* we've had!'

Morse nodded in half-hearted sympathy as she elaborated the point; but his interest in the Delegacy's roofing problems soon dissipated, and he moved to the reason for his visit. He told the Secretary, in the strictest confidence, almost everything he had discovered about the Bowmans, and he hinted at his deep concern for Margaret Bowman's life. He asked whether Margaret had any particular women friends in the Delegacy; whether she had any *men* friends; whether there might have been any gossip about her; whether there was anything at all that might be learned from interviewing any of Margaret's colleagues.

The result of this request was the summoning to the Secretary's office of Mrs Gladys Taylor, who disclaimed all knowledge of Margaret Bowman's married life, of any possible extramarital infidelity, and of her present whereabouts. After only a few minutes Morse realized he was getting nowhere with the woman; and he dismissed her. He was not at all surprised that she knew so little; and he was aware that his own abrupt interlocutory style had made the poor woman hopelessly nervous. What Morse was not aware of – and what, with a little less conceit, he might perhaps have divined – was that Gladys Taylor's nervousness had very little at all to do with the tone of Morse's questioning, but everything to do with the fact that, after spending the weekend at Gladys's council house on the Cutteslowe Estate in North Oxford, Margaret Bowman had turned up *again* – dramatically! – late the previous evening, begging Gladys to take her in and making her promise to say nothing to anyone about her whereabouts.

The former prison officer at Reception deferred his daily perusal of the Court Circular and saluted the Chief Inspector as Morse handed in the temporary badge he had been given – a plastic folder, with a metal clip, containing a buff-coloured card on which was printed VISITOR, in black capitals, and under which, in black felt tip pen, was written 'Insp. Morse'. A row of mailbags stood beside the front door, waiting for the post office van, and Morse was on the point of leaving the building when he turned back – struck by the appropriate juxtaposition of things – and spoke to the Security Officer.

'You must feel almost at home with all these mailbags around!'

'Yes! You don't forget things like that, sir. And I could still tell you where most of 'em were made – from the marks, I mean.'

'You can?' Morse fingered one of the grey bags and the Security Officer walked round to inspect it.

'From the Scrubs, that one.'

'Full of criminals, they tell me, the Scrubs.'

'Used to be – in my day.'

'You don't get many criminals here, though?'

'There's a lot of things here they'd *like* to get their hands on – especially all the question papers, of course.'

'And that's why you're here.'

'Can't be too careful, these days. We get so many people coming in – I'm not talking about the permanent staff – I'm talking about the tradesmen, builders, electricians, caterers—'

'And you give them all a pass – like the one you gave me?'

'Unless they're pretty regular. Then we give 'em a semi-permanent pass with a photograph and all that. Saves a lot of time and trouble.'

'I see,' said Morse.

A letter was awaiting Morse at Kidlington: a white envelope, with a London postmark, addressed to Chief

Inspector Morse (in as neat a piece of typewriting as one could wish to find) and marked 'Strictly Private and Personal'. Even before he opened the envelope, Morse was convinced that he was about to be apprised of some vital intelligence concerning the Bowman case. But he was wrong. The letter read as follows:

> This is a love letter but please don't feel too embarassed about it because it doesn't really matter. You are now engaged on a murder inquiry and it was in connection with this that we met briefly. I don't know why but I think I've fallen genuinely and easily and happily in love with you. So there!
>
> I wouldn't have written this silly letter but for the fact that I've been reading a biography of Thomas Hardy and he (so he said) could never forget the face of a girl who once smiled at him as she rode by on a horse. He knew the girl by name and in fact the pair of them lived quite close, but their relationship never progressed even to the point of speaking to each other. At least I've done that!
>
> Tear this up now. I've told you what I feel about you. I almost wish I was the chief suspect in the case. Perhaps I *am* the murderer! Will you come and arrest me? Please!

The letter lacked both salutation and signature, and Morse's expression, as he read it, seemed to combine a dash of distaste with a curiously pleasurable fascination. But as the girl herself (whoever she was!) had said – it didn't really matter. Yet it would have been quite extraordinary for any man not to have pondered on the identity of such a correspondent. And, for several minutes, Morse did so ponder as he sat silently at his desk that winter's afternoon. She sounded a nice girl – and she'd only made the one spelling error . . .

The call from Lewis – a jubilant Lewis! – came in at 5.10 p.m. that day.

Chapter Thirty-six

Tuesday, January 7th: p.m.

> If you once understand an author's character, the comprehension of his writing becomes easy.
>
> (LONGFELLOW)

IT HAD BEEN in the inside breast pocket of a rather ancient sports jacket that Lewis had finally found the copied letter. And such a discovery was so obviously what Morse had been hoping for that he was unable to conceal the high note of triumph in his voice as he reported his find. Equally, for his part, Morse had been unable to conceal his own delight; and when (only some half an hour later) Lewis delivered the four closely handwritten sheets, Morse handled them with the loving care of a biblical scholar privileged to view the *Codex Vaticanus.*

> You are a selfish thankless bitch and if you think you can just back out of things when *you* like you'd better realize that you've got another big thick headaching think coming because it could be that I've got some ideas about what *I* like. You'd better understand what I'm saying. If you can act like a bitch you'd better know I can be a bit of a sod.

too. You were glad enough to get what you wanted from me and just because I wanted to give it to you you think that we can just drop everything and go back to square one. Well this letter is to tell you we can't and like I say you'd better understand what I'm telling you. You can be sure I'll get my own back on you. You always say you can't really talk on the phone much but you didn't have much trouble on Monday did you. Not much doubt about where you stood then. Not free this week, and perhaps not next week either, and the week after that is a bit busy too!! I know I've not been round *quite* as long as you but I'm not a fool and I think you know I'm not. You say you're not going to sign on next term for night classes and that was the one really long time we did have together. Well I don't want any Dear John letter thank you very much. But I do want one thing and I'm quite serious about saying that I'm going to get it. I must see you again – at least once again. If you've got any sense of fairness to me you'll agree to that. And if you've got just any plain *sense* – and forget any fairness – you'll still agree to see me because if you don't I shall get my own back. Don't drive me to anything like that. Nobody knows about us and I want to leave things like that like they were. You remember how careful I always was and how none of your colleagues ever knew. Not that it matters much to me, not a quarter of what it matters to you. Don't forget that. So do as I say and meet me next Monday. Tell them you've got a dental appointment and I'll pick you up as usual outside the Summertown Library at ten to one. Please make sure you're there for your sake as much as mine. Perhaps I ought to have suspected you were cooling off a bit. When I was at school I read a thing about there's always one who kisses and one who turns the cheek. Well I don't mind it that way but I must see you again. There were lots of times when you wanted me badly enough – lots of times when you nearly set a world record for getting your clothes off, and that wasn't just because we only had forty minutes. So be there for sure on Monday or you'll have to face the consequences. I've just thought that last sentence sounds like a threat but I don't really want to be nasty about all this. I suppose I've never said too much about what I really feel but I think I was in love with you the very first time I saw the top of your golden head in the summer sunshine. Monday – ten to one – or else!

Morse read the letter through twice – each time slowly, and (much to Lewis's delight) appeared to be highly satisfied.

'What do you make of it, sir?'

Morse put the letter down and leaned back in the old black leather chair, his elbows resting on the arms, the tips of his middle fingers tapping each other lightly in front of a well-pleased mouth. 'What would *you* say about that letter, Lewis, eh? What do *you* learn from it?'

Lewis usually hated moments such as this. But he had been asking himself exactly the same question since he'd first read the letter through, and he launched into what he hoped Morse would accept as an intelligent analysis.

'It's quite clear, sir, that Margaret Bowman was

unfaithful to her husband over quite a while. He talks in the letter about night classes and I think they were probably held in the autumn term – say, for about three or four months – after he first saw her, like he says, in the summer. I'd say from about July onwards. That's the first thing.' (Lewis was feeling not displeased with himself.) 'Second thing, sir, is this man's age. He says he's not been around quite as long as she has, and he's underlined the word "quite". He probably teased her a bit – like most people would – if she was a little bit older than he was: let's say, six months or a year, perhaps. Now, Margaret Bowman – I've found out, sir – was thirty-six last September. So let's put our prime suspect in the thirty-five age-bracket then, all right?' (Lewis could recall few occasions on which he had seemed to be speaking with such fluent authority.) 'Then there's a third point, sir. He asks her to meet him outside the library at ten minutes to one – so he must know it takes about five minutes for her to get there *from* the Locals – and five minutes to get back. That leaves us with fifty minutes from the hour they're given at the Locals for a lunch-break. But he mentions "*forty* minutes": so, as I see things' (how happy Lewis felt!) 'he must live only about five minutes' drive away from South Parade. I don't think they just went to a pub and held hands, sir. I think, too, that this fellow probably lives on the *west* side of Oxford – let's say off the Woodstock Road somewhere – because Summertown Library would be a bit of a roundabout place to pick her up if he lived on the *east* side, especially with such a little time they've got together.'

Morse had nodded agreement at several points during this exposition; and had been on the point of congratulating his sergeant when Lewis resumed – still in full spate.

'Now if we add these new facts to what we've already discovered, sir, I reckon we're not all that far off from knowing exactly who he is. We can be far more precise about where he lives – within five minutes' drive, at the outside, from Summertown; and we can be far more precise about his age – pretty certainly thirty-four or thirty-five. So if we had a computerized file on everybody, I think we could spot our man straight away. But there's something else – something perhaps much more helpful than a computer, sir: that night-school class! It won't be difficult to trace the people in Mrs Bowman's class; and I'd like to bet we shall find somebody who had a vague sort of inkling about what Margaret Bowman was up to. Seems to me a good line of inquiry; and I can get on with it straight away if you agree.'

Morse was silent for a little while before replying. 'Yes, I think I *do* agree.'

Yet Lewis was conscious of a deeper undercurrent in Morse's tone: something was worrying the chief, pretty surely so.

'What's the matter, sir?'

'Matter? Nothing's the matter. It's just that – well, tell me what you make of that letter *as a whole*, Lewis. What *sort* of man is he, do you think?'

'Bit of mixture, I'd say. Sounds as if he's genuinely fond of the woman, doesn't it? At the same time it sounds as if he's got quite a cruel streak in him – bit of a coarse streak, too. As if he loved her – but always in a selfish sort of way: as if perhaps he might be prepared to do anything just to keep her.'

Morse nodded. 'I'm sure you're right. I think he *was* prepared to do almost anything to keep her.'

'Have you got any idea of what really happened?' asked Lewis quietly.

'Yes! – for what it's worth, I have. Clearly Bowman found this letter somewhere, and he realized that his wife was going with another fellow. I suspect he told her what he knew and gave her an ultimatum. Most men perhaps would have accepted the facts and called it a day – however much it hurt. But Bowman didn't! He loved his wife more than she could ever have known, and his first instinctive reactions mustered themselves – not against his wife – *but against her lover.* He probably told her all this, in his own vague way; and I think he decided that the best way to help Margaret and, at the same time, to save his own deeply injured pride, was *to get rid of her lover*! We've been on a lot of cases together, Lewis – with lots of people involved; but I don't reckon the motives are ever all *that* different – love, hate, jealousy, revenge . . . Anyway, I think that Bowman got his wife to agree to collaborate with him in a plot to get rid of the man who – at least for the moment – was a threat to both of them. What *exactly* that plan involved, we may never know – unless Margaret Bowman decides to tell us. The only firm thing we know about it so far is that Bowman himself wrote a wholly genuine letter which would rather cleverly serve two purposes when lover-boy was found murdered – that is, if any suspicion were ever likely to fall on either of the Bowmans: first, it would put Margaret Bowman in a wholly sympathetic light; second, it would appear to put Tom Bowman some few hundreds of miles away from the scene of the immediate crime.'

'Didn't we know most of that already—'

'Let me finish, Lewis! At some particular point – I don't know when – *the plan was switched*, and it was switched by the only person who could switch it – by Margaret Bowman, who decided that if she had to take a profoundly important decision about life (as she did!) she would rather throw in her lot with her illicit lover than with her licit husband. Is that clear? Forget the details for the minute, Lewis! The key thing to bear in mind is this: instead of having a plot involving the death of a troublesome lover, we have a plot involving the death of an interfering husband!'

'You don't think the letter helps much at all, then?' Lewis's initial euphoria slipped a notch or two towards his wonted diffidence.

'My goodness, yes! And your own reading of that letter was a model of logic and lucidity! But . . .'

Lewis's heart sank. He knew what Morse was going to say, and he said it for him. 'But you mean I missed some vital clue in it – is that right?'

Morse waited awhile, and then smiled with what he trusted was sympathetic understanding: 'No, Lewis. You didn't miss one vital clue, at all. You missed two.'

Chapter Thirty-seven

Tuesday, January 7th: p.m.

Stand on the highest pavement of the stair –
Lean on a garden urn –
Weave, weave the sunlight in your hair

(T. S. ELIOT)

'APART FROM YOUR own admirable deductions, Lewis, there are, as I say, a couple of other things you could have noticed, perhaps. First' (Morse turned to the letter and found the appropriate reference) 'he says, "You remember how careful I always was and how none of your colleagues ever knew". Now that statement's very revealing. It suggests that this fellow *could* have been very careless about meeting Margaret Bowman; careless in the sense that, if he'd wanted to, he could easily have made Margaret's colleagues aware of what was going on between them – pretty certainly by others actually *seeing* the evidence. It means, I think, that the pair of them were very often *near* each other, and that he very sensibly agreed to avoid all contact with her *in the place where they found themselves.* And you don't need me to tell you where that might have been – *must* have been – do you? It was on the Locals site itself, where twenty-odd workmen were employed on various jobs – but mostly on the roof – between May and September last year.'

'Phew!' Lewis looked down at the letter again. If what Morse was saying were true . . .

'But there's a second thing,' continued Morse, 'that's more specific still. There's a rather nice little bit of English at the end of the letter – "but I think I was in love with you the very first time I saw the top of your golden head in the summer sunshine". Now you were right in saying that this tells us roughly when he first met her. But it also tells us something else, and something even more important. Don't you see? It tells us from which *angle* he first saw her, doesn't it, Lewis? *He saw her from above!*'

Lewis was weighing up what Morse had just said: 'You mean this fellow might have been *on the roof*, sir?'

'Could be!' Morse looked extremely pleased with himself. 'Yes, he could have been on the roof. Or he could have been – *higher*, perhaps? The flat roof at the Locals has been causing a lot of trouble, and last summer they had a complete new go at the whole thing.'

'So?'

'So they had quite a few workmen there, and they'd need something to lift all that stuff . . .'

'A crane!' The words were out of Lewis's excited lips in a flash.

'It makes sense, doesn't it?'

'Did they have a crane on the site?'

'Don't know, do I.'

'Do you remember,' said Lewis slowly, 'that it was *me* who suggested he might be a crane-driver?'

'Nonsense!' said Morse happily.

'But I—'

'You may have got the right answer, Lewis, but you got it for the wrong reasons, and you can't claim much credit for that.'

Lewis's smile was as happy as Morse's. 'Shall I give the Secretary a ring, sir?'

'Think she's still there? It's gone half-past five.'

'Some people stay on after office hours. Like I do!'

The Secretary was still at her desk. Yes, there had been a crane on the site – a big yellow thing – from May to October! And no, the Secretary had no objection at all to the police coming to look at the security passes kept all together in a filing cabinet in Reception.

Morse got up from his chair and pulled on his greatcoat. 'And there's something else, you know, Lewis. Something to crown the whole lot, really. They keep all their records carefully at the Locals – well, the chap on the desk does. All passes have to be shown and I'd like to bet that those workmen were given semi-permanent passes so that they could make use of the facilities there without having to get a badge every time they went to the lavatory or whatever. Just think of it! We sit here and rack our brains – and all the time the fellow we're looking for is sitting there on a little card – in a little drawer at the Locals – with a photograph of himself on it! By Jove, this is the simplest case we've ever handled, my old friend. Come on. On your feet!'

But for a while, Lewis sat where he was, a wistful expression across his square, honest face. 'You know, it's a pity in a way, isn't it? Like you say, we've done all this thinking – we've even given the fellow a name! The only thing we never got round to was deciding where he lives, that's all. And if we'd been able to work that out – well, we wouldn't need any photograph or anything, would we? We'd have, sort of, *thought* it all out.'

Morse sat on the edge of his desk nodding his balding head. 'Ye-es. 'Tis a pity, I agree. Amazing, you know, what feats of logic the human brain is capable of. But sometimes life eludes logic – and sometimes when you build a great big wonderful theory you find there's a fault in the foundations and the whole thing collapses round your ears at the slightest earth tremor.'

Morse's voice had sounded strangely earnest, and Lewis noticed how tired his chief looked. 'You don't think we're in for an earthquake, do you?'

'Hope not! Above all I hope we get a chance to save Margaret Bowman – save her from herself as much as anything. Nice looker, you know, that woman. Lovely head of hair!'

'Especially when viewed from the top of a crane,' said Lewis, as he finally rose to his feet and pulled on his coat.

*

As they were leaving the office, Morse paused to look at a large white map of Oxford City that was fastened on the wall to the left of the door. 'What do you think, Lewis? Here we are: South Parade – that's where he picked her up. Now we want somewhere no more than five minutes away, so you say. Well, one thing's certain – he either turned left or he turned right at the Woodstock Road, agreed?' Morse's finger slowly traced a route that led off to the south: it seemed most unlikely that the man would be living in any of the large villa-type residences that lined the road for most of the way down to St Giles', and Morse found himself looking at the map just below St John's College playing fields, and especially at the maze of little streets that criss-crossed the heart of Jericho. For his part, Lewis's eyes considered the putative route that might have been taken if the man had turned right and towards the north; and soon he spotted a small cluster of streets, between the Woodstock Road itself and, to the west of it, the canal and the railway. The writing on the map was very small but Lewis could just about read the names: St Peter's Road; Ulfgar Road; Pixey Place; Diamond Close . . . All council property, if Lewis recalled correctly – or used to be until, in the 1980s, the Tories remembered Anthony Eden's promises of a property-owning democracy.

Chapter Thirty-eight

Tuesday, January 7th: p.m.

I keep six honest serving-men
(They taught me all I knew):
Their names are What and Why and When
And How and Where and Who.

(RUDYARD KIPLING)

THE MOST OBVIOUS improvements effected by those who had bought their own red-brick houses had been to the doors and the windows: several of the old doors were replaced completely by stout oaken affairs – or at the very least painted some colour other than the former regulation light blue: and most of the old windows, with their former small oblong panes, were now replaced by large horizontal sheets of glass set in stainless-steel frames. In general, it seemed fairly clear, the tone of the neighbourhood was on the 'up'; and number 17 Diamond Close was no exception to this pattern of improved properties. A storm door (behind which no light was visible) had been built across the small front porch; and the front fence and garden had been redesigned to accommodate a medium-sized car – like the light-green Maestro which stood there now.

Under the orange glare of the street-lamps, the close was strangely still.

The two police cars had moved slowly along St Peter's Road and then stopped at the junction with Diamond Close. Morse, Lewis and Phillips were in the first car; two uniformed constables and a plain-clothes detective in the second. Both Phillips and the plain-clothes man had been issued with regulation revolvers; and these two (as prearranged) got out of their cars and without slamming the doors behind them walked silently along the thirty or so yards to the front of number 17, where, with the plain-clothes man rather melodramatically pointing his revolver to the stars, Sergeant Phillips pushed the white button of the front-door bell. After a few seconds, a dull light appeared from somewhere at the back of the house, and then a fuller light and the silhouette of a figure seen through the glass of the outer door. At that moment the watching faces of Morse and Lewis betrayed a high degree of tension: yet, in retrospect, there had been nothing whatsoever to occasion such emotion.

From the outset the man in the thick green sweater had proved surprisingly co-operative. He had requested to be allowed to finish his baked beans (refused), to collect a packet of cigarettes (granted), to drive to Police HQ in his own car (refused), and to take his scarf and duffel coat (granted). At no stage had he mentioned writs, warrants, lawyers, solicitors, civil rights, unlawful arrest or Lord Longford, and Morse himself was beginning to feel a little shamefaced about the death-or-glory scenario of the arrest. But one never knew.

In the interview room it was Lewis who began the questioning.

'Your full name is Edward Wilkins?'

'Edward James Wilkins.'

'Your date of birth?'

'Twentieth September, 1951.'

'Place of birth?'

'17 Diamond Close.'

'The house you live in now?'

'Yes. My mother lived there.'

'Which school did you go to?'

'Hobson Road Primary – for a start.'

'And after that?'

'Oxford Boys' School.'

'You passed the eleven plus to go there?'

'Yes.'

'When did you leave?'

'In 1967.'

'You took your O levels?'

'Yes. I passed in Maths, Physics and Engineering Drawing.'

'You didn't take English Literature?'

'Yes, I did. But I failed.'

'Did you read any Milton?' interrupted Morse.

'Yes, we read *Comus.*'

'What did you do after you left school?' (Lewis had taken up the questioning once more.)

'I got an apprenticeship at Lucy's Ironworks in Jericho.'

'And then?'

'I didn't finish it. I stuck it for eighteen months and then I got offered a much better job with Mackenzie Construction.'

'You still work for them?'

'Yes.'

'What's your job, exactly?'

'I'm a crane-driver.'

'You mean you sit up in the cabin and swing all the loads round the site?'

'That's one way of putting it.'

'This company – Mackenzie Construction – they did some re-roofing last year at the Oxford Delegacy – Oxford Locals, I think you call it. Is that right?'

'Yes. About April to September.'

'You worked there all that time?'

'Yes.'

'Not *all* that time, surely?'

'Pardon?'

'Didn't you have any summer holiday?'

'Oh yes, I'm sorry. I was off a fortnight.'

'When was that?'

'Late July.'

'Where did you go?'

'Up to the north of England.'

'Whereabouts exactly?'

'The Lake District.'

'And where in the Lake District?'

'Derwentwater.'

'Did you send any postcards from there?'

'A few. Yes.'

'To some of your friends here – in Oxford?'

'Who else?'

'Oh, I don't know, Mr Wilkins. If I'd known I wouldn't have asked, would I?'

It was the first moment of tension in the interview, and Lewis (as Morse had instructed him) left things there for a while, saying nothing; and for a little while the silence hung heavily over the bare, rather chilly room at the rear of Police HQ in Kidlington.

From the doorway Sergeant Phillips, who had never previously been present at such an interrogation, watched events with a touch of embarrassment. The prolonged period of silence seemed (as Phillips saw things) particularly to affect Wilkins, whose hands twice twitched at his hip pocket as if seeking the solace of a cigarette, but whose will-power appeared for the minute in adequate control. He was a large-boned, fairish-haired, pleasantly spoken man who seemed to Phillips about the last person in the world who would suddenly display any symptoms of homicidal ferocity. Yet Phillips was also aware that the two men in charge of the case, Morse and Lewis, had great experience in these affairs, and he listened to Lewis's further questions with absorbed fascination.

'When did you first meet Mrs Margaret Bowman?'

'You know all about that?'

'Yes.'

'I met her when I was working at the Locals. We had the use of the canteen and some of us used to have a meal there and that's when I met her.'

'When did you first meet her outside working hours?'

'She had a night-school class, and I used to meet her for a drink afterwards.'

'Quite regularly, you did this?'

'Yes.'

'And you invited her back to your house?'

'Yes.'

'And you made love to each other?'

'Yes.'

'And then she got a bit fed up with you and wanted the affair to stop – is that right, Mr Wilkins?'

'That's not true.'

'You were in love with her?'

'Yes.'

'You still in love with her?'

'Yes.'

'Is she in love with you?' (Morse was delighted with such a beautifully modulated question.)

'I didn't force her along, did I?' (For the first time a little hesitancy – and a little coarseness – had crept into Wilkins's manner.)

'Did you write this?' Lewis handed over a Xeroxed copy of the letter found in Bowman's jacket.

'I wrote it, yes,' said Wilkins.

'And you still say you weren't forcing her along a bit?'

'I just wanted to see her again, that's all.'

'To make love to her again, you mean?'

'Not just that, no.'

'Did you actually see her that day – in South Parade?'

'Yes.'

'And you took her to your house?'

'Yes.'

'Was anyone following you – in a car?'

'What do you mean?'

'Mr Bowman knew all about you – we found that copy of the letter in one of his jackets.'

Wilkins shook his head, as if with regret. 'I didn't know that – honestly, I didn't. I always said to Margaret that whatever happened I never wanted to – well, to *hurt* anybody else.'

'You didn't know that Mr Bowman knew all about you?'

'No.'

'She didn't tell you?'

'No. I stopped seeing her after that day I met her in South Parade. She said she couldn't cope with the strain and everything, and that she'd decided to stay with him. It was a bit hard to take, but I tried to accept it. I hadn't got much option, had I?'

'When did you last see her?'

For the first time in the interview, Wilkins allowed himself a ghost of a smile, showing regular though nicotine-stained teeth. 'I saw her,' he looked at his wrist-watch, 'just over an hour ago. She was in the house when you called to bring me here.'

Morse closed his eyes momentarily in what looked like a twinge of intolerable pain; and Lewis began 'You mean . . .?'

'She came about a quarter to six. She just said she didn't know what to do – she wanted help.'

'Did she want money?'

'No. Well, she didn't mention it. Not much good asking *me* for money, in any case – and she knew that.'

'Did she say where she was going?'

'Not really, but I think she'd been in touch with her sister.'

'She lives where?'

'Near Newcastle, I think.'

'You didn't tell her she could stay with you?'

'That would have been a mad thing to do, wouldn't it?'

'Do you think she's still in your house?'

'She'd be out of there like a bat out of hell immediately we'd gone.'

(Morse gestured to Sergeant Phillips, spoke a few words in his ear and dismissed him.)

'So you think she's off north somewhere?' continued Lewis.

'I don't know. I honestly don't know. I advised her to get on a boat or something and sail off to the continent – away from everything.'

'But she didn't take your advice?'

'No. She couldn't. She hadn't got a passport, and she was frightened of applying for one because she knew everybody was trying to find her.'

'Did she know that everybody was trying to find *you*, as well?'

'Of course she didn't! I don't know what you mean.'

'I'm sure you know why we've brought you here,' said Lewis, looking directly across into Wilkins's eyes.

'Really? I'm afraid you're wrong there.'

'Well she *did* know that everybody was looking for you. You see, Mr Wilkins, she went back to her own house in Chipping Norton, at considerable risk to herself, to remove any incriminating evidence that she thought might be lying around. For example, she took the postcard you wrote to her from the Lake District.'

There was a sudden dramatic silence in the interview room, as though everybody there had taken a sharp intake of breath – and was holding it.

'It's my duty as a police officer,' continued Lewis, 'to tell you formally that you are under arrest for the murder of Thomas Bowman.'

Wilkins slumped back in his chair, his face ashen-pale and his upper lip trembling. 'You're making the most terrible mistake,' he said very quietly.

Chapter Thirty-Nine

Tuesday, January 7th: p.m.

When angry, count four; when very angry, swear.

(MARK TWAIN)

'AM I DOING all right?' asked a slightly subdued Lewis as, five minutes after this preliminary interview, he sat in the canteen drinking coffee with Morse.

'Very good – *very* good,' said Morse. 'But we've got to tread a bit carefully from now on because we're getting to the point where we're not *quite* sure of the ground – by which I mean it's going to be difficult to *prove* one or two things. So let's just recap a minute. Let's go back to the beginning of things – Plan One, let's call it. Bowman follows his wife up to Diamond Close that day, and later he confronts her with the evidence. She's getting desperate anyway, and she goes along with the quite extraordinary plan he's concocted. As we've seen he fixes up the phoney address and books a New-Year-Package-for-Two at the Haworth Hotel. She tells Wilkins that her husband's gone off on a course and that they can spend all that time together; and he jumps at the chance. Once she's safely in her room, she rings Wilkins – we still haven't checked on that, Lewis –

to give him the room number and soon she's giving him the happy hour between the sheets. Then they both get ready for the fancy dress – which she's already told Wilkins about, and which he's already agreed to. If he *hadn't*, Lewis, the plan couldn't have worked. At about seven o'clock she makes some excuse to go out, when she gives the key to Bowman himself, who's waiting somewhere near the annexe, and who's dressed up in exactly the same sort of garb as Wilkins. Now Wilkins is a stronger man, I suspect, than Bowman ever was, and I should think that Bowman wouldn't have taken any chance about letting the whole thing develop into a brawl – he's probably got a knife or a revolver or something. Then the deed is done, and the next part of the deception begins. They could disappear from the scene straight away, but they agree that's far too risky. Somebody's going to find the body immediately if they do, because the "Ballards" as they called themselves won't be there for the party. There's virtually no risk in their being recognized anyway: they're both in fancy dress for the rest of the evening – he's got his face blacked, she's wearing a veil; and the only time a busy receptionist had seen Margaret Bowman was when she'd been muffled up in a scarf and hood – with a pair of dark skiing glasses on, for all we know.'

Lewis nodded.

'That was the original plan – and it must have been very much as I've described it, Lewis; otherwise it's impossible to account for several facts in the case – for instance, the fact that Bowman wrote a letter to his wife that would give them both a reasonable alibi – if the worse came to the worst. It wasn't a bad plan, either – except in one vital respect. Bowman was beginning to know quite a bit about Wilkins, but he never quite knew *enough*. Above all, he didn't know that Wilkins was beginning to dominate his wife in an ever increasing way, and that she'd become so sexually and emotionally dependent on him that she came to realize, at some point, that it was her husband, Tom Bowman, she wanted out of her life for good – not her lover. Maybe Bowman had become so obsessed with this revenge idea of his that she saw, perhaps for the first time, what a crudely devious man he really was. But for whatever reason, we can know one thing for certain: *she told Wilkins what they were planning*. Now you don't need to be a genius – and I don't think Wilkins *is* a genius – to spot an almost incredible opportunity here: the plan can go ahead as Bowman had devised it – exactly so! – but only up to the point when Bowman would let himself into the room. This time it would be *Wilkins* who's waiting behind the door *for Bowman* with a bottle of whatever it was to smash down on the back of his head.'

'Front, sir,' murmured Lewis if only, for conscience' sake, to put the unofficial record straight.

'So that's what happened, Lewis; and it's Plan Two that's now in operation. After murdering Bowman, Wilkins is all ready to go along to the party in exactly the same outlandish clothes as the murdered man would be found in. The two men were roughly the same height and everybody is going to assume that the man in the Rastafarian rig-out at the party is the same as the man in the Rastafarian rig-out later found dead on the bed in Annexe 3. Almost certainly – and this is in fact what happened – the corpse isn't going to be found until pretty late the next day; and if the heating is turned off – as it was – and if the window's left half-open – as it was – then any cautious clown like Max is going to be even cagier than usual about giving any categorical ruling on the time of death, because of the unusual room temperature. I'm not sure, myself, that it wouldn't have been far more sensible to turn the radiator on full and close all the windows. But, be that as it may, Wilkins clearly wanted to give the impression that the murder had taken place *as late as possible.* Agreed?'

'I can't quite see *why* though, sir.'

'You will do, in due course. Have faith!'

Lewis, however, looked rather less than full of faith. 'It's getting a bit too complicated for my brain, sir. I keep forgetting who's dressed up for what and who's planning to kill who—'

'"Whom", Lewis. Your grammar's as bad as Miss Jonstone's.'

'You're sure he *is* the murderer? – Wilkins?'

'My son, the case is over! There are bound to be one or two details—'

'Do you mind if we just go over one or two things again?'

'I can't spell things out *much* more simply, you know.'

'You say Wilkins wanted the murder to look as if it took place as late as possible. But I don't see the point of that. It doesn't give him an alibi, does it? I mean, whether Bowman's murdered at seven o'clock or after midnight – what does it matter? Wilkins and Margaret Bowman were there *all the time*, weren't they?'

'Yes! But who said they'd got an alibi? *I* didn't mention an alibi. All I'm saying is that Wilkins had a reason for wanting to mislead everyone into believing that the murder was committed after the party was over. That's obvious enough, isn't it?'

'But going back a minute, don't you think that in Bowman's original plan – Plan One, as you call it – it would have been far more sensible to have committed the murder – murder Wilkins, that is – and then to get out of the place double quick? With any luck, no one's going to suspect a married couple from Chipping Norton – even if the body's found very soon afterwards.'

Morse nodded, but with obvious frustration.

'I *agree* with you. But somehow or other we've got to explain how it came about that Bowman was found dressed up in identically the same sort of outfit as Wilkins was wearing at the party. Don't you *see* that, Lewis? We've got to explain the facts! And I refuse to believe that anyone could have dressed up Bowman in all that stuff *after* he'd been murdered.'

'There's one other thing, sir. You know from Max's report it says that Bowman could have been eating some of the things they had at the party?'

'What about it?'

'Well – was it just coincidence he'd been eating the same sort of meal?'

'No. Margaret Bowman must have known – she must

have found out – what the menu was and then cooked her husband some of it. Then all Wilkins had to do was just eat a bit of the same stuff—'

'But how did Margaret Bowman know?'

'How the hell do I know, Lewis? But it *happened*, didn't it? I'm not making up this bloody corpse you know! I'm not making up all these people in their fancy dress! You do realize that, don't you?'

'No need to get cross, sir!'

'I'm *not* bloody cross! If somebody decides to make some elaborate plan to rub out one side of the semi-eternal triangle – we've got to have some equally elaborate explanation! Surely you can see that?'

Lewis nodded. 'I agree. But just let me make my main point once again, sir – and then we'll forget it. It's this business of *staying on after the murder* that worries me: it must have been a dreadfully nerve-racking time for the two of them; it was very complicated; and it was a bit chancy. And all I say is that I can't *really* see the whole point of it. It just keeps the pair of them on the hotel premises the whole of the evening, and whatever time the murder was committed they haven't got any chance of an alibi—'

'There you go again, Lewis! For Christ's sake, come off it! *Nobody's got a bloody alibi.*'

The two men were silent for several minutes.

'Cup more coffee, sir?' asked Lewis.

'Augh! I'm sorry, Lewis. You just take the wind out of my sails, that's all.'

'We've got him, sir. That's the only thing that matters.'

Morse nodded.

'And you're absolutely sure that we've got the right man?'

'It's a big word – "absolutely" – isn't it?' said Morse.

Chapter Forty

Tuesday, January 7th: p.m.

Alibi (n.) – the plea in a criminal charge of having been elsewhere at the material time.

(*Chambers 20th Century Dictionary*)

It was, in all, to be an hour or so before the interrogation of Wilkins was resumed. Morse had telephoned Max, but had learned only that if he, Morse, continued to supply the lab with corpses about twenty-four hours old, he, Max, was not going to make too many fanciful speculations: he was a forensic scientist, not a fortune teller. Lewis had contacted the Haworth Hotel to discover that one local call had in fact been made – untraceable, though – from Annexe 3 on New Year's Eve. Phillips, who had returned from Diamond Close with the not unexpected news that Margaret Bowman (if she *had* been there) had flown, now resumed his duties in the interview room, standing by the door, his feet aching a good deal, his eyes idly scanning the bare room once again: the wooden trestle-table, on which stood two white polystyrene cups (empty now) and an ash-tray (rapidly filling); and behind the table, the fairish-haired, fresh-complexioned man accused of a terrible murder, who seemed to Phillips to look perhaps rather less dramatically perturbed than should have been expected.

'What time did you get to the Haworth Hotel on New Year's Eve?'

'Say that again?'

'What time did you get to the hotel?'

'I didn't go to any hotel that night—'

'You were at the Haworth Hotel and you got there at—'

'I've never played there.'

'Never played what?'

'Never *played* there!'

'I'm not quite with you, Mr Wilkins.'

'We go round the pubs – the group – we don't often go to hotels.'

'You play in a pop group?'

'A jazz group – I play tenor sax.'

'So what?'

'Look, Sergeant. You say you're not with *me*: I'm not with *you*, either.'

'You were at the Haworth Hotel on New Year's Eve. What time did you get there?'

'I was at the Friar up in North Oxford on New Year's Eve!'

'Really?'

'Yes, really!'

'Can you prove it?'

'Not offhand, I suppose, but—'

'Would the landlord remember you there?'

'Course he would! He paid us, didn't he?'

'The group you're in – was playing there?'

'Yes.'

'And you were there *all the evening*?'

'Till about two o'clock the next morning.'

'How many others in the group?'

'Four.'

'And how many people were there at the Friar that night?'

'Sixty? – seventy? on and off.'

'Which bar were you in?'

'Lounge bar.'

'And you didn't leave the bar all night?'

'Well, we had steak and chips in the back room at about – half-past nine, I suppose it was.'

'With the rest of the group?'

'*And* the landlord – *and* the landlady.'

'This is New Year's Eve you're talking about?'

'Look, Sergeant, I've been here a long time already tonight, haven't I? Can you please ring up the Friar and get someone here straight away? Or ring up any of the group? I'm getting awfully tired – and it's been one hell of an evening for me – you can understand that, can't you?'

There was a silence in the room – a silence that seemed to Phillips to take on an almost palpable tautness, as the import of Wilkins's claim slowly sank into the minds of the detectives there.

'What does your group call itself, Mr Wilkins?' It was Morse himself who quietly asked the final question.

'The "Oxford Blues",' said Wilkins, his face hard and unamused.

Charlie Freeman ('Fingers' Freeman to his musical colleagues) was surprised to find a uniformed constable standing on his Kidlington doorstep that evening. Yes, the 'Oxford Blues' had played the Friar on New Year's Eve; yes, *he'd* played there that night, with Ted Wilkins, for about five or six hours; yes, he'd be more than willing to go along to Police HQ immediately and make a statement to that effect. No great hardship for him, was it? After all, it was only a couple of minutes' walk away.

By 9.30 p.m. Mr Edward Wilkins had been driven back to his home in Diamond Close; Phillips, at long last, had been given permission to call it a day; and Lewis, tired and dejected, sat in Morse's office, wondering where they had all gone so sadly wrong. Perhaps he might have suspected – and he'd actually *said* so – that Morse's ideas had all been a bit too bizarre: a man murdered in fancy-dress outfit; and then another man spending the night of the party pretending he *was* the murdered man and dressed in a virtually identical outfit. Surely, surely, the simple truth was that *Thomas Bowman* had been the man at the party, as well as the man who'd been murdered! There would be (as Lewis knew) lots of difficulties in substantiating such a view;

but none of them were anywhere near as insurmountable as trying to break Wilkins's alibi – an alibi which could be vouched for by sixty or seventy wholly disinterested witnesses. Gently, quietly, Lewis mentioned his thoughts to Morse – the latter sitting silent and morose in the old black leather armchair. 'You could be right, Lewis.' Morse rubbed his left hand across his eyes. 'Anyway, it's no good worrying about it tonight. My judgement's gone! I need a drink. You coming?'

'No. I'll get straight home, if you don't mind, sir. It's been a long day, and I should think the missus'll have something cooking for me.'

'I should be surprised if she hasn't.'

'You're looking tired, sir. Do you want me to give you a lift?'

Morse nodded wearily. 'Just drop me at the Friar, if you will.'

As he walked up to the entrance, Morse stopped. Red, blue, green and orange lights were flashing through the lounge windows, and the place was athrob with the live music of what sounded like some Caribbean delirium at the Oval greeting a test century from Vivian Richards. Morse checked his step and walked round to the public bar, where in comparative peace he sat and drank two pints of Morrell's bitter and watched a couple of incompetent pool-players pretending to be Steve Davises. On the wall beside the dartboard he saw the notice:

7th January
LIVE MUSIC 7–11 p.m.
Admission Free!!
The fabulous
CALYPSO QUARTET

Morse pondered a quick third pint; but it wanted only a couple of minutes to eleven, and he decided to get home – just a few minutes' walk away, along Carlton Road and thence just a little way down the Banbury Road to his bachelor flat. But something thwarted this decision, and he ordered another pint, a large Bell's Scotch and a packet of plain crisps.

At twenty minutes past eleven he was the last one in the public bar, and the young barman wiping the table-tops suggested that he should finish his drink and leave: it was not unknown (Morse learned) for the police to check up on over-liquored loiterers after a live music evening.

As he left, Morse saw the Calypso Quartet packing away its collection of steel drums and sundry other Caribbean instruments into the back of an old, oft-dented Dormobile. And suddenly Morse stopped. He stopped dead. He stopped as if petrified, staring at the man who had just closed the back door of the vehicle and who was languidly lolling round to the driving seat. Even in the bitter late-night air this man wore only a blood-red, open-necked shirt on the upper part of his loose-limbed body; whilst on his head he had a baggy black-and-white checked cap that covered all his hair apart from the beaded dreadlocks which dangled on either side of his face like the snakes that once wreathed the head of the stone-eyed Gorgon.

'You all right, man?' enquired the coloured musician, holding both hands up in a mock gesture of concern about a fellow mortal who seemed to have imbibed too freely perhaps and too well. And Morse noticed the hands – hands that were almost like the hands of a white man, as though the Almighty had just about run out of pigment when he came to the palms.

'You all right, man?' repeated the musician.

Morse nodded, and there appeared on his face a stupidly beatific smile such as was seldom seen there – save when he listened to the love duet from Act One of *Die Walküre.*

Morse should (he knew it!) not have left things where they were that night. But his eyelids drooped heavily over his prickly-tired eyes as he walked back to his flat and in spite of his elation, he had little enough strength left, little appetite for anything more that day. But before throwing himself on the longed-for bed, he did ring Lewis; and prevailed upon Mrs Lewis (still up) to rouse her husband (an hour abed) for a few quick words before January 7th drew to its seemingly interminable close. And when, after only a brief monologue from Morse, a weary-brained Lewis put his receiver down, he, too, knew the identity of the man who on New Year's Eve had walked back to the annexe of the Haworth Hotel with Helen Smith on the one side and Philippa Palmer on the other.

Chapter Forty-one

Wednesday, January 8th: a.m.

Matrimony is a bargain, and somebody has to get the worst of the bargain.

(HELEN ROWLAND)

AT THE DESK of the Haworth Hotel the following morning, Sarah Jonstone greeted Sergeant Lewis as if she were glad to see him; which indeed she was, since she had at last remembered the little thing that had been troubling her. So early in the day (it was only eight thirty), her excessively circumferenced spectacles were still riding high upon her pretty little nose, and it could hardly be claimed, at least for the present, that she was being hectically overworked; in fact Lewis had already observed her none-too-convincing attempt to conceal beneath a pile of correspondence the book she had been reading when he had so unexpectedly walked in – on Morse's instruction – to interview her once again.

It was just a little corroboration (Lewis had pointed out) that was needed; and Sarah found herself once again seeking to stress the few unequivocally certain points she had made in her earlier statement. Yes, she *did* remember, and very clearly, the man coming out of the Gentlemen's lavatory just before the New Year's Eve party was due to begin; yes (now that Lewis mentioned it) perhaps his hands *hadn't* been blackened-over as convincingly as the rest of him; yes, the two of them, 'Mr and Mrs Ballard', *had* kept themselves very much to themselves for the greater part of the evening – certainly until that hour or so before midnight when a series of eightsome reels, general excuse-mes and old-time barn-dances had severed the last ties of self-consciousness and timidity; and when 'Mr Ballard' had danced with her, his sweaty fingers leaving some of their dark stain on her own hands, *and* on her blouse; yes, without a shadow of doubt that last fact *was* true, because she remembered with a sweet clarity how she had washed her hands in the bedroom washbasin before going to bed that night, and how she had tried to sponge the stain off her blouse the following morning.

A middle-aged couple stood waiting to pay their bill; and while Sarah fetched the account from the small room at the back of Reception, Lewis turned his head to one side and was thus able to make out the title on the white spine of the book she had been reading: MILLGATE: *Thomas Hardy – A Biography.* O.U.P.

The bill settled, Sarah resumed her seat and told Lewis what she had remembered. It had been odd, though it didn't really seem all that important now. What had happened was that someone – a woman – had rung up and asked what the New Year's Eve menu was: that was all. As far as she could recall, the little incident had taken place on the Monday before – that would be December 30th.

Knowing how pleased Morse would be to have one of his hunches confirmed, Lewis was on the point of taking down some firm statement from Sarah Jonstone when he became aware of an extraordinarily attractive brunette standing beside him, shifting the weight of her beautifully moulded figure from one black-stockinged leg to the other.

'Can I have my bill, please?' she asked. Although the marked Birmingham accent was not, as he heard it, exactly the music of the spheres, Lewis found himself staring at the woman with an almost riveted fascination.

The whispered voice in his ear was totally unexpected: 'Take your lecherous eyes off her, Lewis!'

'Thank you very much, Miss Arkwright!' said Sarah Jonstone, as the woman turned and left, flashing a brief, but almost interested, glance at the man who had just come in.

'Good morning, Miss Jonstone!' said Morse.

'Oh, hello!' There was nothing about her greeting that could be construed as even wanly welcoming.

'Is she the same one?' asked Morse, gesturing after the departed beauty. 'The one who was due for the New Year?'

'Yes!'

'Well, well!' said Morse, looking quite extraordinarily pleased with himself and with life in general; and quite clearly pleased with the sight of Miss Doris Arkwright in particular. 'Could you please ask *Mrs*

Binyon to come along to Reception, Miss Jonstone? There's something rather important—'

'She's not here, I'm afraid. She's gone up to Leeds. She *was* going there for the New Year, but—'

'Really? How *very* interesting! Well thank you very much, Miss Jonstone. Come on, Lewis! We've a busy morning ahead.'

'Miss Jonstone remembered something—' started Lewis.

'Forget it for the minute! Bigger things to worry about just now! Goodbye, Miss Jonstone!'

Morse was still smirking to himself with infinite self-satisfaction as, for the last time, the two men walked from the Haworth Hotel.

An hour later, a man was arrested at his home in south-east Oxford. This time, there were no revolvers on view; and the man in question, promptly cautioned by Sergeant Lewis of the Oxfordshire CID, made no show of resistance whatsoever.

Chapter Forty-two

Wednesday, January 8th: noon

> Lovers of air travel find it exhilarating to hang poised between the illusion of immortality and the fact of death.
>
> (ALEXANDER CHASE)

THE BOEING 737 scheduled to take off from Gatwick at 12.05 hours was almost fully booked, with only four or five empty seats visible as the air hostesses went through their dumb-shows with the oxygen masks and the inflatable life-jackets. It was noticeable that almost all the passengers were paying the most careful attention to the advice being offered: several tragic air crashes during the previous months had engendered a sort of collective pterophobia, and airport lounges throughout the world were reporting a dramatic rise in the sales of tranquillizing pills and alcoholic spirits. But quite certainly there were two persons on the aircraft (and there may have been others) who listened only perfunctorily to the safety instructions being rehearsed that lunchtime. For one of these two persons, the transit through the terminal had been a nightmare: and yet, as it now seemed, there had been no real cause for anxiety. Documentation, baggage, passport – none had brought any problem at all. For the second of these two persons, worries had sprung from a slightly different source; yet he, too, was now beginning to feel more relaxed. As he looked down from his window-seat on to the wet tarmac, his left hand quietly slid the half-bottle of brandy from his anorak pocket, allowing his right hand to unscrew the cap. The attention of those passengers sitting immediately around him was still focused on the slim-waisted stewardesses, and he was able to pour for himself a couple of tots without his imbibings being too obvious. And already he felt slightly better! It had been a damnably close-run thing – but he'd made it! A sign came on just above him, bidding all passengers to fasten their seatbelts and to refrain from smoking until further notice; the engines vibrated anew along the fuselage; and the stewardesses took their seats, facing the passengers, and smiling perhaps with slightly spurious confidence upon their latest charges. Gradually the giant plane moved forward in a quarter-turn, took up its proper station, and stood there for a minute or two preparing, like a long-jump finalist in the Olympic Games, to accelerate along the runway. The man seated by the window knew that any second now he would be able to relax – almost completely. Like so many fellow criminals, he was under the happy delusion that there was no extradition treaty between Spain and the United Kingdom, and he had read of so many criminals – bank robbers, embezzlers, drug-peddlers and pederasts – who were even now lounging lazily at various resorts along the Costa del Sol.

Suddenly the aircraft's throttles were opened completely and the mighty power seemed almost a tangible entity.

Then the engines seemed to die a little.

And then they seemed to die completely.

And two members of Gatwick Security Police boarded the aircraft.

For the man in the window-seat, beside whom these men stopped, there appeared little point in even thinking of escape. Where was there to escape to?

The Boeing was only very slightly delayed; and five minutes behind schedule it was shooting off the earth at an angle of forty-five degrees and heading for its appointed destination. Very soon, passengers were told that they could unfasten their seatbelts: everything was fine. And six rows behind the now-empty window-seat, a woman lit a cigarette and inhaled very deeply.

Chapter Forty-Three

Wednesday, January 8th: p.m.

No mask like open truth to cover lies,
As to go naked is the best disguise.

(WILLIAM CONGREVE)

MORSE SAT IN Superintendent Bell's office in St Aldates awaiting Lewis – the latter having been deputed the task of taking down in his rather laborious longhand the statement from the man arrested earlier that day at his home in south-east Oxford.

'Damned clever, you know!' reiterated Bell.

Morse nodded: he liked Bell well enough perhaps – though not overmuch – and he found himself wishing that Lewis would get a move on.

'Well done, anyway!' said Bell. 'The Chief Constable'll be pleased.'

'Perhaps he'll let me have a day or two's holiday before the end of the decade.'

'We're *very* grateful, though – you know that, don't you?'

'Yes,' said Morse, honestly enough.

*

It was a highly euphoric Lewis who came in at a quarter past one, thrusting a statement – four pages of it – on the desk in front of Morse. 'Maybe a few little errors in English usage here and there, sir; but on the whole a splendid piece of prose, I think you'll find.'

Morse took the statement and scanned the last page:

in the normal way, but we were hard up and I lost my job in November and there was only playing in the group left with a wife and my four little children to feed and look after. We'd got the Social Security but the HP was getting bad, and then this came along. All I had to do was what he told me and that wasn't very difficult. I didn't really have any choice because I needed the money bad and it wasn't because I wanted to do anything that was wrong. I know what happened because I saw it in the *Oxford Mail* but when I agreed I just did what I was told and I never knew what things were all about at the time. I'm very sorry about it. Please remember I said that, because I love my wife and my little children.

As dictated to Sergeant Lewis, Kidlington CID, by Mr Winston Grant, labourer (unemployed), of 29 Rose Hill Gardens, Rose Hill, Oxford. 8 Jan.

'The adverb from "bad" is "badly",' mumbled Morse.

'Shall we keep him here?' asked Bell.

'He's your man,' said Morse.

'And the charge – officially?'

'"Accessory to murder", I suppose – but I'm not a legal man.'

'"Party to murder", perhaps?' suggested Lewis, who had seldom looked so happy since his elder daughter announced her first pregnancy.

Back at Kidlington HQ, Morse sat back in the old black leather armchair, looking (for the while) imperturbably expansive. The man arrested at Gatwick, almost two hours earlier, was well on his way to Oxfordshire, expected (Morse learned) within the next fifteen minutes. It was a time to savour.

Lewis himself now knew exactly what had happened on New Year's Eve in Annexe 3; knew, too, that the murderer of Thomas Bowman had neither set foot inside the main hotel building, nor bedecked himself in a single item of fancy dress. And yet, as to how Morse had arrived at the truth, he felt as puzzled as a small boy witnessing his first conjuring performance. 'What really put you on to it, sir?'

'The *key* point was, as I told you, that the murderer tried desperately hard to persuade us that the crime was committed *as late as possible*: after midnight. But as you yourself rightly observed, Lewis, there would seem to be little point in such a deception if the murderer stayed on the scene the whole time from about eight that night to one o'clock the next morning. But there was every point if he *wasn't* on the scene in the latter part of the evening – a time for which he had an *alibi*!'

'But, sir—'

'There were three clues in this case which should

have put us on to the truth much earlier than they did. Each of these three clues, in itself, looks like a pedestrian little piece of information; but taken together – well . . . The *first* vital clue came largely from Sarah Jonstone – the only really valuable and coherent witness in the whole case – and it was this: that the man posing as "Mr Ballard" ate virtually nothing that evening! The *second* vital clue – also brought to our notice, among others, by Miss Jonstone – was the fact that the man posing as "Mr Ballard" was still staining whatever he touched late that evening! Then there was the *third* vital clue – the simplest clue of the lot, and one which was staring all of us in the face from the very beginning. So obvious a clue that none of us – none of us! – paid the slightest attention to it: the fact that the man posing as "Mr Ballard" won the fancy-dress competition!

'You see, Lewis, there are two ways of looking at each of these clues – the complex way, and the simple way. And we'd been looking at them the wrong way – we've been looking at them the *complex* way.'

'I see,' said Lewis, unseeing.

'Take the food business,' continued Morse. 'We almost got in some hopelessly complex muddle about it, didn't we? I read carefully what dear old Max said in his report about what had been floating up and down in the ascending and descending colons. You, Lewis, were bemused enough to listen to what Miss Jonstone said about someone ringing up to ask what the menu was. Why the hell *shouldn't* someone ring up and ask if they're in for another few slices of the virtually inevitable turkey? And do you know what we didn't do amid all this cerebration, Lewis? We didn't ask ourselves a very simple question: if our man had eaten nothing of the first two courses, shouldn't we assume he might be getting a little *hungry*? And even if he's been told he'd better go through the evening secretly sticking all the goodies into a doggie-bag, you might have thought he'd be tempted when he came to the next two courses on the menu – especially a couple of succulent pork chops. So why, Lewis – just think simply! – why didn't he have a mouthful or two?'

'Like you say, sir, he was told not to, because it was vital—'

'No! You're still getting too *complicated*, Lewis. There's a very *simple* answer, you see! Rastafarians aren't allowed to eat pork!

'Now let's come to this business of the stains this man was leaving behind on whatever he touched – even after midnight! We took down all the evidence, didn't we – we got statements from Miss Palmer, and Mrs Smith, and Sarah Jonstone – about how the wretched fellow went round ruining their coats and their blouses. And we almost came to the point – well, *I* did, Lewis – of getting them all analysed and seeing if the stains were the same, and trying to find out where the original theatre-black came from and – well, we were getting too *complex* again! The simple truth is that any make-up *dries* after a few hours; it comes off at first, of course, on anything that's touched – but after a while it's no problem at all. Yet in this case it *remained* a problem.

And the *simple* answer to this particular mystery is that our man *wanted* to leave his marks late that evening; he deliberately put *more* stain on his hands; and he deliberately put his hands where they *would* leave marks. All right, Lewis? He had a stick of theatre-black in his pocket and he smeared it all over the palms of his hands in the final hour or so of the New Year party.

'And then there's the last point. The man won a prize, and we made all sorts of complex assumptions about it; he'd been the most painstaking and imaginative competitor of the lot; he'd been so successful with his make-up that no one could recognize him; he'd been anxious for some reason to carry off the first prize in the fancy-dress competition. And all a load of *complex* nonsense, Lewis. The fact is that the very last thing he wanted was to draw any attention to himself by winning the first prize that evening. And the almost childishly *simple* fact of the matter is that if you want to dress up and win first prize *as*, let's say, Prince Charles, well, the best way to do it is to *be* Prince Charles. And we all ought to have suspected, perhaps, that the man who dressed up in that Rastafarian rig-out and who put on such a convincing and successful performance that night *as* a Rastafarian, might perhaps have owed his success to the simple fact that he *was* a Rastafarian!'

'Mr Winston Grant.'

'Yes, Mr Winston Grant! A man, in fact, I met outside the Friar only last night! And if anyone ever tells you, Lewis, that there isn't a quite extraordinary degree of coincidence in this world of ours – then you tell him to come to see me, and I'll tell him different!'

'Should you perhaps say "differently"?' asked Lewis.

'This man had been a builder's labourer; he'd worked on several sites in Oxford – including the Locals; he'd lost his job because of cutbacks in the building industry; he was getting short of money for himself and his family; he was made an extraordinarily generous offer – we still don't know *how* generous; and he agreed to accept that offer in return for playing – as he saw things – a minor role for a few hours at a New Year's party in an Oxford hotel. I doubt we shall ever know all the ins and outs of the matter but—'

Sergeant Phillips knocked and announced that the prisoner was now in the interview room.

And Morse smiled.

And Lewis smiled.

'Just finish off what you were saying, will you, sir?'

'Nothing more to say, really. Winston Grant must have been pretty carefully briefed, that's for sure. In the first place he'd be coming into the hotel directly from the street, and it was absolutely essential that he should wait his time, to the second almost, until Margaret Bowman had created the clever little distraction of taking Sarah Jonstone away from the reception desk to inspect the graffito in the Ladies' – a graffito which she, Margaret Bowman, had herself just scrawled across the wall. Then, I'm sure he must have been told to say as little as possible to anyone else all the evening and to stick close to Margaret Bowman, as if they were far more interested in each other than in the goings-on around them. *But there was no chance of him opting out of the fancy-dress competition!* I suspect, too, that he was told not to eat anything – if he could manage not to without drawing too much attention to himself; and remember, he was helped in this by the way Binyon had scheduled the various courses at different tables. But it may well be, Lewis, that we're overestimating the extent to which the plan was completely thought out. Above all, though, he had to carry through that final, extraordinarily clever, little deception: he was to make every effort to *pretend* that he was a black man – even though he *was* a black man. And there was one wonderfully simple way in which such a pretence could be sustained, and that was by rubbing dark-stain on to his hands – *hands that were already black* – so that everyone who came into physical contact with him should believe that he was *not* a black man – but a white man. And that, Lewis, in the later stages of that New Year's party is what he did, making sure he left a few indelible marks on the most obvious places – like the shoulders of the light-coloured winter mackintoshes worn by both Miss Palmer and Mrs Smith—'

'—and the white blouse of Sarah Jonstone.'

'Cream-coloured actually,' said Morse.

For Sergeant Phillips it was all somewhat *déjà vu* as he resumed his vigil at the door of the interview room, his feet still aching, his eyes scanning the bare room once again: the wooden trestle-table on which stood a white polystyrene coffee cup (full) and an ash-tray (as yet empty); and behind the table, the same fairish-haired, fresh-complexioned man who had sat there the previous evening – Mr Edward Wilkins.

Chapter Forty-four

Wednesday, January 8th: p.m.

Felix qui potuit rerum cognoscere causas.

(VIRGIL, *Georgics*)

AT 5 P.M., Mr James Prior, Security Officer at the Locals, put on his bicycle clips and prepared to leave. Before he did so he had a final look round Reception to make sure that everything that should be locked up *was* locked up. It was odd though, really, to think that the only thing the police had been interested in was the one drawer that *wasn't* locked up – the drawer in which he kept all the out-of-date security passes, elastic-banded into their various bundles. Like the bundle for the last lot of building workers from which the police had already taken two passes away: that of Winston Grant, a Rastafarian fellow whom Prior remembered very well; and that of a man called Wilkins, who'd operated the giant yellow crane that had towered over the Delegacy building throughout the summer months. After Morse's call early that morning, Prior had looked briefly through the rest of that particular bundle, and had wondered whether there were any other criminals lurking among those very ordinary-looking faces. But the truth was that one could never tell: he, far more than most people, was fully aware of that.

That afternoon, Wilkins had been resignedly co-operative about every detail of the whole case – with the exception of the act of murder itself, which he stubbornly and categorically refused to discuss in any respect whatsoever: it was as if that single, swift dispatch (to which he now confessed) had paralysed his capacity to accept it as in any way a piece of voluntary, responsible behaviour. But for the rest, he spoke fully and freely; and there was nothing surprising, nothing new, that emerged from his statement. Naturally enough, perhaps, he expressed the hope that Winston Grant should be treated with appropriate leniency, although it seemed to others (certainly to Lewis) that such an accomplice must have been rather more aware of the nature of his assignment than either Grant or Wilkins was prepared to admit.

About Margaret Bowman, the only piece of new information Wilkins was able to give was that he had more than once picked her up from a beauty clinic in Oxford, and Lewis shook his head ruefully as he learned that this clinic was the very first one he had rung – the one refusing to divulge any confidential details. About Margaret's present fate Wilkins appeared strangely indifferent. He hadn't (he said) the faintest idea where she'd finally drifted off to; but presumably the police would be concentrating on her various relatives up around Alnwick or Berwick or Newcastle or wherever they were. For his part, he was perhaps glad to get shot of the woman. She'd brought him nothing but trouble, although he fully accepted that it had been far more his fault than hers that things had finally . . . But that was all over now. And in an odd sort of way (he'd said) he felt relieved.

It was just after 6.30 p.m. when Sergeant Phillips escorted Wilkins down to St Aldates where temporarily, together with Grant, he would be held, awaiting (in the short term) the provision of alternative custodial arrangements and (in the long term) the pleasure of Her Majesty.

Morse insisted that both he himself and Lewis should call it a day; and Lewis was just closing the box-file on the Haworth Hotel case when he noticed a letter which he had never been shown: one beginning 'This is a love letter . . .' He read the first few lines with some mystification – until he came to the quite extraordinary statement that the anonymous correspondent had been 'reading a biography of Thomas Hardy . . .'!

Should he tell Morse? He read the letter through again with the greatest interest.

Well, well, well!

At 7 p.m. Morse (Lewis thought he had gone) came back into his office once more. 'Listen, Lewis! This Wilkins is one of the cleverest buggers we've ever had! You realize that? He's pulled the wool over my eyes about the most central, central, central issue of the lot! And you know what that is? That he, Wilkins, was – is!

– hopelessly in love with this woman, Margaret Bowman; and that he'd do anything – *did* do anything – to keep her. In fact, he murdered her husband to keep her! And likewise, Lewis, the fact that he'd do anything to protect her *now*! You remember what he said last night? Just get the transcript, Lewis – the bit about the passport!'

Lewis found the document and read aloud:

'I advised her to get on a boat or something and sail off to the continent – away from everything.'

'But she didn't take your advice?'

'No, she couldn't. She hadn't got a passport and she was frightened of applying for one because she knew everybody was trying to find her . . .'

'God, I'm a fool, Lewis! I wonder how many lies he *has* told us? That she was at his house last night? That she was up with her sister in Newcastle? Has she *got* a sister, Lewis? Oh dear! She hasn't got a passport, he says? And we believe him! So we don't watch all the boats—'

'Or the planes,' added Lewis quietly.

'I don't believe it!' said Morse softly, after a pause.

'What's worrying you, sir?'

'Get a telex off to Gatwick straight away! Get the passenger list of flight number whatever-it-was!'

'You don't think—?'

'*Think?* I'm almost *sure*, Lewis!'

*

When Lewis returned from the telex office, Morse already had his greatcoat on and was ready to leave.

'You know that letter you had from one of your admirers, sir?'

'How do you know about that?'

'You left it in the box.'

'Oh!'

'Did you notice the postmark on the original letter?'

'London. So what?'

'London? Really?' (Lewis sounded like a man who knows all the answers.) 'You get a lot of people going up to the London sales from all over the country, don't you? I mean anyone from anywhere – from Oxford, say – could go up to the January sales and drop a letter in a postbox outside Paddington.'

Morse was frowning. 'What exactly are you trying to tell me, Lewis?'

'I just wondered if you had any idea of who'd written that letter to you, that's all.'

Morse's hand was on the doorknob. 'Look, Lewis! You know the difference between you and me, don't you? You don't use your *eyes* enough! If you *had* done – and very recently, too! – you'd know perfectly well who wrote that letter.'

'Yes?'

'Yes! And it so happens – since you're suddenly so very interested in my private affairs, Lewis – that I'm going to take the particular lady who wrote that particular letter out for a particularly fine meal tonight – that's if you've no objections?'

'Where are you taking her, sir?'

'If you must know, we're going out to Springs Hotel near Wallingford.'

'Pretty expensive, so they say, sir.'

'We shall go halves – you realize that, of course?' Morse winked happily at Lewis – and was gone.

Lewis, too, was smiling happily as he rang his wife and told her that he wouldn't be long.

At 7.50 p.m. the telex reply came through from Gatwick: on the scheduled 12.05 flight that had left that morning for Barcelona, the passenger list had included, apart from a Mr Edward Wilkins, a Mrs Margaret Bowman, the latter giving an address in Chipping Norton, Oxfordshire.

At 8.00 p.m., Lewis pulled on his overcoat and left Kidlington HQ. He wasn't at all sure whether Morse would be pleased, or displeased, with the news he had just received. But the last thing he was going to do was to ring Springs Hotel. He just hoped – very much he hoped – that Morse would have an enjoyable evening, and an enjoyable meal. As for himself, the missus would have the egg and chips ready; and he felt very happy with life.